I0762624

Praise for
Inheritance

"A riveting and realistic glimpse into the complex struggles that newcomers face in the process of rebuilding their lives, communities, and sense of self. Jane Park gifts readers with an honest and nuanced protagonist, Anne, who discovers she can only move forward by going back—to her old home, childhood memories, and family secrets. *Inheritance* is an authentic and layered exploration of identity, sacrifice, and healing. Compelling with an emotional clarity, Park's debut novel balances heartbreak and hope."

—Ann Y.K. Choi, author of
All Things Under the Moon
and *Kay's Lucky Coin Variety*

"With *Inheritance*, Jane Park peels back the familiar, exposing the unfamiliar that lies beneath. It is a novel about unearthed family secrets . . . secrets maybe best kept buried, but impossible to ignore. Propulsive from the start, this debut showcases one Korean Canadian family facing heartbreak, turmoil, and unspoken histories in a way that is both intimate and unforgettable. Certainly, an important contribution to Asian writing in Canada and beyond."

—Jenny Heijun Wills, award-winning author of
Older Sister. Not Necessarily Related.
and *Everything and Nothing at All*

"A powerful and gripping novel about a Korean Canadian woman who returns to her childhood home in small-town Alberta, where she is forced to confront the consequences of her complicity in a decades old incident that left her family in tatters."

—Edward Y. C. Lee, author of
The Laundryman's Boy

"Brilliantly paced and beautifully told, *Inheritance* is above all about family and how, despite our best intentions, we so often do damage to the ones we most love. Jane Park's characters are ones we can all relate to, working their way through a minefield of past traumas and misunderstandings and misplaced expectations in the hopes of reaching, finally, a place of acceptance and healing."

—Nino Ricci, Governor General's Literary Award winner for *Lives of the Saints* **and** *The Origin of Species*

"*Inheritance* is a searching and devastating portrait of a family reckoning with historical trauma, and the cost of migration and assimilation. A tender, finely observed, insightful debut."

—Su Chang, author of *The Immortal Woman*

"In an unforgettable debut novel, Jane Park has crafted a finely wrought family drama about the ties that bind and the horrific cost when one commits an unspeakable act. While set in the desolate plains and bustling cities of Canada, the indelible echoes of a Korea ripped apart by war and families forever torn haunt this novel. The Korean word *jeong* can mean 'the ties that bind' and implies that sacrifices are required to be part of a family. But this untranslatable word also speaks to connection, the love that exists in families, the warmth and joy we foster and receive. The Kim family at the heart of *Inheritance* loses their homeland in more ways than one, endures harsh conditions in their adopted country, becomes unraveled by violence. And yet, they forge new bonds and weave themselves back together stronger, more resilient. With her beautifully written novel, Park reminds us that hope is precious, redemption is possible, and forgiveness is always within reach."

—Helena Rho, author of *Stone Angels*

"Jane Park has written a well-crafted, nuanced story about a family aching to present well, expressing love through duty and atoning for past sins. *Inheritance* is a must-read for all children of immigrants, doubly so if you're Korean in North America."

—Ins Choi, playwright of *Kim's Convenience*

"A beautiful debut. A wide-ranging meditation on the Korean immigrant experience that explores family, ambition, longing and belonging."

—Suji Kwock Kim

"Sparsely written and deeply affecting, *Inheritance* lingers long after the final page—a quiet, devastating meditation on guilt, parental expectations, and the lasting consequences of generational silence. As a Canadian child of immigrants, I know this book will stay with me for a long time."

—Rachel Phan, author of *Restaurant Kid*

Inheritance

Inheritance

A Novel

Jane Park

PEGASUS BOOKS
NEW YORK LONDON

INHERITANCE

Pegasus Books, Ltd.
148 West 37th Street, 13th Floor
New York, NY 10018

First Pegasus Books cloth edition April 2026

Interior design by Maria Fernandez

Library of Congress Cataloging-in-Publication Data is available.

ISBN: 979-8-89710-068-2

10 9 8 7 6 5 4 3 2 1

Printed in the United States of America
Distributed by Simon & Schuster
www.pegasusbooks.com

For Oliver and Theo

AUTHOR'S NOTE

For Hangeul spelling, on most occasions I used the Revised Romanization of Korean, but also, on a few occasions, I deviated from this system.

ONE

2014

My father passed away yesterday. It was a sudden death from a stroke that occurred, poetically, near the stroke of midnight. My father was driving home with my mother after visiting my brother at the rehabilitation centre, when he fell forward onto the steering wheel. My mother gripped the wheel and gently steered the car onto the shoulder of the highway. When she recounted this moment, she omitted all emotions that a wife of forty years would have felt and methodically outlined what happened next: how she called the ambulance, the time it took for the ambulance to come, the rush into the emergency room, how the doctor shook his head when he saw my father's condition, and how, six hours later, he was declared dead. She ended her story using that phrase in perfect English, "He was declared dead," with a drama and finality which made me realize even my own mother, at times, enjoys being histrionic.

I'm sure this will be the story my mother will share with her friends and acquaintances at the funeral. What happened prior to the stroke will be reserved for the few she loves and trusts. She recounted the story about the visit to my brother with exhaustion because she had not slept that night. My father finally agreed to visit Charles, who had been at the centre for a couple of months. Charles had relapsed again when he found out that his ex-girlfriend was engaged to a wealthy Texan who worked trading oil commodities in Calgary. A co-worker found Charles lying in his bare apartment with empty whisky bottles scattered around him after he had missed work for three days.

My mother brought Charles a container of *kimchi* rice—my brother's favourite dish—with the rice wrapped in a layer of fried egg and accompanied by packets of ketchup. In the lobby, the container accidentally broke open inside her shopping bag, releasing a sharp, sour aroma. My mother believes the security guard was more annoyed at the pungent smell than alarmed for the security of the people. He called his boss, who called his superior, and soon a crowd of uniformed men surrounded my mother, who tightly held onto her container of kimchi rice. The men began questioning her about the curious contents of the bright red rice dish with its distinct odour. One man commented, "You eat this stuff?"

My father, not realizing that this was a comment and not a question, answered, "Yes, we eat kimchi like you eat bread." He scooped some of the rice from the bag with his fingers and ate it in front of them. To break an embarrassing silence, the head guard asked my mother to throw away the bag with its container and informed her that all food brought for patients must first be submitted to the nutritionist, who worked only on these specific days. He then gave her the phone number of this specialist, and the men dispersed. At this point of the story, my mother giggled and said that my father had a gift for embarrassing the white man, with his knack for violating every sense of social decorum.

Finally, she spoke of the last conversation they had in the car, moments before he became unconscious. During the ride home, my parents were discussing the passage of time, and how, suddenly, they had arrived at becoming old people with children who were now adults. What would they do differently if they could go back in time? They agreed they would still immigrate to Canada. Then, after qualifying they could not cheat and make themselves more fluent or affluent in this imagined past, they both could not think of a different life. The implicit conclusion is that my father's last thought was how he would not want a different life. And so, my mother ends this story that my father "died happily ever after," ending on a victorious note.

When I arrive in Edmonton for the funeral, Charles waits for me at the airport.

"Mom was planning on coming, but she finally fell asleep, and I didn't want to wake her," Charles says, his voice heavy. I sense he hasn't slept that much either. The last time I saw him was over five years ago. I appraise his grey hair, unsure if he has purposely dyed it this shade or if that's his natural hair colour. I notice a piercing in his ear for the first time and wonder how long it's been there. I assess his outfit: oversized hoodie, baggy jeans, expensive sneakers—Richard, my boyfriend, bought the same pair last spring to train for a marathon.

"Where did you get the money for those shoes?" I ask.

"Seriously? That's the first thing you're saying to me after dad just died?" Charles looks hurt, as he leans in to give me a hug though I remain standing erect. I extend an arm and give him a stiff pat on the back. "These are high-performance shoes. I've had them for over a year, and they still give firm support," he says matter-of-factly.

"You're not a professional athlete," I say as lightly as I can. He ignores this remark and stares intently ahead of him as we walk out of the airport and into the parking lot. When we enter the car, his displeasure at my remark is shown through his silence: He blasts EDM music. We're both tired and say little as the car goes onto the highway, driving past monotonous warehouses, which turn into big-box stores, and then, after a series of turns, rectangular condos and townhouses, and finally into my parents' neighbourhood, where each house seems identical to the next. When we arrive at my mother's house, Charles parks in the driveway, turns off the engine, and sits still, staring ahead at the garage door.

"Listen, Anne. I'm not going back to rehab. I'm staying with mom until everything's settled. Then I'll go to Calgary and look for a job. I'll need some money, enough to tide me over for this next while."

A familiar guilt descends, and I'm reminded why I rarely visit home. "How much do you need?" I ask softly. I dig into my purse, take out the cheque book for my Canadian bank account, which was one of the first things I packed last night, and write down the amount he requests.

I wake the next morning to my mother's knocking on the door. She enters and opens the bedroom curtains. Suddenly, the darkness transforms into light. Outside my window, I see yellow leaves on branches swaying and falling in the wind, their shadows dancing along my walls. She tells me we're late for our appointment with the funeral director. I scramble to find my black skirt suit with matching nylons, an iron to loosen the creases, and my brush, which I realize I've left back in New York.

We drive to the cemetery caught between an industrial plant and farmland. At the entrance is a manicured garden with scattered gazebos covered in plastic latticework. I glimpse into the rearview mirror at

Charles. His tall body is cramped into the back seat, and he's wearing a suit he bought yesterday—likely, the first he's worn in his life. I gaze at his square jaw, angular cheekbones, large eyes; if he were in New York and earned decent money, women would be clamouring to date him.

"Where did you get the money for this?" I ask my mother as we slow down to turn into the wide, gated entrance surrounded by rows of hedges. I was surprised at how prepared my parents were for death: they both had crisp burial clothes hanging in their closet, recent portraits taken at Sears already framed, the burial plots bought years ago.

"We save from bonus money you send every year," my mother says in her English, our default language as I am no longer fluent in Korean.

"That was your spending money. You and Dad were supposed to use that to enjoy yourselves, instead of saving it to buy cemetery plots," I say, trying not to show my irritation; I gave them a part of my annual bonus so they could finally live a little and go to restaurants or develop hobbies by taking classes. They refused, and instead, continued their habit of saving, this time to buy their gravesites.

When we enter the funeral home, my skin prickles against the chilled air, my eyes adjust to the dim light. Muted violin music plays amongst silk flowers and battery-operated candles. The funeral director appears in the lobby. My mother nods as he apologizes for her loss. She tells him how her husband loved gardening and would have appreciated—will appreciate—these well-groomed grounds. When my brother Charles and I are introduced, he says he can see resemblances of my father in both of us.

"What resemblances?" Charles asks curtly.

The funeral director's smile freezes, and he glances at my mother. "Would you like to see your husband before the guests arrive?" He leads us into the room where my father lies and softly closes the door to give us privacy.

My father would have fought with whoever prepared him for viewing. A yellow—too yellow for my father's ruddy skin—is applied to matte perfection on his face and hands. The hair, which he never combed, is shellacked into a firm arch. Our family falls silent.

My mother takes a tissue from her purse and wipes her tearing eyes. She reaches into the coffin, grabs one of his calmly folded hands and brings it towards her. She strokes the back of his hand and, with the damp tissue, wipes off the makeup. She stretches one of his fingers and places it firmly into her palm. Then, with her other hand, she digs into her purse, takes out a nail clipper, and begins clipping his nails.

Charles scowls. "Mom, what're you doing?"

"Your father vision getting worse. He keep cutting his skin when he clip the nails, so I clip. These days, his nails getting too long, but we too busy, so I tell him I clip later," she says, her face composed, even though tears fall down her cheeks. She cups one hand to catch the falling crescents, which she then places inside her coat pocket. "In the end, everything turn out better than we expect," she says, and begins to weep. Charles embraces my mother and holds her as her voice heaves and her body shakes.

After the funeral, guests come to our house bearing their crockpots, casseroles, condolences. Many of my father's friends approach me. I'm surprised that these elderly Koreans—most of whom I have never met—know who I am: my name, my profession, and my achievements. "Your father was so proud of you. You are a good daughter, Anne, graduating from Yale, becoming a lawyer," they say. "How is living in New York?" they ask.

I try not to boast, minimize my accomplishments and do not tell them that I work at Warren & Sterling in midtown Manhattan, in a tall building with tinted black windows and a smooth granite façade. It is the leading firm in America for tax law, which is my specialty. When my parents first visited me in New York, they wanted to see my workplace. They entered the building like pilgrims entering a cathedral, lifting their chins towards the high ceilings to see the light streaming in, treading the ground quietly with their hands tucked behind their backs, raising their hands to slide their fingers against the cool marble walls decorating the building's lobby. They were tactile people, and so they touched everything, to the dismay of the security guards and my assistant: the leather chairs, the crystal glasses, the brass doorknobs. "It is all real," my father whispered in Korean as he set foot into my office. I did not know if he meant the mahogany wood was authentic, or that his dream for me was finally realized. Later, I went into the supply closet and gave them free golf shirts, umbrellas, water bottles—promotional items stamped with our company logo, which our firm gave away in our sponsorships of golf tournaments. When they returned home, my father wore his golf shirt so often that the seams gave way, and my mother had to request that another be sent to him.

I am in the kitchen when an elderly woman approaches me. She wears a black gabardine dress, which elegantly drapes across her clavicle. I recognize her hawk nose, angular cheekbones, sharp chin. "Mrs. Yoon?" I say.

"You were small child when I last see you, but how you've grown," she says, smiling, as she embraces me. "Such sad news."

"Thank you for coming. How are you? How is Yura?" I eagerly ask. The last time I saw her daughter, we were girls. I have often wondered what became of her. Occasionally, I search for her name online, but find nothing.

"Fine, we all doing fine. Mr. Yoon sell the dry cleaners, and we retire now in Coquitlam. Lucky I was here visiting so I can come. Mr. Yoon recovering from hip surgery. How about you? I was so proud when I hear you get into Yale, even receive scholarship. How is New York and being lawyer?" she asks, her tattooed eyebrows rising, revealing delicate lines on her forehead.

"It was a small scholarship, nothing really," I say modestly. "What is Yura up to?"

"Ah, our Yura busy travelling. She in Caribbean right now. She doing fine. We all doing fine, but nothing like your life in New York. You dating someone?"

"I am. The Caribbean sounds lovely. Yura must be doing well then?" I ask, hoping she will reveal more. If Yura is vacationing there, that must mean, at least financially, she's well-off, and I'm curious if it's because she has a good job, or married someone rich, or both.

"Yura is fine. But I wanna hear about your life. Last time I see you was when you were a girl," Mrs. Yoon says with a wide smile. "What does your boyfriend do?"

A familiar feeling of submission returns. Even though I'm an adult, my childhood deference towards Mrs. Yoon prevents me from interrogating her more about Yura, whom she seems resolute on not discussing. "He's also a lawyer."

"How you meet him?"

"We work at the same firm. We've been dating for over a year."

"Ah, lawyer power couple! Is he Korean?" she asks cheerfully. Because I don't know how I compare with her daughter, I can't be certain if I sense jealousy in her tone.

"No, he's white," I say quietly.

"I always knew you would become the success. Is he here? Introduce me to him," she says, as she scans the room. I'm surprised she approves of me dating a white man, as that wasn't her opinion in the past, but that was over two decades ago and her views have changed along with her and my parents' generation.

"He wanted to come, but I asked him not to," I say, though I wish Richard were here now. He would sense my discomfort and could gently find some exit strategy.

Mrs. Yoon looks disappointed. "Well, it's time for you to marry. You need to give your mother grandchildren. What's taking your boyfriend so long to propose?" she asks. I give a polite smile, though my eyes wander around the room, hoping to find Charles or my mother so I can leave this conversation. "Did your father meet him?"

"Yes, they met. I'm so glad they did," I say. I don't see either of them, so I excuse myself to get a drink of water.

The first and only time Richard met my father was last winter, when my parents visited me in New York. Richard wanted to take my parents to the best Korean food the city had to offer even though I told him they would prefer a casual place in Koreatown. He refused, as this was how he liked to host, and I knew no arguing would change his mind, so I kept quiet. Richard knew a little Korean from an ex-girlfriend and greeted my parents with an awkward one-line greeting, to which my parents politely smiled—I am not sure if they understood that he was attempting to speak their language. He took us to a new Korean fusion restaurant which combined *galbi* with goji berries, *doenjang* with duck breast. This restaurant charged kimchi by the plate when it normally comes complimentary, and I could tell this troubled my parents. Throughout dinner, both Richard and I spoke about New York—the recent ice storm, the decreasing diversity, the increasing real estate prices. My parents said very little, and Richard was unsure if they did not understand him or if they did not feel very talkative. Afterwards, the only comment made by my parents was from my mother, who said we had ordered too much food—we left the table with the plates half eaten. My father, when I asked him what he thought about Richard, paused and said quietly, "Richard is different people from us."

Richard thought the dinner went well, and probably assumed that my parents always ate their dinner in silence. I didn't tell him this was not the case, and that my parents felt extremely uncomfortable sitting on velvet seats and being served water imported from Europe.

I'm in the kitchen making more coffee when my mother enters. "Everything okay?"

"I just spoke with Mrs. Yoon. Did you know she was here?" I ask.

"Yes, it was good she come. It's been long time since we last see her. People say Mrs. Yoon change a lot, especially after what happen to Yura." I lean my ear forward as my mother's voice drops. "I find out Yura marry Korean doctor and has a son. But she divorce, and leave son with father. She work for dancing in cruise company and not talking to Mrs. Yoon anymore—that's what I hear."

I stay silent as I process my disappointment. All these years I imagined her leading a glamourous life, performing in front of royalty or making her way into high society with her social prowess—a skill I observed from her and employed throughout my life. Yura, not I, should have been the one who made it.

She pauses, then leans into my ear again. "You see Charles?" she whispers.

"I thought he was with *Gomo*." I'd seen Charles standing in the living room next to my father's sister, who arrived yesterday from Korea for the funeral.

"Gomo's tired and resting upstairs. I check entire house, but don't see Charles." Her voice trembles even though the rest of her face is composed.

"Are you serious?" I say in disbelief.

"Listen, we don't know what he doing. You find him, okay?"

I storm off, upset at the possibility that right after our father's funeral, in front of all our guests, Charles can't keep himself together. I walk into the living room, and an elderly group approaches me and talks about the goodness of my father, his pride in me. How is living in New York? they ask. Do I live in an apartment or a house? Do I rent or own? How much do I pay in rent? I give them short answers, but when they continue to ask more questions, I apologize, say I'm looking for someone, and I bow in multiple directions. When my unease becomes overwhelming, I find my purse, go into the bathroom, and take out the anti-anxiety medication that I brought specifically for a situation like this. There is a knock at the door.

The door cracks open. "You find Charles?" my mother whispers.

I quickly remove the prescription pill bottle from her vision, lest my mother see it and question its contents. "I'm still looking," I reply brusquely. Frustration arises as I think about Charles's potential absence, which all the guests would notice: As the oldest and only son, he is the new patriarch of our family, and he knows he needs to be here. What if Charles is drinking somewhere in our house and will soon be out of control? I sigh out my frustration.

"I know Charles put you through a lot, but he suffering too. Don't be angry. Find Charles and make sure everything okay. Everyone your father know is here," she says softly as she closes the door.

I linger a few more moments in the bathroom to calm down before I go looking for Charles. I walk through the house, trying not to show my panic as I scan each room for my brother. I open the back door, put on plastic slippers, and walk towards the garden, calling his name. I find him sitting behind the shed, hidden from sight, on a lawn chair.

"Charles?"

Charles doesn't turn around. "Just needed to step away. I hate being around Koreans. One old lady didn't even know Dad had a son. She thought it was just you. They ask all these questions about my personal life when Dad's just died. They're so nosy," he says flatly. As the sky darkens, his face is engulfed in shadows. He rattles the ice in his plastic cup before taking a sip.

"What're you drinking?" I ask, trying to remain composed as I stare at his drink. I sit on the lawn chair next to him.

"Cranberry juice."

"Can I have a sip?" I ask casually, though my thoughts race with fear that he's drinking alcohol. Charles rolls his eyes. Then, without turning his head, he passes me his plastic cup. I take a sip, and am relieved to taste only a fruity, tart flavour. I sit next to him as we stare off onto our neighbour's orderly backyard.

"You're lucky, Anne. At least you made him proud."

"Charles, he loved us both the same."

"I've been dreaming about him lately, even about that last night in Crow Plains," he says, gazing ahead. He takes the cup from me and takes a long sip. "I think I wanted to prove that I could be a man and fight back because Dad never did. That's the only way I can explain what happened."

We have never spoken about that night, so I stay quiet, unsure what to say. Along the horizon, a red line burns against the descending blackness. "At least you fought. I never had the courage to fight," I say after some time passes, and we stare off into the approaching twilight.

Eventually, the guests rest their forks on the empty china. They put on their shoes at the door, hold my mother's hand or give her a strong embrace, stare intently into her eyes, and speak of how she and my father lived a hard life, but now, look at the success of her daughter who is a lawyer, her tall, handsome son, this beautiful house.

After they leave, we sit at the kitchen table, exhausted, except for Gomo, who has rested and not adjusted to the time difference. She talks with great animation as my mother pours freshly brewed coffee into her mug. I stare at her face, recognizing the hooded eyelids my father had, the same cautious silence as she waits for us to ask her questions. Her tight curls and pale skin are such a familiar trait of the Korea *ajummas* that I know and grew up with. She is an English teacher in Seoul and speaks to us in both English and Korean.

"What sort of brother was he?" Charles asks. This is something we've never known: my father as a young boy.

My aunt tells us a story about an egg. My father, as a child, wanted to give my aunt something special for her birthday but did not have any money. So, he went into a market and stole an egg. During the day, he carried the egg in his pocket, and at night, placed it into the hollow of his neck to keep it warm so that it would hatch, and he could present her with a pet chick on her birthday. The egg never hatched, so the frustrated boy began to cry and on his sister's birthday came to her empty-handed. I am mesmerized by the image of my father as a boy who slept with a fragile egg placed inside the hollow of his neck. What fascinates me most is the intensity of his conviction and self-restraint that, during the night, he did not crush the egg.

"What was he like when he met Mom?" my brother asks, his eyes becoming lively with curiosity. We have never known the story of my father as a young man. Growing up, my mother only told me they were introduced by a common friend, but never elaborated, and I never asked to hear more.

"He chased her for five years until she finally accepted his proposal. The day of his wedding, he couldn't stop smiling," Gomo says, and tells us the story of how my father fell in love. He saw my mother before meeting her. He spotted her at a local market on an autumn day when she accompanied her sister to purchase chestnuts for *Chuseok*. He followed her home, to the next village, and inquired about who her family was. Every day, he walked in the scorching sun or sleeting snow to watch my mother go to school with her sister. Her eldest sister, Aunt Jung-ja, was the town beauty, and every male—with the exception of my father—wanted to marry her. After they had been introduced by a common acquaintance, my father composed poetry for, and on occasion sang a few songs to, my mother.

My brother and I break out laughing as we try to imagine him singing love songs to our mother, unlike the stoic father we knew. "Your father different when he young," my mother says, with a grin.

"He wouldn't even get you a gift for your twenty-fifth anniversary," Charles says as I snicker. My father believed that anniversary presents were a Western-imposed tradition and that it was a ridiculous notion to have to prove his love. Only through the promptings from Charles and me did he take her to a steakhouse for dinner to celebrate their silver jubilee.

"Anne, you look like your father," Gomo says to me. She turns her head and addresses Charles. "But you look so much like *Maknae.* I was shocked when you come to the airport this morning. I felt like Maknae was standing in front of me again, pulling a prank after all these years."

"Who is Maknae?" I ask.

My aunt raises her eyebrows and looks at my mother.

"I don't think he told them," my mother says quietly.

"Dad once told me about Maknae," Charles mumbles.

"He did?" I say.

"Maknae was our youngest brother." My aunt sees my startled face, but continues. "He and your father were best friends. He was smart. He learn to speak English just by studying books. It was Maknae's dream to immigrate to Canada to study and become a doctor. He convinced your father to come with him. Maybe because of Maknae you are here. He was very mischievous, like Charles. He used to get in fights, steal at the market, and skip class to hike in the mountains. The day we left North Korea, your father told him to stay behind and we never see him again," she says with a resigned sigh.

I widen my eyes. "Dad's from North Korea?" I am filled with a sense of betrayal. Why didn't my father tell me any of this?

"Yes."

"I thought he was from Seoul."

"That's where we ended. During the war, our father wanted us to go to Seoul to be safe, but someone had to take care of the animals. So our father stayed home, and the other family would walk to Seoul to be with our relatives until things became stable. The morning we left, your father asked Maknae to remain with our father. We thought we would only be gone a few months. We never thought overnight Korea would become two countries.

"That was the last time we saw them. Once we reach Seoul, your father went to school but always worked to support our family. He was the oldest son and felt great responsibility. It was very hard times. Your father had guilt for telling Maknae to stay. And that guilt haunted his entire life." Gomo shakes her head and sighs.

I examine my mother's face, which is impassive, unlike mine, which twists with this revelation.

"We have enough sadness for today. Maybe time to sleep," my mother says gently, standing up and putting her mug into the sink.

We walk upstairs and I bring Gomo towels. She takes my hand. "Your father was not an expressive man, but he was so proud of you," she says.

"Thank you," I say, with a polite smile.

"In Korea, we believe it is the duty of the eldest son to bring honour to the family. Charles inherited that role, but your father always told me you were the one fulfilling it."

Tears fall down my face. I'm surprised, as I have not cried since arriving in Edmonton. I have been busy ordering floral arrangements and deli trays, making small talk with guests in the parlour room, worrying if we made enough coffee or had a sufficient selection of teas.

"Thank you," I force myself to say, wiping my cheeks with the back of my hands. I'm embarrassed by these tears. I feel betrayed—my father never told me he was from North Korea or had a missing brother, yet Charles knew.

"He was so proud of you," she says again, staring into my eyes.

“Thank you,” I say again, looking away, not wanting her to see the rage erupting inside of me.

The next morning, my mother knocks softly on my door.

I wake, startled that I am in Edmonton, in my parents’ house. Suddenly, I’m reminded that my father has passed, that I’ve just learned he’s from North Korea and left a brother there.

My mother enters and stands beside my bed. “Charles not in room and his car gone. Gomo sleeping but will wake up any time. We need to find him,” she whispers.

“Okay,” I say, sighing in frustration. Charles behaved so well at the funeral, but all my gratitude disappears as I rise out of bed, change into a sweater and a pair of slacks, grab the keys, and walk towards my mother’s car. I’m hoping Gomo will sleep through the morning and afternoon and not realize Charles is gone. Although my parents only moved into this house five years ago, I’m familiar with the neighbourhood. I drive slowly past a nearby strip mall and see my brother’s car in front of a local bar. I force calm as I go to his car to find it locked and empty. I look around and see my brother sleeping on the outskirts of the gravel lot, curled into a fetal position, holding his cell phone. When I walk towards him, I smell the sickly-sweet scent of alcohol. Before rousing him, I take his phone, scroll down it, and see his attempts, throughout the night, to call my father.

TWO

My parents' house is located in a neighbourhood development called Fair Estates, where retirees masquerade as modern-age lords. They live among Corinthian columns mixed with faux-marble Jacuzzi tubs and resin chandeliers. Outside these homes, trimmed hedges grow along the driveways, and flowerpots anchor the porches and garages. Here, my parents have met many other Korean retirees, and recently, Fair Estates—likely to the chagrin of the original house buyers who wanted a different demographic—is increasingly populated by Koreans: so much so that last year, a Korean church opened on its outskirts. To my mother, this house was the last chapter to my father's life, and represents, perhaps, the castle the hero finally returns to after a life of exile and adventure.

When my parents first moved in, they got rid of the grass in the backyard in exchange for a vegetable garden. Contractors brought in their machinery to dig and dump heaps of soil, and out of this chaos they created a paradise of cabbages, carrots, zucchini blossoms. They erected a greenhouse, a shed, and a drying house where they transformed wild fiddlehead ferns into *gosari*, acorns into jelly—they spent summer weekends foraging for these delicacies at local parks. Occasionally, vegetation from my parents' garden blows through the wire fence and scatters onto their white neighbour's otherwise pristine lawn—a backyard so lacking in blemish that my father once admitted to poking his fingers through the fence to confirm that the grass was real. My brother told me that a few times this neighbour has sat on his deck, drinking a glass of wine and muttering aloud how my parents' sprawling farm was affecting everyone else's property value.

It is early evening, a few days after the funeral. After I found Charles drunk in the parking lot, I dragged him home hoping that my mother would reprimand him. But because Gomo is here, the next morning we all behaved as if that night never happened, and I wonder if she can sense our strain.

Gomo and I are sitting on plastic chairs in the backyard, viewing the vegetable garden. Despite the heat, Gomo is drinking hot tea. I had not expected my family to be here tonight. I have been feeling emotionally exhausted. I craved time alone to process all of the drama and revelations that have happened over the past few days. I wish Gomo was not here so I could ask my mother more about why my father did not tell me about Maknae. I asked Charles to drive Gomo and my mother to Banff for a few days. They left early this morning, but when they arrived, all the hotels in Banff were booked except for an overpriced deluxe Jacuzzi suite that my mother, upon principle, refused to rent, even though I had given them enough spending money. Instead, they drove back home and interrupted my much-needed solitude.

Gomo shares with me her unsolicited opinions about Canada. She is stingy on praise: She has taken walks along the long stretches of sidewalk, not running into a single person the entire time, she says in disbelief. She finds fault with the houses that are identical to the next, wide lawns that are manicured yet devoid of children playing, flowers that carry no scent. The more expensive houses are along the ravine, its beauty tamed by workers wearing bright orange vests and helmets:

They climb ladders, clip stray branches, sterilize the flora with spray, then collect the debris to put into black plastic bags where they will be trapped forever in distant landfills.

"Here in Canada," Gomo complains as she brings her portable electric fan closer to her pale face, protected by her wide-brim visor, "even in a city like this, you can go for days without talking or seeing another human being. But in Korea, you cannot get away from one another. That's why Koreans have *jeong*—a kind of emotional bonding. We don't ask ourselves who we are or write books about our identity. We know our blood, it's pure, not mixed like in Canada," Gomo says as Charles appears at the back door.

Gomo's small eyes widen and light with fervour as she relays to us the pride and resilience of the Koreans: Centuries of invasions and oppression from the Chinese and Japanese have given them a drive to create one of the greatest modern societies in the world. American technology companies and billionaire tycoons visit Seoul to find the next trend because Koreans are on the vanguard of the technological revolution. Cosmetics companies come from all over the world to scout the newest beauty fad.

I glance over at Charles, who is trying to restrain what could be a smirk. Like me, he must find this overbearing.

"If you and Charles grew up there, you would understand. You would be different people," she says, unable to conceal the disappointment in her voice. Then she pauses, and reconsiders what she has just said. "Actually, Anne was better to grow up in Canada, but Charles would be better to grow up in Korea. Here, the men are weak." I'm surprised by Gomo's forthrightness, which, I remind myself, is probably cultural, as I have seen many Korean elders speak with bold bluntness. Charles's face darkens.

“That’s funny because I don’t recall Dad ever being very strong,” Charles snaps back.

“That’s what I remember when he was young. He had to survive. But maybe he changed after immigrating. Without family and friends, the soul weakens. I don’t know how your parents survived. I could never live here so isolated. Perhaps Canada broke him.”

Charles turns around and slams the back screen door. Gomo’s face remains composed, refusing to react to his outburst. She waits a moment before telling me she needs to give me something. She goes inside and returns carrying a parcel.

“Your father said you liked to read and write.”

“I do.”

“This is for you,” she says. It’s a small stack of envelopes, roughly a dozen, bound by burgundy raffia. “Your father wrote letters to Maknae and sent them to our mother’s house hoping one day Maknae would return to read them. When your father first immigrated, he wrote lots, but over time, he sent less, and then the letters stopped. I never knew what to do with them.”

I pick up an envelope, a red stamp dating it from 1977, the candy cane stripes of oxford blue and cherry red decorating the edges. It’s written in Korean, which I can no longer read.

“They’re not opened,” I say. There are a dozen sealed envelopes, and by the date stamp, I organize them chronologically, from 1977 to 1994.

“Your father believed Maknae was still alive,” Gomo says. “When the North Koreans opened their borders to reunite families, I applied so many times, but nothing happen. Once, he sent a newspaper article that show a picture of Kim Jong-il’s generals. He circled a face that look like Maknae, but the image was so small it could have been anyone. I don't think it was him. You know, having relatives in the South would make life hard for Maknae, probably impossible to get a good government job. But I never tell that to your father, let him hope. Knowing if Maknae was dead or alive would give your father peace. If Maknae died, but did not get proper burial, then his spirit is forever wandering. That is the Korean belief. Hopefully, these letters will bring healing, maybe even give rest to Maknae's spirit."

After Gomo goes to bed, I sit in my bedroom holding these envelopes. I pick one up, find a tiny gap along its flap, lengthen my index finger, then lift and tear. I take out a single sheet of paper, scrawled in neat but indecipherable lines, slants, and circles. The letter has a crisp fold. I hold it cautiously, so the paper does not tear off. I study the letters and form syllables but the words hold no meaning, as I understand nothing. I get up and find my mother in the living room, watching a Korean drama on television.

"Gomo just gave me these letters that Dad wrote to Maknae," I say as I hand her the one letter that I peeled open.

She grabs the remote control, pauses her show, and takes the letter. Her face lacks emotion as she reads it. I wait patiently as her eyes scroll down the page. "What does it say?" I ask.

"Just update on how family doing."

I wait for her to say more.

"Your father say we move to Crow Plains and we doing the store." She sighs, exasperated, takes off her reading glasses, and begins rubbing at her temples.

"I was hoping you could let me know what it says sentence by sentence."

She sighs loudly. "Listen, we know what happen. Just forget about it, okay?"

"We have forgotten about it. We never talk about it. He wouldn't have written about that night anyway. I just want to know what these letters say. You know I can't read Korean."

"I tell you already. Letter say we find the store. We move to Crow Plains. Anne and Charles doing the study well. Blah, blah, blah."

"I know but—"

She gets up from the sofa. "Boring update, that's all! I done the talking. This is noying." Although I'm not surprised by her reaction, as we never speak about the past, especially about Crow Plains, her irritation grates on me. I thought reading her deceased husband's letters and translating them to me would be a way for us to bond, not quarrel.

"What do you mean this is knowing? Knowing what?" I ask, my voice rising.

"*Noying*! How you describe Charles."

"The word you're trying to use is *annoying*," I say, trying not to yell, lest it provoke her to more anger.

"You are annoying!" she yells, then walks away.

"Mom, I want to know what these letters say. It could help us heal from what happened."

My mother stops, arches her back and lets out a jarring snort. "We don't need to heal. We need to forget! Easier! Past is past. We need to move on, not go back to bad things," she says as she waves her arm, then goes into her bedroom and slams the door shut. I sigh. For my mother, healing would be too easy. Rather, we should adopt a hard-earned forgetfulness. She has her own rules for suffering and for not showing suffering. And I have seen her face transform, her lips stiffen, and her heart harden from the life that slowly broke before her.

My cell phone rings. It's Richard. He's finally calling me.

"I'm so sorry, babe. It was an insane week. I was doing all-nighters and we just closed. But, I've been thinking about you the entire time."

"Hi," I say icily. I'm angry that it's taken him this long to check in on me.

"How did everything go?" He pauses and waits for me to respond. I don't. So he decides to fill in the silence. "I take it things have been tough?"

"Yeah. I don't like coming here. It's suffocating. I can't explain it."

"I have a funny story to cheer you up. You know that famous fashion designer who's my client? You know what he did? Every time he needed to make a major decision, he would step out of the room to call his fortune-teller so she could guide the closing. Meanwhile, his wife kept calling and interrupting our meeting over their Hamptons renovation. There were five of us sitting at the table being paid thousands of dollars to listen to her cry because another architect quit on her. She wants to build her yoga room around an oak tree, and each firm she spoke with told her it was structurally impossible."

A silence ensues as he waits for my reaction. Although I want to punish him for not calling me until now, I also sense his boyish desire to make me laugh, so I soften towards him. "You know, Cathy's firm specializes in that sort of thing," I say reluctantly. Cathy is my closest friend in New York and works as an architect. "You should recommend her firm. I think it's called Jorgensen or something Scandinavian sounding. I can give you her number."

"That would be great," he says. There's a long pause.

"I wish you had come," I say without emotion.

"You told me not to come. I said I could have taken that weekend off to come to your father's funeral. I didn't call until now because you told me you wanted time and space to take care of your family affairs, and I wanted to respect that."

I begin to cry.

"Babe, don't cry. I'm sorry. You're going through a lot. You need to grieve. I get it. You know what? I'm going to fly out this weekend. The case just closed, and I don't have any pressing work. I was even thinking of taking Friday off and leaving Thursday afternoon."

Richard's sudden announcement catches me off guard. Although I wanted him to be there at the funeral to comfort me, now it's too late. I want to be alone and not burden my mother with his visit. Also, there's resentment: When I told him that my father passed, he only offered once to come to my father's funeral. When I said no, he dropped it and did not insist when I wanted him to. "I'm sorry, I just got emotional. I don't know what came over me. Please don't come. I don't want my mom to stress out about being a good host. I just need to wrap up my father's affairs."

"But I want to see you. I want to be there for you."

I don't respond. There's residual anger, so I refuse to reassure him.

"You know, Anne, I finally understand this about you. Your power comes from your ability to withhold. You told me that you didn't want me to come, and now you're telling me the opposite."

"You should have insisted."

"I can't read your mind. You have to tell me when you want something. Listen, I get that you're grieving, but you have to open up to me more. You're an oyster that I need to dive for and crack open, so I can claim you as my pearl."

"I felt like you didn't care when you just offered to come once and then easily accepted my no," I manage to say. It's out of character for me to spell things out like this. He's right that I am closed, but he should know this is how I handle emotion. It's my way of being considerate: I don't want others to feel burdened by my strong feelings.

"I do care. But you need to tell me when you really want something," he says with a defensiveness which is unusual, coming from him. "I was thinking about how little I know about your past. You never talk about your childhood. I don't recall a single story that you've ever shared with me about your childhood except for that one time you went skiing in Banff—"

"—I have a terrible memory, you know that, Richard."

"Your forgetfulness seems selective. You have a great memory recalling things I've done wrong. And you never tell me what's going on with your family. For instance, you never talk about Charles. Is he there?"

"Yes."

"So he's out of rehab?"

"Yes."

"Is he working?"

"No. He's going to stay with my mom for a while."

"Is he searching for a job anytime soon?"

"Richard, our father just passed, okay?"

"Fine. Let's talk about your father. We've been dating for over a year and you never talk about him."

"I don't know that much myself," I say as my voice rises. "I just found out that he was originally from North Korea, and that he left behind my grandfather and uncle during the Korean War."

"He never told you that?"

"No. Apparently, this lost uncle was my father's best friend. My aunt gave me a stack of unopened letters that my father wrote to him and sent to my grandmother's home just in case he returned.

But they're written in Korean, which I can't read, and my mother refuses to translate them for me." I start crying, and I appreciate that Richard is quiet.

"I wish I could be next to you right now," he says with affection.

I pause as I struggle to find words that won't separate us further. "It's hard being back," I finally manage to say.

"The reason I didn't call is because you told me you'd be busy and wanted space. I wanted to respect that since you've told me it's hard for you to be there."

"You're right, I did say that."

"I miss you."

"Hey, it's late. I should be going to bed."

"Fine. Tell me good night in that voice I love."

"Good night, Richard," I say, so quietly that I can barely hear my own voice.

Richard fell in love with me, he will tell our friends, because of the sweetness of my voice: *Your voice, it did something to me.* His voice is loud and commanding, learned from a father whose own father was a commander in the army. Richard's words move like bullets: lean, economical, targeted towards a specific point. In contrast, my own voice is barely audible, and I find myself repeating words to cashiers, co-workers, and colleagues. It's a trait that always comes up on my performance review at work, my soft voice, though luckily most of my work consists of reading dense documents. My words move like feathers: light, inoffensive, always accommodating the currents moving around me.

We met at a benefit dinner for a humanitarian group operating in North Korea. I'm hardly a political person, but my firm sponsored a table, and, well, I had nothing better to do on a Thursday evening. A co-worker promised to attend with me, but cancelled at the last minute. I was sitting at the table not knowing anyone, feigning interest in the speaker: a French NGO director who went to Pyongyang and saw the atrocities of the dictatorship firsthand. Outside, an ice storm was pelting, while my stiff fingers—leaning against the cutlery—softened against the steamed salmon soufflé I was eating.

Richard appeared. He sat down on the empty chair next to me.

"Is this seat taken?"

I shook my head.

"Hi, I'm Richard," he said, grinning. I noticed his piercing blue eyes, the ease of his manner, his steely brown hair. He smelled of bergamot.

"I'm Anne."

"Sorry, I didn't catch that. What's your name again?"

"Anne."

"I've seen you before. Don't you work on the fortieth floor?"

"I'm actually a few floors above," I said. A woman who my co-workers jokingly call my doppelganger works on that floor. Although I don't see the resemblances, she has a similar slim physique and height, but she's Chinese.

"I recognize your face. I've seen you in the elevators."

This is how we met. When we first started dating, I felt awkward in the restaurants Richard would take me to. Even though I have a strong sense of taste, I never knew what to order, which wines to pair with which dishes. Not wanting to seem opportunistic and following in the footsteps of my parents, I picked the cheaper dishes on the leather-bound menus: the roasted chicken as opposed to the braised sea bass.

Richard, on the other hand, selects only the finest. He researches the restaurant's specialty, their seasonal offerings, what the reviewers say, and with this knowledge, orders a seamless feast. Yet, when he indulges in fine things, he has a calculated dissatisfaction that prevents him from fully embracing the experience: The Kobe steak is too tender, the sauvignon too dry. Sometimes, I fear he feels the same towards me: that I am too thoughtful, too thoughtless, too little, too much.

He believes he is entitled to this finery. After all, he believes he is a self-made man. His father, a partner at a law firm, refused to support him financially after high school to teach him independence. At best, his father offered to loan him money, but at an interest rate higher than what his college's financial aid office was charging. Richard believes he deserves the best that life has to offer since he has earned it. This includes me, where—despite what I fear are my backwater tendencies—he will say that I am the finest of all women. He loves saying that, pitching me against his colleague's girlfriends or wives, saying sotto voce, "Babe, you're so much prettier than anyone else here," and I will return his proud gaze with a smile, a straightening of my back, trying to believe in his certitude.

When Gomo returns to Korea I finally have time to go through the letters. I select an envelope and pull out a page. The letter's date is when we lived in Crow Plains. The last time I read Korean was when I was a child. I enunciate each syllable aloud, unsure of the words forming. I understand only a few words, and the rest I look up, verbatim, in my parent's dictionary. I try to understand the whole by the parts. In the dictionary, there are some Korean words that will be one symbol, one syllable, and the English definition requires an entire phrase, sentences, multiple entries to describe the meaning. *Han: 1) one 2) mid-winter 3) a grudge 4) a resentful lamentation 5) limits.* I know I am not fully comprehending things, and, in frustration, I return the letters to the pile.

It's Richard who brings up the letters again when he calls a few days later. "Listen, I've been thinking about what you said, about your uncle and those letters. I emailed an acquaintance I know who works for an NGO that has a network of translators throughout North America. Anyway, he found a Korean translator in Edmonton who teaches at the university and comes highly recommended. His name is Hugh MacDonald."

"He hardly sounds like a Korean translator," I say, trying to hide my annoyance.

"He seems legit. Search him online. He taught there for over two decades. He's even written some articles about feminism in Korea. He's married to a Korean woman," Richard says with eagerness. This gesture reminds me of when we first started dating, of how he would always go out of his way to dote on me, and my heart softens.

"Thanks for thinking of me."

"You know I'm there for you, right, babe?" He mentions again that he'd like to visit, and this time counters my refusal by insisting again, but I'm firm: Although I admit I wanted Richard to be with me at the funeral, having him here now would complicate things. I need to complete my father's taxes, close his accounts, cancel his identity, and organize my mother's finances. I want to be alone while I undertake the dreary paperwork of post-death.

The translator does have impressive credentials—he's translated some books from Korean to English—so I contact Hugh and arrange to meet him at his office, inside a Brutalist building on campus. The room is small and decorated with celadon vases covered with white cranes and clouds. Before we sit down, he bows and greets me in Korean. I have never spoken Korean with a white person before, and on instinct resist his attempt at camaraderie. Instead, I shake his hand and respond in English; he doesn't make another attempt to speak with me in Korean. I hand him my envelopes, and after we agree on a price, he tells me to give him the weekend.

When I return to his office on Monday, he hands back my envelopes and a folder containing the translations. I eagerly flip through the pages. I see the names of people I have forgotten, places I have left and never thought of again. I'm surprised when I find myself suppressing a rush of tears. I blink successively, pretending to be absorbed in his translations, holding the papers up, trying to shield my glassy eyes.

The translator notes that in one letter my father shifts grammatical tenses and conjugates his verbs using honorifics, which would be out of place, as he is addressing his younger brother. I wonder if this is playfulness, or a sober moment when he desires to revisit his lost brother? The translator outlines which tenses are being used, and when there are changes to these tenses, but he will not get involved in discussing the reasons behind these shifts and refuses to relent under my pleading stares when I try to corner him—this stranger—and force him to explain to me the inexplicable.

"What is he really saying here?"

"He wrote that the family is moving back to Edmonton."

"Does he sound sad?"

"All I know is that he's using the polite, formal tense when he writes that the family will be moving."

"Why does he shift to honorifics? Is he trying to distance himself from his brother?"

"I can't answer that for you. I'm only a translator. I can only translate. I can't speak on behalf of your father."

I burst out crying. The translator looks down at the floor, embarrassed. Minutes later, I dry my eyes. I'm apologizing, he's understanding, and we're sharing an awkward silence as I count out the bills for his service.

He starts talking to fill the silence. "You know, one thing I must say about my time when I taught there was how difficult it was to read Koreans. I felt they were constantly saying one thing yet meaning another. I never fully understood what people actually meant, if their *no* really meant no or was really a yes and that it was my responsibility to keep insisting. I never knew what was expected from me, or when I was being rude. I remember this one co-worker. After years of knowing him, one night we both got extremely drunk and he told me of the many times I had unknowingly insulted him. I was so shocked. The next morning, he acted as if nothing happened. I still don't know if he remembers telling me about all his grievances towards me. I lived there for over twenty years, but I never felt like I fully knew what was going on. I guess it needs to be in your blood."

THREE

After retrieving the letters from the translator, I stop by a Korean grocery store to buy a bag of soup bones. When I arrive at my mother's house, I rinse the chunks of fleshy bone, then put them into a pot of water. Once the pot boils, I turn the dial to simmer, and look at the quiet ring of blue flames that rise from the burner. Whenever I need comfort, I crave bone soup: the broth clear, the taste complex, sprinkled with thinly sliced scallions.

My mother walks into the kitchen and pauses when she sees me cooking. "Where you learn to make this soup?"

"Do you remember Mrs. Song? She taught me when we were at Crow Plains."

A flash of recognition passes my mother's face. "She was nice lady. I hear they retire somewhere in Vancouver. We lose touch," she says simply. She picks up a spoon, goes to the pot, and samples some of the broth. "Need more salt," she says as she scoops a generous heaping of salt with her fingers and sprinkles it into the soup. "You do the cooking in New York?"

"This is probably the only thing I can make aside from instant ramen."

"My children helpless, don't know how to take care of themselves."

"I don't know how to cook because I work all the time and I can afford to eat out. But you should stop cooking and doing everything for Charles," I say, pointing to the table, where a place setting waits for his arrival. On the placemat are his utensils laid out between an empty bowl, small plates of banchan are covered under plastic wrap, *miyeokguk* simmers on the stove, and rice warms in the cooker.

"Charles helpless, you know that," my mother says affectionately.

"It's because you allow him to be helpless."

"He going through hard time."

"When is he ever not going through a hard time?" I say, annoyed.

"You so hard against Charles," she says, hurt. "Try and be nice to him. You never here. It's so small, the time you spend together."

"I didn't realize how much you still pamper him. He's a grown man. You're not letting him learn to take care of himself," I say to my mother, who shows no penitence. I leave the kitchen frustrated.

I go back to my room and lie on my bed. After I calm down, I pick up the letters and the neatly typed pages I received from Dr. MacDonald. I reread them, but there is a flatness to the words, a dimness to this past—though, at the same time, a forgotten world resurfaces: the Yoons, Crow Plains, Essex Academy. I'm hungry for some sort of revelation, but the sentences refuse to descend beyond the surface narration of these letters.

The earliest letter takes place before my birth. It is the story of my father as a young man, fresh immigrant, new husband. It is May 1977. The letter is one page and is written in pencil. The script is dark, showing the writer pressed the pencil deeply into the page. There are no traces of erasing, no sign of hesitation or regret. Also, the consistency of the angles makes it certain that this letter was composed in one sitting. My father was consumed with happiness, writing about his first account of Canada, gripping his pencil, writing without self-doubt, in the exhilarations of first love.

He was in love with the square street blocks, the huge houses, the cruising cars, the air. At the Edmonton airport, Mr. Kang, a distant relation of my mother's, picked them up, and drove them to his house for temporary residence. I imagine, at some point, Mr. Kang drove my parents around the city and gave them an edited tour—predominately going to the neighbourhoods of splendour and wealth—so that in my father's ignorance and imagination he assumed everyone in Canada had made it, with their lush gardens, fenced property, stretched driveways. He felt that by finally landing on this blessed ground, he too would make it. It's an easy letter to comprehend, for he uses simple adjectives to describe simple nouns: big houses, green grass, fresh air. He's happy.

Another letter is written roughly a year after their arrival. His words are less generous, the details more sparse, the comments vague. By now, their reality has settled in, like a dark fog, obscuring his previous declaration that Canada is like *haneul*, heaven. He doesn't mention they are struggling. They have rented an apartment, bought a used car, enrolled in an English language class, and my mother has started working as a janitor in a retirement home. My father is searching for work and unable to pass the few interviews he gets because he cannot understand the questions asked. He does not openly admit this in his letters, though, and only alludes to some job prospects. I only know about these rejections because when I was interviewing for jobs during law school, he brought up this anecdote to comfort me.

Inside another envelope is a photo of Charles and me as toddlers sitting on a brown sofa in front of our coffee table. When I show my mother this photo, I'm told this apartment is one from a series we moved through—each apartment having a new surprise about Canadian life: bursting pipes, melting radiators, Canadian cockroaches.

"Your father never believe this country have them until he finally find one crawling on his forehead when he sleeping. That night is first night I find out my husband can scream like a woman," my mother says as she hands back the photo, the corners of her lips lifting.

1983

February 25, 1983
To our beloved Maknae,

I wish you could see a Canadian winter. Right now, as I write to you, there is a storm. The snow may pile up, tonight, as high as to my waist, so that tomorrow morning, when I open the front door to shovel, the snow will come pouring down onto the floor. Chul-min's mother has asked her mother to mail me another set of long johns so that when I shovel, I will have two layers of long johns underneath my pants. When I told her I could just buy a pair from Woodward's (a department store), she told me she does not trust Canadian long johns and thinks their quality is inferior even though we have not actually bought any or shopped for them here. Even with two layers of long johns, I will be cold.

In the mornings, when I shovel, I take breaks and run inside to drink the hot barley tea Chul-min's mother makes for me before she goes to work. Even though Chul-min's mother complains about the cold, she admits the falling snow is beautiful to watch.

She is still working at the hospital, and I am now working in restaurants. You would be shocked at the prosperity of these people. After Canadians finish their meals, they leave coins on the table, to thank the waiter for bringing them their food. People are so wealthy they freely give money away like that. Once, Chul-min's mother brought the children to the restaurant, and they began collecting the coins on the tables. I had to apologize to my supervisor and make them return the money.

Here is a photo of the children. We went to a studio and had our family photo taken. Our Eun-ah is very much like her mother, with her egg-shaped face and high nose and her love for art. She likes to draw all day, and she's quite good. But with Chul-min, aren't you shocked at how much of yourself is in him? Sometimes when he is eating at the table or talking to his mother I will watch him, stunned at how much he resembles you, even his mannerism. He is a quick learner and is already reading books from the library. Remember how you and I used to take turns stealing books from the marketplace, then spend entire nights reading them by the candle? I read to them every night. They speak perfect Korean, so when you meet them, they will not be strangers to you.

With Love,

Hyung

My father is holding our favourite book, which has a tiger lying on a pillow, smoking from a pipe on the cover. My father reads from this book before we go to sleep. It is our nightly ritual.

Inside this book are pictures of animals conversing with peasants, of the heavens opening, and the gods watching mortals through parted clouds. At the end of every story, my father asks us what is the moral, for there is always a purpose to these tales. My brother quietly searches for the moral, whereas I get lost in the terrain with its talking bears, filial women, and tragic lost loves.

This is Korea, your true home, my father reminds us. At this point, we interact entirely in Korean. English is spoken only to the outside world—mailmen, neighbours, our building superintendent—but we rarely speak it, and never to one another. Korea is not separated by a vast ocean but is our true home, a place of familiarity and refuge—never mind that we have never been there.

My brother's favourite tale is the one about the nymph and the woodcutter. Long, long ago, there lived a woodcutter who was hard-working, obedient to his mother, but single because he was so poor. One day, he saved the life of a deer and, as recompense, the deer told him of a lake where seven nymphs descended from heaven to bathe. Choose a wife and take her robe, the deer instructed him, and she will be unable to return, but never give her that robe, or she will escape. He followed the deer's advice and trapped a beautiful nymph and made her his wife. She was deeply grieved, but, over time, bore him children, and eventually, her sorrows subsided. Years later, she convinced him to show her the robe. When he did, she put on the robe, grabbed her children, and flew back to heaven. He was devastated.

By chance, he met the same deer again, who told him of a bucket that drew water from earth to heaven. Sneak into the bucket, the deer said. When he did, he entered heaven and reunited with his family. But, over time, he missed his mother. When the mother was about to die, his wife arranged to have him visit her on a flying horse. But, she instructed him, do not dismount from this horse or you will never be able to come back. When he flew down and met his mother, she asked him to have some pumpkin soup, his favourite dish. He ate it while on the horse, but accidentally dropped some onto the horse's back, startling it, and he was thrown to the ground. The horse returned to heaven, leaving the poor woodcutter on Earth, where he never saw his wife and children again. This is why the cockerel cries so mournfully into the sky, for it has the spirit of the woodcutter, and his crowing is his longing to be back in heaven.

My brother likes this tale because, he tells me, he likes the heavenly being. The tale praises her beauty, obedience, and submission. She loves this woodcutter even though he is low in status, has no money, and is ultimately her trickster and tormentor.

"Why does she love him when he stole her robe and trapped her?" I ask, thinking this an obvious problem to the story, but my question goes unanswered.

"Chul-min, would you visit Mommy if she were dying?" my father asks in Korean. My father is smiling in a way that we know this is a test question with only one right answer. The sound of my mother chopping garlic in the kitchen stops.

"But I don't like pumpkin soup," Charles replies in Korean.

"What if she made your favourite, seaweed soup?" my father asks, looking at him in mock seriousness.

"Yes!" Charles shouts, and we hear my mother chuckling in the kitchen.

My father turns stern, his voice sober. "Canada is a good country, but they don't take care of their parents. Your mother comes home crying from work because even though these elderly patients have money, no one visits them. Korea is different. The eldest son takes care of his parents for life. If my parents were alive, they would be living in our home, and I would be taking care of them. It would be my duty. Do you understand?" There is a gravitas that has descended into our conversation, a moral we need to understand.

"Because I'm the eldest son, does that mean I have to take care of you and Mom?"

"Only if that is something you want." My dad quizzically asks Charles, "Is that what you want?"

"*Yeobo!* Stop it. Leave the poor boy alone," my mother shouts from the kitchen, although a weighted silence follows.

Charles avoids eye contact with me or my father. He runs out of the living room and shouts, "Yes!" in the hallway. My father looks pleased.

I believe that in Korea tigers talk, foxes mutate, and the gods commune with people. Anything is possible in Korea, unlike here, where, from my parents' whisperings at the kitchen table, everything seems impossible. I don't know why we left Korea, especially since my father told me we descended from a great king. That logic would make my father a king, my mother a queen, my brother a prince, and me a princess. I cannot understand why we are here, where my father is always searching for work, and my mother holds a cleaning job at a retirement home. I understand our situation is shameful, for my mother instructs my brother and me to not offer more information than necessary, especially about what our father does, or, rather, does not do.

Sometimes we shoot marbles on the sidewalk with the neighbourhood children. We rarely talk, because we don't really understand what they are saying, but I like to observe them: to inhale the scent from their freshly laundered clothes and observe their bright candies, which

I am always hoping they offer to share so I can have a taste. I've even won a few cat's eyes that I treasure.

One particularly hard day, my father comes home early. After a week of work, my father has been fired because he has marinated the forks in a tub of herb sauce, rather than the pork.

"In my last job, they made me put the forks into a tub of warm lemon water. I thought he said fork," my father says in Korean to my mother.

That night, my mother calls her mother. The times they call home are infrequent, usually reserved for New Year's Day. But tonight, my mother's eyes are raw and swelled, and my father looks very tired. My brother and I stand behind them, waiting to *insa*, to pay our respects to our grandmother.

My mother is shouting Korean into the phone as if the distance between her and her mother can somehow shrink if she shouts from her Canadian hilltop to reach her mother's Korean hilltop.

"*Eomma?*" she yells. It's strange to hear my mother address someone by that name: Mom. "It's me, Jung-soon. Yes, everything is fine. The children are fine. How are you? How is your health?"

There is a pause. I can hear my grandmother shouting in her thick country accent. "We sent you a cheque last month. Did you receive it? Please spend it on yourself . . . How is Jung-ja?" My mother is always worried about her sister, and oftentimes, at night, I hear my parents fighting over how much money to send to her and my grandmother.

Now my grandmother is shouting louder, speaking faster, and my mother quietly murmurs yes, yes, yes. She bites her lower lip—a sign I recognize that something is not right.

"Jung-ja always stops eating when she gets into those moods." My mother now speaks hoarsely, as her tears wet the phone's mouthpiece.

"Yes, yes, everything is fine. The children are growing up so quickly. I will send you photos soon. Here is Chul-min's father."

My father takes the phone as my mother wipes her tears with her fingers. He reassures her that we are all fine, that he is working hard, that the children are happy and eager to speak with her. Then he passes the phone to my brother.

"Hi *halmeoni*," he says in Korean. "Yes, I am fine. Yes, I am eating lots even though Father never buys us any candy or toys." My mother smacks Chul-min on the back of his head. When we hear my grandmother's cackle over the phone, my mother looks relieved. Charles passes the phone to me.

"Hi, halmeoni. Yes, I am fine. Yes, I am obeying Mother and Father. Yes, I am eating well."

My mother takes the phone from me and confirms that Chul-min and Eun-ah are very good children who obey their father and mother, and there is nothing to worry about, for we are all fine and very happy in Canada. She then hangs up the phone and begins to weep.

Later that evening, I hear the mention of my name as my parents speak quietly at the kitchen table. I tiptoe towards the kitchen's entrance, squat inside the door's shadow, and cup my ears to listen.

"Things would be so much easier if we were in Korea. My mother or Jung-ja could help watch them while we work. Yesterday, the Polish neighbour came over and accused Chul-min of hitting her son and said she doesn't want the children coming over to their house anymore. Now, I have to find someone else to watch them while you search for a job," my mother says.

"I won't have a job if we return to Korea. It's better to be jobless among strangers rather than among our friends and family. Besides, the future is here, in Canada, not Korea. We have to think about Chul-min and Eun-ah. Last Sunday, after church, someone mentioned they are hiring welders up north. The pay is good. If I can take night classes for welding, I can get my certificate and get a job."

I'm confused because my father, who keeps telling us that Korea is our true home, doesn't want to go back and somehow this is my and my brother's fault.

"*Appa*, let's just go back to Korea," I say in Korean, standing in front of the kitchen door, arms akimbo.

My father stops smoking and turns his head towards me. "Do you know why we moved to Canada?" my father asks.

"No."

"For you and Chul-min."

"I want to go back to Korea. I want to be a princess."

My parents laugh. I'm not sure why they think this is so funny, since I think it incredibly logical, but I'm glad that the weariness—even for this moment—has lifted.

1984

It's my first day of school. We have just moved into a new neighbourhood where my parents can barely afford rent, but they like that there are no immigrants, just white people. My mother is dressed in an orange-and-brown polyester print dress. She wears purple eye shadow and frosted pink lipstick. Her hair is feathered around her face. It's early in the morning, and she needs to take the bus to work after she walks us to school and enrolls me. After taking night classes at a local college, she now works at a telephone company doing data entry. She's proud of her office job: Every morning she colours her eyelids and lips, applies mousse to her hair, wears skirts with nylon pantyhose. Her name is now Susan. She doesn't really understand what her boss says, but every time she punches data into the machine, she double-checks, then triple-checks the dreary string of numbers with a hypervigilance driven by desperation: She can't afford to ever lose this job.

My father has also taken night classes and gotten his welding certificate and works in Fort McMurray during the winter when the ground freezes. He returns every couple of months and, during this time, takes us to the shopping mall and buys us each one toy. For the rest of his time back, we are told to be quiet, to leave our father alone. He likes to sleep, or read the Korean newspaper, or play *baduk*—a Korean version of chess is how it is explained to me—with his friends. Sometimes, if we are shouting or laughing too loudly, he snaps at us or at my mother to keep us in line. We learn to be more cautious when he returns; going up north has made him less patient, more protective of his space. I secretly am relieved when my father boards the bus, a week later, to disappear again to a vast, unimaginable place that swallows my father for months at a time. We are then released from catering to his comforts and can return to roaming freely around the house. Even my mother seems more relaxed and lets us shout and laugh as much as we please; sometimes she even joins us.

My mother takes a comb, dips it into a bowl of water, and straightens my hair, then ties it into a braid. My new clothes are laid out on my bed, bought from Woodward's Department Store's clearance rack: a plaid shirt with puff sleeves, a beige corduroy skirt that stops at my knees. I also have new shoes: black patent leather. When I wear these shoes, I see my reflection: the bottom of my chin, the holes of my nostrils, my peering eyes. I'm excited to wear all this newness.

When we get to the school, my mother speaks to the office people, and later, I am escorted into my classroom. As I walk in, the kids peer at me. They're sitting at their wooden desks, turning their heads and swinging their legs as I walk past them to my seat. I take a quick inventory of the kids with dark skin or black hair: There are none.

My teacher, Miss Duda, is a round woman—her large, owl-like glasses exaggerate the round eyes beneath, rimmed in peacock blue. I look at her in wonder, perhaps with the same curiosity that some of my classmates look at me now. She smells of stale saliva and floral perfume. She's speaking to me: I don't understand what she's saying. Instead, I focus on breathing through my mouth, trying not to inhale her scent. Her mouth moves slower, though her voice remains the same heightened pitch. I sit, staring at her mouth. The class giggles. She pauses, then writes something on a piece of paper and places it on my desk. She's just written my new name, Anne. It's been crudely derived from Eun-ah, but I don't understand the significance of this moment: that I have just been christened with my Canadian identity. Instead, I sit and stare straight ahead as she begins to speak and the children chant in unison. Then she walks away and no longer addresses me for the rest of the day. I am relieved.

Soon, I'm making sense of the salutations, the way my classmates interact among one another. I enjoy sitting in class, but dread when the bell rings for lunch. I'm always the one lingering behind, the slowest to go to the cloakroom. I wait for the other children to take out their lunchboxes and, when they are distractedly holding on to their sandwiches and juice boxes and chatting amongst one another, I dive into the cloakroom, take out my lunch, and either hide in the closet or sit furtively at my desk. I force the food into my mouth, trying to make the food disappear, fast.

I'm holding a piece of dried seaweed, which I bring to my mouth.

"What *is* that?" a boy asks. He is tall and heavyset, with angry freckles scattered across his face.

I don't say anything. I don't know what to say.

"Why don't you talk?" he asks, his bright green eyes peering at me.

"What's that smell," another girl says, sniffing towards me. She wears a cardigan with embroidered dogs, which I admire. She scrunches her nose, then walks away displeased, whispering to her friend as they slowly turn around and stare at me.

When I arrive home, I cry because I don't know what I am doing wrong. I'm scared of provoking this hidden offence that I'm not aware of.

Charles tells me not to be a sissy.

"Don't they make fun of your lunch?" I ask back in Korean.

"Just throw it away."

"What would I eat then?"

"No one notices if a banana goes missing from the cloakroom."

I decide not to bring my lunch anymore. I take the rice and seaweed sheets and fermented vegetables that I love and quietly place the container beneath my bed before leaving for school, then ferociously eat it when I return home. I don't speak, and I spend my days obsessing about how I will avoid everyone.

It's recess, and some older girls are skipping with two ropes on the pavement, singing. I stand against a wall, watching. A girl with a mint headband and matching pom-pom socks looks my way. "Do you want to join us?" she asks in a high-pitched voice.

I nod, pleased that I've been noticed by the older girls. "What's your name?"

"Anne," I say, to which the girls giggle and whisper.

I've never skipped in my life. She begins jumping from side to side, explaining how to jump double Dutch. I imitate her motions. Her two friends set up their two ropes around me, then slowly rotate their arms so that the ropes take on the form of two elliptical spheres.

> "In China was a girl named Anne,
> Whose name was also Chingaling Chan,
> She smelled like garlic and onion and fish,
> Which she ate then puked then ate again from her dish!"

They start snickering, though I'm not absorbing these words. I'm too busy skipping from side to side, trying to avoid each rope that lashes against the pavement. The skipping becomes faster, the whipping more severe. I jump harder and higher until I stumble and fall, scraping my knees against the cement in a tangle of rope. I wipe blood off with my fingers. The girls laugh.

"Leave her alone." It's Charles. He's approaching us, holding a stick, glaring at the girls.

"It's Chinaman Charles! He's lost his marbles!" the girl with the pom-pom socks squeals.

There's a crowd of children now surrounding us. Charles grabs the rope from her hand, and violently whips it onto the ground, almost hitting her shoes. She recoils.

"We're not Chinese!" he yells angrily.

"Chinese, Japanese, Dirty Knees, Look at These!" the children chant, stretching their eyes upwards, then downwards in a slant, slapping their knees, then chests as my brother continues to whip the ground, glaring at everyone circling us. We hear a whistle. It's Miss Duda, on recess supervision. She runs towards us, waving her arm. The children scatter. The girl walks up to Charles, gives him a defiant glare, snatches the jump rope from his hands, then runs off with her friends. It's just Charles and me left standing on the pavement.

"Carry on, children, carry on," Miss Duda says nervously, and the bell rings.

I receive my first report card. *Anne is very quiet. I encourage her to practise speaking English at home.* My parents look up the meaning of these words in the dictionary. The problem is that they don't know the English which I am to learn, that they are being told to teach me.

Tonight, it's parent-teacher interview night. My father traded shifts with a co-worker in Fort McMurray so he could come a few days earlier and attend this conference. He wears his only suit: the suit he married my mother in, wore to his immigration interview, and brought to Canada. My mother wears a new skirt suit she bought at Woodward's in the clearance section. She frosts her eyelids and lips and heats the curling iron to add a slightly vertical puff to her bangs. She has wrapped two boxes of After Eight chocolate mints to present to each teacher.

When they return home, my mother's pouf has punctured, her smile is deflated. She carefully unfolds a list of words from her purse. They're ones she has gleaned from the interview, which she did not understand the meaning of. We open the Korean-English dictionary to diagnose my deficiencies.

"You need to talk more in class," my mother says in Korean.

"There's nothing I want to say," I answer in Korean. This is a partial truth. I have nothing to say because I can barely understand or speak English.

"The teacher said we need to speak English at home." And so, my mother decrees that our family—in spite of our very limited vocabulary—will speak only English to one another. The next day, we're addressed by our English names when she arrives home from work.

"How is your day, Anne?"

"Good."

"How is school, Charles?"

"Good."

We are staging our dialogue for an imagined audience—as if my teacher has somehow climbed a ladder and is proudly watching through the window at this stilted exchange. Conversation becomes clumsy as language is reduced to its most basic function.

This new rule lasts only for a day, because my mother struggles to communicate at all. So we return to speaking Korean, but with a smattering of English words; Korean nouns have articles and Korean verbs now have gerunds. The next time our father visits from Fort McMurray, he buys us a television set. Charles and I are hooked: When we return home from school, while waiting for our mother to return from work, we watch beautiful people say hilarious things, and even though I laugh with the audience, I have no idea why. It's a mystery I'm intent on solving. I force English to slowly overtake my thinking, as if it were a type of cleansing agent, and over time, the goblins, dragons, and nymphs of my Korean imagination begin to fade.

FOUR

2014

I wake to the sound of my cell phone ringing. It's Cathy, my architect friend from New York. I picture her, tanned and sloe-eyed, with a beauty that attracts white men over Korean men who prefer their women pale and doll-like, which Cathy is not. She has long given up on trying to find a Korean man. I imagine her in one of her crisp work shirts, the buttons just low enough to leave some room for an admirer's imagination.

"Hello?" I say, trying to mask my groggy voice.

"Oh, I totally forgot, it's early morning out there, isn't it? Go back to sleep. I'll call you later."

I clear my throat. "No, I'm fine. I need to get up anyway. Aren't you at work right now? Is everything okay?"

"It's slow today. We're in between projects, and I wanted to check in with you. How are you doing? I didn't reach out because I figured you were busy with everything going on."

"It's been a blur," I say, and give her a brief account of the funeral. I don't tell her that some attendees didn't even know that my father had a son. Rather, I tell her a story one of the congregants shared: how one summer, my father invited church kids over to teach them how to garden.

"Your parents have a garden?" she asks, impressed. She is envisioning gorgeous flora surrounded by pastoral hedges and trees rather than the utilitarian vegetables my parents grew for the sole purpose of reducing their grocery bill.

"Yes, but I don't want to talk about funeral stuff anymore. Tell me what's going on with you," I say, changing the topic, lest she ask more detailed questions.

"Richard called," Cathy casually mentions.

"Oh? I didn't realize he had your number," I say, trying to recall why he would call her. My memory has been failing me lately, and I'm concerned when these lapses arise.

"He didn't, he found my work number through our company website. Thanks for telling him our firm could be a possible fit for his client. He wanted to ask about the work we do before he referred us."

"Of course," I say, now remembering his troublesome client. "I forgot to give him your number. Did you get the business?"

"We're bidding on the project, so keep your fingers crossed. He's so thoughtful and sweet," Cathy says. She has told me numerous times that Richard is a catch and not to let go. She likes that he texts me in full sentences, takes risks with his selection of metals for watches, reaches for the check without hesitation. "I told him that if we get the project, I would take you guys out to dinner."

"Oh, you don't have to."

"I insist."

The thought of Cathy buying us dinner feels excessive, but, I tell myself, I should be proud for having such a generous friend, a thoughtful boyfriend. "That's nice of you to offer," I say.

"You should see some of the fish out there," she bemoans, and chats away, regaling me with tales of her most recent bad dates. Some people could find her self-absorption irritating, but I find it comforting: It's a way to feel close yet not have to reciprocate that intimacy by sharing my own personal information. She complains of the doctor—a surgeon, no less—who is smart but short, the banker who is tall but dull, and the artist who is fun but broke. She wants an enlightened gentleman: someone who understands the need for chivalry but doesn't compound this with chauvinism.

"Did you hear that Scott, the Korean banker who just made managing director last year, went to Korea, found a wife, and is getting married this summer in Newport? He barely speaks Korean." There's a pause, and I can sense she's exhausted from her tirade. "When are you coming back?" she asks.

"I've asked for another week off. I need to take care of my dad's stuff," I say. I can't explain why, but after reading the letters, I know I need to be here, exiled and immersed in my childhood world.

"Does Richard know?"

"I haven't told him yet. I should, but he's been so sensitive lately when I'm the one grieving," I say, trying to mask my annoyance.

"Don't you have a brother who can help?"

"I'd rather just do it all myself. It's easier that way."

"How old is your brother?"

"He's a year older."

"For some reason I thought he was much younger. What does he do?"

"He's in between jobs," I say vaguely. I hear a soft knock. "Hey, I should get going. I think my mom's at the door."

"Come back soon. I miss you," she says as she air kisses into the phone. I do the same.

Like me, Cathy is a child of Korean immigrants although there is a divide between us that I'm unsure if Cathy senses. Cathy grew up in a predominately white and wealthy town in Connecticut, where her father was a gynecologist and her mother a pianist who studied at Juilliard and later became a housewife. Her childhood was free from stressors like working at a store or helping parents navigate immigrant life by filling out their paperwork. It was only at Princeton that she became involved in Korean circles, and this has been her social network since moving to New York; we met at a Korean American fundraising event in the city.

After meeting Cathy, I shopped the labels she wore, read the magazines and websites she referenced, tried my best to understand her world, as if it were a currency I needed. And my efforts have paid off. Richard often praises me for my sophisticated taste even though I'm a grocer's daughter who grew up in the prairies.

When I first met Cathy, what drew me to her was her resemblance to Yura. They both exuded an Asian exotica. They both attended schools where their peers were privileged white children. Also, they were proud of their Korean heritage—Yura learned traditional Korean dance, whereas Cathy played the *geomungo*, a stringed instrument learned from her musician grandmother. I, on the other hand, was always trying to hide my ethnicity, which I saw as a source of shame—my parents and I so readily accepted our inferiority, which, I realized through Yura or Cathy, not all immigrant kids did. Whereas Cathy made it, Yura did not: Ever since meeting Mrs. Yoon at the funeral, I have been thinking about the news of Yura's divorce and her self-imposed exile to the Caribbean.

I go to the door to see who's knocking. It's Charles.

"You're up early," I say, the sarcasm leaking through my voice. Charles usually wakes around noon, then goes to the kitchen for his laid out meal.

He enters my room without being invited and sits on my bed. "Mom told me you got the letters translated. Can I read them?"

I go to my desk and take out a slim stack of papers. "Dad wasn't expressive in life, so it's no surprise that these letters are very bland."

Charles flips through the translated pages, his eyes darting across and down each page. I wait as he quickly glosses over the words, turning each page. Then he tosses them to me on the bed. "You're right, these letters don't say much except to describe how happy we were," he says with a smirk.

"When did he tell you about Maknae?" I ask.

"He only mentioned him to me once. It was during one of his visits to the centre. For some reason, Mom couldn't make it, so it was just him, and it was very awkward at first. But then he started opening up. He said I reminded him a lot of his youngest brother, Maknae, even the way I rebelled. He told me that Maknae was a genius who taught himself English and even had an interest in Communism: He read all of Marx's and Lenin's work. Dad thinks it may have helped him succeed in North Korea, though having family flee to the South could have ruined his chances to get a government job. When Dad was talking about him, his eyes went glassy, as if he was about to cry. He stopped talking, and then we spent the rest of the evening watching golf on television. That was the only time we spoke about Maknae."

"He never told me about Maknae or that he was from North Korea," I say, trying not to show my hurt.

"He probably thought you didn't care. You never showed any interest in being Korean. Growing up, you were the *banana*," he says mockingly.

This term, *banana*—yellow on the outside, white on the inside—never offended me. It almost felt like a compliment.

"Well, you were my banana brother," I say in defence.

"At least I have an interest in Korea. I listen to K-pop. I eat Korean food. You, on the other hand, always distanced yourself from anything Korean, unless it helped you, like getting a job."

"I didn't get my job because of my ethnicity. I got it because I went to the right schools and I'm smart."

Charles rolls his eyes. "Sure."

"Remember Yura? I stopped eating kimchi because she told me it would help me fit in. Did you see her mom at the funeral? I've been thinking about her lately."

"I saw Mrs. Yoon but didn't talk to her. She just stared at me like I was some freak and looked away when I stared back."

"Apparently, Yura works for a cruise line, dancing," I say.

Charles raises his eyebrows in surprise. "Does that make you happy, knowing that she failed?"

"I don't get pleasure knowing Yura's life didn't turn out the way she wanted it to," I say, unsure where this accusation of schadenfreude is coming from.

"I'm sure you don't," he says in a tone where I sense, but can't confirm, sarcasm. "Wasn't it Yura who gave you that knife?"

My mind blanks, though this knife sounds familiar, like some remnant from my past. "What knife?"

"You wore it as a pendant on a necklace," he says, peering intently into my eyes.

I look away in discomfort as my heart begins to race. "I don't know what you're talking about," I say in a mild tone, trying to control a sudden panic surging inside of me.

"Doesn't ring a bell?" he asks.

"Am I supposed to remember every item I owned from childhood?"

"You wore it pretty often," Charles says as he continues to stare at me.

I shake my head firmly. "I don't know what you're talking about." The more I say this with certainty, the more I keep the unease at bay.

After an uncomfortable silence, he coolly says, "Okay, we can talk about it later. How's work?"

"Fine."

"Fine?"

"Yeah. I'm happy," I say matter-of-factly.

"You don't sound happy."

"I don't have to prove to you that I am."

"Well, I'm glad you found a job that suits your personality."

"What does that mean?"

"I think anyone who's a successful lawyer probably has some questionable, amoral tendencies. That's your job, isn't it? To manipulate and find loopholes in tax law so you can make your clients as rich as possible? Isn't that why they pay you so much, because you find ways for them not to be held accountable?"

"Charles, what's your problem?"

"Come on, I have to pretend I don't see that you're always deciding what's right or wrong in order to maintain your conscience?" he says.

"Well, someone had to get a solid job to take care of Mom and Dad because they couldn't depend on their oldest son, so maybe you could show a little more appreciation," I say. I can't help my response: It's been years of trying to rein in my resentment, and these words allow just a little release, a little relief.

He stands up and leaves without looking at me. I resist the urge to go after Charles and try to placate him. I'm unsure what he's thinking or how I should handle the situation. It's been five years since I've been back, and I rarely talk to Charles on the phone. I have forgotten how moody and quarrelsome he can be, and I wonder if it's his jealousy over my achievements—which I can't help—exacerbated by all the attention and praise I received from the funeral attendees.

I organize the scattered letters on my bed and read the top letter which praises Charles: he's the smartest in his class, smart enough to become a doctor—the dream Maknae wanted to pursue. There's no mention of me. I'm reminded that when we were young, I was the one with the least promise for success; it was Charles and Yura who were supposed to succeed. And yet here I am, the one who made it: a tax lawyer working for one of the top firms in America. Whose fault was it for their wasted brilliance, themselves or our parents? Or are there more deeply rooted forces that carried over from the old world? Either way, success or not, none of us ended up happy.

1987

When my parents go to a shopping mall or take a neighbourhood stroll, they take note of the Asian families and speculate on that couple's ethnicity—are they Chinese? Japanese? Or, maybe, even, Korean? If they believe the couple is Korean, my father—usually a reserved man—walks up to them, introduces himself, and asks where they are from. This is embarrassing. Charles and I walk faster or slower while this is happening, hoping to dissociate ourselves from our parents.

In one of these instances, my father introduces himself to the Yoons, and the conversation accelerates.

"We are Korean."

"We are also Korean."

The language then crosses into Korean, a very personal territory. When did you come? Which part of Korea did you come from? What do you do?

They have one daughter named Yura, who is two years older than me, and stares at us cautiously. "You have a new friend," the adults say, turning to me, smiling, when in fact they are speaking of themselves.

When we first visit the Yoons, Yura opens the door. She wears a pale pink dress with a glittering headband. She welcomes us in perfectly enunciated Korean and moves every lithe limb with dignity and deliberation as she graciously bows to my parents. My mother, delighted, remarks on what a pretty daughter Mrs. Yoon has. I silently take note that this comment is not reciprocated. I study Mrs. Yoon's powdered face, marvelling at how perfectly coloured her eyes, cheeks, and lips are.

Mr. Yoon used to weld, but now he owns a dry-cleaning business in Glenora, an affluent neighbourhood in Edmonton. Like my father, he comes from Seoul, although he is three years younger. They both graduated from Seoul National University, the most prestigious school there, the "Harvard of Korea" my father says whenever he explains his alma mater to anyone not from Korea. At university, Mr. Yoon studied literature and published a book of poetry, which he presents to my parents as a gift. He is a thin man with delicate hands and a quiet voice. When he offers me dried persimmons, I immediately like him. He eagerly tells my father about the alumni chapter he is starting with other immigrants he has met. After some chatting, it's revealed they have a mutual connection: My father's classmate and friend, Mr. Hong, is Mr. Yoon's cousin. The conversation becomes livelier as my father proudly announces that before leaving Korea he gave his job as an electronics engineer to Mr. Hong, and Mr. Yoon says his cousin plans to visit Canada in the near future. Mr. Yoon pours whisky into a crystal glass and with both hands offers it to my father. Mrs. Yoon brings a bowl of fruit, which my mother insists on helping her peel. My mother takes a knife, and together they begin filling a plate with apple and orange slices.

Charles and I sit in the living room with Yura. We listen as the adults roar with laughter next door. Charles turns on the television and rotates the dial in search of a cartoon show.

"Do you like our table?" Yura asks in Korean, pointing to the coffee table. The coffee table matches the credenza. The furniture is black, lacquered with an elaborate, inlaid, mother-of-pearl design of cranes and clouds. The room smells of dried fish.

"It's pretty," I reply in Korean.

"My mom brought this over when they came here. She also brought over all her fancy clothes. Would you like to see them?"

I nod, and Yura leads me down the hallway, into her parents' bedroom. She opens a closet full of pastel pinks, swirls of peaches and creams. The fabrics are fine to the touch, with silks and delicate wools. There is a stack of brightly patterned silk scarves; I want to examine each piece individually and study its intricate details. She kneels and brings out a wooden box with the same crane-and-cloud design from the living room furniture.

"This is her jewellery," she says, opening the box and taking out strands of pearls, rings of gold. "My grandfather was a *yangban*. Do you know what that is?"

"No."

"Yangbans were the rulers of Korea."

This is not true, since it is our family who would have ruled Korea had things been different, but since I do not want to damage our potential friendship, I stay silent.

"Does she still wear these fancy clothes?" I ask, noticing the clothes are too light and delicate for the harsh winters.

"Only on Sundays for church or when we have guests over. When she married my father, she thought he was rich, so her family bought these clothes for her new life in Canada."

Mrs. Yoon calls for Yura. She hastily puts the jewellery back into the box, shuts the closet door, and walks out of the bedroom.

"Yes, Mom?" she says in a high-pitched voice.

"Come into the kitchen," Mrs. Yoon says in Korean.

Yura's back becomes erect. When we go into the kitchen, the adults, all in a merry mood, turn around and look at Yura.

"Show us what you are practising for the Christmas recital," Mrs. Yoon says.

"Yes," Yura says softly, then bows obediently. This sudden shift into formality makes me uncomfortable: Do I also need to act like this in front of Mrs. Yoon?

"Just let the girls play," Mr. Yoon says, irritated.

"Go to your room and change into your dress," Mrs. Yoon says.

Yura nods, then disappears down the hallway to her room. Mr. Yoon reluctantly leads the adults into the living room, turns off the television, and clears an area to make space for her performance. I hear Mrs. Yoon instructing Yura to redo her ponytail, readjust her stockings, straighten her crown. Finally, Mrs. Yoon enters the living room, clasping her fingers together, hands pressed against her chest. The scene, Mrs. Yoon explains, is from the *Nutcracker*, in which Yura was selected to be the Sugar Plum Fairy for her ballet school's Christmas production. It was the first time someone who wasn't white was selected for a lead role, Mrs. Yoon adds. She drops the needle onto the record player, and the music plays.

Yura walks in with a tiara, a frothy skirt, and satin ballet shoes. She takes tiny steps, tips and teeters, leaps and lunges her delicate limbs. I am spellbound: I have never seen a performance like this, nor witnessed such artistry. When the dance is over, the adults burst into applause. Yura bows gracefully.

"Such a fine performance. She is so tall for her age," my mother says.

"She is the tallest in her class," Mrs. Yoon answers. "The teachers don't know what to make of her. Even though she is only in Grade 5, she is taller than some of the girls in Grade 6, and smarter too. At the last parent-teacher interview, her teacher said she could skip a grade. But our Yura is so popular with her classmates that she begged to remain in her class."

Yura takes my hand, and we exit the living room and go to her bedroom. "When I grow up, I'm going to move to New York and become a dancer," she says. "I want to dance in front of presidents and kings, just like Karen Kain."

"I also want to live in New York," I say, trying to sound just as certain, although this thought has never occurred to me until now.

"Then we will go together," she says matter-of-factly.

"Really?" I'm thrilled that she has chosen me to be a part of her brilliant future.

"Sure, we will be roommates."

"Have you ever been there?" I ask.

"No, but I have an uncle who lives there. He owns a jewellery store and promised to send me hairpins from New York."

"Are the hairpins nice?"

"Eun-ah, they're from New York."

I have never seen hairpins from New York, but I imagine sapphire crystals, jet beads, and plumed peacock feathers. I have seen *Breakfast at Tiffany's*, so I know that the people in New York are more beautiful, better styled, and more genteel than the people of Edmonton.

On the ride home, my parents speak in light, mirthful voices. My mother speaks about the coincidence of it all: of how Mr. Yoon and my father grew up in the same city, attended the same school, and yet they meet here of all places, in a mall in the middle of the Canadian prairies. Whereas in Korea, because my father was poor and Mr. Yoon rich, they would never socialize together, here they can, even be considered equals. My father nods while my mother says this. He turns around and asks what Charles and I did tonight.

"Watched television," Charles answers in English, chipping the frost off the car window with his fingernails.

"Looked at the living room furniture. It's from Korea," I say. I do not mention viewing Mrs. Yoon's fancy clothes or fine jewellery.

My parents stay silent, enjoying the afterglow of this new friendship, until my mother softly remarks in Korean, "The furniture was out of place in that house. It must have cost them a fortune to bring all that from Korea. They should have known better and left it behind."

FIVE

1990

After church on Sundays, we usually go to the Yoons' for dinner. Mrs. Yoon enjoys entertaining, so rarely do they come over to our house. I'm always eager to spend time with Yura. Even though we have only known one another for three years, Yura is like close kin, the only person aside from my family that I can count on. Throughout the week, I prepare for this visit by collecting stickers, stories, or pretty things to bring to her. When we arrive at their house, Charles automatically goes to the television set and sits in front of it. I stretch my neck until I see Yura, and shyly walk towards her. Mrs. Yoon smiles and says how wonderful it is that we have found one another because Yura has always wanted a *dongsaeng*—a younger sister—and my mother responds with mirth that I have always wanted an *unnie*—an older sister.

Yura is now in Grade 8, and I am in Grade 6. She is in junior high school and is growing at a pace faster than her classmates. "I'm becoming a woman," she says, and points out her developing curves and sunken cheeks. She shows me the training bras her mother has bought for her. Sometimes, while we are talking, she presses her breasts with folded arms, in the hopes that they will not protrude, not betray her dreams to dance. She uses words that I memorize and look up in our dictionary when I return home. These words are clever and sophisticated. At a later date, when I speak with her, I will use them back, always casually: you are so *capricious*; that was so *serendipitous*; what he said was so *facetious*. But these attempts fail, and she calls out my blunders: One day, she corrects my pronunciation and accuses me of committing a *malapropism*. Only after I return home to look up this word in the dictionary do I feel ashamed.

In exchange for my motley stories and piecemeal offerings, Yura shares with me her observations of the world her mother desires her to partake in, that she is becoming a part of, at Saint Lidwina Junior High School, which is in a wealthy neighbourhood in Edmonton. I imagine her friends and their parents as if they are part of a British television drama from the Victorian era, where they wear puffed-sleeve dresses, speak in refined accents, and drink tea with their pinkies arched.

I'm sitting cross-legged on Yura's bed. She leans against the wall, painting her toenails mauve, which she will later hide from her mother by wearing socks. She tells me about her best friend, Sharon Rosewood. She is not only beautiful (from the school photo Yura shows me, Sharon looks like a movie star with her high cheekbones, luminescent skin, golden hair), but rich: Her father owns the Rosewood Sausage Factory, and his products are sold in every supermarket. Our family buys his kielbasa, which we slice into circles, then fry so that the meat curves inwards like tiny frisbees. We eat this with our rice and kimchi and it's delicious.

Last weekend, Mrs. Rosewood, Sharon's mother, hosted a mother and daughter tea, to which Mrs. Yoon was also invited. They went to Sharon's house in Glenora, which overlooks the North Saskatchewan River.

There were silver trays holding white triangular sandwiches—with the crusts cut off—filled with tuna and mayonnaise, cucumber and cheese, and pitchers of fruit punch—I realize that punch is something you can also drink. The tablecloth matched the napkins, which were neatly rolled into rings adorned with silver butterflies—accompanied by the silver candlesticks that created an interior harmony, according to Yura. Their bathroom had mint-green toilet paper. "It was *fabulous*," Yura says in an exaggerated enunciation different from how she normally speaks. Yura has two distinct voices. With me, she speaks in a grainy voice, her laughter similar to her father's—a low, staccato huff. But if someone else—say my parents—enter the room, her inflection rises, her laughter softens, her demeanour becomes more delicate. It is a privilege that she uses her more intimate voice with me.

She is reading books about artists and tells me about their lives marked by great suffering and hardship. Take Isadora Duncan, the famous dancer whose life was tragic: Her two children drowned, her third child died shortly after birth, her husband committed suicide, and she strangled herself when her long scarf caught onto the spokes of the car she was in. But the tragedies in her life helped convey the inexpressible through the movement of her body. Words cannot possibly say everything you wish to say, which is why we need dance, Yura tells me.

"Close your eyes," she whispers in my ear. "Out, damn spot, out I say. Open your eyes," she instructs me, then repeats these same words with her arms lifted and swaying with such force to prove her point: that movement matters and is the essence of life. "I must feel so my audience can feel. As a result, I will suffer in life," she says matter-of-factly, fully resolved to devote her life to art.

"How do you know you will suffer?" I ask, horrified that she has already resigned herself to this fate.

She lowers her voice. "I overheard my mom telling a friend that when she was a young single woman in Seoul, she went to see a fortune-teller. The fortune-teller predicted that she would marry and live in a foreign land. That's why, out of her many suitors, she chose my dad, because of his desire to immigrate to Canada. Then the fortune-teller told her she would bear a child whose life would be full of sorrow."

"Can't she be wrong?" I say, my words barely audible.

"I know in my heart that I am going to suffer," she says.

On the car ride home, my mother is alarmed when she turns around and sees me silently crying.

"What's wrong?" she asks in Korean.

I blurt out in English that Yura will live a life of suffering because of what the fortune-teller predicted.

"What fortune-teller?"

"The fortune-teller that spoke to Mrs. Yoon when she was a young woman living in Seoul and told her that she would marry and live in a foreign land and have a child who would suffer," I say all in one breath.

"Yura's talent seems to be more in storytelling than dancing," my mother says, and begins to laugh. My father joins in. After hearing their chuckles, I feel both better and foolish for my tears.

"They seem very alike, mother and daughter," my mother says, and my father nods in agreement.

There is no end to Yura's potential. Mrs. Yoon discusses with my mother the various possibilities for her daughter: Her dance instructor declared she has immense potential. Should she attend a prestigious ballet camp in Winnipeg this summer? Her teachers all say she is the top student and is very articulate. Should she become a lawyer? Or, Mrs. Yoon's sister-in-law—a well-to-do society woman in Seoul—has seen Yura's photographs and believes she can compete one day for Miss Korea. Should she begin her training?

My mother begins showing reluctance when my father suggests we visit the Yoons. "She never asks about Eun-ah or Chul-min," my mother says with quiet indignation, while I prepare for our visit. "I heard that Mrs. Yoon framed her husband's Seoul University diploma and hung it behind the cash register at their dry cleaners. Pfft! That might have meant something in Korea, but it has no value here. To Canadians, we're all Chinese peasants."

Increasingly, my mother finds an excuse not to come, so that it's only my father and I who show up at the Yoons—my brother stays at home with my mother. My father apologizes for my mother's absence due to her not feeling well.

"Your wife is frequently ill these days. You should stop making her work so hard," Mrs. Yoon says in Korean as she opens the front door, masking her disappointment with a smile. Normally, she is soft-spoken in front of our family, but today she screams for Yura from the hallway, glares at her when she walks down the stairs. My father joins Mr. Yoon in the living room, where he has laid out a small wooden table to play baduk.

Yura takes me to her room. She's sullen and says nothing as she lies on her bed and flips through a fashion magazine. She seems annoyed, so I sit quietly on the floor and observe the things in her room.

"What's that?" I ask. There's a beautiful silver object on her dresser.

Yura stares at it, then at me as if deciding if she will show it to me. Then she gets up and puts the long silver object into her palm. An ornate design of birds and flowers is etched onto the metal. The ends curve slightly. A red tassel dangles from the middle, which is affixed to a ring. She gently breaks it open to reveal a blade underneath.

"Do you know what this is?" she asks, pointing the blade towards me.

"A knife," I say.

"It's an *eunjangdo*. It has been passed down our family for generations. Noblewomen wore this with their *hanboks*. If a man dishonoured a woman, she would take this knife and stab herself with it."

I gasp in horror. "Why would she do that?"

"To prove her virtue if she was dishonoured." She rotates her wrist towards the sunlight and the blade gleams. Then she offers it to me.

I take hold of the knife, heavy, tarnished. I lightly caress the delicate etchings. "What sort of dishonour would require a woman to kill herself?" I ask.

"Back then, all a woman had was her purity. If she lost that, she was no longer worth anything," she says.

I'm puzzled by her cryptic talk. "How did you lose your purity?" I ask.

"When you lost your virginity to someone who was not your husband."

"What is a virginity?"

She pauses to find the right words. "It's a box that can only be opened once," she says carefully.

"Where is this box?"

Yura puts her hand on her belly and points downwards. "I'll tell you a secret," she whispers. "Sharon Rosewood's sister lost her virginity at a camp last summer."

"She didn't *lose* her virginity, it's only been *opened*, since the box must still be inside of her," I say reassuringly. Yura looks amused but remains silent. None of this makes sense, especially why a woman would kill herself.

"Why would they stab themselves and not the man who dishonoured them?" I ask.

"Suicide is more virtuous than murder," Yura says, pressing her finger against the knife's blade. "This is from my mother, who got it passed down to her from my grandmother. I actually have another one. My gomo only has sons and gave this to me when she heard that I was part of the fan dance to represent Korea at the Heritage Festival. I wore it with my hanbok." She opens her drawer and takes out another silver knife.

The knife handle and lid are etched with vines and flowering chrysanthemums with a silver ring in the middle. A royal-blue tassel juts from one side. I realize I don't own anything from Korea, that my parents have nothing to pass down to me. I have no inheritance. I want this knife.

"Can I have it?" I ask.

Yura looks surprised by my bold request. "I guess," she says with a shrug.

The phone rings and she quickly jumps off the bed and announces that she has to go to the bathroom.

I pick up the knife and admire its beauty before I tuck it into my pocket, grateful that I have caught Yura in a generous mood. Then I lie on her bed and flip through her teen magazines. After some time, I wander into the hallway. I see the phone cord running underneath the bathroom door and realize she's been talking softly on the phone the entire time. When she returns, her eyes are red and raw. As she rubs her eyes, her sleeve drops, exposing several long marks on her arm. I recognize these marks because my father has also lashed Charles and me when he is angry.

"What's wrong?" I ask.

"Nothing."

"What happened to your arm?" I glance at her purple mark.

"An accident," she says curtly, then pulls her sleeve to her wrist.

I'm actually relieved to see those marks, as it means we're not the only ones experiencing this pain. "My father hits us too, although I'm lucky because he hits Charles harder than me," I say reassuringly.

"It's not my father," she says despondently. "It's my mother. She found out I have a boyfriend, and she's trying to stop our relationship."

"You have a boyfriend?"

"Yes. He's best friends with Sharon's boyfriend."

"Is he white?"

She nods. She pulls out his photo from underneath her mattress and reveals a handsome boy with blonde hair and blue eyes. I'm shocked. Yura has crossed the divide, pulled off the ultimate coup of having the desirable find her desirable. Yura tells me that last week, her mother found her diary and read all about her secret dates with Tom Fenson. Mrs. Yoon called every listing under his last name in the White Pages until she contacted his mother who, at best, seemed amused, at worst, was offended and stated that she was fully aware her son was dating Yura and, no, she refused to interfere. They could choose to do as they liked with their relationship.

Infuriated, Mrs. Yoon, knowing Tom's address from the White Pages, parked outside of his house and watched in horror as he returned home from school with a cigarette dangling from his hand. She approached him and began yelling at him, forbidding him to see Yura again, lest he derail her destiny to marry a Korean man and become a world-class ballerina. Tom refused to promise to leave her daughter alone.

After hearing what happened, Yura was devastated, but agreed to Tom's pleas to see him in secret, but it's been tough: Mrs. Yoon now picks Yura up from school every day and chaperones her to all her extracurricular activities. She's no longer allowed to visit Sharon's house.

Yura tries to sound casual as she mentions that it's been a month since she's last seen Tom and that maybe their relationship was just a fling to him.

"Have you kissed him?" I ask, unable to resist my curiosity.

"Yeah."

"How was it?" I ask, enthralled.

"It was okay, but . . . he sweats a lot. White guys have this smell, which is why they need to wear deodorant."

"What's that?" I ask, marvelling at Yura's worldly knowledge.

"It's something you or I don't have to worry about," she says as she scrunches her nose, pausing as if she wants to say more, but then decides against it.

Because she's being so generous right now, I ask a question I have been wanting to ask her for a long time. "How did you become best friends with Sharon Rosewood?"

"You become like them," she says bluntly. "It's not so hard. Small things are what create a barrier. You just remove them so nothing is offensive. For instance, I never eat kimchi. Why? Because I don't want to smell like garlic. Smells offend them."

I must look confused, because she continues. "There's one other Korean girl in my school who I avoid. I'm so embarrassed by her. She's super fobby. When she passes me in the hallway, she leaves a scent trail of garlic. Even though she brings sandwiches for lunch, she eats so much garlic at home that the smell oozes out of her skin. I think she's oblivious, but everyone around her can smell it. And it makes them uncomfortable."

"Do I smell like her?"

Yura buries her nose into my neck, then down my arm, and then the back of my hand. I catch a whiff of her pleasant drugstore floral scent. "Yes."

"Really?"

"You need to take care of these details so that people won't look down on you. Maybe get a better haircut."

"My mom cuts my hair."

"I know. Your goal is to make them comfortable, and the only way to do that is to look like them, act like them, become them," Yura says. I scan the stacks of fashion magazines in Yura's room, and I realize she dresses like the models with her hoop earrings and brightly coloured cardigan.

"Doesn't that make you fake?"

"You're just trying not to be offensive, but first you need to know what is offensive. Korean fan dancing isn't offensive. They appreciate beauty, so you don't have to get rid of everything Korean, just pick and choose. Also, try to be a little more upbeat. People like Sharon don't like to be around people who are so . . . heavy." I feel a personal sting because her directives are aimed precisely towards my personality. I wonder how long she's been compiling this list. She glances at me as if she wants to say more. "Besides, we're lucky."

"Why?"

"Most people are trapped by their traditions or their ancestors' beliefs, but we don't have that," she says reassuringly. "We can decide for us what's right and what's wrong."

"What do you mean?"

"We're not from Korea, but we're also not from here. So, we get to decide which beliefs we want to go with for whatever works for us."

I shake my head in confusion.

"Here's an example. My mom thinks she's being a really good mom and that it's Tom's mom who is terrible, without discipline, almost irresponsible. But Tom's mom doesn't see it that way. She thinks she's the good mom and that it's my mom who has all the problems. Who do you think is right?"

"I can see why both think that way."

"Exactly, we can see both sides. That's our gift of belonging neither here nor there. We get to decide what is good or bad, and that can be our gift, if we let it."

Her words are dense, and I need time to process them, to comprehend what she's saying. When I don't respond immediately, she picks up a teen magazine and studies the pages intently, indicating she doesn't want to talk anymore.

I think about what Yura has said, how not belonging to either culture is to my advantage, which is a thought I have never considered. I think about Mrs. Yoon and Tom's mom, and am sympathetic to both as good mothers, and yet I can see why they would view the other as bad. I start imagining a privileged freedom where I can decide what is right and what is wrong, but my mind balks. Seeing morality as something I can construct rather than having to be held accountable to is overwhelming, something I'm not ready for yet.

The following week, Yura calls me. Even though we have been friends for three years, this is the first time I have ever received a call from her.

"Did your mom hang up?" Yura asks when I get on the phone.

"Yes, I just heard her phone click."

"Do you think she would be listening again from another phone?"

"No, she's cooking in the kitchen right now," I whisper.

"How do you know?"

"I can hear her chopping in the kitchen."

"Tom wants to see me, and I told him we could meet by your house. I told my mom that you invited me over to watch a video. Your father will be over at my house playing baduk. Can you try and get Charles out of the house? I plan to be there on Sunday after church, okay?"

I am filled with fear. Though Mrs. Yoon is not my mother, I fear disobeying her. "Sure," I say weakly.

On Sunday, I tell Charles that Yura will be coming over after church to watch a girly movie, so, without asking, he goes to a friend's house. Yura arrives in high spirits. From our front porch, she waves to her mother and says that she will call her once the movie is done. I follow Yura into our bathroom, which she locks shut. She takes off her baggy sweater to reveal a lacy leotard. She leans into the mirror and applies thick eyeliner, glossy lipstick. She teases her bangs and flash freezes them with hairspray.

"You look like someone who could be on TV," I say, in awe of her transformation.

"Have you ever seen anyone that looks like us on TV?" she asks lightly.

"No, but you could be the first."

She turns her face from the mirror, pleased by my answer.

My mother is in the kitchen, cooking dinner. I blare the volume on the TV downstairs, and we sneak out of the basement's back door and walk along a side of the yard that my mother cannot see from the kitchen. When we reach the back fence, a tall blonde boy stands in the alleyway. He waves.

Yura rushes to him. I've never seen her like this: nervous.

"Hey," she says shyly as he leans in for a kiss.

I stand there watching them make out. After a few minutes pass, Yura turns around and widens her eyes at me.

"Who's that?" Tom asks.

"That's my dad's friend's daughter."

He checks me out. "She looks like your younger sister."

"Seriously?" Yura laughs, and I don't think he catches the displeasure in her voice. "No one's ever said that about us," she says, then impatiently looks at me. "So, I'll be back in an hour," she says in a high-pitched voice. Tom strokes Yura's hair and whispers something into her ear. She giggles as she nestles in closer to him.

"See ya," I say in a casual voice, and I walk back home.

It's been less than an hour when the doorbell rings. I'm sitting in front of the TV in the basement, and my heart sinks when I hear Mrs. Yoon greet my mother in Korean.

"Yura, your mom is here!" my mother yells from the front door.

"We're still watching the movie, why don't you wait upstairs until it's over?" I plead back in English.

I hear the steps of the adults descending to the basement, and Mrs. Yoon's Korean words ricochet against the walls. "Your math tutor called and said he found some extra exercises to help you for the upcoming exam. I went to his house to pick them up, not realizing how close he lived from here. So, I just decided to come here, and I will have tea with Chul-min's mother until the movie ends. I just—" Mrs. Yoon and my mother enter. Mrs. Yoon scans the room. "Where's our Yura?"

"Outside," I say, terrified that Mrs. Yoon will uncover our scheme. Because I am complicit, I also feel responsible for their tryst.

"What is she doing outside?" Mrs. Yoon asks. I lower my eyes as Mrs. Yoon searches my face. "Eun-ah, you must tell me where Yura is."

I stare at the floor.

"She's with that boy, isn't she?" After a long silence, she says, "You're very loyal. You follow her around like a little, helpless puppy, but she does not care for you the way you care for her. It would be foolish trying to protect someone like that. Where is she?"

"I don't know," I say with an unconvincing shrug. Mrs. Yoon runs upstairs to get her shoes, then returns to the basement, where she exits the back door, and walks around the yard, following the perimeter of the fence. I scamper behind her. Upon reaching the back gate, she stretches her neck until she finally pauses.

Yura is cuddled in Tom's arms, their backs against a neighbour's garage. Her eyes and lips are smeared with colour, their cheeks are flushed.

Mrs. Yoon starts screaming in Korean as she opens the latch and runs towards Yura. She yanks Yura's arm as if she were a doll. When Tom holds Yura's other arm, Mrs. Yoon pushes it off, then begins yelling at him. "Leave my daughter alone! No contact! You understand? You never see my Yura again!"

"That's not what Yura wants," Tom says angrily.

"Tom, be quiet," Yura says.

"She don't know what she wants. I know what she wants," Mrs. Yoon hisses. Mrs. Yoon and Tom lock eyes. "She's not gonna ruin her future just because you wanna little fun. She's not a prostitute."

Tom's face cringes at this accusation. "What are you talking about? I love her, Mrs. Yoon."

Mrs. Yoon gives a violent guffaw.

"Tom, go away," Yura whispers.

“Come on, Yura, tell your mom what you want. Like what we talked about,” Tom pleads.

“Just leave,” Yura scolds Tom, unable to meet his eyes. “I didn’t mean any of it. I just said it because I know that’s what you wanted to hear.”

Tom winces at these words. Abruptly, he turns around and starts walking down the alley, shoving his hands into his jean pockets. Yura watches, colour draining from her face as his pace starts to quicken, then he breaks into a run and turns the corner and disappears.

Mrs. Yoon jerks Yura’s arm and drags her across our yard towards their car, then pushes her inside the car with great force as if she might spill out.

I follow them, trying to make eye contact with Yura. “I’m sorry,” I mumble.

After Mrs. Yoon slams Yura’s door shut, Yura rolls down her window and says in a barely audible voice, “I got in trouble for giving you my aunt’s knife. My mother told me to ask for it back, but I know you liked it, so I didn’t. I was expecting that type of loyalty back.” With that, the car jerks forward and roars down the street until it disappears.

Later that evening, my mother enters my room.

“Mrs. Yoon found a cigarette in Yura’s backpack,” she says with gravitas in Korean.

“So? Dad and Mr. Yoon smoke,” I reply in English.

“They’re men. They learned that in the military. Her boyfriend is still a teenager, and he taught her how to smoke. Imagine what other things he would have taught her.”

“His dad’s a doctor,” I say, hoping this might hold some weight.

“His father is a doctor?” My mother looks confused. “Maybe he likes Yura, but what if he is not serious? What if he just wants to have a good time? Then what? Yura will end up with many more problems. In Korea, a respectable woman would never be seen with a white man.”

“But they love each other.”

“She is too young to understand love. It may feel good now, but you have to think of everyone, including the whole family, when you decide to love someone. Yura has many talents, but she is also very selfish.” She pauses, then clears her throat. “What if you bring a white boy home to Mom and Dad? What would we talk about? What would we feed him? Our family has nothing in common with a white boy.” She pauses as she stares at me. “Do you understand?”

I nod submissively. I don’t want to be selfish. I never want to alienate my parents because of my choices.

“Korean is best. Maybe your dad and I will accept a Chinese boy, but we prefer Korean. Not white. Don’t ever bring a white boy to our house.”

“What about Charles?”

“He is the eldest son of the eldest son. Our family line has always been Korean. He needs to carry on the family responsibilities. Not even Chinese for Chul-min. She must be Korean.”

“What if he doesn’t fall in love with a Korean girl?”

“Then we will take him to Korea and find someone for him.”

“Mrs. Yoon is crazy.”

“No, she is right. Yura is selfish. Mrs. Yoon doesn’t want a daughter that will go through divorce.”

“Just because a couple are from different races doesn’t mean they’ll divorce.”

“If not a divorce between wife and husband, then a divorce between the daughter and parents,” she says, then shuts the door.

SIX

2014

A delivery man brings a large bouquet of flowers to my mother's house. Without reading the card, I know they're from Richard. The bouquet is filled with more choice flowers—ranunculus over roses, lisianthus over lilies. Immediately, I become suspicious: In the past, he only sent flowers after a big fight—were our recent conversations so tense as to necessitate this extravagance? Why is he spending so much money like this, especially if he thinks I'm leaving the following day? But I remind myself that I need to appreciate Richard's generous nature, despite my discomfort.

Early in our relationship, Richard took me to have dinner with his parents in Massachusetts. His father is a lawyer, his mother, a Latin professor, and throughout dinner I struggled to join in by throwing a bon mot here, some choice repartee there. I laughed louder, thought faster, tried my best not to come across as boring. His parents touched one another unknowingly, fingers carelessly brushing shoulders, arms, hands. Since then, I've learned not to flinch when Richard's arm wraps around my waist in public places, not to cringe when he praises or flatters me in front of others. He's called three days in a row, and I haven't called him back, so I call him now.

"Thank you for the flowers."

"Did you see my calls? Did you get my messages? I haven't heard from you and I've been worried."

"Sorry, I've been overwhelmed."

"I know you're going through a lot, so this weekend I booked a little getaway for us at the Cape. I want to take you to that chowder house you love."

"Oh, I asked for another week off from work. I won't be coming tomorrow."

There's silence. I know Richard is recalibrating, trying to compose himself. "Why didn't you tell me?"

"I'm sorry. Can you cancel and get a refund?" But I don't feel bad. This surprise weekend trip feels like an attempt at an apology, at trying to pay off his guilt for not accompanying me to my father's funeral. But I'm too proud to tell him this.

Richard sighs into the phone. "You're avoiding my calls and didn't tell me that you've extended your stay. What's going on?"

"I forgot, okay?"

"You're not letting me in."

"Being back has been intense."

"You never need anyone. You never ask for things. I thought this was something I would like or even get used to, but I can't. I wish you would call me when things are tough. After a year of dating, I still don't know who you are or what you want." When we first dated, Richard would comment on how independent I was, how little I needed people, and back then, this felt like a compliment; now it feels accusatory. I know he wants to feel wanted, but I can't manage to fake this.

"I just need some space to be alone for a while, and then I'll be fine."

"Everything is fine until it isn't. Then there's these flashes of rage because it's always there, brewing inside of you."

"When have I ever been angry with you?"

"Do you even know it's there?"

"It seems you know me better than I do."

"Babe, I don't mean to offend you. I just wish you would let me in."

"You know I like my space. Why do you even want to be with me?"

There's a long pause before Richard speaks again. "Because you have a good heart. You take care of your family. You're beautiful," he says tenderly. "I just wish you would let me in more."

"You know what I'm like."

"Can I come there? I really want to see you. It could be just a short weekend trip. I've never seen Canada. We could get away. I've always wanted to see the Rocky Mountains."

"My mom wouldn't think it's appropriate for me to go on a rendezvous right after my dad's funeral. Also, if you came, she would be burdened to host. It's better that I see you back in New York."

He's silent for a long time before he says, "I thought you hated being back."

"I do. But I need to be here. I can't explain it."

He pauses. I know he's hurt, and wants me to reassure him with my affections, but instead, I tell him I need to go and catch up on sleep. Cathy is always amused whenever she sees me interacting with Richard and making such little effort for him to feel needed. What she doesn't understand is that this is my way of being considerate, of not burdening anyone with my presence. Cathy, on the other hand, goes out of her way to do and say things to make her boyfriends feel desired, in charge. Perhaps this is why she's always been popular with men—this is the first time she's been single since college.

I look at the flowers—their brightness wears on me. I am too tired to remove the plastic wrap, so I place the bouquet on the floor, out of sight. I am exhausted. I haven't been sleeping well because of the letters, especially the ones about Crow Plains. Last night, I dreamt I was back there, and woke up in a panic. To calm my racing mind, I reached for the letters, but they brought back forgotten memories, and I lay awake for the rest of the night, unable to sleep.

I go into the kitchen. My mother sits at the table, sipping her tea. "You need to put flower in water or they die," she says, and hands me a glass jar with its label taken off, already filled with water.

I look at her annoyed. "I'll do it later."

She leaves the kitchen and returns with the bouquet. She nods approvingly at it. "I never see this type of flower before. Looks expensive," she says, pleased. She clips the stems into the sink.

I see the stack of papers concerning my father's finances on the counter. "We're meeting the accountant this afternoon," I remind her as I pour myself a cup of coffee.

"You go and tell me what happen after."

"You need to be there in case he asks any questions I can't answer."

"You see the stink bugs in garden? Today, I need to spray, or tomato go bad," she says, placing the bouquet on the table. The elegant flowers are out of place on my mother's kitchen table, in a glass jar, next to her Bible and hymn book.

"Mom, I can't do this all by myself. You'll need to look over some documents and help me make decisions."

"All the talking, talking, talking, I don't understand. I trust you take care of everything. If you need signature, bring home and I will sign. I know you do the right way," my mother says.

My brother comes downstairs dressed in a nylon shirt and shorts.

"Hey, I'm meeting the accountant in a couple of hours. Mom can't come, so it would be helpful if you came instead," I say to Charles, trying to maintain an even tone.

"You're the hotshot lawyer. You don't need me," Charles says, sitting at the table.

"I'm a tax lawyer. This isn't what I do. I may not be able to answer some of his questions."

"I need to go to the gym."

"Do I really have to do this all by myself?" I ask loudly as they both ignore me. My mother places soup and rice for Charles as he sits there, reading his phone. I glare at him, resentful at how useless he is.

"It should be pretty straightforward since everything just gets transferred to Mom," Charles says without looking up.

"You are right that the little Dad has is going to be transferred to Mom. But he did leave us a small inheritance," I say. Charles looks up. I pause, and then say carefully, "Dad owned land at Crow Plains, which he's divided between us. Apparently, when he bought the store, he also got the adjacent lot next door, and he never sold it."

With the mention of Crow Plains, both my mother and I glance at Charles. We rarely speak about this town, especially around Charles. I have been waiting to find the right moment to bring up news of our inheritance, and I wonder if I should have waited for a better time. His jaw clenches.

My mother joins us at the table and begins talking quickly. "When we sell store, we rushing. We forget about the land, but later, when we remember, we decide to keep because they find the oil nearby. Who knows if they develop the oil and price go up? We decide to hold onto just in case."

There's a long pause as I wait for Charles to speak. "How much is it worth?" Charles asks quietly.

"It's on Main Street, but it's still a Ukrainian farming community, so definitely not city prices. But, from what the internet says, Crow Plains is booming, alongside every other town in Alberta. I need to meet with the Realtor to see how much it's worth and put it up for sale. I was planning on driving there tomorrow if you want to join," I say, glancing at Charles to see his reaction.

"Sure," Charles says as he rotates a glass in front of him with both hands, considering it all. "And if there's oil underneath that land, I'm going to dig a hole, light a match, drop it into the ground, and wipe that shithole off the face of the earth."

1991

The problem, these days, is money. When visitors come, the adults will separate from the children, the women will separate from the men, and the men will gather around the kitchen table and talk about money. I know that my father is not a greedy person, and that this is a matter of survival, like fighting for rationed air.

The richest man among them is Mr. Kang, the distant relation who helped sponsor my parents' immigration. He does not seem rich because he has a hunched back, thinning hair, and wears a lumpy sweater, but the other men revere him because he owns a bustling gas station and restaurant by a busy highway, which affords him a large house, a wide American car, and a family vacation to Disneyland last summer. My father, secretly, does not like Mr. Kang, but he smiles, bows, and pours whisky into Mr. Kang's glass, using one hand to hold the bottle, the other to hold up his elbow as a gesture of respect. Later, when I read Shakespeare's *The Merchant of Venice*, I think of Mr. Kang when I study Shylock, imagining Mr. Kang's stumpy fingers, his fists filled with ducats.

I will also think of Mr. Kang when I learn about King Midas. Money, apparently the making of it, comes easily to Mr. Kang, who reveals to my father that wealth lies in the small business, not the salary man's job. Mr. Kang tells anecdotes: A Korean dentist approached him to borrow money for his impending debts. Imagine! Mr. Kang is a mere gas station proprietor and yet he is lending money to a professional. Or Mr. Kang's brother—who also has the golden touch because he followed Mr. Kang's advice—quit his job as a welder and bought a motel, which has slowly evolved into a portfolio of highway motels. This allowed his brother to afford tutors for his son to attend the prestigious Essex Academy high school and then get accepted into Cornell University, Mr. Kang says, as the final argument. Small business is where success lies.

My father is convinced. When he returns for a week of rest from Fort McMurray, he is fatigued, irritable, and lies on the sofa during most of his stay. I overhear him complaining to my mother about his younger counterparts. He can't lift as high, push as far, or endure as much of the extreme cold as they do. One co-worker lost his glove while working in this subarctic weather, and upon returning to the camp, the tips of his fingers turned black. Later, a finger had to be amputated. My mother massages my father's cracked hands with lotion and tells him this cannot go on.

So, it does not continue. One day, my mother dresses me in my favourite outfit: a pink lace dress with scalloped sleeves that Yura's grandmother mailed to her, and has been handed down to me. Charles wears a button-up shirt and pants, the sleeves and pant hems stopping before his wrists and ankles. Earlier this morning, my mother ground glutinous rice into a mortar to make *mujigae-tteok*—rainbow rice cakes—which she has arranged into neat slices of pink, light yellow, and pale green, next to a plate of melon slices. We have been forbidden to touch them until Mr. Kang is first served. When Mr. Kang arrives, my father enthusiastically shakes his hands, leads him to the living room and pours him a glass of whisky. Charles and I are brought in. We are told to bow, then exit the room. Afterwards, we stand in the hallway, debating about when we should walk into the living room again to take this precious tteok. We listen to the adults converse in Korean.

"How much?" asks Mr. Kang.

"Forty thousand dollars. I will pay you back in monthly installments over a five-year time frame," my father says as he rustles a sheet of paper ripped from his ledger book.

There's a long pause, as I hear Mr. Kang counting aloud.

"I will give you twenty thousand dollars with repayment in three years' time. I will decide the terms of interest."

"Interest?" my father says, confused.

Mr. Kang's response comes too quickly for a proposal that my father has been working on for weeks, sitting at the kitchen table with a calculator and pencil, furiously erasing, then recalculating, then rewriting on this sheet of paper. I know twenty thousand dollars is not as big a difference to Mr. Kang as it is for my father. I burn with hatred for Mr. Kang.

"Well, I must get back to the store and work hard, as it seems I am operating a bank as well as a gas station," he says, and my parents laugh nervously. I hear the pushing of chairs as Mr. Kang appears in the hallway with a jacket in one hand. “Your children have grown since the last time I saw them,” he says, appraising us. His mouth is open in a way that exposes his yellow teeth.

“Chul-min is the top student in his class,” my father says with exaggerated cheer.

“How many A’s did you get in your last report card?” Mr. Kang asks in a falsetto voice. Charles says nothing, to which my mother’s eyes widen at him, prodding him to speak, to not be rude.

“Our Chul-min received straight A’s,” my mother says enthusiastically. “Eun-ah is also getting many A’s on her report card.”

“Ah, a smart daughter! But be careful, boys don’t like girls that are too smart!” he says, tapping his forehead with his finger as my parents give a hollow laugh.

“I don’t care about boys,” I say boldly.

“Oh. An opinionated girl that speaks her mind! You better watch out,” he says, wagging a disapproving finger at my father. “You are lucky you have a smart son and a pretty girl. Having the reverse would be a curse.”

I look away, refusing to reply or bow to his hateful face. To my annoyance, my insolence hasn’t been noticed. After Mr. Kang puts on his shoes, he lights a cigarette at the door’s entrance, then tilts his head in thought.

“Twenty percent. The bank is lending at eleven percent, but you would never qualify for a loan if you applied, and I am taking a risk since this will be your first business. So you figure that out,” he says as he flings the ledger sheet back at my father. As Mr. Kang walks out, my parents bow. Their smiles disappear as the door shuts.

Charles and I are told we are moving to a small town named Crow Plains, where my parents have purchased a grocery store. Charles's face shows no emotion.

"How far is Crow Plains?" I ask in English.

"A two-hour drive from Edmonton," my mother replies in Korean.

"How will I be able to go to school, then?" I ask.

"You will change schools," she says.

I begin to cry. I'm not particularly attached to my classmates, but this is the only world that I know; I cannot imagine another.

"You will make new friends there," says my mother, spreading her lips thin.

For the next two weeks, I am in despair and Charles avoids me.

We pack our belongings into the boxes that the local grocery store manager has set aside for us. While my mother is packing, she picks out things that she plans to throw away. From this pile, I salvage a burgundy *norigae*, a tasseled ornament from Korea. It must have been a gift from the church or a visiting guest. I cut out pieces of its string, then tie them to create one long piece, and pull it through the ring attached to Yura's knife. Then I tie the ends of the rope to make a necklace. The cool silver slides against my skin and anchors me. I dig underneath my sweater and hold its weight in the palm of my hand. I imagine Yura's aunt, and all the women before her, carrying this knife. I try to imagine this ancient world, of hanboks and hangul, but I can't. Still, I feel this knife will protect me. And maybe that will be enough for this new rupture ahead.

The day of our move, my father pulls up in a rented moving truck. When the truck is almost loaded, Mr. and Mrs. Yoon arrive, bringing a final bag of Yura's hand-me-downs and a paper bag containing roasted sweet potatoes, which my parents gladly receive and eat. No one mentions Yura. A month after her mother caught Yura with Tom, they sent her to a boarding school on Vancouver Island. I asked my mother to contact Mrs. Yoon for Yura's dorm address and mailed her a letter, but did not hear back from her.

I am too tired, my eyes puffy from crying throughout the week. Charles says I resemble an angry bullfrog. I avoid Mrs. Yoon. I don't want her to see the silver knife protruding beneath my sweater. When it's time to go, I feel dread when she approaches me.

"Yura mistakenly gave you something she wasn't supposed to give away. It was a silver knife that belongs to our family. Do you know where this is?" Mrs. Yoon asks me in Korean.

I look at her blankly. I don't want to hand over the eunjangdo to Mrs. Yoon. Even if it is not from my family, it has become my talisman and I am hoping it will protect me, my honour.

"Leave the poor girl alone. All their belongings are put away—how could she possibly find it now?" Mr. Yoon says.

"It belonged to my sister-in-law and has been passed on for many generations. If you find it, please ask your mother to mail it to me. It's an inheritance I would like Yura's future daughter to have," Mrs. Yoon says gravely.

"She already has your mother's," Mr. Yoon says impatiently.

"What if our Yura has two daughters? Or three?" Mrs. Yoon says, shaking her head at her husband's short-sightedness.

I imagine the future Yura with her future daughters, and cannot fathom this as something she would want to pass down to them, so I don't feel bad. Rather, I give her a reverent bow. The silver knife pendant dangles against my chest, then hits my sweater. I immediately stand erect, lest she see it through my collar gap. A look of pity comes across her.

"The countryside is a harsh place, but you seem to be a hardy girl. You will form roots and learn how to survive. You will do well," she says, her voice softening. Then Mrs. Yoon mentions how her husband also wanted to buy a grocery store in the countryside because the price was much cheaper, but she refused and threatened divorce if he made her live anywhere other than the city. She's the only one who laughs after sharing this story.

Soon my parents declare that they are ready for the journey ahead. My father drives the moving truck, while my mother follows in the car. I turn around in the rear seat and look out the back window: The Yoons stand and wave as we leave the driveway. They get smaller until they disappear. We pass the familiar blocks of houses where the neighbourhood kids are playing on the sidewalk, and soon we leave the busy streets for the highway with its continuous farmland. The monotony lulls me to sleep. I wake when the car slows down.

I see a billboard that says WELCOME TO CROW PLAINS! HOME OF THE WORLD'S LARGEST CABBAGE ROLL! Near the sign is a statue of a large fork piercing a giant cabbage roll. A grain elevator stands at the entrance of the town. My mother signals to turn and goes into the main strip. My brother and I roll down the windows, looking at either side of the street and the businesses we pass—a video store, a grocery store, a Chinese restaurant, a pizza parlour. I'm pleasantly surprised the downtown core comprises several blocks; the town is larger than I imagined. At the end of the block, next to a drugstore, is a small, white clapboard building with a faded wooden sign that reads BILL'S GROCERY.

"We're here," my mother says in Korean as she drives to the side of the building and parks the car.

I open the door and my feet land on soft ground. I'm standing beside the store, on a graveled lot with patches of grass. There's a shed and a garbage dumpster. The sky is clearing from a rain shower, and the air smells clean.

"Where are we going to live?" Charles asks in English.

"At the back of the store," my father replies in Korean. "This is our home now," he says as he unlocks the back door, then opens a window from inside and shouts through the screen, "Come inside!"

Charles and I walk through the mud. We take off our shoes before entering through the back door, which opens into the kitchen, furnished in honey oak cabinetry and white appliances. Behind this is a windowless living room. Adjacent to the living room is a hallway, carpeted in beige. As I walk down the hall, I count three bedrooms and a bathroom. I breathe in the scent of stale cigarette smoke.

My father takes my hand and leads me to the living room, where he opens a doorway that leads to the store. He turns on the switch. Fluorescent light glares down at us. We're in the back office, surrounded by shelves of boxes, and a walk-in cooler. "New lighting just installed," he says. He stamps his feet on laminated, beige terrazzo. "New tiles," he says proudly. We walk to the retail space where there are aisles of food. I slide my fingers on a bottom shelf of cans and observe that my fingers come out darkened.

"It was a bargain," he says. The previous owner, Bill, inherited the business from his father, which was started by his grandfather: three generations of Ukrainian grocers. Bill is widowed and in his sixties. His sons work in the oil patch up north, and he's ready to retire. My father pauses dramatically before saying, "They've found oil nearby, and there's talk that this town could become another Fort McMurray."

My father is smiling, almost maniacally. I walk out the back door to find my mother unloading the boxes crammed in the back seat, swatting the air from the clouds of mosquitoes and black flies. From how she is pushing the boxes, lifting the bags, and yelling at Charles and me, I can tell she does not want to be here. I go outside and help pull a garbage bag full of clothes from the back seat of the car. I drag it towards our house, but am not aware that the plastic tears and my mother's dresses fall into the mud. I hear her shouting at me, and I turn around.

My mother angrily picks up her office clothes, which are smeared with fresh mud. My father is inside, humming happily, oblivious. "Mom, I'm sorry I ruined your clothes," I say.

She places one hand across her forehead, closes her eyes, and stands still until the redness in her face drains. "It's okay, I won't need these clothes anymore," she says, and quietly drops the soiled polyester dresses into the dumpster.

SEVEN

2014

My father called the stretch of road north of Edmonton, on Highway 28, Van Gogh country. During the day, the sky maintains a cheerful cornflower blue, periodically interrupted by the drama of thunderstorms, hail, or blizzards. In the spring, verdant green shoots forth from the earth. The brilliance intensifies in the summer with canola yellow, prairie-flower magenta and violet, and the endless variations of green that sway in the summer wind. For fall, the colours burn into gold, citron, and rust, and then a blanket of white coats the black bones of trees when the snow arrives. In the dark of winter, you might see sudden bursts of luminous green or pink dancing against the black sky. "Watercolours leaking from the gods," Mrs. Reeves, my high school teacher, would say as she encouraged us to brave the freezing nights to view the aurora borealis.

We pass by the exit sign for Vernet. Last night, while suffering from insomnia, I googled news about Crow Plains and came across an article about Vernet—named after a French missionary's favourite landscape painter—which is in the process of being reclaimed with the new name Wâwâskêsiwacîs.

My brother is beside me, and we're driving to Crow Plains to meet the real estate agent on this unusually hot September day. Although I was pleasantly surprised at how easily Charles agreed to come with me, I now wish he wasn't here, as we've been bickering throughout the entire ride.

"I'm freezing," Charles says, and sighs out his frustration.

"Don't touch the AC. This is the temperature I like when I drive."

I'm resentful. After all, I have been doing all the work: filing my father's final taxes, calling people and terminating his accounts, taking care of the business of death, whereas Charles wakes up late every morning, eats the food laid out by my mother, leaves the house to go to the gym, and returns in the evening. A few times he's gone out at night—I am unsure where he goes or with whom—and has come back smelling of alcohol. Not once has Charles asked about what I'm doing or if I need any help. Charles turns on the radio and scans for stations. A discordant mélange of noise jumps from an announcer to classical music, then to heavy metal. He stops at a guitar riff and turns up the volume, which blares angrily into the car. I lower the volume. He sighs, exasperated.

Charles turns down the air conditioner. "I know you're frustrated being back and taking care of things, but I also helped look after Mom and Dad."

I laugh sarcastically. "By going into rehab? By not being able to hold down a job? That's your idea of being a great son?"

"We all know you're the golden child, alright? But I also took care of them. Especially when Dad got into one of his stretches of depression."

I'm surprised by this comment, but I quickly reason that it's a natural reaction to how my father would have felt about Charles's life.

"I'd be depressed too if you were my son. Whenever we talked, Dad was always in a good mood. The last time I spoke with him on the phone, Dad told me how grateful he was for the house and having the garden to work on."

"We all know you bought that house and this car, okay?" he shouts, rolling down the window. "We all know I'm the fuckup, alright?" He lights a cigarette.

I also roll down my window, annoyed at the smell. I'm tired. Strands of my hair whip across my face as the hard sun burns onto my skin. We pass fields of bales in silence, as the smell of grass rushes through the windows. I want, so badly, to return to New York, to be away from Charles and the needs of my family. I want to be in my apartment, controlling the temperature, the exposure to light and noise, all through remote controls and motorized solar shades.

"Dad was depressed as hell," Charles says, flicking the cigarette butt out of the window. "But you probably didn't notice because you were so busy being perfect. You were always good at ignoring or forgetting or editing it all out so that somehow it worked out to your advantage, and you always won in the end. I made the mistake of holding on and remembering and trying to fight."

I feel betrayed: If my father had mental health problems, why didn't my mother tell me? Especially since she knows I also struggle with depression.

"How dare you accuse me of not being a good daughter when you're the one that's a wreck. Everything you touch gets destroyed, but you don't seem to notice it because you're so self-absorbed," I shout into the wind.

Charles taps another cigarette out of his packet, which he lights and takes several drags of. "They always kept bad news away from you. Dad would fall into these strange spells. Last winter, Mom called to tell me that he'd been gone since lunch, and he left his car and cell phone at home. It was going to get dark soon, and she didn't want to walk on the icy paths by herself to find him. So I drove up from Calgary. I found him walking by the ravine, and when he saw me, he gave me a strange look of recognition. He said he shouldn't have left me behind. I didn't really think about what that meant until now. I realize that he thought I was Maknae."

"You never told me this," I say quietly. Charles is right—I didn't know about the day-to-day details in my family.

"Mom didn't want to burden you. I told her Dad was depressed and to take him to the doctor, but you know how Mom and Dad are. They refuse to acknowledge that mental illness exists in their world. You were lucky to be the one to leave and be able to send money and help from a clean distance. I stayed and got my hands dirty."

We drive in silence. I reflect on the last letter my father wrote from Crow Plains when our prospects began improving: *We are finally making our dreams here*, he wrote proudly, unleashing his optimism because business was improving, and my brother and I were both excelling at school. I stare ahead, my eyes watering, my vision blurry. I can't apologize or thank Charles. I'm too tired and upset. Charles throws out his cigarette. His hair tosses violently in the wind.

"Charles?"

"What?"

"Did you bring alcohol?"

"So, what, you're going through my stuff now?"

"When we get there, I'm going to need a drink," I say.

Without turning to me, Charles reaches into his jacket pocket, pulls out a bottle filled with amber liquid, and places it in the cupholder between us.

1991

It's my first day at Crow Plains High School. I am in Grade 7. I wear my cracked leather shoes and one of Yura's hand-me-downs: a baggy navy dress with a bright red sash. I meet Miss Schlueter, my new teacher, who leads me down the row to my desk. I stare directly ahead, not meeting the curious eyes on me. Without surveying my classmates, I know they are all white. I decide to be as invisible as I can. If no one notices me, I won't incur their ridicule. When Miss Schlueter introduces me, I'm proud of how normal my name sounds: Anne Kim. I dare not speak, and sit still, staring straight ahead, focusing on the barrettes adorning the girl sitting in front of me.

After school, Charles and I walk home. I feel the gaze of the townspeople: eyes that peer out from the rearview mirrors of cars, the windows of homes, the storefronts of businesses.

The busiest store is Stanley's Grocery, with cars crowding the angle parking in front of it. There's a sign on the door that boldly proclaims PROUD SPONSOR OF THE CROW PLAINS BUFFALOS HOCKEY TEAM! An elderly woman walks out with a bulky youth carrying her grocery bags. The teen stops when he sees us, and as his hard blue eyes meet mine, I instinctively know he's the owner's son. He appraises me and Charles as we quickly walk past him.

"Thank you, Jeffrey," the woman says as he loads her bags into her trunk. Though I don't dare look back, I can feel his glare pushing against us.

When we arrive home, dinner is not made because the store's freezer broke, and an electrician from Fort Athabasca is taking apart the components. There is a grocery cart filled with soggy bags of peas, melting boxes of ice cream, and limp microwaveable dinners. Charles and I each take out a box of thawed dinner, enter our home from the doorway at the back of the store, microwave the food, and quietly eat by the television. We're watching a sitcom: A father is spying on his daughter, who has just started dating and has brought over her boyfriend. The young lovers sit on the sofa, while the father prances in the background. The house is enormous. There's a spiral staircase from which the father dangles. He cups his ears with his hands, and the audience laughs at his changing expressions. But he clumsily gets tangled up with a vacuum and is found out. The daughter affectionately drags her father out from hiding, and says *Oh Daddy, I love you*, to which the father hugs his daughter and says, *I love you too. Come on, let's go get some ice cream*, and comically shuts the door on the boyfriend's face. I poke a pea onto each of the fork's prongs and eat them one by one, the room quiet except for the audience's laughter, applause, and then a collective sigh at the show's end when the father hugs his daughter.

The next day, a customer opens the soda cooler, and the hinges snap off. My father tries to screw it back on, but he accidentally drops the glass door so that it crashes to the ground, cracking into a web of shards. My father is to blame. My mother says this with more conviction as each machine breaks down or refuses to turn on. If there is no electrician, mechanic, or plumber in Fort Athabasca, then he has to hire someone from Edmonton, and pay for the four-hour roundtrip drive, and all this because before purchasing this store, to save some money, my father foolishly did not hire an inspector who could have caught these malfunctions and prevented this purchase. My mother cries in the back office, and Charles and I pretend we can't hear him shouting his justifications or feel her hard silences.

But worse than these failing machines is the empty store: No one is shopping with us. It's been two weeks since we've taken over Bill's Grocery, and his customers have stopped shopping here.

"Bill's customers must be running out of food. But they're not coming here to shop," my mother says, nervously gazing out the window where no cars are parked in front of our store. She then walks outside and counts the many cars parked in front of Stanley's Grocery.

While my mother is resigned, my father is indignant. "The only person that walked in today had the nerve to ask me to donate to the hockey team. No way! Canadians have so much, why are they asking me for money? No way!"

My parents call Bill, who has just moved into his retirement home in Penticton. He sounds puzzled and says he will call a few of his loyal customers to see what's going on. When he calls back a few days later, he gently says that the townspeople aren't familiar with us yet and encourages my parents to engage in chit-chat. He promises one of his loyal customers, Edna, will visit next week.

"What is 'chit-chat'?" my father asks me when he hangs up. I take out the dictionary and am disappointed when this word isn't there.

I cry every day in front of my mother and father. After I walk home from school, I enter the store, stand in front of the cash register, and begin to cry, saying that I cannot bear to be inside that classroom where no one speaks to me except to call me "chink." My mother asks if I have shame, for I should never cry inside the store, what will the customers think? But there are no customers in the store, I say, so I do not feel any shame. My father takes my hand and walks me down the candy aisle, telling me to take whatever I want. But as the grocer's daughter, knowing that I am already entitled to have any of our candy makes this offer unappealing, and I refuse everything.

At night, it is my mother who cries in front of my father, although she waits until the store closes and they are in their bedroom. I am surprised when I hear her sobbing—a sonorous cry different from her usual soft voice. I stand by the door and wonder why she cries: After all, wasn't this their idea? Only then does it occur to me that my mother might feel the same terror I do, perhaps even a deeper fear. Throughout the day, my parents walk outside and nervously count the number of cars parked in front of Stanley's Grocery. We never have cars parked by our store. And even I know that no customers equals no money.

Though we have plenty to eat. Every day my mother brings to the kitchen wilting lettuces, limp cucumbers, and tomatoes so soft that they burst open at the mere tap of a knife. She marinates them with sesame oil, soy sauce, red pepper flakes, even though we cannot possibly eat all this food. The garbage bin fills and then the fruit flies appear, circling listlessly in front of the television that Charles and I silently watch every day after school.

My parents are working hard, harder than they've ever worked, and anything outside of work is a luxury, including sleep. Though there are no customers, there is always something to do: vegetables to rotate, cans to dust, dairy expiration dates to consider. They are at the store when I rise, and still there when I go to sleep. Without being told, Charles and I try to be as self-sufficient as possible, subsisting on canned ravioli and frozen dinners. We don't ask our parents for anything: It is understood that to express need is an act of great selfishness.

One day, Charles and I are sitting in front of the television, and my father walks in, and sees us leisurely lying on the carpet. He turns off the television.

"Get up and study," he says in English, as little balls form a frown on his eyebrows.

"Aw, Dad, the show's about to end. Can't we just finish?" Charles asks.

"Why we work hard? So you can watch TV? Do you see how hard Mother and Father working?" he says. I lift myself off the floor and go into my room. A few minutes later, Charles follows suit. It's only when I hear Charles slam his bedroom door shut that I hear my father return to the store. Afterwards, this becomes our evening routine: After dinner, we go into our individual rooms to sit at our desks and study, and the house falls silent.

The few customers who shop with us come in because of the drugstore next door—when the weather gets too cold for them to make another stop at Stanley's Grocery, they shop here for items that the drugstore doesn't carry: a bag of dinner rolls, a carton of cream, a sack of potatoes. When these customers arrive at the front counter, my father searches for the price sticker and diligently punches it into the cash register. He places the food into a paper bag with an exacting alignment. He presents the receipt with both hands. I watch as customers impatiently tap their feet and stare at my father, who tries his best to show his dignity and not his desperation.

He was an engineer back in Korea, I want to say aloud, as if this were a punchline to a joke we're all participating in. The English that my father has mastered through his exercise books leaves him at a loss here as he—a man clever enough to graduate from the Harvard of Korea—can't conduct the simplest transaction without some inevitable fumbling. Language is reduced to its most basic function: Paper or plastic bag? Receipt in bag? Yes? No? These daily, repetitive conversations dim my parents' minds, alienating them not only from the townspeople but, more importantly, from themselves.

A man stands in front of the counter. I look up from my comic book. I immediately notice that he's not white. Although he is taller, he has an uncanny resemblance to my father: the same almond-shaped eyes, dark skin, unkempt black hair, rounded nose. My father, sensing there's a customer, rushes to the front counter. The man grins at him.

"Hey, are you my brother?" he announces as he widens his arms, examining my father.

My father's countenance brightens as he tries to match his exuberance.

"You new to town?" the man asks.

"We been here two months. We buy store from Bill."

"You look like me! Where are you from?"

"From Edmonton."

"No, I mean what country are you from?"

"From Korea. Where you from?"

"Vernet. It's a reserve half an hour from here."

"Which country you from?" my father asks.

"We're Cree . . . You're standing on my land!" he says with a chuckle.

"You Indian?"

The man nods. "Hey, you look like Bruce Lee!" he says, assessing my father approvingly. He stretches out a hand. "I'm Jim. I'm the Chief of Vernet."

"I'm Jung," my father says, struggling to keep pace with this gregarious man.

"How do you like it here?" Jim asks.

My father shakes his head. "Business not so good."

"Really? It's a good business. This store is always busy."

"Used to be busy. After we come, now empty. No one shopping."

Jim considers this answer, then guffaws. "Yup, I know these townspeople well. Listen, here's what I'm gonna do for you. I'm gonna tell everyone in Vernet to come shop here. Tired of how Stanley treats us anyway. He don't need our money. I'm gonna tell them all to shop at Bruce Lee's store."

"Thank you," my father says with appreciation.

"You wait, I'll spread the word about your store. You're gonna see a lot of people that look like me, that look like us, shopping here."

An elderly lady with pale skin and silver hair parks her grocery cart next to the front counter. "Oh dear, is this man causing you trouble?" she asks as she winks at Jim.

"Hello, Mrs. Martin. Me and Bruce Lee, we're just having a good chat. I'm gonna make sure everyone I know shops here," Jim says as he pays for his cigarettes and leaves the store.

"Jim's a good one to know. Hi, I'm Edna. I'm a friend of Bill's, and I kept meaning to drop by. I was just recovering from a cold, but now I'm feeling better. Bill called and told me about you. Well, it's nice to finally meet you."

My father returns her generous smile. "Bill tell me you coming."

"And how are you doing today?" she asks.

"How I doing?"

"Yes, how are you feeling?"

"Feeling not so good," he says as he shakes his head.

"I like a straight shooter," she says with a laugh. "Just between you and me, I can't stand Stanley. Once Stanley knew Bill sold, he's done all he can to get the town to shop with him. Suddenly, he's trying to turn old enemies into friends. Overnight, he's sponsoring the curling club, the hockey team, and putting up their signs in his front window as if he's the patron saint of our community. But he won't give a dime to the organization I'm involved in to help the kids in Vernet. Stanley will only be your friend if he can get something from you. He's a bad apple. But I can tell that you are a good egg. As a grocer, I think you can appreciate my example," she says as her crow's feet wrinkle with delight.

My father smiles in a way that I know means he's puzzled by her idioms. My father tallies, then packs her groceries. After she pays and waves goodbye, she exits the store.

"Dad, when someone asks you how you're doing, it's not a question more than a greeting, like saying hello. You need to smile and say everything is fine."

"Ev-lee-ting is fa-een," he says slowly, accentuating each syllable.

"Everything is fine," I say again, and at that moment, I almost believe what I say.

In class, I'm not paying attention to the lessons, but rather, under a feigned aloofness, observing the people around me. Sometimes, I pick up a pencil and surreptitiously draw the students around me, which brings me calm. I try to understand the hierarchy operating in our classroom. The most popular girl is also the prettiest. Her name is Meredith Sweeney. She resembles a doll with her porcelain skin, sharp nose, blue eyes, and blond hair, which she often plaits into one or two French braids. Once, during lunch break, the popular kids decide to play Boys Catch Girls, and the boys chase Meredith the most. I watch from the sidelines as Trevor Miller—the most popular boy in Grade 9—runs after her. I'm convinced she runs slower when he pursues her, squeals louder when he finally catches her and wraps his arms around her, and that it's blush, not exhaustion, that reddens her cheeks. She has two friends that she continually passes notes to in class: Crystal and Tess.

Crystal is her best friend, and she has edge. She knows all the cool bands and brands. Crystal is the only girl in our class who's allowed to wear makeup. She crimps her brunette hair and ties it back with lace ribbon. She wears oversized plaid shirts with denim that she rips and frays. She brings her Discman with CDs of the newest bands that she buys from the music store when she visits her father in Fort Athabasca; the other girls take turns listening to her headphones at recess. She walks around in combat boots. Later, I learn from magazines that her style is grunge, and this look is inspired by these bands.

Tess, on the other hand, is completely ordinary with her short blonde hair and colourless eyelashes. Once, she comes with crimped hair which frizzes, then flops around her freckled face, and when she enters the classroom, Meredith and Crystal exchange a meaningful glance, conferring with their eyes. From her wardrobe and lunch offerings, I infer that, like me, she's poor: she cycles through the same few sweaters and pants every day and eats the same peanut butter and jelly sandwiches. However, my advantage is that I have Yura's stylish hand-me-downs, and access to our store as my personal pantry. Tess's entry into this group is her persistence: She is always ingratiating to Meredith, deferential to Crystal. If either girl has a need, Tess is immediately there, eager to help.

The smartest person in class is Roger Korchowski. I know he is the smartest because Miss Schlueter accidentally leaves out her grading book on her desk one day, and through my quick scan, I see that he has the most A's next to his name. I'm surprised, as Roger is frequently making obvious statements or asking questions that create even more questions, whereas I'm comfortable in my muteness; if I speak, I want to say the most profound thought, and because these thoughts do not come often, if at all, I never raise my hand.

I'm not surprised when the first assignment I've written receives a C grade. "We're working so hard. Why can't you?" my mother says, exasperated.

"Here's my test," Charles says proudly as he digs into his backpack and hands over his science test, triumphantly marked with an A+. Recalling facts comes easily for him: He reads an article once and is able to remember the dates, the names of people and places, the concepts underlying it all.

"Thank you, Charles," my mother says as her face softens and her eyes tear up in gratitude. "You are good *adeul*, good son."

I am bothered that my mother is not too upset with my poor marks. Though it is unspoken, I wonder if it matters less that I succeed because I'm a girl. Even still, I want to be praised, like Charles, so I motivate myself to study harder, to get higher grades. I want this goodness not only for myself, but for my parents.

One night, after the store closes, the doorbell rings. A Korean couple stand at the back entrance with a gangly boy behind them.

"One of my customers told me that a Korean family moved into Crow Plains, and we wanted to introduce ourselves. My name is Song Young-gil and this is my wife and my son Samuel. Our oldest son goes to the university. We own a gas station in Comet," he says in Korean. His wife holds a box of clementines.

"Welcome," my father says, opening the door wide.

I notice Mrs. Song's rough hands as she sets down the box of clementines. Mr. and Mrs. Song are short, portly, and of the same height.

Samuel is tall and lanky. He gives an awkward bow to my parents, then greets them in Korean with a squeaky, adolescent voice. Charles and I bow to Mr. and Mrs. Song and we go to the living room and turn on the television. The boys find a hockey game to watch so I go to the kitchen and take a seat next to my mother at the table and help her peel fruit. My father takes two mugs from the cupboard, pours whisky into them, then hands over a mug to Mr. Song with both hands. I'm grateful for Mrs. Song's boisterous laugh and Mr. Song's animated voice, which bring a joviality into our otherwise silent house.

"This place feels like the end of civilization. Who knew other Koreans lived here," my father says, offering Mr. Song a cigarette with both hands, which he accepts.

"When I first moved here, the quiet was unbearable, but now, I've turned into a country hick. I can't stand the city anymore, it's too busy. Now, whenever I visit Edmonton, I want to immediately leave," Mr. Song says.

Mr. Song then identifies the small community of Koreans scattered along this highway stretch. The closest family runs a gas station an hour from Comet. From there, another family owns a grocery store close to the Saskatchewan border. The wife is famous among her largely Ukrainian customers for her cabbage rolls, which she spikes with Korean pepper flakes.

"When we first moved here, we didn't know anything about Canada. We thought the tins with dog pictures on them were canned dog meat. We were surprised that Canadian people would eat this type of meat, but they kept coming in and buying so many week after week. So Mr. Song brought it home to taste it," Mrs. Song says in her thick Daegu dialect. She exchanges a glance with her husband, and they burst out laughing. Mr. Song, impressed by the frequency and regularity that his customers bought these tins, finally asked a customer how she prepared this meat, for didn't she find it bland? The customer asked him to repeat his question. After several times of making sure she understood his question, she finally said, "Mr. Song, these cans are food for my dog."

"Which is a good thing, since it tastes awful," Mr. Song says. My mother starts tearing from the hilarity.

"If you're a country hick in Korea, you're still a country hick in Canada. Immigration can't take that out of you," Mrs. Song says teasingly to her husband.

"I heard Mr. Kang was asking around on where to get dog meat here," Mr. Song says with a mocking smile.

"Do you mean the Mr. Kang who owns the truck stop off of Highway 16?" my father asks.

Mr. Song nods. "Yes, everyone knows he's the richest of us all."

"He is a distant relation of ours and lent us money to buy this store," my mother says. The laughing stops and a sobriety enters.

"He has a reputation for being harsh. I imagine he's like that with money he's lent, even to his relatives," Mrs. Song murmurs.

"We've been struggling since arriving here, and he keeps calling us for payment," my mother says.

"Everyone is shopping at the other store in town now. No one is shopping with us," my father says sombrely.

Mr. Song clears his throat. "We struggled a lot in the beginning too. But we're lucky we are the only gas station in town and customers need to fill up their cars no matter who is behind the counter."

"We feel so helpless being in that empty store all day, every day," my mother says in a tone laced with desperation.

"I hear that the government is going to privatize liquor stores because they don't want to deal with the unions. This might be an opportunity for you," Mr. Song says.

"Won't selling alcohol bring in a difficult clientele?" my mother asks.

"At least we'd be getting customers," my father says.

"If they don't buy alcohol from you, they will buy it somewhere else. Anyone needing alcohol around here has to drive to Fort Athabasca. For the people of Vernet, you'd be a closer drive for them. Either way, someone will be taking their money," Mr. Song says.

"For a country this wealthy, it's shameful how they leave Vernet with dirt roads and filthy water," Mrs. Song says disapprovingly as she shakes her head.

A silence descends as the adults consider this. When it's time to leave, Mr. Song's face beams red from the alcohol, and Mrs. Song quietly takes the keys from her husband's jacket.

"Thank you for coming. It's good to know we are not alone out here," my mother says in an earnestness that moves Mrs. Song, who takes my mother's hands and holds them.

"It is hard living here," Mrs. Song says gently, to which tears roll down my mother's cheeks. Even though a few hours ago we did not know that the Songs existed, they now leave like family, with my parents promising to pay a visit to their home in Comet. My parents' spirits are lighter, and for this, I am grateful for the Songs' visit.

Mrs. Song looks thoughtfully at my mother. "I can get used to a lot of things in Canada, like the bitter cold or the bland food. But one thing I still haven't gotten used to is the isolation. There's so much land, and yet you're completely alone in it."

Following the Songs' advice, I help my parents complete the forms with the Alberta Liquor Control Board, and we are delighted when we receive our liquor license. My father sections off a corner of our store with a makeshift wall of milk crates to create a separate store. He buys a secondhand cooler from Edmonton. When the alcohol is delivered, we unpack the bottles and tag them with a price gun.

After the liquor store opens, the townspeople slowly appear, and while they are picking up their alcohol, they also venture into our grocery store. One of Charles's classmates, Clint, has a father who becomes one of our first regulars, coming in with crumpled bills jammed inside his jean pockets. Jim stops shopping at our store, but the family and friends he has sent our way continue to come, some even more frequently after the opening of the liquor store. Jim's brother becomes a regular: He drives in every second Friday when his government cheque arrives and spends it on vodka. Once, I see Jim across the street, shaking his head as he watches his brother exit our store carrying jugs of alcohol.

Edna views the new addition with discomfort. Finally, after a few visits, she makes a comment to my father that ever since the liquor store opened, she has noticed that some of the kids in the program she volunteers at in Vernet eat less and wear dirtier clothes. My father responds that he just sells the alcohol and it's not his job to be responsible for how his customers consume it. But he does agree to donate expiring food to her church's meal program. Every week, Edna comes and picks up boxes of stale bread and overripe fruit and other expiring food products. She still shops with us but is no longer chatty, just cordial.

Her composure slips only once, when she greets Jim's brother as he leaves the store. Her eyes follow him to his running car, where his wife is holding an infant and his children play in the back seat. Edna murmurs under her breath, "Damn it, those kids need shoes."

We also become acquainted with a group of teenage boys from town that Edna calls the "arcade boys"—they hang out at the video store, which also has an arcade. The oldest of them is eighteen, and he comes regularly to purchase beer on behalf of the group. He always comes with the other boys during the dinner rush, when my parents are busy at the cash register. While he waits in line, the other boys scatter throughout the store. My father swears that the snack and soda inventory is lighter after their visits, and has ordered more ceiling mirrors to be installed.

Jeff, Stanley's son, belongs to this group and now regularly enters our store with his friends. Sometimes while walking home from school, Charles and I hear their roaring truck as they drive past us. When they loiter in front of the pizza parlour and we walk past them, they stare, or rather, glare at us, beer cans and cigarettes in hand.

Once, one of them comes in to buy a pack of cigarettes and spits on his coins before handing them to my mother. She calmly takes his coins, wipes them with a tissue, and places them in her till. Later that night, after the store closes, she confesses to my father it was the first time she ever wanted to hit somebody.

"Why didn't you?" Charles asks from the living room. My mother reminds him that we don't want retaliation from a town that doesn't want to shop with us.

"What did he look like? Who was he?" Charles asks, his eyes darkening.

"They all look the same, all those boys look the same to me."

EIGHT

2014

The giant cabbage roll statue still stands next to the town's welcome sign. I'm reminded of the eccentric statues built by Eastern European settlers dotting the towns of Alberta. The grain elevator still overlooks the town's entrance, where I slow down and turn left onto Main Street. I'm surprised when we pass a new development of houses under construction. The wooden frames shoot forth from the black earth next to a billboard: TUSCAN VILLA—NEW HOUSES STARTING AT $400,000. On Main Street, Charles and I turn our heads and survey the streets. Businesses have changed—the video store is now a quilting store, our old store is a hair and tanning salon. The buildings are painted in sunny colours, and flowerpots anchor the streetlamps with banners that cheerfully declare CROW PLAINS, COUNTRY LIVING.

We drive slowly until we see the Realtor's office. Inside, a woman sits at her desk.

"Anne Kim? Jordan Chafalt—nice to meet you," she says, smiling, as she walks towards me and reaches out her bronzed hand embellished with silver bracelets and rings, her fingernails lacquered in lilac. There is a framed picture behind her of her family in sombreros with palm trees in the background.

"So your family owns that lot down the street?"

"Yes."

"I've always wondered who owned it. You've come at a great time. Our town is experiencing what you'd call a renaissance. You probably saw the new subdivision being built on your way here. There's going to be more demand for retail space, and your location is prime."

"Who wants to live here?" my brother asks.

"The town's done a good job marketing to the workers up north. They work at Fort Mac for two weeks outta the month, then get two weeks off, and by then, they just wanna get outta there. Lots of young families come here. They wanna escape the fast-paced city life in Edmonton or Calgary. We're building a swimming pool in the rec centre and a splash park outside," she says proudly.

"We grew up here as kids. It's changed a lot since then. Our parents ran a grocery store, which is now the hair and tanning salon," I say.

"That happened before my time. Stanley's is now the only grocery store in town, but he's always talkin' 'bout closing it down. Once Stanley's closes, town's hoping to start a weekly farmer's market. We still need fresh produce. Everyone shops at the Wal-Mart in Fort Athabasca, and there's talks they're opening up a Costco there. The gas station also sells groceries, but most people just go there for their fried chicken and potato wedges. It's run by an Asian family," she adds, as if boasting.

"Lucky them," Charles says with a deadpan expression.

"Yeah, our town is getting more diverse. That's another thing we're proud of. We have the Chinese gentleman who runs the restaurant, some really nice Filipino ladies who work at the retirement home, and then there's another family from . . . give me a sec while I try to remember . . . It's on the tip of my tongue . . ."

"Did they ever do anything with the oil they found here?" Charles asks after it's apparent she can't recall the name of the country.

"There were talks of developing that, but no investors pulled through. We've carved out a niche of being the town that supports the oil patch. Our businesses service the oil companies, and our towns provide a place for their workers to live in. So it's growing and people have money and want stores to shop at. You've got a great location, and it's a decent-sized lot."

"How much is it worth?" Charles asks.

"Let me get that appraised. It's a good time to be selling. There's so much money in Alberta, people don't know what to do with it. We're at record highs. People want to live here. It shows in the rising real estate prices." She picks up the telephone and punches the keys with her long acrylic nails. After a pause, she leaves a voicemail to her appraiser.

We walk outside and see the Twin Dragons restaurant across the street. The Chinese restaurant still has the wooden double dragons with their twisted necks spiraling into the prairie sky. These creatures are bright orange, indicating that they have been recently painted, and they contrast against the backdrop of cornflower blue. Below the sign TWIN DRAGONS CHINESE RESTAURANT is another, newer sign which reads WE SERVE CHINESE AND THAI AND VIETNAMESE FOOD. I notice a patch of freshly painted white against the side of the restaurant. I study and squint at this patch and see the faint outlines of the words GO BACK HOME, which the white paint doesn't entirely conceal. I glance at Charles, who also studies the almost invisible words.

"Very diverse and divisive," he says dryly.

When we walk in, an elderly Asian man I do not recognize greets us, menus in hand.

"Excuse me, but is the owner here a Mr. Wong?" I ask. When I realize that I'm speaking slower and louder, I change my enunciation mid-sentence.

"No, I owner. I buy from Mr. Chan. I never hear of Mr. Wong," he says as he leads us to a booth by the window. He studies my face. "You Korean?"

I nod.

"Another Korean family in town. They own gas station," he says. I ask how long he's lived here and how he likes the town.

We order food that comes out too fast: deep fried pork balls accompanied by a bright, almost neon-pink sauce, and fried rice with shiny green peas and yellow corn kernels and small cubes of orange carrots. He passes us pre-bundled napkins with a fork and knife inside. I ask him for chopsticks.

"When we lived here, I never came inside here. Isn't that strange?" I say, more as a confession to myself.

"I remember you were a snob to Euphemia. You would think as the only other Asian girl in town you two would be friends," Charles says. Euphemia was Chinese, and her parents ran this restaurant.

"I felt like I couldn't be friends with her," I say. "It's hard to explain."

Charles chews silently, contemplating my words, but says nothing.

Once, while I was on a plane flying home to visit my parents, I came across an article written by Euphemia in a national newspaper. She wrote about how racism—seemingly sterilized out of Canada's conscience—still existed in more subtle, less obvious forms. Despite Canada's pride in its glorious mosaic, she still second-guessed herself if the hostess at a nice restaurant seated her in a dark corner instead of the better empty seats elsewhere, or if a boss promoted the white male co-worker over her when she felt she performed better—each ambivalence stacked into a growing pile that she could not continually dismiss as paranoia, yet could not say with certainty amounted to an act of racism. I understood her anxiety. Cathy and I would sometimes discuss this over drinks, labeling these instances "Am I Paranoid or Was That Just Racist" moments. I was surprised reading her article, as I always believed that Canada was more progressive, less xenophobic than the States.

When I go to the counter to pay, I notice a phone book, which I open. I immediately flip to the Crow Plains section and search for the name Reeves. Since reading the letters, I've been reflecting on my past and thinking about Mrs. Reeves, my old teacher. There are several entries, and I cannot recall her first name—Mrs. Annabelle Reeves, Mrs. Beth Reeves, or Ms. Sara Reeves—even though I remember her soft eyes, cleft chin, the heavy bosom that stirred a commotion among the boys in my class whenever she leaned forward. I have often wondered about her after leaving this town. Around her, I felt seen and understood. I have a sudden urge to contact her and I don't resist. I call all three numbers on my cell phone. There is no answer at the first number, another is disconnected, and the third belongs to a woman with a Newfie accent who recently moved here. I run my fingers down the column, looking for familiar names, old classmates. A few names I recognize, though I have no business calling them during this hot autumn afternoon to say, "Weren't you in my Grade 7 class?" or "Didn't you lick the flagpole during lunch one freezing winter afternoon so that they had to call the fire department to scrape off your tongue?"

We exit the restaurant and walk to my car when I recognize the bird-like face of an old woman walking towards us: her cropped, feathered hair, her retreating chin, her bright red glasses.

"Excuse me, aren't you Mrs. McKenzie, the librarian?" I ask, going up to her.

"I guess you could say I *was*," she says, lifting her bifocals towards me. "I'm now retired."

"I used to live here as a child. I'm Anne. Do you remember me?"

"Why yes, your parents owned the restaurant, didn't they?"

"That was Euphemia Wong. My parents owned the old Krowski grocery store."

"Oh, how could I forget! You came and borrowed so many books," she says.

"Yes, that was me."

She glances at Charles, and I'm unsure if she is uncomfortable or not. "And you're the brother?"

"Charles," he says, then looks away, not wanting to engage.

She appraises my champagne diamond earrings, my cashmere sweater, my Italian lambskin purse. "Well, what have you done with yourself?"

"I'm a lawyer in New York."

"New York? My goodness, what a giant leap from Crow Plains. I hear the Twin Dragons girl lives in Toronto and writes for a big newspaper. You kids have all become successful. It's because you watched your parents work hard and became hard workers yourselves. And how about you, Charles?"

"I've been in Calgary," he says.

Mrs. McKenzie waits for him to elaborate, and when he doesn't, she smiles politely and says, "Your parents raised city folks, I see."

We're pausing, unsure who should talk next, wondering if we need to continue or end this polite conversation. Charles turns his back and stares at the businesses along the street.

"Do you remember Mrs. Reeves who taught at the high school?"

"Annabelle? Of course, she's a dear friend of mine. She lives in the retirement home—it's a short walk from here. I'm headed that direction and could pop in with you if you want to see her. Would you like that?"

I nod and am taken aback for the simple kindnesses offered in small towns that can live so easily alongside other erstwhile behaviour. I look at Charles, who says he will wait for me in the car, so I give him my keys.

When we arrive at the retirement home, Mrs. McKenzie leads me down a hall and stops by a half-open door.

From time to time, I have imagined visiting Mrs. Reeves, and now here I am, standing in front of her: an aging woman sitting on a recliner, the television blaring loudly, her hand on the remote control. She peers at me suspiciously. Blurry watercolours are taped to the wall. She has shrunk—her body is propped like a sitting doll resting on a homemade quilt on her chair.

"Annabelle, guess who I bumped into?" Mrs. McKenzie says, entering the room.

"Who, Dorothy?" she asks, taking her remote control and lowering the volume.

"Remember the Koreans who ran Bill's old store in town? It's their daughter, Anne."

"Was she one of my students?" she asks in a clear, intelligent voice.

Mrs. McKenzie looks apologetically at me. "Yes."

"Nice to meet you, Anne," she says, smiling politely. Mrs. Reeves peers at me with her pale blue eyes, then nods and turns her head back to the television. I try to hide my hurt when she doesn't recognize me.

Mrs. McKenzie leads me outside into the hallway. "Don't take any of this personally. Sometimes she'll remember her old students, and I was hoping she would remember you, but she's been getting worse. These days she recognizes the cafeteria staff over her own sister."

"I'm sorry to hear. How long has she been ill?"

"It's been a slow decline. She's waiting to be transferred to a more specialized facility in Edmonton. Her sister lives near Fort Athabasca, so it'll be a shorter drive for her to visit."

"Did she paint those watercolours on her wall?" I ask.

"I don't know," she says, frowning. "You remembered that about her, that she loved to paint."

I nod and feign interest as she talks about the art classes that the recreation centre will have and how the centre is also building a new pool with a spiral slide that is being imported from Denmark. I wait until she pauses, then say that it was good to see her and Mrs. Reeves and that I need to return to Charles.

"I'm sorry she didn't remember you. If you remind her of the past, she may not necessarily remember everything, but it may help her return to the person she once was."

1992

During lunch, a group of boys follows me.

"Chink! Chink! You're a chink, riding on a horse's dink!" they chant, circling me as other kids gather around them. I angrily walk past them, although there's nowhere to go: The schoolyard is a fenced field of yellow grass and patches of snow. I don't have anywhere to run to.

"Get lost, you mean bullies," a girl says, emerging from a crowd of kids. I turn around and see a girl who looks Chinese, with thick glasses and frizzy, coarse hair.

The boys scowl at her, until one of the group members leaves, and the others follow him. I hear them muttering *stupid ding dong wong* underneath their breaths.

"Hi, my name's Euphemia. Don't listen to them, they're just ignorant," she says.

"Hi, I'm Anne."

"I heard your family bought Bill Krowski's store. My father came by to introduce himself to your parents the other day. We own the Chinese restaurant in town. I'm in Grade 9. What grade are you in?" Euphemia asks. She wears a wool sweater that fits loosely, in a drab colour that emphasizes her brown freckles.

"I'm in Grade 7," I say. I see girls from my class standing nearby pointing at us—two Chinese girls, both wearing brown sweaters and baggy jeans. I hear someone call out "Twin Dragons," and the girls giggle.

"Our restaurant is on the same street as your store. If you want, I can wait for you today after school so we can walk home together," she says.

I examine the freckles that spot her face, the heavy glasses that make her eyes shrink, and the metal braces that correct her crooked teeth. I hear girls behind us snickering. Yura would caution me against ever associating myself with her if I wanted to make any other friends. If we became friends now, I instinctively know that my fate in this town will be sealed as one of the Twin Dragons. This thought terrifies me.

"I can't. I volunteered to reorganize the art supply closet after school," I say in a heightened voice, a voice that Yura would use. It's not entirely a lie. Miss Schlueter asked for helpers to make room for new supplies, and I decide then that I will now volunteer.

"Oh, you'll like Miss Schlueter. She's an easy marker. If you need help with anything, you can always ask me. I'm always at the restaurant, so drop by anytime," she says, then lingers as if she wants to say something more, but decides to walk away.

A girl in class asks why I don't hang out with Euphemia. I tell her we're not friends because she's a chink, but I'm Korean. The kids surrounding us laugh.

"What's the difference between a Chinese and a Korean?" the girl asks.

"Chinese people have slanty eyes, but mine aren't like that," I say, widening my eyes until I can't make them any larger.

"Yes they are," the girl says, and places her fingers on her temples and pulls them upwards to supposedly mirror mine. I laugh, alongside my classmates.

That night, I ask my parents what the difference is between a Chinese and a Korean. My father says that the Chinese once ran a great empire that heavily influenced Korean culture. So, I ask what the difference is between a Chinese and a Canadian. My father says there are many differences but that we are more Chinese than we are Canadian. I'm confused. I have never been to China, I was born here, so how can I be more Chinese than Canadian?

"When the townspeople watch you, they will judge all Orientals," my father says in Korean, "which is why we need to work hard so we can be better than white people in every imaginable way." Our behaviour will not only impact our family's reputation but how white people will esteem Koreans, Chinese, even the Indians who, according to my father, are also related to us. I sense my father is exaggerating, but if there is truth to his words—that my actions will affect how the townspeople view whole countries and swaths of races—then I have an even greater need to be good, to achieve a moral purity, so I can both become superior and exact revenge on this oppressive town.

Because of the liquor store, we are no longer on the brink of bankruptcy, and our new challenge is to keep up with the daily demands of the stores. With both a grocery and a liquor store, my parents are busy. They need to watch customers at two cash registers in addition to the many tasks involved in maintaining two bustling stores. Eventually, they hire a farmer's wife who has never travelled beyond Fort Athabasca to work part-time. My parents are grateful that she is punctual, takes orders from them, and, more than anything, is kind.

When school ends, it's understood that I am to help at the store, but I don't mind: I don't have any friends or plans to be excited about summer break. Charles, though, must study.

My father has spoken with Mr. Wong, who told him that Euphemia is spending the summer studying for the SSAT, the entrance exam for Essex Academy—a prestigious high school in Edmonton that her cousin attends. Its graduates go on to reputable universities out east and in America. Euphemia will apply to their IB program for Grade 11. She will take the SSAT in the fall and apply the following year. Though it's in Edmonton, they offer full scholarships to exceptional students. If Euphemia gets accepted, she will live with her aunt, whose son also attends this school. According to her cousin, in spite of the fierce competition, there is a disproportionate number of Chinese kids at Essex.

My father tells Charles to study for this entrance exam. My brother complains to my mother at the absurdity of studying for an exam that he won't take for another year, and my mother nods in sympathy.

"Dad, my grades are good. Why can't I just play with my friends this summer and study next year?"

"No, you study."

"I got straight A's, and I can easily do it again," Charles protests.

"Just let Charles enjoy after studying so hard," my mother says in Korean. I'm watching television, though also eavesdropping. Usually, my mother doesn't stand up to my father, so I tune out of my show and listen carefully to their conversation.

"He will study," my father says.

"Yeobo, Charles did well this year. Let him relax. He needs to have a refreshed mind for the fall," my mother pleads. My father glares at my mother.

"He needs to understand hard work. If he listens to you, he will become rotten. Is that why I'm working so hard, so my son will be spoiled?" my father snarls, his face hardening.

"Let him enjoy playing with his friends. Why can't he be like the other—"

My father slams his fist onto the kitchen table. Startled, I look up from the television.

"I did not come to Canada so I can have a son like the other boys who will never amount to anything. Charles needs to study." Though my mother looks upset, she says nothing. And with that, Charles's summer is set.

Mr. Wong writes down the titles to Euphemia's SSAT prep books—which she got from her cousin—and my mother drives to

Fort Athabasca Mall to order these titles from the bookstore and then, a month later, makes another trip to pick them up.

I complain to my mother that it's not fair that I have to work at the store while Charles gets to stay in his room. My mother explains that we're both working, Charles even more so. Because he is a male and the eldest son, he has great responsibilities to shoulder—he must provide for his future family—a burden I have evaded by being born female. My mother tells me that I'm lucky, and I try to direct my thoughts to gratitude, but I'm annoyed because Charles does not study. During the day, he goes into the shed to read through a stack of discarded comic books without their covers—my parents rip off the covers then mail them back to the distributor to get a refund on unsold periodicals. I don't blame him; it's too hot in our house. The prairie sun bakes through all our bedroom windows. Eventually, I decide that I enjoy being at the store: Even though work is dreary, the coolers and freezers keep the temperature cool, which I prefer to the dry heat outside. I get to eat endless chips and candy. I drink unlimited soda. I read through all our comics and magazines.

My favourite job is sitting at the front counter and keeping watch so my parents can work in the back. I munch on a bag of chips, sip on a soda, and read teen magazines—through them, I learn how to French kiss (later, in my bedroom, I practise on my arm), how to French braid, how to dress Parisian chic.

Today is milk day. I'm at the front counter reading a fashion magazine while my parents unload the dairy crates in the back. A boy enters the store. It's Trevor Miller, who I consider the handsomest boy in town. He's two grades ahead of me. I'm embarrassed being behind the counter to serve him and pretend to read my magazine as he slowly walks down the aisles. But I look up often and see him glancing at me every now and then. He's the only customer. We've never spoken, so we don't speak now, continuing our feigned formality. He stops at the candy aisle and turns his back towards me. I stare into the convex mirror that hangs in the corner of the store. I admire his spikey hair with its frosted blonde tips, his rolled jean cuffs, the metal chains dangling from his neck and wrists. I watch as he stuffs his pockets with chocolate bars, packages of licorice and candy. The plastic wrapping makes a squeaking noise, which he doesn't try very hard to mask. When he turns slightly and gives a furtive glance in my direction, my eyes obediently fall to the ground. He continues to reach and to grab.

I hear my father slamming the door of the back cooler, then walking up the centre aisle. The squeaking sound stops. Without turning around, Trevor goes to the front door and leaves.

"Did he take anything?" my father asks in Korean. My face blanks. He stands at the window, watching Trevor walk away. "He's stolen before. I told myself I'd call the police the next time I caught him. Did you see anything suspicious?"

I stare at my father, confounded. I want to tell my father that he just stole. But if Trevor gets arrested for shoplifting, then when school starts, I will have to pass him and his friends in the halls. News of me squealing on him would spread and ruin my chances of ever fitting in. This thought terrifies me, so I shake my head. "I was watching him the whole time," I reply in English, not wanting to respond this way but unable to say otherwise.

·

The rest of the summer passes unremarkably. The highlight is summer's end when my mother takes us to Fort Athabasca Mall and I shop for new school supplies and clothes. On the first day of Grade 8, I am elated when my new teacher, Mrs. Reeves, assigns me to sit in front of Crystal. Meredith sits a few desks in front of me, and during class, I pass their notes. I get complicit glances and giggles from both girls as I deliver their folded papers, trying to evade Mrs. Reeves's notice.

One day, we are working on a social studies project, and Mrs. Reeves is going around the class consulting each student with their ideas. It's a warm autumn day and the students are chatting amongst one another. I'm wearing my necklace with the pendant knife, and its burgundy satin rope shows behind my neck.

Crystal is bored and taps me on the back. "Can I see your necklace?"

I fish out the knife pendant and pull the rope over my head.

"What is that?" Crystal asks as her fingers trace the intricate chrysanthemum design.

"It's a knife," I say, looking around to make sure no one is watching, then breaking the case in half to reveal the blade.

"You brought a knife to class?" she whispers, her eyes widening. "Is that from your country?"

"Yes."

Meredith sees us talking and walks over. "What are you looking at?" she asks, and then sees the blade.

"It's a knife. Anne wears it as a pendant."

"Anne, I had no idea you were Goth," Meredith says, impressed. I don't know what she is referring to, but I smile as if complimented.

Tess, seeing that we're all gathered together, joins us. "Is that a knife?" she asks nervously.

"Shh!" the girls shush her and turn around to make sure Mrs. Reeves has not heard.

Crystal touches the etched design. "Want to see it?" She offers it to Tess.

"No."

"Are you scared of it?" Meredith asks, almost as if testing Tess.

"I'm not scared . . . I think it's cool," Tess says quietly.

"I dare you to carve your name on the desk with it," Meredith says with a hint of malice.

"Mrs. Reeves would know it was me," Tess mumbles. "I don't want to get in trouble."

"Fine, I dare you to take the knife and . . ." Meredith scans the classroom, "take the lemon off of Mrs. Reeves's tree." Mrs. Reeves has a potted lemon tree on her desk that she planted from a seed. To her great excitement, over the summer it produced a sole lemon for the first time, and she brought in her plant to discuss citrus trees, and horticulture in general.

"Mrs. Reeves loves that lemon," Tess says.

"Mrs. Reeves is a cow," Crystal says.

"It's so tiny, and not even ripe!" Tess protests.

"Crystal is right. Mrs. Reeves is a cow. Tess, give it to us," Meredith says flatly as she hands the knife to Tess.

Tess reluctantly grabs it, then walks over to Mrs. Reeves's desk. She searches for Mrs. Reeves, and sees that she is bent over, helping a student. Meredith and Crystal burst into giggles. Tess frowns and motions them to shush up. In a quick motion, Tess takes the knife and cuts off the tiny lemon, which disappears into her palm and up her sleeve. No one seems to notice, least of all Mrs. Reeves, who is speaking to a student with her back towards us. Tess returns and plunks the lemon on Crystal's desk, where we're all huddled. Tess hands the knife over to me and gives me a cool look.

Meredith smiles triumphantly. "Now, I dare you to eat it."

When the lunch bell rings, we run outside. I'm thrilled to be with them. I take out my knife and slice the small lemon into pieces. I give the first slice to Tess, who reluctantly puts the piece into her mouth and almost gags amidst our giggles. Then we all take a slice to consume: Its sour taste deforms our faces. After the lemon is gone and the laughing stops, an uncomfortable silence descends. I don't want to leave. I can't leave. Ever since I have arrived in this town, I have wanted to be standing here, among these girls. I think of Yura, charming Sharon and Tom, and muster up the courage to be bold and fun, yet conforming and pleasant. I pull my jacket sleeve to my elbow, exposing my arm. "Do you guys want to learn how to French kiss?" For the remainder of lunch, I teach them how to manoeuvre their tongues with the expertise I have gleaned from the teen magazines I read all summer.

The rest of the afternoon, we sit in class eyeing one another and giggling as we take turns sucking on our arms. The next day, during lunch, I boldly walk up to them and offer to demonstrate an asymmetrical side braid, a variation on the French braid that I also learned from the teen magazines. I offer them a big bag of ketchup chips that I have brought.

"You're so fun!" Meredith says, viewing her side braid approvingly in Crystal's purse mirror.

"You're so nice!" Crystal and Tess say, as they take fistfuls of chips. I've made sure to pack my lunches according to my observations of what is considered in good taste. I am the grocer's daughter, and I have unlimited resources to create inoffensive and enviable lunches: two slices of white bread around two perfect lines of pink bologna with orange cheese at the centre. I soon upgrade my snack-size bags of chips to the family-sized bags, a bar of chocolate into several, with a handful of sour soothers, Swedish fish, and strawberry marshmallows for good measure. At home, heeding Yura's warning to not smell, I stop eating kimchi and any other Korean food with garlic that my mother makes.

At lunch, I go to my newfound friends with my offerings. They compliment me on my generosity. We have debates over which tastes better, the O'Ryans Sour Cream'n Onion or Sour Cream'n Bacon flavour? Which is more exotic, the Cuban Lunch or the Big Turk? Which has the better prize, Lucky Elephant's Pink Popcorn or Cracker Jack? We adorn our fingers with gem ring pops, drape ourselves with ropes of candy necklaces and bracelets. We suck on our Popeye's candy cigarettes, blowing fake smoke into the air. We crunch gobstoppers during class, and sizzle Fizz Wiz on our tongues with a straight face, to the bewilderment of Mrs. Reeves.

"Meredith, Crystal, and Anne, I'd like you to stay after class."

We glance at one another. Mrs. Reeves looks calmly at us as she dismisses the class. Tess has not been in school for the past few days, but we assumed that she probably was sick. When class is dismissed, Mrs. Reeves motions us to sit in the desks in front of her.

"Tess is suspended for a week," Mrs. Reeves says, giving us each a meaningful look.

"That's terrible," Meredith says in a high-pitched voice.

"Oh no," Crystal chimes in.

"Last week, during class, the lemon on my plant disappeared. I inquired around, and one student saw Tess tear off the fruit. I spoke with Tess, and she cried and admitted to doing this. I asked her if others were involved, but she refused to say anything more. Do you know if someone made her do something that she didn't want to do?" As Mrs. Reeves peers at us, my eyes fall to the ground.

"Did she tell you someone made her do it?" Meredith asks.

"No," Mrs. Reeves says sternly. "But it seems unlike her to do something like that. I don't sense that vandalizing my property would be something Tess would do unprompted. And if someone did ask her to do it, that's not really being a friend to her, is it?"

Meredith's face flushes, and Crystal starts twirling her hair. None of us meets her eyes.

"That's all. Anne, I'd like you to stay for a quick word, but you girls are dismissed. Please close the door on your way out."

Meredith and Crystal seem worried, but I give them a reassuring smile. Mrs. Reeves waits until the girls shut the door.

"Anne, I'm just wondering how you've been settling in. Is everything okay?" Mrs. Reeves asks.

"Yes," I say quietly.

"What Tess did seems very out of character." There's a long pause as she studies my face. "I know you moved into town last year. It can be hard to find your group of friends. I'd be careful as to who I select as my friends."

My face burns with shame. "Yes, Mrs. Reeves," I mutter.

"You're dismissed."

I plod my way to the classroom door and walk down the hallway. When I go outside, Meredith and Crystal are waiting for me.

"What happened?" Meredith asks.

"Nothing, Mrs. Reeves was just making sure I was settling in well."

"Did she say anything else?"

"No."

"What a cow!" Meredith exclaims.

"Yeah, I can't believe Mrs. Reeves guilt tripped us when she has no evidence!" Crystal says.

"No, not her. The other cow, Tess. Should we tell Anne why we no longer like Tess?" Meredith says.

Crystal giggles. "You mean why no one likes Tess."

"You guess why, Anne," Meredith says.

Whatever the reason is, it must be something that deserves this collective scorn. My mind fills with the sins Tess could have committed—saying things that are annoying or even being entirely plain—that need to be discussed and judged.

"She doesn't have any style," I say. Tess rotates through the same bland items of faded jeans and her brother's ill-fitting sweaters. She doesn't try. I, however, have pulled out all of Yura's hand-me-downs, assessed each piece, ripped holes in her jeans, shortened the hemlines of her skirts, fastened safety pins with beads on her denim jacket. I've taken my mother's scarves to wear as hairbands, my father's ties to use as sashes. "She eats garlic," Meredith says.

"You can smell it on her, especially when she sweats in phys ed," Crystal says with a sneer.

"Which is why we no longer want to be her friend," Meredith says.

I fake indignation even though inside I feel dread. I wonder how my sins would fare with our packages of dried fish, jars of spicy sour cabbage, blocks of bean paste.

"She's as stinky as that ding dong girl," Meredith says.

"Euphemia?" I say.

Crystal starts giggling. "Ding Dong is such a dork. When you first came here, we thought she was going to be your best friend, so I said we should call you two the Twin Dragons," she says proudly.

I force myself to laugh.

"I remember. That was a good one," Meredith says. "But we can't use it anymore because Anne is our friend now."

When Tess returns, she instinctively knows that she is no longer welcome in our group. In class, I join Meredith and Crystal as we giggle and pass notes amongst one another. During lunch, Tess stands alone, reading a book, or walks along the perimeter of the schoolgrounds, until, one day, she doesn't show up at all and we're told she has decided to finish the rest of the year through correspondence. Once, I see her coming out of the drugstore with her mother, and she stops when she sees me. I quickly turn and walk the opposite way, trying to suppress the guilt arising inside of me.

The Songs are visiting. The adults are in the kitchen, the men drinking whisky and smoking while the women drink tea and peel fruit. Charles and Samuel rented a movie from the video store, and they are now watching a horror film. I'm in my room, the door open, eavesdropping in case something interesting is revealed, while also studying.

Mr. Song complains that his sons are addicted to the *bee-dee-oh* game. They are constantly playing, prioritizing this before anything else, and as a result, their grades are dropping. They are worried that their eldest son is flunking university and Samuel may not even be able to get in.

"This bee-dee-oh has screwed up our sons," Mr. Song says, lamenting that the video game has brought discord with his sons and strife with his wife. Twice, in a fit of rage, Mr. Song threw it in the garbage, but their sons always managed to repurchase another console. Now, he's resigned, and blames his wife for purchasing the bee-dee-oh in the first place. It is his life's biggest regret. The bee-dee-oh is destroying their sons' lives. Mrs. Song defends herself, saying all her sons' friends have consoles, how could they be the only family that deprives them, and soon the couple begin arguing, until Mr. Song violently shouts over her until she falls silent.

Then the conversation turns to me.

My mother complains that I have become increasingly vain, experimenting with her makeup in the bathroom, begging to wear eyeshadow or lipstick to school—which she forbids—and spending hours flipping through the Sears catalogue for clothes that we can't afford. I am embarrassed and want her to stop talking about me, so I go to the kitchen to get a glass of water. The adults stop talking, and I sense Mrs. Song appraising me. Mrs. Song motions me to come over. She examines me. She instructs me to close my eyes and presses her rough thumb over each of my eyelids.

"You could be so pretty. Do you want to be pretty?" she asks me in Korean, a note of pity lining her voice.

"Yes," I eagerly answer back in English. I notice that Mrs. Song looks different, and realize that she now has a double eyelid accenting each eye. She catches my gaze and proudly smiles.

"I went to Korea last month and got eyelid surgery. When I came back, my husband and sons didn't notice anything changed, but some customers told me, 'Julie, you look so amazing, so good. What happen to you?'" She giggles as she says this last phrase in English. "But you don't need to go to Korea or even get surgery. You can get big eyes at night using tape," Mrs. Song says brightly, and she instructs me to bring a roll of scotch tape, a pen, a mirror, and a pair of scissors. She sits in front of me, measures the length of my eye against her thumb, and draws two crescent moons on the tape, which she then cuts. She presses them against my closed eyelids, then asks me to open them as she holds up a mirror. I open my eyes, and my eyelids have miraculously folded against the tape, creating a double eyelid.

"So beautiful," Mrs. Song exclaims. My mother spreads her lips, and I'm unsure if it is a grin or a grimace.

I can't see clearly; the rigid tape unravels and obstructs my vision.

"If you do this every night before sleep, one day, you will wake up and have big, beautiful eyes. Maybe you can try out for Miss Korea, or maybe a doctor will marry you. Do you want that?" Mrs. Song asks merrily.

"Anne needs to focus on her studies," my mother says, and when she tightens the corners of her lips, I realize that she is trying not to reveal her annoyance.

"Don't listen to your mother. A girl needs to focus on being pretty, not studying. It's more fun being a doctor's wife than becoming a doctor. It's the man's job to make money and his wife's job to spend it. Working isn't fun; spending your husband's money is," Mrs. Song says with a chuckle. Then she tells me about her two female cousins who are sisters: The oldest studied hard and became a dentist, whereas the youngest was too busy dating boys and flunked out of university. With nothing better to do, the youngest got both eye and nose surgery and decided to try out for the Miss Korea pageant. Even though she did not win, she married a doctor and now lives in a big apartment in Apgujeong—the Beverly Hills of Seoul. The dentist sister is still single and now, in her thirties, is considered too old to marry. "Even though the youngest sister wasn't that smart, she became the success of the family," Mrs. Song says approvingly.

"Here, it's better that she doesn't get any attention from boys. My sister was very beautiful, but it got her into trouble," my mother says.

"Yes, but your sister made bad decisions. I don't think Anne would make those decisions. She seems very sensible," Mrs. Song says in a voice mixed with pity and hope. The reference to my aunt brings a pang of hurt: Mrs. Song, a friend that my mother has only known for a little more than a year, knows more about our family's history than I do. The few times I ask about it, my mother reveals little. "They're in Korea. What more do you want to know?" she says impatiently in Korean, after which I don't insist, as I doubt I will get a truthful account of why she avoids talking about them. The rare time my mother speaks about her sister, it's always with a pitying tone.

The following week, every day when I return home from school, I cut a pair of crescent moons from scotch tape. I press them against my eyelids. The tape scratches my skin, often falling off at inconvenient moments so that I need to recut the tape. I look obsessively into the mirror, and sometimes I see my eyelids fold and crease. Other times, they remain flat. I want, so badly, to be pretty, or at least to change my features. When my mother sees me, she tells me to focus on studying; but she's too busy maintaining the store to chastise me further. At night, before I sleep, I take a clothespin and grip the tip of my nose. My mother tells me that Vivien Leigh did this. The pain is excruciating, and it only lasts for a few minutes before it pops off. After I shower, I squeeze lemon juice into my hair. I've read in a teen magazine that this will lighten the colour. Weeks pass but nothing changes. I wish I could take our exfoliating cloth and peel off my skin to unveil a fairer undertone, brush off my coarse hair to reveal finer, lighter-coloured strands. One day, I'm standing next to Meredith and Crystal, and I see our reflection in the school's windowpane. I see how different I am from them with my shorter stature, my alien eyes, my rounded nose, and I realize the futility of all my efforts.

NINE

Charles becomes friends with Clint, a lanky boy whom Meredith has referred to as a "geek." He lives in a trailer house on the outskirts of town with his mother, who waitresses at the pizza parlour, and his older brother, Paul, who works at the Radio Shack in Fort Athabasca. Paul has amassed an expansive Nintendo video game collection using his employee discount. Charles is addicted. Every day, after school, Charles goes to Clint's house and stays for hours trying to save a pixelated princess or fight off serpents and monsters to restore world order. My parents are too busy to notice his absence. Besides, Charles continues to bring home high grades, so they leave him alone, assuming that he is diligently studying in his room even though he is not.

I say nothing because if Charles gets caught, more drama will unfold: Last month, my father was walking to the bank on Main Street and saw Charles and Clint entering the arcade. Furious, my father followed them inside, grabbed Charles by the ear and berated him in front of the arcade boys, who watched with amusement: the squabbling Chinaman and his son. That night, my father raged, using his wooden backscratcher to lash Charles's limbs while my mother wailed beside her bruising son. Charles sobbed and screamed, "Clint's mom is fine with him visiting the arcade! She even gives us the quarters from her tip money so we can play!" My father, horrified at Clint's mother's negligence, forbade Charles from being friends with Clint and yelled at my mother for daring to side with her son.

After this event, to avoid further drama, every day I call Clint's house and plead with my brother to come home before the store closes. Charles will race home either on foot or by bike, and so far, he has managed to be in his room by the time my parents return. When no one picks up the phone at Clint's house, that means they're at the arcade.

One day, my father is in an especially sour mood: Mr. Kang has called to confirm that he's finally received his cheque in the mail, but because of several late payments, he has decided to increase the interest rate on their loan. After slamming down the phone, my father screams at my mother for ordering too much milk that has now expired. I sense his tension needing a release, so I call Clint's house, but no one answers. I walk out our back door to the arcade. It's a chilly fall evening, and the arcade windows are steamed and show the darkened silhouettes of a crowd inside.

When I open the door, the air is heavy with sweat and cigarette smoke. A few girls sit at a Formica table, drinking soda and chatting. A group of boys stands in front of an arcade machine, shouting and cheering. I walk towards them, stand on my toes, and see Charles at the race car machine, seated next to Jeff, whose father owns the competing grocery store in town. They both grasp a steering wheel as music blasts in the background. Their postures are tense. Every time Jeff jerks his steering wheel, the boys cheer. Suddenly, I hear the sound of tires screeching, and the boys jeer as Jeff's car crashes and crumples on the screen. Jeff, frustrated, slams his fists against the steering wheel. Charles looks triumphantly at the screen as it dings a victory song and a trophy appears.

I break through the crowd and tug at Charles's arm. "Come home," I hiss.

The boys begin to chant, "Rematch! Rematch! Rematch!" Jeff inserts quarters and grabs the steering wheel again. They hoot as Jeff's car reappears on the screen.

"Get lost!" Charles yells as he wipes the sweat dripping down his forehead with his forearm and digs into his jean pocket for more quarters.

Both boys grip their wheels. Clint and his brother, Paul, are the lone voices chanting for Charles. I turn around and see a red-haired girl with curly hair coyly watching Charles. The boys cheer as Jeff approaches the finish line. Without warning, a brick wall appears out of nowhere and Jeff's car crashes into it. The audience boos. Frustrated, Jeff rises from his seat and kicks the arcade machine. The room goes silent.

"Fuck! Fuck! Fuck!" Jeff yells as he glowers at Charles.

"Hey, man, cool it," Paul says, appearing by Charles's side. Clint stays in the crowd, his face blanching. Charles gets out of the car and slowly turns towards the entrance.

"Get the fuck out of here, you fucking chink!" Jeff screams as we run out the door.

Every lunch hour, I join Meredith and Crystal to whisper and giggle. Everyone in class, including the popular boys, now know who I am. Because of my acceptance, this town transforms: The people and houses that once were impenetrable and interchangeable now become nuanced and real. After school, I walk home with Crystal, who discloses the town's secrets: about Edna and her gay son who live together in a house thought to be haunted, or Stanley's mistress, who lives with their love child in a house where the curtains are always drawn shut. One day, Meredith invites me to a sleepover. I'm elated.

The Sweeneys' house is large, surrounded by forest and fields. My mother looks around to find the property's perimeter while driving down the long driveway. I nervously hold a box of Laura Secord chocolates in one hand while I ring the doorbell with the other. Mrs. Sweeney greets me in an apron and is surprised when I present her with a gift.

"A gift, how charming," she says with a smile that I cannot tell is grateful or fake.

Mrs. Sweeney is blonde and tall, and her face casts a rosy glow as if she's just returned from a hike in the Alps. She doesn't dress like the other townswomen with their brightly coloured clothes and frosted-tip, teased hair. She wears a light lavender sweater and matching skirt. The knife pleats at the back of her skirt open when she turns around and places the chocolates on a console table holding stiff flowers. When Mrs. Sweeney isn't looking, I touch the petals and realize with disappointment that they are not real but made out of a tough fabric.

Mrs. Sweeney goes to the door and calls to my mother, who is watching me from our car. "Mrs. Kim, why don't you come inside for some coffee or tea?" It's an offer of cordiality, possibly friendship.

My mother shakes her head, terrified, and rolls down her window. "Solly, need to go back to store, busy, busy," she says, inelegant though polite. Although I'm warmed by Mrs. Sweeney's invitation to my mother, I feel threatened by her progressiveness.

Their house smells of gravy and roses. I scan the living room and adjoining dining room from the entrance as I take off my shoes. Their house looks like it's from the women's magazines that I read at the store: The sofa matches the curtains and valances, satin stripes cover the walls, and a plate of pastel chocolate almonds sit on the coffee table, accompanied by a small pair of silver tongs—even though we sell these almonds, they look better, taste better here. The coffee table gleams against the afternoon light, and I'm certain that if I were to run my finger against its surface, it would not pick up any dust.

Mrs. Sweeney leads me to Meredith's room, where Meredith and Crystal have just finished braiding their hair. Meredith's room is covered with wallpaper where unicorns gallop endlessly among rainbows and clouds. Her furniture matches: lacquered white wood with gold drawer pulls and bowed table legs. The blanket on her bed folds into sharp corners and matching pillows lean against the headboard. Porcelain figurines decorate a glass shelf. They all have blonde hair and blue eyes. I make a comment that these figurines resemble her, and Meredith says thank you in a polite adult voice.

"You own a lot of pretty things," I say, almost to myself.

"You want to see more?" Meredith asks, and before I can respond she gets up and leads us to her closet. She pulls out a wooden chest.

"What's that?" I ask.

"My grandma gave me her hope chest. It's where you put your family heirlooms."

"What's an heirloom?"

"Things that get passed down to you. Every girl has things that their mom or grandma wants to give to the next generation."

"Sure," I say, as if this is something I also have.

Meredith opens the cover, and inside there are folded pieces of fabric, leather-bound books, silk sachets, and a polished wooden box. She takes out the wooden box. Inside is a velvet tray holding sparkling jewellery.

"My grandfather was a lawyer in Toronto. He knew my grandmother had a weakness for gems." We embellish our fingers and necks with cocktail rings and necklaces. There are also brooches, which I pin along my collar. I am envious of these brilliant jewels.

"My mom promised I would get her engagement ring," Crystal says.

"What is your mom going to give you?" Meredith asks me.

I try not to look stumped. I fish under my sweater and bring out the silver knife. "This knife is probably older than anything you have in your hope chest," I say proudly.

"Why would you give a girl a knife as an inheritance?" Meredith asks.

"Ladies would wear them in case they got raped. If that happened, they would have to kill themselves," I say matter-of-factly, for added shock.

"That's so barbaric," Meredith says, lifting the rope from my neck and breaking open the silver pendant to reveal the knife. "Do you think any ancestor has killed herself with this blade?"

I haven't considered this thought. I remember Yura telling me it was a gift from her aunt, but what do I know of her family's hidden secrets?

"Is that blood?" Crystal asks, pointing to some dark matter at the base of the knife. We peer in closer. I'm unsure how ancient, dried blood would look on a knife.

"So savage having to carry around a knife," Meredith says. "And to expect a woman to kill herself if she got attacked."

Even though I agree with her, I'm offended by Meredith's judgment: Only I should be authorized to judge it as savage. I want to say something hurtful back, so I say, "This hope chest is so big and heavy. It could trap someone inside and stifle them to death." I envision a corpse-like Meredith curled inside with her golden hair and dried flowers. "Even if I had one, I wouldn't be able to carry it with me to New York," I say. I remember Yura's declaration that she would move there and how much this impressed me.

"You're moving to New York?" Crystal says.

"Yes, I'm going to live there one day," I say, and their hush reveals that they are in awe. I haven't seriously considered my future or career, but my mind automatically latches onto Yura's lofty ambitions so I can make the same impression.

"What are you going to do there?" Meredith asks.

"I'm not sure yet," I say, and the girls seem disappointed.

"Well, I want to be a choreographer," says Crystal. She takes jazz-dancing classes on the weekends when she visits her father in Fort Athabasca. Later, she will teach us dance moves from pre-recorded shows of *Video Hits*. She has brought her VHS tapes, and in a painfully slow process, she will push play, then pause, then rewind as she breaks down dance moves and then teaches them to us in Meredith's basement.

"I want to be a wife and a mother," Meredith announces proudly.

"What job would you have before that happens?" I ask.

"I don't know. Everything seems like a waiting time until I find my soul mate and get married," she says in a dreamy voice. "Okay, I have a question for you. If you could have only one trait and be either smart, rich, or beautiful, which one would you pick?"

I realize this is a trick question and that there is only one right answer. I don't have any of these traits, so I want them all equally. But being smart or beautiful would only benefit myself, whereas if I were rich, I could help my parents.

"I would be beautiful," Meredith says.

"But you already are," I respond.

Meredith is pleased with my answer. "I want to be the prettiest girl out there. Then I could marry a man who is handsome, smart, and rich. Being smart for a girl is useless. Did you know that my mother has a master's degree?"

"What's that?" I ask.

"It's a degree higher than your bachelor's degree . . . that's your first degree in university," she adds when I look confused. "Originally, my mother wanted to study medicine, but my grandfather would only allow her to go to university if she promised to study something useless or else it would scare off potential suitors. So, my mother studied German literature. She got her master's degree and wanted to study for a PhD, but then she met my father and married him and is now a housewife." I almost sense pity from Meredith's tone, and it is jarring for me to think of Mrs. Sweeney—in her charming outfit and house—as pitiful.

"I would pick being beautiful too," Crystal says.

"I would be rich," I say.

"Why?" both girls ask.

"So I could buy my parents a nice house."

"I'm actually surprised you picked rich," Meredith says as she turns to the mirror and unravels the braids in her hair.

"Why?"

Meredith gives Crystal a glance. "We thought you would say you wanted to be smart."

"Even I know that being smart isn't helpful when you're a woman," I say.

"I guess we all agree on something," Meredith says, and I realize that even though I imagined a great divide between us, perhaps Meredith and I have more in common than I thought.

There's a knock on the door, and Mr. Sweeney walks in.

"Daddy!" Meredith says, and jumps up to hug and kiss him. I look away from this burst of affection. He's dressed in a suit and has loosened his tie, just like how I've seen fathers do on television. Mr. Sweeney,

I'm told afterwards, heads the chemical plant in Fort Athabasca. They moved here because of Meredith's love for horses: so that Mystique, her horse, has a proper field to roam in.

"Hey, Fred!" Crystal says with casual cheer. I try to contain my horror that Crystal is addressing Meredith's father so rudely: She's calling him by his first name.

"Where's my present?" Meredith asks, grabbing the bag her father carries. Her father has just arrived from a business trip in Michigan. She opens a box and brings out a beautiful porcelain doll whose wavy blonde hair sweeps away from her face, off her shoulders. The delicate figurine wears a flouncy peach dress that drapes and dips into a gradation of auburn, with a matching bonnet.

"Thank you, Daddy!" Meredith shouts, kissing her father as he gives her a tight embrace, then swings her.

"Who's your new friend?" Mr. Sweeney asks as he puts his daughter down. I am embarrassed at being acknowledged.

"Hello, Mr. Sweeney," I say solemnly.

"She's our newest addition," Meredith says.

"Welcome newest addition," he says, smiling warmly at me. "Do you have any other name that you go by?"

"My name is Anne."

"Nice to meet you. Please call me Fred."

"Yes, Mr. Sweeney," I say automatically, and I see Crystal give Meredith a smirk. At dinner, I sit between Meredith and Crystal, trying not to show my unease. Everything matches: the table linen with the napkins, the dishes with their inner dishes, the cutlery with their floral handles. When Mr. Sweeney takes his napkin and casually tosses it onto his lap, I follow suit.

"Anne, please start," Mrs. Sweeney says.

I pick up a chicken drumstick with my fingers, then pierce some green beans with my fork. Everyone watches me. I wonder if this is out of deference; in our family, we wait for my father or the oldest male to take his food before anyone else can help themselves, and perhaps in their household, this is translated to the newest guest.

"Feel free to use the serving spoons," Mrs. Sweeney says in a taut voice.

I hear Crystal snicker. It's then that I see the shiny spoons jutting out of each dish. When I drop my fork and reach for this spoon to take some mashed potatoes, I see Mrs. Sweeney's face relax. Then she begins passing the dishes to everyone else.

"How is it?" Mrs. Sweeney asks.

"Delicious," I say too enthusiastically.

"Where are the drumsticks?" Meredith asks, using the serving spoon to search beneath the carved chicken parts.

"You can have mine," I say as I pick up my drumstick with my fingers and drop it on her plate.

Meredith's eyes glint with amusement. Mrs. Sweeney takes a gulp of her wine and afterwards gives a quick exhalation of air.

Mr. Sweeney takes over the conversation and relays stories of people he met on his business trip, imitating these comical figures with their Detroit accents. Everyone is laughing. Meredith and Crystal interrupt to ask questions or share their own stories in front of her parents. The entire time, I don't speak. So, it is true. All the television sitcoms that depict the family dinner scene with a jovial father, well-coiffed mother, and children participating in lively conversation are real. I'm watching them as I would one of these shows, laughing on cue as an audience participant when someone says something funny. But I am also on set, a participant in the meal.

"Anne, you're awfully quiet. Tell us a little about yourself," Mr. Sweeney says, and everyone looks at me. My cheeks burn as I stare down at my plate. "Where are you from?"

"I was born in Edmonton," I say, but knowing this is not the correct answer, I quickly add, "but my parents are from Korea."

"From North or South Korea?" he asks.

I'm surprised that he knows I come from a divided country. It's the first time anyone outside my family has conveyed this understanding. But I also know this question still reveals an ignorance since North Koreans can't leave their country. "My parents are from Seoul, so we're from South Korea," I say.

"My uncle went there for the war," Mr. Sweeney says. I look at him, puzzled.

"You know, the Korean War?" he says, his brow furrowing. "Uncle Bob was posted near Seoul. It was his first time being away from home, and though it was a hard period for him, he said the people were very warm and welcoming. He brought me back some coins and stamps."

Mr. Sweeney pauses and waits for me to comment, but I don't. This is the first time I'm hearing about a war in Korea, so I try to hide my surprise. I do a quick calculation: Mr. Sweeney is probably my parents' age, and if he saw his uncle serve, then that must mean my parents were alive for this war. My mind scrambles trying to connect my family to this war, but I don't say anything because I have nothing to say.

"Great Uncle Bob is *so* weird," Meredith says, rolling her eyes.

"He said he would never forget the children. Kids would follow him around everywhere for the army chocolates from his suppers, and once they got it they would scurry away like sparrows. When he came back to Canada, he sent a box of children's shoes to an orphanage. He wanted to adopt a child from there, but his wife ultimately vetoed that idea. She said it would be hard on a child to grow up in a place where everyone was so different from them," Mr. Sweeney says.

"Maybe that's for the best given how Uncle Bob changed after he came back," Mrs. Sweeney adds gently.

"He was never the same after that. He couldn't adjust back to small-town life. When the Vietnam War broke out, he went to fight with the Americans," Mr. Sweeney says quietly, as if in thought.

Meredith crosses her eyes, points her index finger to her ear and draws circles in the air.

"Where does he live now?" I ask, wanting to change the topic.

"He's back in Saskatchewan, living among my Cossack relations," says Mr. Sweeney in a playful tone.

I am confused. "What's a Cossack?"

"That's what they called Ukrainians, which is my mother's side. Luckily, my father's from England, so he rescued her from her horrible last name, Kravchenko. I don't know if my wife would have married me if that meant she had to carry that last name," he says, looking at his wife.

"Well, if I'm going to be perfectly honest, I prefer the name I have now," Mrs. Sweeney says firmly.

"Grandpa had a problem with my mom marrying a Ukrainian," Meredith says to clarify.

"Yes, but we sorted that all out, didn't we? He forgave us once we had you," Mr. Sweeney says with a chuckle.

"Why would he have a problem?" I ask.

"There's a hierarchy here, even among white people. Ukrainians are at the bottom; the Brits are on top. Canada once considered Ukrainians enemy aliens during the first war. My grandfather had to register as an enemy and report to the police. He had it lucky though.

Some other Ukrainians went to prison camps where they were forced to build our highways and national parks, like Banff."

"Really?" I say, surprised. It never occurred to me that among the white townspeople, there's an order of superiority.

"Luckily, we had a British last name, even though my father left us when I was young. It was my mother's family who raised us. Bigots are the worst, aren't they, Anne?" he says, giving me a conspiratorial glance. "I understand what it's like being an outsider."

I nod, accepting this pretend camaraderie, but I'm too diffident to say it's different: Being a white outsider is better than looking like me, with my dark colours and alien eyes.

"Daddy, you're being *so* depressing," Meredith interrupts, annoyed.

Mrs. Sweeney takes an audible breath and exhales to express her annoyance, then raises her eyebrows. "Enough about these heavy subjects. Let's talk about sweeter things, like what we're having for dessert."

When my mother arrives to pick me up the next day, I hear our car rumbling down the driveway from Meredith's room. When the doorbell rings, I notice the faded colour of my mother's wool coat as she greets Mrs. Sweeney at the doorstep. I am silent on our ride home.

"Did you have fun?" she asks in Korean.

"Yeah."

"What did you do?"

"Stuff," I say. I roll down the window, letting in the winter air. Experiencing Meredith's world has shown me how much I lack, even though I know this comparison is unfair. To compare assumes an equality I don't—and will never—have. I am both angry with my mother and angry at myself for this anger.

When we return home, I go to my room, shut the door, and lie on my bed, reflecting on the weekend. Mrs. Sweeney frequently used the word *charming*, and I realize that this word embodies all that I envy about Meredith's family: They are a charming family in their charming house. Through Meredith, I experienced my first horse ride. I savour the memory of the cold, crunchy frost-covered snow, the sound of Mystique's hoofs, the white mist of her breath, her moist tongue licking the sugar cubes off my hand. I cannot imagine a world where the decision to live somewhere would be dictated by a daughter's love for horses. I remember the dinner afterwards, how Mr. Sweeney rose, went to the sink, put on an apron, and washed the dishes while Mrs. Sweeney sat, sipping on a glass of wine and smoking a cigarette. Instinctually, I rose and offered to help, but Mr. Sweeney refused and laughed at the horror I showed that he—a male—should wash the dishes, something I have never seen. I felt immense guilt watching him clean off my dish, and I could not enjoy the second portion of flan that Mrs. Sweeney offered. When he was done washing the dishes, I averted my eyes as he kissed his wife and his daughter and tried not to flinch as he placed his hands on both Crystal's and my shoulders to wish us a good night.

I wait until the store closes and my father is watching the nightly news.

"Dad, were you alive during the Korean War?" I ask.

My father continues watching the screen. "Why?"

"When I slept over Meredith's, her father mentioned that his uncle fought in the Korean War."

"I was boy when it happen. After war, Korea divide to North and South," my father says matter-of-factly without looking up from the television. A silence follows.

"Why didn't you tell us?"

"You and Charles have nice life here. Don't need to remember past bad things."

I wait for him to say more. I wait until the news goes into a series of commercials, but his eyes remain stubbornly fixed on the television. I quietly withdraw and go back to my room. I bitterly remember Mr. Sweeney joking with his daughter, and the many words they exchanged. For the first time in my life, I am dissatisfied with who my father is, or rather, who he is unable to be.

I am walking home from school when someone taps me on my shoulder: It's Euphemia. "Hey," she says excitedly, picking up her pace to walk alongside me.

"Hey," I say back. I scan behind her and am relieved there are no other classmates around, no one to report a Twin Dragons sighting. We are walking side by side.

"How are you liking this town?"

"I'm liking it," I say, grateful that I mean it. "Are we the only non-whites here?"

"There was a Japanese family that lived near town, but they left for Vancouver a few years ago."

"What were they doing here?"

"They moved here from Lethbridge. There was an internment camp there."

"What's that?"

"During World War Two, Canada was suspicious of the Japanese, so they rounded them up and put them in camps around BC and Alberta.

After the war, the Tanakas opened a ranch nearby, but the mother got cancer and they eventually moved."

I've never seen Japanese people, but my parents told me that Japan is the enemy of Korea. Once, in a rare moment of openness, my mother commented she would never buy a Japanese car, and when I asked her why, she told me it was because of what the Japanese did to her aunt. My mother's grandfather was a gambler, so her aunt took a factory job in Japan to help pay off their family debt. She was never seen again, and it was a great source of shame for the family. When I asked more about where she could have disappeared to, my mother steeled her countenance and merely said that I must never befriend a Japanese as they are not to be trusted, nor buy anything Japanese if I can help it.

"They should be wary of the Japs," I say.

Euphemia stops walking and stares at me, shocked. "How can you say that?"

"My great-aunt disappeared working for the Japanese, and my mom said it destroyed her family." I don't know what happened in detail, but my mother's indignation is rising in my voice.

"You can't hold an entire nation responsible for something that happened to your family two generations ago. If you want to think that way, then you should hate Canadians as much as you do the Japanese. If Canada participated in the Korean War, there's definitely Korean blood on their hands, maybe even against your relatives." Euphemia speaks with a certainty and confidence that is disconcerting.

"It's easy to be open-minded when it doesn't cost you anything," I say. If Japanese people kidnapped her relative, I wonder how high-minded she would be.

"Some of the Japanese are like us, born here, which makes us as Canadian as the Canadians."

"You know we'll never be as Canadian as the Canadians," I say, and we both nod.

We walk in silence to the sound of our boots crunching on the freshly fallen snow. Out of all the townspeople, Euphemia and I should be the ones looking out for one another. And yet she's basically accused me of being a racist. We pass a few long blocks without saying anything.

I swallow my annoyance and change the topic by asking, "Do you like it here?"

She's quiet, recovering from our heated exchange. "It's alright, although I'm applying to Essex Academy in Edmonton. It's the best high school in Alberta. I hope I get in. If I do, I'll live with my aunt. My cousin goes there, and he tells me that some of his classmates go on to universities out east, even to the States."

"Your parents told my parents about it. Now, they want Charles to go there."

"What about you? Are you interested in applying?"

I shake my head. Now that I have become friends with Meredith and Crystal, I don't want to leave. Besides, because I'm a daughter, it's not as important for me to succeed, as I won't have the responsibilities Charles has as the eldest son. I wonder if Euphemia, as an only child, understands this dynamic.

When we reach her restaurant, she turns to me and says, "I know you're friends with Meredith and Crystal, but you shouldn't let them boss you around. Those girls always seem to cycle through their third wheel. Tess wasn't the first friend they dropped."

"Thanks for the advice," I say, trying not to allow my sarcasm to show. I stop myself from saying more. If the girls heard what Euphemia said, Meredith would know how to put Euphemia in her place, and I could certainly christen her with a mean nickname. It would be easy since Wong rhymes with so many words. But I silently decide that I will not tell them what she's just said. Euphemia Ding Dong, although she seems nice enough, is already unpopular and I will spare her more ridicule.

TEN

2014

When I get back to my car, Charles is passed out in his seat, reeking of alcohol. I'm relieved that this is the only drama that's resulted from our return to Crow Plains, which hasn't been that bad considering it's Charles's first time back since he left as a teenager. I open the windows for the sickly sweet smell to escape and decide to take one more walk down Main Street before driving home.

I walk over to our old store. The wooden siding is freshly painted. Through the glass, two portly women chat at the cash register, and I decide against going inside. I don't know what I would say, nor do I want to make small talk. I walk to the back of the building to our former home, and a FOR RENT sign is posted on an outside window. I press my nose against the glass and find the space vacant and changed; faux grey wood panels have replaced the brown carpet, though the kitchen's honey oak cabinetry and white appliances remain.

I find the window to my old room, which is unrecognizable with its grey flooring and lavender walls. I try to remember my old room but can no longer picture it. A few days ago, while searching for some of my father's documents, I found a storage box of my old journals that

I wrote as a child. I flipped through one and stopped at a page that outlined my life's goals. I had drawn a neat line against a ruler and slotted my goals according to the decade of my life. According to my childhood myopia, by thirty, I should be married with a son named Bruce and a daughter named Courtney. I should be living in a BIG house—in my journals I always capitalized words that were important to me. I even drew a picture of this life: a Chagallian dreamland where stick people floated among flying teacups and layered cakes below a boxed house with a smiling face. I'm reminded that once my only aspiration was to get married and have kids and live in a big Victorian house in this town.

A photo dropped out of the pages. It was a magazine portrait of a lawyer that I ripped out and taped above my desk as motivation to study; at some point, my goal changed from wanting a family to becoming a successful lawyer. I wanted so badly to become her. Staring at this lawyer's photo became my way of praying for escape even though I didn't even know what a lawyer did. I studied the article's headline above her declaring: "Women Trailblazers: The New Vanguard." I reassessed her bulky blazer, the overly dyed blonde hair, the garish fuchsia blush, and realized she was trying too hard. Now, I'm the poster child for progress. When I first started at the firm, the HR department asked me to be part of a group photo for their recruiting material. I stood next to a black colleague and a Hispanic counterpart. We grinned widely in our neutral-coloured suits and flaunted our diverse skin tones even though the majority of the lawyers who make partner at our firm are white males.

Richard is proud of how progressive our firm is, though I have asked whether it bothers him. To him, affirmative action means more competition, but he is confident that he is among the best. Once, I asked if he thought I was hired, in part, because of my ethnicity, and rather than answering my question, he accused me of trying to start a fight.

I walk back to my car, where Charles is quietly snoring in the passenger seat. As I start the car, the phone rings. It's Richard. I turn off the ringer, but it's too late, Charles wakes. Instead of going back to sleep, he stares out the window at the passing stores. I also scan Main Street as I drive along it, thinking how ridiculous it was for me that this town—with its cheerful street banners and hanging baskets of flowers—was the source of my darkest anxiety.

"You okay being back?"

Charles watches the landscape passing before us. "Yeah. Mom always tells me to forget everything and forge ahead. The past is the past, right?"

I nod, pleased.

"What's going on between you and Richard?" Charles asks.

"Nothing, why?"

"His name popped up on your screen. Why didn't you pick up?"

"I don't feel like talking to him right now," I say coolly.

I'm still puzzling over why Richard would send me flowers the day before what he thought would be my departure. He usually sends flowers as a peace offering, so what is he trying to atone for? The possible reasons I imagine make me anxious. The entire time we have been dating, I have always wondered why Richard would want to date me, especially since I don't disclose very much of my personal history.

We drive in silence for a while before Charles speaks again. "Have you mentioned me to Richard?"

"Barely."

"Does he know about my past?"

"No. It's not something I like to broadcast to the world."

"What about your other friends, do they know about me?"

"Just that you exist. I don't really like elaborating on you."

"You're embarrassed about me, aren't you?"

"How would I describe you? You don't have a job. You're always studying for some certification, but you're not actually attending a school, so you're technically not a student. You need to get a job. Find a career," I say, foolishly hoping maybe Charles is receptive to my advice right now. Although my words come out harshly, I don't regret them. This visit has confirmed what I've suspected all along: that my mother coddles him and stunts his ability to grow. I sense this was probably a great source of tension in my parents' marriage when my father was alive.

"You sound just like dad," he murmurs.

"Dad did a lot of things wrong, but one thing he did right was speak honestly, and you need people in your life to do that," I say resentfully—now that my father is gone, I'm the only person left who can talk candidly about his life.

"Seriously? You're the one applauding yourself for being the honest one?" Charles hisses.

"Are you accusing me of lying?"

"Yes."

"I hardly talk to you, Charles. When would I have that opportunity?"

"Not lying to me, but to yourself."

"What are you talking about?"

"I keep remembering that night and wondering where the knife came from."

I grip the steering wheel, trying to quell the feeling of vertigo, a drop inside of me, as if I am falling into an endless void. When

Charles asked me about Yura's knife the other day, though I blanked out, the question made me panic enough to reach for my anti-anxiety pills. I wished I had them with me now. "Why are you bringing this up?"

"I've just been reevaluating my life lately, trying to figure out where it all went wrong. Once that knife entered the scene, it changed everything."

"That was over two decades ago."

"Fine, but what do you remember about that night?"

"Nothing, I have no memory of it," I say and it's true. Charles's glare drills into me, but I refuse to look at him. I am annoyed that I still have two hours left in this car with him. I am desperate to change the topic. "Even though you think I have it all together in New York, I don't, okay?"

"What do you mean?"

"I'm not on partner track. Richard is, but I'm not. That means I need to find another place to work because I'll never get promoted. But the thought of interviewing at other firms in New York is depressing. I've considered moving, possibly back here. It would be less stressful, and I know Mom will need me more now that Dad's gone."

"What about Richard?"

"He would have to decide if he would follow me."

"That's a huge ask, for him to leave his career and move here." There's a pause as Charles thinks about what I've said. "But even though you're unhappy with your job, at least you get to live in New York."

I say nothing back. I've never invited him to visit me in New York because we both know he would be denied entry for his criminal record. Charles leans into the stereo and turns up the volume as the car speeds down the highway into a canopy of dark grey clouds.

1992

I'm now a regular visitor at Meredith's house. Every weekend, I'm invited to either visit or sleep over. Crystal comes on alternating weekends because she also has to visit her father and stepmother in Fort Athabasca. I bring discarded *Teen*, *Bop*, and *YM* magazines without their covers. We lie on her carpet or bed and follow their beauty advice. We apply cucumber slices on our faces to calm our skin. We grind oatmeal in Mrs. Sweeney's blender and make an exfoliating paste. We paint our fingernails to match our toenails. Sometimes, Meredith's mother drives us to Fort Athabasca Mall, and I spend all my savings at The Body Shop. Afterwards, we try on the confectionary gels and lotions in her bathroom. I've eaten caramel balls and Rice Krispies squares. My adolescence is unfolding just like how I see it in the magazines. Meredith gives me a photograph of the three of us in our pyjamas, our heads peeping out from beneath the blankets, our grins huge. I proudly place this photo inside my photo frame, over a stiff family portrait taken at Sears when we lived in Edmonton.

I'm fascinated with the Sweeneys' house, where I consider myself an observer more than a participant. At dinner, Mrs. Sweeney serves food that I know only in its raw or packaged form. I'm surprised at how delicious carrots or zucchini taste inside a cake, or as julienne confetti inside a jelly mould. But I also make my quiet judgments as I watch from a distance. Mrs. Sweeney has a pleasant demeanour, smooth skin, delicate fingers because she has a life freed from the worries of money. When we speak, I catch her casual, disparaging remarks about the townspeople she finds dull, who lack any understanding of culture. She divides her adjectives into "charming," which is the desired state, and "ill-mannered," which is the worst sin one can commit, and I try hard to understand what comprises the latter so as not to do it. During my first few visits, she seemed a little irritated at having me at the dinner table, but I have since learned to chew with my mouth closed, use the respective serving spoon for each entrée, and say thank you when someone passes me a glass bowl filled with salad. Once I had a vision of my own father seated at this table—dipping his bread stick into the olive oil and balsamic vinegar mixture twice, slurping his soup, burping freely at the table—and I had to stifle a laugh. Being here feels subversive or disloyal; I can't quite tell which.

At dinner, when she complains about how boring their life is in this town, I nod, stay silent, but do not allow myself to see her as someone whose struggles are of worth. When before, her crisp outfits and perfectly made-up face impressed me, now I realize this upkeep is her way of killing time, which is too plentiful. In contrast, my own mother rushes to the store as soon as she wakes, and her only moment of vanity is at night, when she slathers Nivea cream onto her face while watching the evening news. Mrs. Sweeney is too engrossed in her own dissatisfaction to pick up on my disdain of her, and I'm too fascinated with their household to deny myself their company.

My disapproval of Mrs. Sweeney is offset by my admiration of Mr. Sweeney. Sometimes, when Mrs. Sweeney is tired, he drives us into town, where we eat inside the vinyl booths of the pizza parlour. There, I've tried things I've only seen in comic books: milkshakes, banana splits, pie à la mode with a maraschino cherry on top. Mr. Sweeney talks about his own childhood, and his Baba and Dido—the farmer and his wife from Saskatchewan—become familiar to me like beloved characters in a novel. When I think of grandparents, I envision Dido Kravchenko, who shot cougars to protect his livestock, and

Baba Kravchenko, who made cougar pies afterwards. Mr. Sweeney is surprised that I remember every detail of these stories. When I watch the televised movie of *Anne of Green Gables*, Baba and Dido Kravchenko take on the physicality of Matthew and Marilla.

I lack any knowledge of my own grandparents. Aside from my maternal grandmother, they have all died, and my parents refuse to explain how. As for uncles and aunts, I have two aunts: my father's younger sister and my mother's older sister; I have spoken only briefly with either of them over the phone in my broken Korean.

Tucked inside my mother's dresser is a plastic bag containing a few black-and-white photographs of what is presumably family. I sneak into their bedroom while my parents are busy at the store and take out the bag: There are pictures of Korean adults and children crowded together glaring at the sun. These photos are taken from a distance and there is no detail, so everyone looks the same. I scan the round, unsmiling faces and can barely identify my own father or mother. I wonder if some of the children crowding the photos are my parents' siblings—but the rule is not to ask. The one time I do ask, my father grimaces and says, "You don't need to know. Focus on school," and my mother shakes her head and says, "Enjoy your life. Korea, nothing but sorrow." So, there's an unspoken understanding that I may have dead aunts and uncles.

When we learn about Remembrance Day, Mrs. Reeves asks if anyone has stories of war in our families. Meredith has a grandfather who fought during World War II. He received a medal for his valour, saving a comrade in Normandy. Other classmates tell similar stories. A few have even brought photos of these heroic relatives dressed in uniform.

"Is there anyone else with relatives who participated in a war?" Mrs. Reeves asks, and a long silence descends. Finally, she addresses me. "Anne, what about you?"

"No," I say and her face falls in disappointment. I'm not sure how else to answer. Last night, I asked my parents what they remembered from the Korean War. My mother said she was very young and only remembers the hunger. My father also remembers the constant hunger. There was no heroism, just fear. The heroism, according to my father, belonged to the Americans, who walked along the dirt road, handing out military chocolates to my father and his neighbourhood friends. He tells this story about the candy with a deep reverence. I imagine Mr. Sweeney's uncle giving chocolates to my father. "Without America, Kim Il-sung rules all of Korea, and we probably there, not here."

I want to tell Mrs. Reeves that I feel more of an affinity with the white soldiers, not the Korean civilians who, from the several photos I see in the books from the library, are huddled together in collective misery. I want to boast that last Remembrance Day, when we gathered in the auditorium for our two minutes of silence, I cried thinking about the soldiers who died in Flanders Fields. The Korean War stirs nothing in me.

I try to learn more about my mother's family by eavesdropping when Mrs. Song visits. I hear my mother's low voice as she speaks in Korean. "When the Japanese lost, my aunt was in China. I learned later they killed everyone at those stations, but she survived and managed to return home. But my grandfather refused to let her in, and she disappeared. My grandfather began drinking heavily afterwards and never recovered. My mother would oftentimes walk to Itaewon to see if her sister was alive, but she never saw her again." My mother looks up and sees me crouching in the hallway. She frowns, displeased, and stops talking.

Mrs. Song calls me over in a bright voice and hands me a plate of peeled orange slices. The women don't dare speak again until they hear my bedroom door close, and though I press my ears against the gap between the door and the floor, I can't make out more of this tragedy. I wait a little longer, and when I open the door slightly, I hear the women whispering in Korean again.

"We never knew about this growing up. Such a tragedy," says Mrs. Song.

"The greatest sorrow in my grandfather's life was what happened to my aunt. She was beautiful, and my sister was said to have resembled her. He never forgave himself for not making enough money so that she sought after that job. He drank himself to death. My grandmother passed shortly afterwards, from the heartbreak, leaving my mother to raise her siblings." My mother instinctively turns around and sees me crouched in the hallway. Her face flashes with annoyance. For the rest of the evening, there is an iciness in her voice as she only talks about business, complaining about her wholesaler and difficult customers.

Later that night, I try to make sense of this story, but I can't. Why would they kill everyone at her work station? Why wasn't she allowed to return home? I go to the library and look through the few books about the Korean War, but the texts, which celebrate the American and Canadian armies, ring hollow. There is something about this story that I know is part of the dark sorrow in my mother's family that I cannot access.

I study the photo frame atop our television: My maternal grandmother wears a lavender hanbok with embroidered flowers. Her greying hair is tied into a tight bun, and she refuses to smile. Next to her is her daughter, my Aunt Jung-ja, who is beautiful but sad—jet-black hair against her pale skin, eyelids powdered with shimmering mauve, and lips frosted with a dark pink. She's wearing a cream silk blouse which elegantly ties at the neck. Her eyes are large but void of any emotion.

Although I've spoken to both of them several times over the phone, somehow their voices—soft, cheerful, warm—do not match the seriousness of these portraits.

Through another visit from Mrs. Song, I piece together that my Aunt Jung-ja was in love with a man who belonged to a wealthy family, and though he loved her, he could not marry her. His mother hired an investigator to uncover that in addition to my aunt's family being poor, her father was riddled in so much debt that he passed away—blemishes that a wealthy family would never tolerate. Instead, the man gave my aunt an apartment, bought her diamond earrings and dresses made in America. When she became pregnant, the man—heeding the advice of his mother—cut off all communication with her. Shortly thereafter, he married another woman from a similar social standing. My aunt lost their baby very late in the pregnancy, which resulted in lifelong health issues. Since then, she's had a string of failed relationships, and because of her age, is no longer considered eligible for marriage. She now works at a restaurant for a man who, my mother phrases delicately, won't leave her alone, and it is hard on her body and the pay barely covers their living expenses.

Her father's death, her sister's miseries, her family's financial stress, these must be the reasons for the perpetual sorrow that my mother carries, making it so that she refuses to be happy. Once, it's a glorious spring day: A burst of rain brings forth a rainbow with colours so intense, they look opaque. I stare, dazzled by the intensity and beauty of the display and excitedly point it out to my mother, but after a quick glance out the window, she returns despondently to her boxes to unload groceries. I don't sense this cloak of sadness at the Sweeneys. These tragic women from my mother's family, one disgraced and banished, another impregnated and scorned, are not my inheritance. Their stories may belong to my parents' lives, but not mine. I have no connection to this past. I am a clean slate. My friends, not my parents or ancestors, will guide me in the new world.

I am struggling in class. I'm distracted by the constant note passing with Meredith and Crystal where we discuss the daily drama of our classroom: who is flirting with whom, who is slighting the other, their observations on the nuanced communications between friends and enemies. I ignore Mrs. Reeves. It's only when I come home that I peruse the textbooks and try to understand the class lessons. Even though Charles is always spending time at Clint's playing video games, memorizing and processing facts come easily to him. Though his exercise books remain blank and his pencils unsharpened, Charles leaves his flawless quizzes and exams with the coveted A+ on the kitchen table for my parents to see. I also need to present these offerings.

In order to get an A, at home, I memorize flashcards and do additional math exercises. I go to the drugstore and buy index cards and a pack of highlighters. The next time we visit Fort Athabasca Mall, I buy the only supplemental math exercise book at the bookstore and order a few more, which will arrive in six weeks' time. I make a schedule that accounts for every hour in the evenings and weekends when I'm not with Meredith, rotating subject matter, giving myself five-minute breaks. I need to maintain my friendship with Meredith and Crystal but also fulfill my duty as a daughter.

One day in class, Meredith spots my timetable and pulls it out of my backpack.

"What's this?" she asks as she silently reads my schedule. Then she opens my backpack and pulls out my supplemental math exercise book. "*Math Fun*? *A Guide to Unlocking Geometry*?" She digs further and finds my flash cards of vocabulary words. "How ironic that you don't know what *charlatan* means," she says with a smirk. She calls Crystal over and shows her the contents of my bag. Crystal snickers. My cheeks flush with humiliation.

"Listen, Anne, you're either smart or you're not. You can't make yourself into someone you're not. For instance, take Tess. We all know she's not pretty. But she tried very hard to be pretty. She would wear makeup, but she looked like . . . a clown. A sad, eager clown." Meredith looks at me knowingly. "You need to chill. All this hard work is, how should I put this . . ." she says. She pauses dramatically as her eyes wander to find the right word: "Uncool."

I say nothing as this admonishment burns inside of me.

"You need to chill," Crystal repeats.

"I can chill," I say, but I come off as defensive.

"Then prove it," Meredith says.

"How?"

"Fail with me."

"What do you mean?"

"Fail the next math quiz with me. I dare you."

"Sure," I say, though my heart immediately sinks. I have to accept her dare, or else face her judgment and endless taunts. My mind does a quick calculation: A math quiz is weighted less than an exam. I can afford to fail this one time to appease Meredith. I just can't make any more mistakes for the rest of the term if my goal is to get an A average for my report card.

On the morning of the test, I feel immense guilt as Mrs. Reeves hands me the quiz. Meredith turns around and gives me a thumbs-up and an exaggerated wink. A few days later, when Mrs. Reeves returns our quizzes, her eyes avoid mine as she hands me my quiz marked with red ink. At lunch, Meredith gives me a high five and is pleased that she's scored higher than me but still fails nonetheless. She is extra chatty. I say little as resentment blooms inside of me, towards my best friend.

Now, our conversations revolve around who scored the lowest grade. Meredith makes me show the papers I get from Mrs. Reeves to confirm that I'm slacking. For the next few weeks, I smother my ambition. I get an essay back marked with a C. I try not to care. Rather than taking notes in class, I begin doodling, which brings me comfort—when I draw, a calm descends, and I enter into a trancelike state. Both Meredith and Crystal inspect my notebook to make sure I'm not being a "keener" and are pleased when they see my doodles, proof that I have not been paying attention. When I tell Meredith and Crystal that I got a C, it ends up becoming a brag because they've gotten C minuses.

I imagine what it would be like if, instead of trying so hard, I just chilled. School isn't the only thing in life. Last year only a handful of the high school graduates from town went on to a college or university. The majority of people never get past a high school diploma, so why should I? I imagine a life freed from the anxiety and fear that pushes me to study. I would spend more time with Meredith and Crystal. My money would be spent on nail polish and spiral perms rather than on supplementary math exercise books. I would work alongside my parents and eventually take over their store—that thought comforts me, as I don't know what they would do without me to translate and help with all the paperwork. But Meredith's cruelty confuses me. Is her meanness temporary, or is it a fury that will always keep me in check, to ensure that I'm not better than her in any way? I don't believe I am and have never inferred that I am.

These days, during lunchtime, we sit against our lockers and discuss the future where we all plan to live next door to one another. We discuss our future children's names. Both Meredith and Crystal want to name their sons Corey, and after some negotiation, it's decided that Meredith will name her son Corey, and Crystal will name her son Kory. We will time our pregnancies together so that our future children will become best friends, possibly future spouses. We will take turns hosting our families for dinner. Thinking about this future makes me deeply unhappy, though I'm too scared at this point to articulate it to them, or to myself. I feign excitement as Meredith and Crystal plan our future.

"Guess what? My cousin told me that Chad asked about you," Crystal says.

Meredith lets out a hoot. He's two grades ahead of us. I've seen him in the hallways, though we've never spoken. I'm surprised he's expressed interest.

"Chad's not bad-looking. Plus, he drives a car," Crystal says.

"I've never spoken to him. Wasn't his last girlfriend from Vernet? That bothers me," I say, and I immediately regret saying this aloud.

"That's very racist of you to say," Meredith says, knitting her eyebrows together. "Why are you offended that his last girlfriend was Indian?"

"I'm not saying I'm better than her. I'm saying that Chad seems to go after girls that aren't white and that bothers me," I say.

"You're being nitpicky. He's cute in a rugged sort of way. Plus, he's tall, and you know what they say about tall guys," Crystal says, raising her voice teasingly to imply something secret and grown-up.

“What?” I ask.

“Tall guys have big feet. And big feet mean big shoes,” Crystal says, slyly glancing at Meredith, who giggles. I don’t understand what she’s implying about the big shoes, but I know it has something to do with sexuality; whereas theirs seem to be blossoming, I’m lagging behind, but I don’t care. With all my responsibilities and pressures to excel, I don’t want another thing to have to worry about and have to succeed in.

“He’s not much for conversation,” I say.

“So he’s not a talker, he’s a guy,” Meredith says, her eyes narrowing as she stares at me.

“He’s seems a little . . . thick,” I say.

“You think you’re too good for him, don’t you?” Meredith says abruptly.

“No, it’s not that. I just don’t think we have anything in common. I mean we’ve never spoken to each other,” I say gingerly.

“You don’t have a boyfriend to talk with. That’s what your friends are for,” Crystal says. “You have a boyfriend to feel like a woman. Don’t you want to feel like one?”

They start giggling. Suddenly, Trevor appears in the hallway with his friend Brent. The girls quiet down and stare at the floor demurely while they walk past us. When they turn the corner, Meredith and Crystal burst into nervous giggles.

“Trevor was checking you out,” Crystal tells Meredith, who beams.

“I can’t wait until we all grow up,” Meredith says dreamily.

It will all work out for Meredith. I have confidence in her confidence: of riding horses, of finding her soul mate, of devising a life freed from struggle. More than her nice clothes and house, I envy most her insouciance: of not taking life so seriously, not being crushed by one bad test mark. I want this chill, but I can’t: I’ve got an engine that refuses to relent or be restrained. At night, I often wake in a panic, feeling trapped. But maybe I can pull the brakes on my ambition and be content with the friends I have, this life I lead.

My parents announce that for Christmas break, we will go skiing at Banff for two days: Christmas and Boxing Day. It's a six-hour drive to get there, and it will be our first time closing the store. I'm elated. I have never wanted to go skiing, but I know this experience is part of a Canadian childhood. I boast to Meredith and Crystal and all my classmates that I'm going to ski at Banff during the Christmas holidays. The weeks leading up to our vacation, my parents take pleasure in chit-chatting: proudly telling our customers about this ski trip, listening attentively to the customers' tips on what to do après-ski, which restaurants to visit on Banff Avenue, how to get to the hot springs.

"Melly Klis-mas!"

"Merry Christmas!"

"What you doing for Klis-mas?"

"Oh, just visiting family in Fort Athabasca. How about you, any plans?"

"We go to Banff and do the ski."

"Good for you. How long are you there for?"

"Two days."

"Only two days? That's a lot of driving. You should stay longer."

"We close Klis-mas and Boxing Day. Two day enough."

"Well, you have a good trip. You deserve a break. You're hardworking people."

"Thank you, Melly Klis-mas."

"You too. Merry Christmas."

The night before we leave, I help my mother make *kimbap*. Though I no longer eat kimchi, I will eat more neutral, less-garlicy flavoured Korean foods like kimbap. Our kitchen fills with the comforting smell of fried hot dogs, eggs, and sesame oil. We make enough rolls to eat for dinner while driving, and then for lunch the following day at the ski slopes. I imagine our family eating our strange, home-brought food in a chalet while everyone else will be buying their lunches at the cafeteria, and I brace myself to be embarrassed. On Christmas Eve, after the predinner rush, we close early and pile into the car in high spirits. My father opens a Neil Diamond Christmas cassette that we sell at our store, and we listen to it as we drive in the dark, eating our kimbap.

The next morning, groggy from our midnight check-in at the motel, my father wakes us early. When we arrive at the ski resort, the parking lot is full, and we are directed to the overflow parking. By the time we reach the base, there are long lines for tickets and rentals. When we're finally fitted into our rental boots, skis, and poles, we go up the gondola, and I see the pointy tops of fir trees, an aerial view of the skiers, the surrounding mountains. I breathe in the crisp air. We ski on the beginner slope, and though I'm cold, and I frequently fall, I know this is what Canadians do for winter break, so I'm grateful rather than miserable to be here. By lunch, I'm too hungry to be self-conscious about eating kimbap while the surrounding families eat pizza and french fries on their plastic trays. I don't care anymore. It is liberating to live without the demands of the store or school.

After two days of this altered reality, we start our journey back home. When we drive through Calgary, we see a Dairy Queen, and my father slows down and signals to turn into the drive-thru. He asks us, "You want a Friday, a Saturday, or a sundae?" It's the first time we have ever heard him tell a joke—and English at that. Charles and I stare at one another, astonished. We break into laughter as my father proudly joins in.

After getting our ice creams, we stop at a traffic light, and a blonde girl in the next car curiously observes us: two Chinese kids giggling, licking our sundaes in the back seat, the father at the steering wheel, the mother beside him, everyone in full smiles. For the first time, I have a rising hope that we can finally be that happy, Canadian family.

We return home after midnight. The car abruptly stops, and a bitter cold rushes in as my father flings open his door. The headlights shine onto the broken glass in front of our store.

Chief Jim from Vernet was the person who reported it. On Christmas, he drove into town with his family to eat at Mr. Wong's restaurant, and upon passing our store and seeing the smashed door, he called the RCMP. Afterwards, he went over to Mr. Wong's restaurant—the only business that was open—and both men boarded up the front door with a wooden plank.

Stanley's brother, Darryl, is our town's RCMP officer. He estimates that the robbery took place on the night between Christmas Eve and Christmas Day. The robbers broke the glass door, opened the lock from inside, and pillaged the liquor store, leaving the shelves bare. They also ransacked all the cigarettes and even stocked up on chips and candy bars.

My father shrugs when Darryl asks him if he has any suspects. "Can be anyone in town," my father mumbles.

"Well, at least someone got a big holiday party," Darryl says with a chuckle.

My father joins in with a laugh and then offers him a can of soda and chips, which Darryl accepts as he scribbles onto his notepad and says he will file a report and follow up.

Later, Mr. Wong comes over with a bag of food: rice, sautéed vegetables, and a fish that is not on their menu. The fish is delicious: steamed and smothered in a delicate scallion sauce. I recall Meredith and Crystal teasing Euphemia for eating weird food, and yet this fish is more delicious than anything I've ever eaten at the Sweeneys' house.

After talking with Darryl and Mr. Wong, my parents discuss the mistake that led to the robbery: It wasn't the desire to go on a trip rather than the disclosing of it. They made the mistake of believing in an equality with the townspeople, when really, they should have kept quiet. The invisible robber takes on the form of all our customers and so, the conclusion is that no one should be trusted. "Say nothing about family to anyone," my parents warn us. These words enter in, twisting me. What if my bragging was the reason we got robbed?

My parents sweep the glass shards, reorder and restock the alcohol and cigarettes. A few days later, a new glass door is installed so that all traces of the robbery have disappeared. The only thing left is to fill out the insurance claim paperwork, which I do. When I speak with the adjustor over the phone, she laughs and asks, "Sweetie, how *old* are you?" Charles, meanwhile, rages.

The robbery consumes Charles. The idea that some person or people smashed our glass door, then filled their car with our liquor and cigarettes, preoccupies him to the point of obsession. He meticulously searches for clues, and a few days later he shouts that he's found something. As our family gathers around him, he announces that the thief—alongside the booze and cigarettes—has also stolen a box of sour soothers.

"Stanley doesn't sell this candy. I called Clint and he went in and checked. No one in town carries these aside from us, so whoever the thief is will have a hell of a lot of sour soothers to suck on." Charles pauses, waiting for us to appreciate this revelation.

"Forget about it," my father says, his voice tired.

"We probably know this person. I bet he comes in here and looks us right in the eyes."

"Even if we think we know, no evidence," my father says.

"Doesn't this bother you? And why were you so nice to Stanley's brother, Darryl? Especially since we all know his nephew probably did it!" Charles asks, incredulous.

"If I don't be nice, he not gonna help us."

"He's not going to help whatever we do. He doesn't care. He hasn't followed up and he won't. He knows it's Jeff or one of his friends who did it."

"That's enough," my father says, his voice curling at the edges with anger.

"Charles, no more talking," my mother says as she glances at my father's hardening face.

"You think Darryl would turn in his own nephew to help the chinks? Who's going to bring justice? If we let this go, we're telling the town that we're stupid chinks and our doors are open for anyone to rob us," Charles says bitterly.

"Shut up," my father says curtly.

"Charles, you go to your room and study," my mother says nervously.

One day, Charles comes running home, opens my door, and announces that he finally has the proof he needs to accuse the arcade boys. He went to the video store to return a movie, and saw them all sharing a package of sour soothers. He was going to attack them right then and there but decided to wait until he figured out a stealthier way for vengeance.

"They're sour soothers. They could have bought them in Fort Athabasca," I say.

"I stared at them, but they avoided looking at me. I saw the guilt."

"Maybe they just didn't notice you. Why can't you just let it go?"

"What I hate the most about this whole thing is how Dad acts so tough in front of us, but in front of white people, he's so passive and accommodating. Makes me sick."

The next morning, Charles is gone when I wake up to get ready for school. As I walk down Main Street, I notice the RCMP car in front of Stanley's Grocery. Stanley stands next to his uniformed brother, Darryl, and from afar they look almost identical: tall, portly, with pale, thinning hair. They are engrossed, looking at Stanley's glass window: There's a hole at the centre surrounded by a web of cracked lines.

"Ever since those people opened that liquor store, things have gone downhill. Lots of bad activity going on. Those people don't care what happens to our community. That's a line I never crossed. Selling alcohol could make me a lot more money, but I care about the people in this town," Stanley says as he shakes his head. I quietly pass behind them, unnoticed.

Later, that afternoon, when I arrive home from school, I go into Charles's room, where he's in bed.

"I know what you did," I say.

"What are you talking about?"

"You threw that rock at Stanley's window."

"It could have been anyone, just like it could have been anyone who robbed us," he says and rolls over so his back faces me.

Meanwhile, I continue to fail or barely pass. I stack my failing tests, quizzes, and essays and hide them underneath my bed—for some reason, I'm unable to throw them away. Seeing these low marks fill me with guilt and dread, and it has come at a great cost.

One day, during recess, Trevor and his friends approach the girls in our class and declare that at lunch they will rank the girls from prettiest to ugliest. All morning there is a palpable energy among the girls in anticipation. Before the lunch bell rings, several girls take out their pocket mirrors, comb their hair, adjust the bra bands underneath their clothes, put on lip gloss. I go to the bathroom and pat water on my hair to make it sleek, then pinch my cheeks and lips for colour. When we are finally released outside, the girls stand next to the exterior wall, and Trevor and his friends come over. After some deliberation, Trevor walks up to us and casually points to Meredith, declaring her the prettiest, and then, with one hand mimicking a gun, continues selecting the girls as they form a line against the wall, showing their rank. Crystal is the second prettiest.

Everyone watches Trevor's index finger as he, after huddling with the boys between each selection, organizes us according to our beauty. My heart sinks when I'm the only one left standing. Trevor looks at me and nods his head. All eyes watch me as I slog to the end of the line. I burn with shame. I can't control the tears that well up, then run down my cheeks. Suddenly, Brent, one of Trevor's friends, walks up to me and kisses me on the cheek. This sets off a roar among the boys. I look into his blue eyes, their clarity piercing me with shock but also a confused hope. Brent wipes his mouth, then slaps Trevor on the arm and says, "Alien germs, no return!" The kids laugh, and out of the corner of my eye, I see Meredith's and Crystal's amused expressions.

I return home that day defeated. I sit at my desk, holding a mirror, looking at myself in despair. It's then that my mother opens the door, walks to my desk, and plops down a science test with a scrawled C. I've been careless and left it on the kitchen table.

"What happen?" my mother asks. Her face is grim.

I've imagined this encounter and already have my speech prepared: It starts with how a C is a perfectly acceptable grade to have, nothing to be ashamed of. In fact, both Meredith's and Crystal's parents would be proud if their daughters received this mark. Not everyone should pursue academics. Perhaps I could work at the store after I graduate high school. I'm about to start my speech when I look into my mother's eyes—tired, worn, delicate, as if they will break at any moment—and her disappointment unnerves me, exposes my actions as selfish so that I furiously beat back my desires, and I'm left with nothing to say.

I sit, staring at her for a few minutes, until tears begin to form. "I'm sorry. I won't ever do this again," I say meekly.

"I know you will get A on next one," my mother says confidently as I vigorously nod.

She sits down on my bed. "Every morning, we open the store to town that don't want us. We work like ox even though Father graduate from best university in Korea. Why? For you and Charles."

Then she rises and leaves the room, closing the door. I feel it again: my drive. I can't fail. I don't have that luxury, unlike Meredith and Crystal, who have the privilege to allow their victories and defeats to be theirs alone, contained, and not tied to their parents' psyche. I violently slap each cheek, scold myself with the word *selfish* over and over again, until I feel the release of hot tears, and I free myself from my friends who weren't there for me when I needed them.

I pick up a magazine on my desk that I took from the store. The cover has a group of smiling women, all wearing power suits. The headline reads "Women Trailblazers." Though all these women are white, they have plain faces and are not fashion models. Some are full-figured, others too angular, but they command respect. The main article profiles a CEO, a marketing executive, and a lawyer, all of whom are changing the landscape of their respective industry. I'm drawn to the profile of the lawyer, who, like me, comes from a small town in Alberta. Growing up, she had great ambitions and spent all her time studying. She eventually got accepted into Essex Academy, then went to Yale, and now she is a lawyer practising in New York. I study her lacquered nails, frosted hair, and steely composure. Even though she is not conventionally beautiful, she exudes power, demands respect. This lawyer would never sabotage herself and be at the mercy of friends who didn't care about her. She would know better than to disclose any personal information that might be used against her or her family. She wouldn't care what the boys thought about her appearance. She is the opposite of naïve and I want to be her. I tear out her portrait and tape her picture on my wall, above my desk. It's then that I decide that if I can't be beautiful, then I will be smart.

ELEVEN

2014

When we return to my mother's house from Crow Plains, she is sleeping on the sofa. I quietly take off my shoes and walk across the living room. Charles doesn't take off his sneakers and walks on my mother's carpet to his bedroom. He slams the door shut, which wakes my mother. She rises, startled, then relaxes when she sees me.

"When you get back?" she asks.

"Just now. Sorry to worry you. My cell phone ran out of battery, so I couldn't call."

From behind Charles's bedroom door, I hear the muffled sounds of beeps and fans whirring, indicating that his computer has been turned on. When I enter the kitchen, I observe the kitchen table, which is set with three place settings, accompanying water glasses, and in the centre, small dishes of marinated vegetables underneath plastic wrap.

"We already ate," I say. "It rained hard on our way back from Crow Plains, so we pulled over and ate some fast food."

My mother follows me into the kitchen. "Eat more. You losing so much weight. You too skinny."

She goes to the stove and turns off the warming pot of soup. There are a few envelopes addressed to me on the kitchen table. I'm annoyed when I notice that all the sides are slit open, even though they are all promotional letters from the bank.

"How was visit?"

"Good. I don't know if you remember my old teacher, Mrs. Reeves, but I visited her at the seniors' centre."

"She remember you?"

"No, she didn't recognize me. She has Alzheimer's."

"Why you visit her?"

I take a few moments to reflect on my answer. "To thank her."

"For what?"

"She saw a version of myself that I wished I honoured."

"What you mean?"

"She was the only one who saw my artistic potential."

"I remember you good at the drawing. You get that from me."

"I realize I was happiest whenever I was drawing or painting. I stopped doing all that after we moved to Edmonton, but I wished I pursued it more," I say. It's an admission I have never said aloud.

"You can still do it for hobby."

"I can't draw anymore," I say, trying to curb the anger rising within me.

"You keep trying," my mother says in a voice that lacks encouragement. She ladles soup and sets it beside me. She hands me a bowl with a perfectly convex heap of rice. She takes off the plastic wrap covering small dishes of marinated vegetables. We sit in silence as I sample the banchan.

"Why didn't you or Dad ever tell me about Maknae?"

After a long pause, my mother speaks. "After we immigrate, we have new life here. Why burden you and Charles with our suffering?

Why remember the pain? But now I wonder if this was the right way. Maybe we should tell you more. But we want you to be free from past."

We were never free, I want to say. "I know nothing about our family's past. These stories were mine to inherit, and I feel bereft." My mother looks puzzled because I know she doesn't know what bereft means, but I don't have the energy to simplify my language for her.

"Father never talk about Maknae. Only when North Korea is on TV or in newspaper, then he go searching for Maknae's face. Father worry because North Korea don't like people who have relatives in South Korea. They spy on them and sometime send to concentration camp. But your father say Maknae is smart and can play the game. He say if anybody can survive North Korea, it's Maknae."

My mother sighs and stares at her folded hands on the table. "When South and North government reunite families, Gomo try to find Maknae, but she find nothing. Father has hard time not knowing if Maknae dead or alive. I think sorrow kill him in the end."

"You needed to tell me about the past. I'm in my thirties. I can't believe I'm finding out now that I'm also from North Korea."

"North Korea, South Korea, same, you Korean. America and Russia, they make the two country. If Korea unite, it could be so powerful, could be like Japan," she says wistfully. Then, after she looks at me, her face softens. "Maybe we make mistake. Maybe we should tell you more."

"I need to hear these stories. I want to know about what happened to our family in Korea so I can figure out how I got here. Right now, there's just a blank when I think about my past, my heritage," I say. Her mouth tightens, and her eyebrows knot, but I keep talking. "When you're ready, I was thinking of videotaping you telling these stories."

She laughs. "For what?"

"To preserve the past. I was even thinking of making it into a short documentary that I could upload on YouTube."

"Who care?"

"I care. I think other people would want to hear these stories too."

Her eyes twinkle with amusement. "No one caring about North Korea. Anyone who caring is dead or dying. We are last generation with connection there. Even if North Korea wanna unite, South Korea don't want it because it will hurt economy. If *you* wanna know family story, maybe I tell. But don't waste time on a bee-dee-oh clip. No one care." After a long pause, she asks again, "How was visit?"

I stare at my mother intently before answering her. "I'm going to take that as a yes. When you're ready, I want you to tell me the stories from the past. As for Crow Plains, it's flooded with oil money. They're building new houses and renovating the rec centre. Our store is now a hair and tanning salon." My mother guffaws, as if I am telling her a joke. After a moment, I add, "We're waiting for the appraiser's estimate, but the Realtor said prices are hitting record highs."

"So your father smart to keep it," she says, nodding. She leans forward and whispers, "Once you sell, give your money to Charles. You don't need it."

"Mom, it's my inheritance too," I say, wincing as if struck.

"Don't think this is something feminist you need to prove. His government money gonna end soon and he gonna struggle. Anything you give will help him back to his foot. I always so proud of our Anne. Can you do this small sacrifice for your brother?" my mother asks in a voice that gets higher pitched.

"No," I say firmly.

"Money will help Charles get new start."

"His days of starting over are long gone. And how do you know he wouldn't spend this money on alcohol or maybe find another new habit that will give him more problems later on?" I say as my mother's face hardens.

"You so mean sometime. Think about your brother, so helpless."

"Does it occur to you that giving him money and rescuing him may be the reason why he's so helpless? He's a grown man, yet you have his dinner laid out, his laundry folded, his bathroom cleaned. How is he ever going to learn to be an adult?"

"Why you fighting for something that mean so little to you? No contest. Anne is winner. Charles is loser."

"Alberta is flush with money. It's on boom mode, and yet Charles somehow manages to be a bust. I read an article that high school grads in this province expect to make $100K right after they graduate. Everyone is drunk on oil, so it really takes some talent to be financially struggling in an economy like this."

"You always so competitive. You won, but somewhere you forgot your heart," she says, and for added dramatics, she pounds the left side of her chest with her fist.

I don't have the will to convince my mother to believe otherwise. I am exhausted as I blink back the tears wanting to form. "Mom, you can't have a daughter that has it all without paying some sort of price."

1993

I begin distancing myself from Meredith and Crystal, but it goes unnoticed because they are preoccupied with something that makes them whisper more, pass more notes in class. I'm relieved that they no longer demand to see my tests or quizzes or ask about my marks. Before class ends, they go to the bathroom, where they preen themselves, returning with their faces fully made up, their hair lacquered. When the bell rings, they race out the door.

During lunch, I stand alone reading my books. In the evenings and on weekends, I return to my schedule of hourly slots devoted to homework, flashcards, and supplemental exercises. It's the last day before spring break. I see Euphemia leaning against her locker, and I boldly walk up to her and say hi and even exchange a few pleasantries. I imagine all the kids around us are whispering that the Twin Dragons have finally united, but when I turn around, I'm surprised no one is paying any attention to us. Meredith and Crystal are in the parking lot, as if waiting for someone to appear.

The following Monday is the start of spring break. I sit at my desk, but I can't focus because I keep hearing the needs of the store. If the cash register or door chime rings too often, I join my parents and bag groceries or liquor bottles. Charles's absence is seen as being equally dutiful. My parents are grateful for his shut bedroom door because they believe he is diligently studying. No matter that his bedroom is actually empty and that he's at Clint's house playing video games.

I've just helped my parents at the store for the lunch rush, and I'm in my room, taking a break. I'm lying on my bed, rewinding my cassette player to a song that I've been listening to over and over. Bob Seger's sad song fills the room, and I wonder if I will ever experience these emotions of love and longing. I'm fantasizing about having a brunette boyfriend. In these dreams, he's courting me and being patient and loving despite my insecurities of being an outsider. There's a knock on my window. I lie still, wondering if I'm imagining the sound. I hear another knock. I open the curtains. It's Meredith.

"Anne!" she says.

I take out the screen, and Meredith crawls through the window and embraces me.

As Meredith stands in my room, I notice the recent changes in her body. She's grown in height, although she's stretched the same weight into a svelte frame. Twin bumps emerge from her chest. A light rosy sheen glistens across her cheeks. I try to mask my suspicion: Why is she here?

She hugs me. "My mom is at the hairdresser's right now, so I snuck away to say hi . . . and to ask you for a favour."

"Sure," I say, wondering if she can hear the reluctance in my voice.

"I know you've probably noticed I've been out of it lately. Well, it's because last month, Trevor asked me out, and since then, we've been going steady. Now, Crystal and Brent are going out too," she says, beaming.

"That's great news," I say without enthusiasm.

"Trevor's parents will be away this weekend, and he's invited me to go over to his house this Saturday. I plan on telling my parents that I've been invited to sleep over at your house. They'll love that idea. They like you so much, and my dad told me the other day how I should be spending more time with you. So, in case my dad calls, I wanted to let you know." She breaks into a dreamy smile.

"But that would be a lie."

"Anne, you're my friend, not my dad's," Meredith says, her tone sharpening.

"What if he asks to talk to you?"

"You're smart. You'll figure something out. Just tell him I'm in the bathroom or I had to go to the drugstore or something. I'll give you Trevor's phone number so you can call me in case that happens, and

I'll call my dad back," she says. Her eyes narrow. "Wait, you're jealous, aren't you?"

I look up, shocked at how she's perceived this envy burning inside of me. If Mr. Sweeney were my father, I wouldn't be spending my spring break bagging groceries. If Mr. Sweeney were my father, I would be as carefree as Meredith, only I would be grateful for this privilege. If Mr. Sweeney were my father, we would eat pot roasts for dinner and discuss issues like bigotry from a clean distance. In my daydreams, which are endless, Mr. Sweeney is my father, and he's allowing for me to have a nonchalance that I envy in Meredith. And I'm never taking him for granted.

"It's okay. I know Crystal will be jealous too when she finds out that I'm going to sleep over at Trevor's house!" she says as she bursts into laughter.

The weekend passes without drama. I wait for the phone to ring, but it never does. The following Monday morning, Meredith greets me, and I confirm to her that her dad did not call. She gives me a grateful hug.

Because I am no longer part of Meredith and Crystal's note passing, I now start paying attention in class. My favourite class is art—where before, I would slack off the most, now I love bringing out my pencil crayons and sitting in front of a blank sheet of paper. Today's assignment is to draw a portrait from memory of someone we know well, and then tie it to a fairy tale character. I decide to draw my mother. I draw her nervous eyes, her tight lips, the protruding marbles at the end of her eyebrows as she frowns. Behind her are cardboard boxes: It's delivery day and a pallet has arrived from the wholesaler, which she must unpack, sticker with a price gun, and then shelve by herself.

She's wearing my eunjangdo necklace, but the string ties her wrists, like handcuffs. Her tied hands are on a spinning wheel, and an imp dances on one of her shoulders.

As Mrs. Reeves passes my desk, she stops and watches me draw for a long time. Her presence behind me makes me uneasy as I draw. Finally, she whispers, "This is a really strong portrait. It's your mother, but there's so much more going on. Do you mind if I share it with the class?"

I nod, gratified by her praise.

Mrs. Reeves interrupts the class and holds up my portrait and outlines what she perceives are deeper meanings that make it more profound.

"What are her hands clutching?"

"A spinning wheel," I say.

"What fairy tale are you alluding to?"

"Rumpelstiltskin."

"Why did you associate your mother with the maiden who has to spin straw into gold?"

"Behind her are all the boxes of groceries that she needs to unload and sell so that we can make money."

"What about your dad? Doesn't he help?" a boy asks.

"My father likes to stay at the cash register in case people shoplift and to make sure the money is safe, so my mom usually works at the back."

"Isn't that the harder job though?" he responds.

I nod.

"What is that dangling from her wrists?" a girl asks.

"It's a Korean knife," I say. The silver pendant dangles underneath my sweater, but I know that taking it out would alarm Mrs. Reeves. I scan the room for Meredith and Crystal, who might call me out to show my knife, and am relieved they aren't paying attention.

"How beautiful," Mrs. Reeves murmurs. "Could you tell us what this knife was used for?"

"It was worn with the traditional dress."

"Why would a woman carry a knife around?" the girl asks.

"If a Korean woman was raped, she would use this knife to kill herself."

The class erupts as my classmates begin shouting out their questions:

"Why wouldn't she try to kill the rapist in self-defence?"

"Did geishas carry these knives around and stab their customers?"

"Do you know anyone that ever used that knife?"

I stammer and can't answer for my parents' culture when asked why a woman would kill herself and not her attacker. I don't know. It's assumed my great-aunt has killed herself or died tragically, and somehow this knife is complicit. But I cannot offer this story to my classmates. I would be judged by a value system this knife does not belong to. I have a sense of betrayal towards something, someone.

Mrs. Reeves, seeing my bewilderment, calms the class down, and draws attention back to the portrait of my mother. "Such a lovely portrait. Is there anything else you would like to add?" Mrs. Reeves asks, smiling at me.

I need to expose my classmates' heritage as being equally problematic, that it's not just Koreans. "I don't understand the men in the story of Rumpelstiltskin. They're the ones creating the problems. Rumpelstiltskin's father makes the outlandish promise that his daughter can turn straw into gold, and then the king commands her to do this or else he will kill her. When she does the impossible, she has to marry the man who threatened her life. That seems pretty savage," I say, and from Mrs. Reeves's enthusiastic nods, I can tell she's impressed by what I'm saying.

"These are all good points. I don't know how to justify their actions. But, ironically, it's the male imp who saves her, isn't it?" Mrs. Reeves says as she returns the portrait to me and whispers, "You should be proud of this drawing. It's doing so much more than simply rendering your mom. It's doing art, and that's no easy feat."

For homework, Mrs. Reeves asks us to spend some time in front of the mirror and draw a self-portrait. That evening, I set up a mirror at my desk. I take out a box of pencil crayons and a sketchpad. I study my face: My eyes do not slant but are two horizontal almonds with a chestnut inside. My nose is not squished but rounds off quietly. My lips are small but plush. While I draw, I lose all sense of time. I'm in a trance, when I realize that my mother's face appears in the mirror and that she's looking at my drawing.

"Anne has talent," she says as she studies the drawing and smiles. "When I your age, I also good at art. But why you look angry?" She's right. My eyebrows knit and there's an intensity in my eyes. "Next time draw happy face. That way you get A-plus," she says, and then sees her portrait lying on my desk. "What's this?" she asks, picking up the drawing I made of her that afternoon.

"Just an exercise we did in art class today."

She picks it up and studies it with a frown. "You make me look sad."

"Mrs. Reeves asked us to draw a person we know," I say, ashamed that she's found my drawing.

She studies the imp on her shoulder. "Isn't that Appa?" she asks. "Why you draw him funny?"

I feel a pang of guilt.

"No one wants to see sad, Chinese woman. Next time, don't draw us. Draw the beautiful people," she says as she walks out of my room.

Now that I'm finishing my homework earlier, I have extra time on my hands. I decide to pursue a self-directed path for extra learning. I know that a mastery of language is crucial to unlocking a power that my family lacks. So, on our next visit to Fort Athabasca Mall, I buy a dictionary from the bookstore with the goal to read and memorize its entirety. But I can't get beyond the first few pages. After reading an entry, I need to look up more words to understand that entry, which leads to other words that I don't understand. Eventually, I give up. I go to the library and redirect my efforts into reading the encyclopedia. If I can know everything inside these thirty-two volumes, then I will be able to patch the gaps and holes of my cultural understanding that make me feel like an outsider.

I lift the first volume and savour the weight of knowledge, the chemical smell of ink and glue. When I break open the pages, the gilt edges stick together, revealing that I am likely its first reader even though I'm sure these books have been here for a while.

I read the first article, but midway, my mind wanders, and I'm unable to focus. I flip through the pages and stop at a photo of an armadillo and begin reading again, but my interest quickly fades. I search for another article to engage with, when I hear someone calling my name. I look up.

"Hey!" It's Euphemia.

"Hi," I say back.

"Do you mind if I join you?"

"Sure," I say, trying to mask my reluctance. I scan the room and am relieved we're the only ones here aside from the librarian. Even though I no longer hang out with Meredith and Crystal, I instinctively know a judgment will be placed on us if we become too close—which will make us even more alien in this town.

She's carrying a big book entitled *The Canon of Art* and places it beside me. Euphemia tells me that she comes here when the restaurant is slow and reads books in the reference section for fun. I pick up her art book and flip through it. It's my first time viewing a book about paintings or, for that matter, art. About one-third of the book's photos are coloured while the rest are in black and white.

"Who made that?" I ask, stopping at a stunning image of a ballerina completing an arabesque, basking in the audience's attention.

"That's Degas," she says without having to reference the caption underneath.

I lean in and notice brilliant pastel lines which spotlight her ivory skin. "It's beautiful. I had a friend who was a ballerina," I say. I can't explain why looking at this image gives me such pleasure.

"That's a good artist to like. You see that man there?" She points to a black silhouette to the left of the painting.

I view the figure in the wings—a man in a suit, his head hidden.

"That was probably her patron, meaning she got her fame in exchange for giving him pleasure," she says, glancing at me.

"Like a prostitute?"

"Pretty much. A lot of these women came from lower classes and could only rise to fame with the help of a powerful man."

I continue studying the painting.

"Degas had a unique understanding of perspective," she continues. She presses her hand across one side of the painting and explains how the eye is forced to move in that direction. She uses words that I only know from my vocabulary flashcards, that I've never used in conversation: *composition*, *asymmetry*, *foreshortening*. An excitement grows within me because she's articulating something that I've felt but never expressed. Soon, we're flipping through the pages, searching for examples of how the eye is being controlled by the great masters, how perspective is improbable, the proportions problematic.

I browse through *The Canon of Art* book and find another image that intrigues me: It's a painting by Matisse. A woman lies leisurely against brightly patterned fabric. According to the book, he's one of many artists influenced by Orientalism, which, I will later read, is translating Eastern culture into a more refined aesthetic. Although there is a chapter devoted to Asian art, the majority of these pages are devoted to Japan, then China, and then one page represents Korea: a photo of a vase. The caption underneath explains that Koreans were renowned for their pottery, specifically for producing a delicate celadon hue which was coveted all throughout Asia. I don't know what colour celadon is, and it is hard to imagine this when the picture is in black and white.

It seems as if we've been talking a short while, but in fact, several hours have passed because the librarian walks towards us and tells us the library is about to close. A silence descends. When we exchange glances, I sense Euphemia's anxious desire, and my fear for this friendship. We exit the library and walk down Main Street.

"Did you apply to Essex Academy?" I ask.

"Yeah, I sent my application in last month. I didn't get straight A's, so I'm really nervous."

"How was the SSAT?"

"I did better than expected. I studied all summer, so now I know a lot of useless vocabulary words and math tricks. Is Charles going to apply for Essex Academy next year?"

"Yeah."

"I hear he's really smart."

"He gets straight A's without even trying," I say, almost apologetically. "But we don't have any relatives in Edmonton. If Charles got accepted, my parents would search for a Korean family to arrange a homestay."

"Are you going to apply the year after Charles?"

"I was thinking of it."

"If you both got in, how would that work? Would they send both of you?"

"They're hoping Charles gets a scholarship. But if he didn't, they said they would find a way to pay for it. I haven't thought about what would happen if I also got in."

"It's just very expensive, especially if you're also paying for a homestay . . . My cousin's friend does that, and what his family pays for tuition and board is the price of a car. Can your parents afford to buy two cars a year?"

"No," I say, shaking my head.

"Would they consider moving to Edmonton?"

"No. We've started making money since we opened the liquor store and we borrowed a lot of money that we have to pay back."

"So, if Charles gets in without a scholarship, then they would find a way to send him, but they haven't said anything about how they would pay for you if you got in too?"

I nod. Euphemia's demand for details is grating on me, though I realize her probing has revealed a potential problem that I haven't considered until now.

"If Charles got accepted, he would go, scholarship or not. If I got accepted, they probably wouldn't send me if they had to pay for two children. Besides, he's smarter and he's the boy."

"What do you mean by that?"

"He's the eldest son, which means he has to take care of my parents and provide for his future family, whereas I just need to get married," I say flatly, pushing down any emotions.

"Our parents can have their old-world thoughts, but we don't have to. We can have it all. We can get married and have a career. I want to be a journalist."

"Can't you become one by graduating from Crow Plains High School?"

"I don't want to end up writing obituaries and covering local country fairs. My parents subscribe to the *Edmonton Journal*, and I read it every day. I want to eventually live in a big city where I can report on important things," she says proudly. "My cousin goes to Essex, and he told me the students there aren't only smart, but they all have some sort of genius in a particular field. One of his classmates plays in the national youth orchestra every summer; another won the provincial tournament for chess. They're really impressed with applicants who get recognition outside of school, like winning some provincial award or recognition. Even if you come in second or third place, it means something. What are you naturally good at?"

"I don't know."

"Do you have any hobbies?"

I look at her blankly. "No."

"What are your passions?"

I shrug. "I don't have any."

"Well, I like writing and I'm working on an essay to submit to a student writing contest at the *Edmonton Journal*. If my essay gets printed, that means something to the admissions committee," she says as we reach her restaurant.

"What's the essay about?" I ask.

"About growing up in small-town Alberta."

"Sounds interesting," I say in a deadpan voice.

Euphemia pauses as if deciding to say more. "Well, I'm here if you ever want to talk again."

"See you around," I say ambivalently. Euphemia goes into her restaurant.

As much as I've enjoyed our conversation, I still need to maintain my distance, or else, to the townspeople, my identity would merge with hers as the interchangeable Oriental twin. The following day, I see her in her drab brown coat, listening to her Discman and reading a book. I immediately look away and turn the opposite direction. When I go to and from school, I cross the street to avoid passing the restaurant. Once, I make the mistake of walking by her restaurant, where she stares sadly out the window. I give her a robotic wave, which she returns with an eager one, and I notice her posture slumps as I quickly walk past her.

My marks steadily improve. For the parent-teacher interview night, my parents close the store early and transform from grocers to a smartly dressed couple: My mother wears a wool skirt suit she ordered from the Sears catalogue specifically for this occasion; my father wears the blazer from his wedding suit, which stretches tightly across his shoulders. I almost don't recognize them before they leave and wonder at the people they would have been had we stayed in Korea: Would they be this stylish?

They come back with their eyes shining, their voices triumphant, because the teachers have praised both of us for our performance and promise. Charles's teacher calls him a "genius," a rare student who can aspire to anything, so easily does he absorb information and quickly grasp concepts and theories. According to his teacher, he should have no problem getting accepted into Essex Academy. Mrs. Reeves tells my parents that I'm one of the most talented students in her class, and they should be proud.

"What you wanna be when you grow up?" my father asks us, his eyes bright.

We're both silent. The only other careers I know aside from working at the store is to be a teacher, a doctor, a dentist, or a lawyer. I have a basic understanding of what a doctor, dentist, and teacher do, but have no idea what a lawyer does. Although I think of the magazine photo of the lawyer, I'm at a loss as to what she must do all day aside from sitting at a desk. "I don't know," I say.

"You like reading. Become lawyer," he says in a serious voice. And because I have taped the photo of the lawyer on my wall, I nod and accept this as my fate.

My father looks at my brother. "What about Charles?" he asks.

Charles presses his lips together to indicate that he's annoyed. "You get to decide on my life, right, Dad?" he says in a tone steeped with sarcasm that my father does not or chooses not to hear.

"You like to study, so become doctor," my father says.

Charles raises his eyebrows but says nothing, to which my father grins, pleased with how easily our destinies have been set into motion. "You must work hard to achieve your dreams and be happy," he says, though he is speaking more to himself than to us. The only thing I know about being a lawyer is that they hold power and prestige, and I want this to make my parents proud.

"You've really improved this term, but most students applying to Essex Academy will have grades like these, if not better."

I'm sitting with Mrs. Reeves after class. I've decided to speak to her about my chances. We review my report card: I was setback because I followed Meredith's instructions to fail, but with great effort, I've scored both B's and A's. I plan to study even harder next year, when the marks really matter.

"No one from our town has ever applied, but now we have this surge of strong applicants for the next three years: first with Euphemia, then Charles, then yourself. You all have such drive. It must be something in your culture. I did speak with a teacher friend of mine from Edmonton who is familiar with the admissions process, and she told me that what makes an applicant stand out is some trophy or competition that a student has won outside of school. That validation makes a difference to the admissions committee, especially if you're from a small town. What's something you're really good at, that comes naturally to you and can set you apart?"

I shake my head. "Nothing," I say. The A's I have gotten are all due to forcing knowledge into my brain rather than the outcome of true passion.

"Do you have any hobbies?"

I look at her blankly. "No."

"I know you're really creative. I've seen your artwork, and you have talent there."

"Would art be something that would impress the admissions committee?"

"I don't think so. Art is highly subjective. There's no competition to distinguish excellence or rank. Also, it's not academic. But not everything has to be about getting into the program. Sometimes, your path may not be the one everyone expects you to take," she says gently.

"I really want to go there."

"I know. Have you heard the news about Euphemia?"

"Didn't she win the essay contest for the *Edmonton Journal*?" I read her article, a critique on Canada's multiculturalism, which focuses on celebrating ethnic foods and holidays, but there's still a lot more work needing to be done for minorities to feel that they are welcomed. She gave an interview in the town newspaper, which celebrated this recognition, but I still see her reading books by herself during lunch. I wonder if she regrets writing her article, which probably has alienated her more from the townspeople.

"After the essay ran, she got her acceptance letter."

"Wow," I say, feeling jealous.

"Is there any tournament or competition you could enter? You don't have to win first prize, even being a finalist counts for something."

"I don't have any passions," I say robotically. "Maybe I should just want what every girl seems to want in this town: to become a wife and a mom," I say dejectedly. Meredith and Crystal always made me feel odd for not aspiring to this goal. Tempering my ambitions would make my life so much easier.

"There's nothing wrong with not wanting that. I don't have either."

"Did you ever want to get married or be a mother?"

There's a measured pause. "I did have both. My daughter was a baby when she died unexpectedly in her sleep. My marriage didn't last much longer after that," she says flatly. "I'm telling you this because what you want in life and how your life turns out can sometimes be two separate things. But you have to take a chance on the things you want so you won't regret it later on in life."

I nod and awkwardly rise from my chair and collect my notebook. While doing so, a drawing slips out. It's a page where I've drawn my classmates when I was bored in class.

"Did you draw that?" she asks.

"Yes, I'm sorry, I didn't mean for you to see this," I say sheepishly.

She takes off her glasses and brings the sketches closer to her face. "These are really good. You've really captured everyone's personalities. Do you have more?"

"Yes," I say shyly. I go to my desk and bring my folder where I keep the drawings and paintings that I've done at home. I store them in my classroom desk because I know that my parents occasionally rummage through my desk: Though I have never caught them, sometimes the things in my drawers are rearranged, and I know Charles wouldn't do this. I have doodles of classmates, paintings of magazine models, but what I cherish the most are the portraits of my parents: my mother at the cash register holding Yura's knife towards the viewer, my father proudly standing behind a wall decorated with Charles's accolades.

Mrs. Reeves flips through the drawings, but it is only when she reaches these portraits of my parents that she stops and stares at them for a long time, as if searching for a truth. "A lot of times when people first learn to draw, they try to be as realistic as possible. Your drawings don't do that, and yet you've captured the essence of your parents. Your lines are sparse and elegant. These are a real pleasure to view. You have talent."

"Thank you, Mrs. Reeves," I say, trying to contain my pride as I start stacking my pictures.

"You've probably shown your art to the only person in Crow Plains who can give you an outlet for your creative talent. I used to paint when I was younger and had aspirations of becoming an artist. I tried, but it got too tough, so I ended up going to teachers college, thinking I would continue painting on the side, but life got in the way and I never did. Anyway, one of my friends from those days now runs a gallery in Edmonton. Do you mind if I keep these for a few days? I want to take some photos and send them to Glenda. I think she would really enjoy seeing these. I find these images provocative, but in a good way."

"Sure," I say. I'm confused why she would want to send photos of my work to her friend, but I want to be amicable, especially after she confided in me her personal tragedy, so I acquiesce. I hand over my stack of papers to Mrs. Reeves, who still studies the portraits of my parents. "Have your parents seen these?"

"No," I say quietly.

"You should show them. They should be aware of your artistic talent."

They would find anything outside of academics a distraction, but I don't say this. I leave the classroom feeling deflated. Even though she has recognized my love for drawing, if it will not help me get into Essex Academy, then I can't pursue it. Mrs. Reeves doesn't understand my burden: Unlike my classmates, my life does not belong to me. My parents have worked too hard, given up too much for me to pursue my own interests.

On my walk home, I stop by the library and find Euphemia sitting in the reference section reading a book on cathedrals. She moves her books to make space for me as I sit down.

"Congratulations, I heard you got accepted," I say.

"Thanks," she says bashfully. "I didn't get any scholarship or anything like that, but I'm happy I got in."

She tells me that after her acceptance letter arrived, she skipped class and her father drove her to Essex Academy to hand-deliver her signed acceptance letter. She observed there were a good number of immigrant kids. "I'm finally going to be normal," she says, and tells me she's already begun requesting catalogues to universities she wants to attend in Ontario. "Once I leave this town, I'm never coming back," she says.

I begin airing my worries to Euphemia: how I just spoke with Mrs. Reeves, who mentioned that the program is very competitive and most students applying have straight A's.

"I didn't get straight A's. I'm certain I got in because my essay won the *Edmonton Journal* contest. Is there some contest that you could compete in? There's that science fair that happens every spring. The winner goes on to compete in Edmonton at the provincial level. Maybe you should start thinking about that," she says, peering at me behind her thick glasses.

"I'm bad at science," I say.

"Science fairs are different. Think of something that interests you and submit that as your project. My father had a bunch of rusty pots that he was planning to throw away, so I did mine on the oxidation of metals. The principal gave me an honourable mention, and that was from salvaging what was going to go into our garbage."

"I can't think of anything."

She gives me a sympathetic look. "You'll figure something out. You want to succeed more than anyone here, more than me, even," Euphemia says, not in judgment but as a fact. She glances at her watch. "I should get going and help with dinner service. Well, it's nice to talk to you," she says, and gently adds, "I hope you get in." As she walks away, I feel shame because of her kindness despite my constant rejection of her. I hope she knows my reasoning of why we cannot be friends. In this town, we would forever be lumped as identical Orientals, and not only would we alienate ourselves from our peers, but we would lose our ability to become individuals.

I sit at the table alone and slump in my seat. I need to be unique. My mind draws a blank. I haven't the faintest idea on how to do this. I stay at the library and force myself to study my vocab flash cards, an SSAT practice exam book, and my homework until closing.

TWELVE

2014

When Cathy calls, I can tell from the techno-music background that she is at our favourite nail salon. Her exaggerated enunciations mean that she must be onto her second or third cocktail. I instantly miss being in New York, sitting next to her, getting our mani and pedis together.

"Guess where I'm at?"

"Perfect Nail Salon," I say, trying to match her exuberance.

"Yup, getting my nails done. I miss you so much."

"I miss you too," I say. I look down at my fingernails, with their rough edges and unruly cuticles. "How's Mrs. Ahn?" I ask. She is the owner of the salon and knows much about my life and Cathy's. Early on she asked if we were Korean, which, I sense, makes her and the other Korean ladies speak more cautiously when we're there. Mrs. Ahn usually does my nails and asks me many questions about Richard—what he does for a living, where he went to school, if he rents or has bought his apartment. She has two sons who are roughly my age but offers no information on them. She speaks about them with great delicacy, and so, I never pry.

"She's in California."

"Ah, visiting her oldest sister," I say, and we both giggle because over the years, we have come to know all of Mrs. Ahn's siblings: where they live, which colleges her nieces and nephews attended, and what they all do for work.

"Guess what?" she says.

"What?"

"We got the bid, the one Richard referred us to. The partners were pleased and put me on as the lead for the project."

"Congrats! I'm so glad it worked out. I hope this will help you get a promotion, which you totally deserve," I say, trying to shake off my melancholy and sound happy for her.

There's a long pause, and I wonder if Cathy is being distracted at the nail salon. "Richard didn't tell you?"

"No. I haven't spoken to him for a few days."

"You're pushing him away," she blurts out, and then immediately softens her tone with, "You should give him a call to let him know that you care."

"I should but I'm in this bubble right now, and I don't want to break out of it. It's hard to explain," I say defensively. "I should be missing him more."

"You should talk to him about your ambivalence. He deserves to know that," she says brusquely, then changes the topic and crams in all the events that have happened to her since we last spoke. "So, I had this really profound moment last week. I had this super chatty Uber driver. He's a writer and has self-published three novels. Anyway, he told me I should write down my life's events for the past week like it's a story and then, from there, figure out what the themes are so I can see what my life's about. So, when I got home, I wrote down what I did last week. I went to work, I ate out, I came home late. That was my life, and I realized . . . I'm not happy."

At first, I think she's using mock horror, but her voice is tightening, deepening, and she's crying on the other end of the phone. "My whole life I did what was expected of me and never what I wanted to do. My parents pushed me to study architecture. I never lived out my own desires."

"I thought you wanted to be an architect?"

"My grandfather was a famous architect in Korea, so that's the route my parents chose for me because I was good at drawing. I don't even know what I would be if I had a choice. But I don't care about my career anymore. Now, all I want is to be married. I want it so bad, I'll do anything."

"You will get married. You always get what you want. You're probably too intimidating for most, but in time, you'll find someone," I say sympathetically.

"It's my father's fault that I'm so competitive. I have to win at everything or have the best, or else I feel like a failure. You know, when I was a kid, every Saturday morning, my father made me do all the newspaper crosswords? He recorded how long it took me to complete so I knew what time I had to beat. Then he would make up his own math equations. I wouldn't be allowed to do anything else until all my answers were perfect. That's how I got great SAT scores. It made me a success, but I'm such a mess. I'm a bad person."

"No, you're not. You're a good friend and you have a lot going on: You just got put on as the team lead for one of the top boutique architecture firms in the country. You're going to be a rising star, I just know it."

A muffled voice interrupts Cathy, which I assume is a worker taking her from the pedicure seat to the manicure station.

"Hey, I gotta go. You are my dearest friend, do you know that? I love you so much."

"I love you too, Cathy, goodbye," I say, wondering how much she's drunk. Despite all these years of friendship, this is the first time she's been so vulnerable, and her neediness comes as a surprise. I begin to wonder if something happened to trigger these confessions as I imagine her carrying her flute of Bellini, walking on her heels, with foam spacers between her toes.

I bring out my laptop to check my work emails, but the computer doesn't start. I hit the power button again and again, but it refuses to turn on. I knock on Charles's door. He's at his desk, studying.

"My laptop isn't working," I say as I plop it on top of his thick book.

"What am I, your IT support?"

"That's what you're studying, aren't you? Consider this as helping you get work experience."

He presses the power button but nothing happens. "Is it charged?"

"I don't know." I realize my laptop probably just ran out of battery.

"Plug it in, then come back if it doesn't work."

I look at his desk, covered with books on computers and coding. "Why don't you just start interviewing for jobs? I feel like studying is an excuse for not putting yourself out there in the real world."

"I already have a lot working against me when I apply for jobs. I need to get my certification to have a shot at an actual career."

"You have to start interviewing at some point," I say softly. The past few years, he's been in and out of local colleges studying technology but never staying on long enough to graduate. I'm hoping that however long his sobriety lasts, he will be able to push through his studies and pass this certification test.

"Things have changed. You can't just apply to a job because you like computers. Those days are over. Do you remember Paul?" he asks.

"Wasn't he from Crow Plains?"

"He's Clint's older brother. He was profiled by some tech website for selling another start-up and raking in millions."

"I didn't know he ended up a success. He was also into computers, right?"

"Yeah. Remember that job offer in San Francisco that I was planning to take? Well, when everything went down, Paul went instead of me, and he was paid in stock options. When that company went public, he made a killing and has been investing in start-ups ever since. He's a venture capitalist now," he says as he opens Facebook and shows me his profile.

"Wow," I say, gawking at the many photos of him surrounded by important-looking white men and beautiful women.

"Do you still talk to him? Can't you ask him for a job?"

Charles snorts. "He used to visit me back in the day, but he never comes here anymore. He's too busy dating models and summering on yachts."

I look at Charles, studying the screen. "Do you wish that was you?" I ask.

He shakes his head. "I'd never have the rise like Paul had. I mean, it's still a white bro culture. At best, I could have become a mid-level manager. But that would have been something."

"There's still opportunity. As soon as you get your certification, I'm sure you'll get hired right away."

"Sure," he says, his sour tone offsetting my attempt to be positive. "Studying used to come so much easier for me. I could just read something once and get it. I guess I wrecked my brain. Nothing sticks. I've lost my gift."

Charles folds his fingers into a fist and then places his knuckles against his temples as he leans forward, hunched over his desk. I've never heard him make an admission like this. Though he's right, I don't want to confirm it, lest it crush him.

"I know what you mean. Do you remember I used to draw?"

"Didn't you draw those portraits of Mom and Dad?"

"I was proud of those. I picked up a pencil the other day to draw, but it was all chicken scratch, like a kid drew it. I wished I kept going at it." In my room, I found an empty sketch book and pencil, so I attempted to draw. I took the pencil and studied Richard's bouquet in front of me. But the lines were clumsy, and the picture ended up cartoon-like and flat.

"Do you wish you were an artist?"

"Yeah, or that I had a more creative career."

"Do you ever wonder where we would be if we were both allowed to pursue our passions? I'm not sure about money, but we'd probably be happier. Those portraits were really good."

"I killed that passion before Dad ever could. I knew what Dad wanted for me and that's what I went for, but I feel like I went on the wrong path. So you're not the only one that got crushed by him," I say. We're quiet for a long time before I talk again. "It was Dad's fault, not yours."

"He was just doing his best," Charles says quietly.

"I can't believe you're defending him. He derailed your life. If you were allowed to follow your dreams, you would have been the success in our family," I say with reassurance. One thing that struck me when reading my father's letters from Crow Plains was how often he praised Charles and anticipated his bright future. Back then, we all believed that he could achieve anything.

"I'm responsible for how I turned out, not Dad," Charles says as he stares hard into his thick book. A wet sheen forms on his eyes. He shuts them tightly. I stand there, unsure what to do. "Although, I wish I could take back that night."

With the mention of the night, my mind goes blank. Why is he mentioning this? Is this a trap where he's trying to hold me accountable for something I cannot remember? Charles's jaw starts tightening. He stares straight ahead as if considering what to say next. I abruptly turn to leave in case he wants to discuss this more. "You'll get it back. You'll get your second act," I say, my voice trying to sound cheerful as I shut his door.

1993

School finishes at the end of June. I find Meredith and Crystal sitting on the school steps after the final day of class. Though we're no longer close, they motion me over to sit with them. After they teasingly accuse me of being a snob, they update me on their lives and discuss their summer plans: Both are going steady with their boyfriends, though not without obstacles. Last week, Meredith was caught sneaking out of her bedroom window at night. She has been grounded and her mother has arranged for her to stay at her aunt's ranch near Edmonton for the entire summer, where she will attend a horseback riding camp. Crystal is planning to spend time with Brent, and her dad has even invited him to their cabin at the lake. Brent likes to cook over an open fire, and she describes the foods he can make.

I listen to their excited chatter with a detached amusement. To ride a horse in the summer heath or to eat s'mores at a campfire has the same wonder for me as drinking raspberry cordial or wearing a dress with puff sleeves. I'm fascinated, but I'm enjoying their stories for their entertainment value, cleanly separating their reality from mine. I nod, ask appropriate questions, laugh. I don't envy them. I can't envy them. Besides, I have something these girls don't, a report card, my best yet: straight A's, for this term, which has bumped up my final grades. I imagine presenting my report card to my parents when they finish work. It's our family's victory, a deliberate strike against this invisible enemy that lurks in the shadows, always making our happiness precarious. Anticipating their joy makes me happy. Yes, this is a feeling these two will never know.

Our talk ends when Trevor pulls up in his truck with Brent in the passenger seat. They invite me to a party they're headed to, but don't insist when I decline. Besides, Chad has started dating another girl from Vernet. Although I'm relieved they no longer tease me about a potential romance, I wonder if this was my last chance to be a part of their coterie, of being able to fit into this town by having an admirer.

I go home and eat a microwaved dinner in front of the television. Then I decide to take a walk. It's 9:00 P.M. and the sun still hasn't set. The sky is purple, pink, and orange, the cherry-red sun melting into the horizon, tinting my world golden. A breeze rustles through the long grass, shakes the leaves above me, blows the strands of my hair. I silently take in this beauty. My spirit is full. This is enough, for now.

The rest of the summer passes monotonously. I rise, work, and then sleep. If the store is slow, I go to the back office and draw: portraits of my parents, quick sketches of our customers. Or I take a mirror and study my reflection, trying to capture in lead pencil my intense gaze, my unhappy face.

My brother will take the SSAT in the fall and is supposed to be studying. Though his door is always closed, every morning I hear his window open: the sound of his escape. During my periodic walks around town, I always go by Clint's trailer house and see Charles's bike parked there.

Summer ends with the climactic visit to Fort Athabasca Mall, where we shop for back-to-school clothes and supplies. When school starts, I enter Grade 9 feeling freer since, without Euphemia, I'm now the only non-white girl. I spend my lunches either studying or doing extra-curricular activities—I'm starting a school newspaper and am part of the yearbook committee.

Even though school begins, Charles continues to go to Clint's house daily. At first, he comes home right before dinner, then skips it altogether and shows up right before bedtime. One night, he doesn't show up at all, but my parents are too busy closing the store to notice.

At the end of September, the school secretary calls my father, concerned that Charles has missed three consecutive days. When I arrive home that afternoon, Charles says nothing when I open the door to his room. His eyes are raw and red. I see large gash marks on his legs. Only when I close his bedroom door does he start sobbing. My father decrees that as punishment, Charles must come home every day after school and stay in his room to study. My father begins to sporadically check that he's seated at his desk. Though Charles is always there, I instinctively know he's not studying. Even my mother feels this is too much surveillance, but the one time she brings it up, my father glowers at her and warns her that it is his job to discipline his son because she has spoiled him. During one of my father's checkups, Charles asks with restrained resentment if my father can knock before opening his bedroom door, which results in another round of lashes.

One day, my father decides to join us for dinner because an early snowfall has brought business to a halt. Charles has just taken the

SSAT for Essex Academy that weekend, and though he did not study or prepare, he says it was a piece of cake and that he was the first person to finish each section.

"You check every answer right?"

"I looked over all my answers twice. I know I aced that test," Charles says. My father grins, pleased. "Oh yeah, I also got back my math test today. Here." Charles hands the paper to my father.

"I appreciate hardworking son," my father says. Charles is now back in good standing.

Charles chews his food and waits a few minutes to pass before he speaks. "So, Dad, I know my birthday is a little ways off, but I wanted you to start considering my present. You could combine it with my Christmas gift. I'd like a computer."

"A *com-pew-tuh*?"

"Clint's brother works at Radio Shack, and he said I could use his employee discount." Charles timidly pulls out a folded *Time* article about how computers are going to change the world. This article has photos of smiling white men wearing thick glasses in front of black computer screens.

My father studies these photos and snorts. "Isn't com-pew-tuh same thing as bee-dee-oh?" He pronounces each syllable with derision and contempt.

"They're completely different, Dad," Charles says confidently, and as he's about to explain the differences, my father stops him.

"No," my father says. "Right now, Mrs. Song crying every day. Why? Because sons keep playing bee-dee-oh and screw up their lives. You not gonna be loser."

"Dad, it's not the same thing. Computers are different from video games. Read this article. It says that—"

"You know you lucky? I don't have father when I your age. I was the only adeul, so as oldest son I have to study, then get a job to support mother and family. Think about that." He turns to me and asks, "If something happen to Father, what you do? You take care of the family?"

It's the first mention of my father's hardship, and I realize my father never told us how his father passed, but I know he's not in the mood to disclose this. These stories of suffering and sacrifice I can't grasp, nor can I compete with. The impoverishment is too great, the stakes higher than anything I will likely face in Crow Plains. I resent knowing these past traumas that diminish my life as trivial because I don't have war wounds to flaunt or great sacrifices to make even though I'm convinced I have this latent heroism: I just need the right circumstances to prove it. But I suppress these thoughts and answer "Sure" with forced enthusiasm.

My father looks at Charles. "What you do if something happen to Father?"

Charles shrugs. "Nothing."

"What you mean, nothing?"

"The government would take care of it," Charles says. I kick him underneath the table. We both know this isn't the right answer. "Clint's dad doesn't work, but the government sends him cheques."

My father gets up and pours himself a shot of whisky, takes a drink, and considers Charles's answer. "You won't take care of Mommy or Sister?" my father says, both as a statement of disbelief and as a question.

"Yup. Not my job."

My father sits down and continues eating. There is a subtle shift in his expression: his decelerated chewing, his delayed blinks, the hardening countenance.

"Your duty is to take care of family after me," my father says mildly, but I notice his fists begin to tighten. I widen my eyes at Charles, hoping he sees me warning him to shut up.

"Well, those rules don't apply here, because we're in Canada."

With a sudden move, my father reaches across the table and slaps Charles across the face.

Charles stares at my father, his lips trembling, his cheeks red from the blow. Charles sits there, motionless. My father takes another shot of whisky before leaving for the store and says, "The problem is you not grateful enough. I need to make sure this country don't spoil you."

It's early November, and we have a major snowstorm. Heavy snowflakes snap the remaining brittle leaves off branches, leaving the trees bare. Whiteness builds and builds. But then the cold stops and a warmth enters, melting the snowbanks and forming rivulets that run onto the roads. I welcome this respite as I unzip my wool coat on my walk from school. However, the next day, a cool blast transforms the wet surfaces into ice. The boys are euphoric because the entire town has transformed into a gigantic skating rink, and they organize a hockey tournament after school. Charles joins them, and even though I shout for him to come home, he ignores me. My father says nothing when I arrive home alone. He says nothing when he periodically opens Charles's door to find the room empty. Eventually, he sits down to have dinner with me. While we are eating, Charles walks through the back door. My father does not turn to look at him, but rather hardens his gaze against the wall and clenches his fists. I nervously watch Charles taking off his boots.

"I'm sorry I'm late today. All the boys in town organized this hockey game because of the ice," Charles says as he takes off his jacket and boots. His jeans and socks are dark from the dampness of playing on the ice.

My father stands up slowly, then walks to the counter and pours himself a shot of whisky. Charles and I watch in silence as my father takes a sip. "Go outside," he says. I stare out the window, at the falling snow. I know it's getting cold from the way the glass steams on the inside and ice forms along the window seams. Charles also looks out the window, his eyes widening.

"I'm sorry. I won't do it again. It was just this one time. All the boys in town were on the ice and I had to play because—"

"Go outside."

"But the temperature's dropping! It's freezing outside!"

"Get out now," my father says angrily.

"You can't make me," Charles says and, after staring at my father's resolute face, adds, "I'm turning sixteen soon. I'm almost a man."

My father laughs. Then he walks over to Charles and pushes him to the entrance, opens the door, and shoves him outside so that he lands on the snow, in his hoodie and jeans, with only wet socks on his feet. Then my father talks nonstop in Korean. "Manhood is not about serving your desires, but serving the desires of your father, your mother, this family. This is your duty as the son. Why are your mother and I working so hard? So you can waste your life on the *com-pew-tah!* The *bee-dee-oh!* Is that why we moved here, so my son can become a loser? Do you want to become a bum like Clint's father, rummaging for crushed soda cans so he can afford another case of beer? Do you know he digs inside my garbage at night so he can eat day-old bread until his government cheques arrive? Do you know what hunger is like? No, you do not understand hunger because you are spoiled, but I will make sure you will not take your life for granted. Your life does not just belong to just you. It belongs to our family. Later, you will understand what I am doing. You will thank me for disciplining you, stopping you from ruining your life on your friend's com-pew-tuh. You will stay outside until I decide when you can come in. Don't you dare run to your mother and get her involved or I will punish her too." Then he slams the door. This is the first time my father has ever threatened consequences to my mother if Charles tries to involve her. I am uneasy as I peek out the corner of the kitchen window where Charles squirms in the snow.

At first, Charles furiously hops from foot to foot in the snow. Then, after some time passes, he sits on the cement doorstep, shivering and whimpering. He curls himself into a ball and burrows his hands underneath his armpits. I stare helplessly out the window, unable to do anything, knowing that if I go to my mother, it would only exacerbate the situation. My father chews his food slowly, deliberately. After dinner, he pours himself another glass of whisky and sips it, leisurely. Then, once he's felt that enough time has passed, he rises and opens the back door. In a calm voice, he tells me to get dressed because we need to take Charles to the hospital.

We're quiet the entire drive to Fort Athabasca and as we wait in the ER. It's my first time at a hospital, as my parents rarely take us to the doctor, believing most ailments will just go away on their own or can be solved with ginseng tea. After the doctor assesses Charles, he asks why, on such a cold night as this, did this boy decide to walk outside with no jacket on and in damp jeans and socks? Charles has hypothermia and second-degree, possibly third-degree frostbite on his feet. My father clears his throat and begins to talk: He breaks his English—I'm unsure if he's nervous speaking in front of the doctor or if this is on purpose—to sound incomprehensible and become the bumbling Oriental many believe him to be. He mixes verbs as nouns, uses impersonal pronouns as personal, speaks vaguely and incorrectly, and refuses to make eye contact. Even I get lost in his obfuscation. When my father finishes talking, the doctor turns to me, but I say nothing. The doctor quietly watches our family, all of us refusing to look at each other or say anything.

"It's hard to believe a child would voluntarily walk outside in this weather in only wet jeans and socks," the doctor finally says, accusation leaking from his voice.

We wordlessly put on our coats. I feel the doctor's hard stare as we exit. When we return home, my mother begins wailing upon seeing Charles's bandaged feet, and a fight ensues. She accuses my father of harm, and my father accuses my mother of a greater harm: of spoiling their son and teaching him disobedience. My father's anger is now directed at my mother, who he accuses as continually disobeying and challenging him—it's no wonder the children follow suit. More accusations follow, each forming another upward spiral in his tornado of anger, and in a burst of rage, my father picks up Charles's hockey stick and begins smashing our bookshelf with it. My mother's small collection of Korean novels scatters to the floor. Then my father searches for another place to strike and marches towards my brother's room so that my mother cries, admits her guilt, promises not to say another word.

She is true to this promise. I wait for her anger to manifest again, even subtly, but there's only silence. Our emotions flash freeze overnight, and the next morning, we adopt a normalcy that at first feels feigned, then, over time, becomes real. My fear and anger retreats inward, then warps, then numbs.

Rather than think about my family, I think of Mrs. Sweeney and how freely she argues with her husband. Though I can't explain it, I know this is somehow a gift for Meredith. A few days later, I find my mother in the kitchen. When she sees me, she quickly wipes the tears from her cheeks.

"Mom, why do you let Dad talk to you like that?"

She looks perplexed that I should even ask such a question. "He grow up in war, Anne. When he act like that, we need to forgive, then forget." She gives a resolute smile and returns to the store.

It's the first time either parent has referenced this unknown trauma that needs to be forgiven, then forgotten. From then on, I block my thoughts on comparing our family dynamics with the Sweeneys'. To compare is to assume a parity that I will never have.

THIRTEEN

1994

One day, I arrive home to find a shiny black Cadillac parked in the back. When I open the door, it jams from the many shoes crowding the doormat. I hear adults talking Korean in the living room.

"Ah, our daughter has come home," my father says cheerfully. "Eun-ah, come greet our visitors!"

I go to our living room and see my father seated on the floor with Mr. Yoon. I quickly scan the room for Yura and am disappointed that she is not here. Instead, a Korean family sits on the sofa. I glance at them: the man's smart, plaid blazer, the woman's perfectly matte face, two teenagers who look our age. The girl, though Korean, is unlike me. Her hair is straight, shoulder length, with blunt bangs—too severe for her slender face. The boy is unlike Charles with his slim-fitting clothes and expensive-looking glasses. I'm embarrassed by our milk crate storage and makeshift Sears catalogue coasters.

"Eun-ah, *insahae* to Mr. Yoon and his cousin, Mr. Hong, who is also my university friend. They are visiting from Korea," my father says.

I first bow to Mr. Yoon, who addresses me warmly. "Ah, Eun-ah you have grown into an *agassi*! Our Yura came home for the Christmas break, but she just left to go back to her school on Vancouver Island," he says apologetically. I try not to show my disappointment.

Then I bow to the couple. The woman appraises me. I shyly look away, though I also want to study her: She wears layers of muted beige accented with gold jewellery. "Such a pretty girl, so tall and pretty. She resembles her mother, who was such a *meotjaengi* in Seoul," she exclaims. I'm stunned both that she's called me pretty—this is the first time anyone has ever called me that, and I'm flattered that it's coming from such a sophisticated woman—and that she's called my mother a stylish woman. I have never heard anyone outside of our family reference my mother's life in Korea, and the fact that she has called my mother fashionable—the grocer's wife with her shapeless jeans and sneakers—makes me question her judgment. I freeze, unsure how to react to these untruths.

"Our daughter is very vain. She does not need any more encouragement. She's always reading fashion magazines when she should be studying. My children are nothing like yours," my father says, and then turns to me to speak. "Eun-ah, did you know Mr. Hong's kids wake up at 6:00 A.M. every morning to study before school starts, then go to regular school, then attend *hagwon*, which are after-school classes, and return home every day around midnight? They are destined to become Seoul University graduates and successes, like their father," my father says fervidly, impressed by this level of dedication.

"Anne and Charles are good children compared to our Yura," Mr. Yoon interrupts. "When she comes home, she's always in front of the mirror styling her hair and putting on makeup, then calling all her friends. Not only does she refuse to study, but she's lost interest in ballet." He then shifts into a mirthful voice, picks up his shot glass, and declares, "We are having a Seoul University reunion in Crow Plains!"

The adults erupt into laughter, and the men raise their shot glasses and clink. Mr. Yoon and Mr. Hong both ensure that their rims are lower than my father's as a sign of respect to his senior rank. The shot glasses are inscribed with different NHL team logos—they were promotional gifts that dangled on the bottlenecks of whisky, but we kept them all and this is our first time using them.

"I came from the poor countryside in Korea, and I return to the poor countryside in Canada—unlike you, Mr. Hong, with all your successes," my father says with a laugh, taking a drink from his shot glass. He's too cheerful, too talkative, and I wonder if the other men feel his unease.

My father whispers to me to relieve my mother at the store. The adults all watch as I shyly walk across the living room, towards the doorway. I overhear Mr. Hong saying that his accomplishments are all because of my father, who gave his job to Mr. Hong before immigrating to Canada. The company has grown, expanded into other industries, and now Mr. Hong heads the household electronics branch, which has plans to export internationally. The company has sent Mr. Hong to Canada to meet with retail buyers and sell his company's hair dryers and alarm clocks at a cost cheaper than his Japanese competitors.

"Had you stayed in Korea, our fortunes would have been reversed. Before you offered me your job, I was planning to immigrate to America and work for my brother-in-law, who owns several dry cleaners in Virginia. If it weren't for you, I would have been a dry cleaner," Mr. Hong says with a chuckle, and lights a cigarette.

My ears perk up. I have never considered the fate of our family had we stayed in Korea, and, judging from how this family is dressed, I see it would have been the better option. I peer at my father to gauge his reaction: He is pensive and doesn't join in this laughter. I wish

I could study his expression more, but I've reached the doorway, so I force myself to open it and walk into the store to find my mother waiting for me.

She is relieved to see me and asks me to watch the cash register and call her if I have any problems. The part-time cashier is on her way to tend to the liquor store. My mother pulls out a pocket mirror and runs her fingers through her hair and applies lipstick. She selects a cantaloupe, a few oranges, and a can of pineapple slices as she hurries to the doorway.

The adults' laughter and lively conversation can be heard from where I'm standing at the front of the store. I panic when I realize that Charles has not come home. After a brief spell of contrition while he recovered from his frostbite, Charles has become rebellious again; even though I've expressed my apprehension, he continues to go to Clint's house after school, even if it's just for an hour. I call Clint's house and tell Charles to come home immediately because our parents are entertaining guests from Korea and they will notice if he doesn't return soon. Shortly afterwards, I hear Charles greet the adults, who make a big fuss upon his arrival. Later, the door in the back of the store opens, and Charles walks in with Mr. Hong's kids. They stop at the snack aisle, and he tells them in English that they can eat whatever they'd like. They curiously study the packages without saying a word. I walk over to them.

"How do you like Canada?" I stutter in my broken Korean.

"Cold . . . very cold," the girl replies in English.

"You speak English," I say, surprised.

"A little," she says immediately to prove that she can keep up with a conversational pace.

"I'm Anne. I'm sorry my Korean is so bad."

"No, it's good for someone born here. What year were you born?" she asks.

"Um, 1979," I say, trying not to show that I'm baffled this is her first question to me.

She nods. "I was born 1977. You can call me unnie—that means older sister." She appraises my outfit. "You wear that to school?" she says as she points to my purple headband, my hoop earrings, my plastic bangles.

"Yes," I say proudly.

"We wear uniform. We not allowed to wear that. My hair always cut," she says, making scissor motions with one hand.

I then ask about her visit, how she liked Jasper, the mountain goats they saw, the gondola they rode. Finally, I ask about her impression of Yura and the Yoons.

"*Oppa*, what do you think about Yura and her family?" she asks her brother with a sly grin.

"They are . . ." He pauses for dramatic effect. "Nice people." They both giggle.

"Yura is very . . ." She pauses, then pulls out her electronic dictionary and types into it. "Old-fashioned. Korean people don't think like that anymore. They still think like 1970s Korean style. They come to Canada and don't change old thinking. In Korea, no one care they are yangban."

I'm surprised by her critique of the Yoons, but I also appreciate her candour. Suddenly, I see the Yoons' pride in a different light, as something fuelled by their insecurity, rather than for me to feel insecure about. Also, I am shocked at how critical she is of them: I thought Koreans worshipped anything American. Shouldn't Yura and I be the more progressive ones, living in Canada—the next best thing to

America? I understand this girl comes from a wealthy family, but I assumed that our middle-class comforts were enviable, even among rich Koreans.

"My father visit for business, but he also think maybe we move to Canada—my mother move here with us and my father stay in Korea to work. But after we visit, we think no."

"Why?" I ask.

She begins whispering in Korean to her brother and then takes out the electronic dictionary again. They begin arguing about which word to look up, and finally after typing in a word, her brother says, "In Canada, many challenge for us. Korea, there is no challenge."

My brother and I wait for a further explanation. We stare at them, and they stare back at us, and an awkward silence ensues.

"But in Canada we have televisions and cars," my pride forces me to say.

"In Korea, we have many televisions and cars," the boy says. I don't know if he means the country Korea or his household has multiples of these. The conversation stalls again.

"You have game?" the boy asks, pressing both thumbs into the air to indicate a game controller.

"You mean video game? No, I don't, do you?" Charles asks eagerly.

"I bring Game Boy."

Charles's eyes widen. "Really? Can I see it?" The boy disappears through the back door and returns with a rectangular grey box. Charles is entranced as he holds the machine and presses the power button. We all look at the green screen as a tiny man with a cap appears and chipper music plays as he jumps for coins.

A customer walks up to the front counter, so I run to ring up his purchases. The girl stares at me: Does she realize that if my father had stayed, and if Mr. Hong was the one who immigrated, then in all likelihood, she would be the one behind the cash register?

Finally, we hear Mrs. Hong calling for her kids. Even though my mother insists on making dinner, they insist on returning to Edmonton because Mrs. Yoon is preparing dinner. Mr. Yoon tells me if I visit Edmonton next summer break, to come and visit Yura. I politely nod, knowing this won't happen. Mr. Hong walks over to Charles and me. His face is flushed.

"How do they perform in school?" Mr. Hong asks my father in Korean. I smell the sweet scent of alcohol on his breath.

"Charles reads too many comic books, and Anne is too busy spending time with friends," my father complains.

"Dad, we both get A's on our report card," I remind him in English, though it's for Mr. Hong to hear. Mr. Hong guffaws. Some of his saliva sprays onto my face. He says he's glad I have exposed my father's false modesty.

"What university do you want to go to?" he asks, leaning forward as if he's asking us to pick our favourite candy. Charles looks annoyed and shrugs. I'm not prepared for this question.

"I want to go to Ivy University," I say, hoping this is the right answer.

Mr. Hong looks amused. "Even though you were born in Canada, you are Korean. You must never forget your language. But you must also teach your father some English. After all these years your father has lived here, my children speak better English than him!" Mr. Hong says, laughing again. The other adults join, although my parents' laughter sounds forced. Then Mr. Hong's face becomes more serious. "You must study hard. Your father was the smartest amongst us, so you must be the smartest amongst your classmates. He has given up so much to give you this opportunity." While he's talking,

Mr. Hong tightens his fists and shakes them into the air to illustrate how hard we must work.

Though I understand what he is saying, I can't return his swift articulations. I utter my Korean back in clumsy consonants, harsh twangs, stumbling syllables. I know I'm not being honorific enough addressing him with my basic grammar tense. While I speak, the boy cringes and the girl stifles a laugh. After my brother and I bow, Mr. Hong grabs one of our hands and vigorously shakes them. Almost as if it were a magic trick, a wad of hundred-dollar bills appears in my fist. I look over to see that Charles also holds this.

"No, please, there's no need," my father says when he sees our wad of cash, and then, realizing the bills are brown, his voice drops into a deadpan seriousness as he says, "That's too much money for them."

I'm thrilled as I look in disbelief at the bills in my hand. Mr. Hong laughs. Then an awkward exchange follows: My father reaches for his wallet, hands over a twenty dollar bill to each of Mr. Hong's kids and says he has more money in the safe, if only they would just wait a moment for him to get it, to which Mr. Hong refuses because his kids are spoiled and this money is the least he could do. After all, he is deeply indebted to my father for giving him his job which has given him so much success, his family so much to be grateful for, and after more back-and-forth insistence, Mr. Hong physically holds down my father's shoulders as my father indignantly asks Charles and me to return the money because the amount is too much. We stand there, clutching our bills, unwilling to let go. The men continue talking over each other, until my mother clears her throat and humbly thanks Mr. Hong for the money. The men fall silent. My mother's hand suddenly presses my back forward so that I lean into another bow, and this initiates another round of bows among the kids and adults, and a great fuss is made from the Hongs about the hospitality we have provided—especially since they came unannounced—and then great apologies are made by my parents for not having provided enough—surely they could stay for dinner—and finally they get in the car, and we watch Mr. Yoon's shiny black Cadillac disappear.

A silence descends on our family. In contrast to my father's earlier nonstop chatter, now he doesn't say a word and stares absentmindedly while we eat dinner. Charles swears that he saw a car rental tag on Mr. Yoon's keychain.

After dinner, when my father leaves to go to the store, and I'm washing the dishes, Charles asks, "Do you know how much money we got?"

"No," I say. I have been waiting all evening to count the bills, but I instinctively know I should not do this in front of my father.

"A grand."

My mouth drops open. I knew Mr. Hong was rich, but I had no idea he was this rich and would give us such a large amount. I'm elated as I consider that I now have one thousand dollars.

Later, when the store closes, and my parents sit in front of the television watching the news, I hear my father's voice emerge from the living room. "We called him the empty rice cooker. He was so stupid, there was nothing inside his head. There really must be an economic miracle for a fool like him to be so successful."

I count each bill. I am giddy with the power that a thousand dollars affords. I flip through the Sears catalogue with a Jiffy marker and realize that whatever I want, I could buy, in multiples. I find a sweater that I like. I can't decide on the mint or the powder-pink colour so I circle both. Next time we go to Fort Athabasca Mall, I will go to Lewiscraft and buy the expensive set of watercolours from England, the creamy watercolour paper from France that I have coveted.

"What are you going to do with the money?" Charles asks.

I'm lying in bed flipping through the Sears catalogue. I show him the pages I've earmarked, and he shakes his head to show that he disapproves of my selections.

He goes over to my desk and picks up a stack of my drawings. He studies them. "You've really captured Mom and Dad," he says, chuckling at my renderings where I've cross-hatched bags under my father's eyes, anxious arcs above my mother's eyes. He shuffles through paintings that I've done of magazine models superimposed against an Oriental-themed background. "These are really good. You really know how to draw. You could make a lot of money making art."

"I wish," I say with a snort.

"Remember playing *Super Mario* on the Game Boy?"

"Yes."

"Well, someone had to design those images. It's easy, as long as you know the language. If we had a computer, you could learn how to make a graphic."

"What's that?"

"It's basically computer art. You can make a lot of money right now if you know graphic design. Paul knows someone who's my age and self-taught himself this language. This kid does weekend projects for an advertising firm in Edmonton. Everyone at that firm is two or three times his age, yet he's the only one that knows how to make graphics for their customers. He's made so much money that he bought his mother a brand-new Honda Accord. This is money he makes from a weekend job! There's so much work from the firm that he's had to turn away projects, and he's asked Paul if he knows anyone that can help him. I could connect you to him. Think about it, Anne. Adults are too old to learn this technology, so they're throwing money at us kids. This is a once-in-a-lifetime opportunity! Imagine making this sort of money from a weekend job," he says as he shakes the stack of hundred-dollar bills, "instead of sitting at a cash register all weekend to earn a few bucks for Mom and Dad."

"We don't have a computer," I remind Charles.

"You're right. That's the only thing holding us back."

"How much would one cost?"

"With Paul's discount, I could get something decent for around two grand."

"You want all my money so you can buy a computer?"

"It would be *our* computer. And you could easily earn that money back. If you invest one thousand dollars, imagine how much more money you could make doing something you naturally love doing, which is making art. Look at these drawings. You have design sense. The composition and colours don't come easily to just anyone, and you could build this into a career. You'd be so much better at this than being a lawyer. Do you even know what they do?"

"They do law," I say, trying to sound like I know what I'm talking about.

"What does that mean?" Charles asks, glancing at the taped picture of the lawyer on my wall.

"It means that they work with law," I say, though my voice falters from a lack of confidence. I'm trying not to show Charles that he is right: Even though I have taped the lawyer above my desk, I don't actually know what she does.

He lowers his voice and widens his eyes. "Dad thinks computers and video games are the same thing, but they're not. The computer will change every facet of life, every industry, every business. We are on the verge of a technological revolution. Just think about our grocery store. Right now, with the push of a button, accounting software could replace Dad's ledger books and calculator paper rolls. The computer could tally Dad's monthly profit or loss in seconds, rather than the hours it takes him every day to calculate every purchase and expense." He looks at me, trying to see if he's making any headway with his argument. "Think about Mom's painstaking job of reordering food. Every day, she walks down the aisles scanning the shelves for low stock, then fills in an order form, then faxes it to the wholesaler. Imagine if the computer could do all that thinking. There is so much opportunity, but we have to seize the moment now."

I listen and nod in passive agreement as Charles continues speaking. "Paul recently got a modem and showed me the World Wide Web. It's like a BBS, only better because you're not limited to a small group, and you can see it from anywhere! Now you can connect with the entire world!"

"What's a BBS?" I ask.

"A Bulletin Board System. It's a place where you go and share files and have conversations with people!" He holds a magazine article with the headline, "The Information Superhighway" and opens a page that lists website addresses. "All these different topics I can instantly access, just by typing in the website address into Mosaic. Soon we'll be able to exchange any information, discuss anything, even buy things from anyone in the world. But we need to act now."

Charles looks at me pleadingly. I know a thousand dollars, though a handsome sum, will eventually run out. What if Charles is right, and giving him my thousand dollars will reap more in the future? If I made enough money, I would buy my parents nice things. But perhaps the ultimate luxury would be to make my parents' peers—like Mr. Hong—jealous for immigrating to Canada and having children who succeed.

"Fine," I say. I reach for the shoebox underneath my bed and bring out my stack of bills.

Charles grins. "This computer is going to rock our world."

When the computer arrives, Clint and Paul come over carrying big boxes into my brother's room. As usual, my parents are too busy working at the store to be aware of what is taking place at home. Charles's room fills with Styrofoam bricks and plastic film as they begin sputtering out words I don't understand. After it's been set up, a hush descends as Charles presses the power button on the horizontal box and monitor. Seconds later, their faces glow blue.

"You've got a good CPU, but a so-so monitor," Paul says.

"Isn't everything the computer?" I ask, confused.

"Technically, the monitor is just a screen. All the information is here in this case," Paul says, patting the horizonal box the monitor rests on. "As long as this baby is fine, we're all good."

I pick up the CorelDRAW box. "I want to learn how to draw," I say.

"Let me install it," Charles says, inserting a floppy disk into the computer case. It makes an erratic stuttering noise, as if thinking aloud. Once it stops, Charles installs the next disk. I try to read the instruction booklet. My eyes glaze over with the technical language—Bezier tool, screen calibration, vectorizing bitmap images. I flip through chapters while waiting for the software to install, but I still have no understanding of how I will make computer art. After a long time has passed, Charles announces the software is installed.

"A lot of CorelDRAW is learning the commands, but you'll get the hang of it. Here, let me show you," Paul says, motioning me to sit in front of the computer. Once I do, I randomly click on the menu, frustrated that even though I'm clicking on the mouse, nothing is coming out. Paul shows me how to draw lines, how to connect them, how to make an ellipse. The commands do not come intuitively to me. The few rectangles and circles I make are rudimentary and ugly. I'm not sure what I envisioned when Charles spoke about graphic design, but it wasn't this.

I listen to the boys chatter in their incomprehensible language and have a sinking realization that not only have I lost all my money, but I'm helping Charles fuel his new addiction, which will only create more drama at home.

Charles is now always in front of the computer—his eyes fixed, his fingers furiously typing, his voice murmuring words of ecstasy and anguish. My parents are pleased that Charles's door is always closed—they assume he's busy studying and they don't mind that he doesn't even eat dinner with us anymore. My father has stopped checking in on Charles after seeing his perfect exams and essays. They are too busy working at the store to notice the blue light glowing from underneath his bedroom door.

I hear the beeps and whirs of his computer as I drift off to sleep. When I wake up, I open his door and find him still sitting at the computer, his face glowing blue and his eyes glazed with fatigue, indicating that he hasn't slept all night. At first, he missed only a few days a week of classes, but now he doesn't show up at all. He's more careless because his teacher has taken a leave of absence for a month to take care of her ailing mother, and a substitute teacher is receiving the notes that I write and deliver. I don't want to be involved, but I help because, for now, these notes keep my parents unaware, the drama contained.

"How do you spell *bronchitis*?" I ask. I'm writing another sick note to his substitute teacher to apologize for his absence.

"She wouldn't expect Mom and Dad to know how to spell it. Making mistakes will be more authentic." He says with a huge grin. "Want to see my first order?"

"For what?" I ask. He beckons me to his screen where I see a header that reads *Charles's Crazy Comic Book Shop* in a red bubble font against a turquoise backdrop and then a simple list of his comic book collection titles. "What's this?"

"It's my website. Look here," he says as he points to a counter, which states eighty-four people have visited his page. "Almost a hundred people have viewed this page. Paul's friend got me an account on his machine at the university, and it's hosting my site. It went live last week! Anyone in the world can see it. Yesterday, someone from Thunder Bay contacted me to tell me he wanted all six of my limited-edition comic books."

"You've never even seen this person! How will you collect the money?"

"He's going to mail me a money order, and after I deposit that in the bank, I'll mail him his comic books," he says, beaming the entire time. "It's limited-edition. They only printed a thousand of them, but by some fluke, our store received six copies. You can't get them anywhere. The cover price is $1.75. Guess how much I'm selling one copy for?"

"How much?"

"$175! So basically, once I sell all of them, I'll repay you!"

"So, you're going to fail high school to sell a few comic books?"

"I'm not just selling a few comic books, I'm starting a business. My friend is giving me tips. He's selling his dad's hockey card collection on a website and making hundreds of dollars."

I snort. "A friend you've never even met?"

"A friend I met on a BBS." His eyes shine, and he lowers his voice as he speaks about money. "Yesterday, I made in a day what it takes Dad to earn in a week. And unlike groceries, there's no physical labour, no worries about paying off a loan, no humiliation, no standing around all day waiting for customers to come in—I only sit behind the computer and do what I love. All I did was make a website and post the address on different web directories. If I can make almost a thousand dollars in one day from one customer, imagine how much I can make in a year! With the money I make, I'm first going to pay off Dad's debt. If Dad doesn't understand computers, he'll understand money."

"What about graduating?" I ask.

"Christopher Columbus didn't find the New World by studying Latin and getting his high school diploma. He dropped out and sailed when he was young, and that gave him the courage to venture into the unknown," Charles says impatiently, typing vigorously on his keyboard.

"So you're going to become a drop-out so you can sell comic books?"

"You don't understand this huge opportunity! Remember when Mom wanted to buy those SSAT study books? She had to drive two hours round trip to Fort Athabasca to order them, then wait a month, then spend another two hours to pick them up. Bookstores don't carry a lot of specialized books, so when they get an order, they have to contact their warehouse, and if they don't have it, then someone has to call the publishing house to place an order. What if I had these books in stock and I could immediately ship them once I get money in the mail? I could cut down on all that waiting time! And because I wouldn't have to pay rent or employee wages, I could offer the books at a steep discount."

"So you want to operate a bookstore?"

"This is beyond books—it's connecting buyers with sellers for specialized items. Right now, if you wanted to search for specific comic books, you have to drive to every comic store in Fort Athabasca, then Edmonton, to see what they carry. You're limited to where you can drive and which store you can visit. Imagine if it was all listed on a website, like a Sears catalogue, and then all you had to do was go online and see everything offered from anywhere in Canada, even the world, anytime of the day. Whatever the store sold, the inventory could adjust right away. I want to sell everything and anything to everyone and anyone!" He's euphoric. He talks about the gold rush and how he's just found a mine full of gold.

"I think a fake case of bronchitis can only cover you for another week. At some point, you'll have to return to school or else Dad will find out," I say, exasperated. I slam the door shut. Then, in a sober flash, I realize he'll start slacking off, his marks will lower and, as a result, I will no longer be able to fail. The more Charles rebels, the more devastated my parents will be, and the more I will need to excel. This logic is like the logic of integers: The more negative his grades become, the more I will need to compensate their inverse value with my grades to neutralize my parents' crushing disappointment. My spirit writhes as I comprehend the sacrifice I must make.

Luckily for Charles, my father is oblivious. After Mr. Hong's visit, my father has started a self-improvement project, and books start arriving in the mail. When business is slow, my father sits at the front counter and reads books with optimistic titles like *How to Win Friends and Influence People*. He will slowly read aloud, murmuring Dale Carnegie's cheerful dictums in grave tones, mispronouncing words, stopping frequently to reference the dictionary.

Success and money are accessible to anyone, it's just a matter of having the right attitude, is my father's newfound philosophy. I witness this transformation in how he works: When once he silently took money from his customers, now he looks them directly in the eyes, says thank you, asks how they are doing. Sometimes, while conversing, my father watches with elation as the customer reaches for a pack of gum or asks for another pack of cigarettes at the counter.

It's through these casual conversations about the weather and inquiries as to how they're doing that he meets Joe, a manager setting up a lumber camp nearby. Joe mentions that they need to find a grocery store that can supply food to their cook to feed their fifty workers for a project that will last at least until next summer. Joe doesn't flinch when my father quotes a price for delivering the groceries and says his accounts payable department will call him in a few days to set up a direct billing account and place their first order. My father, not having a business card, eagerly writes down his phone number on a piece of paper. He is ecstatic. So, it is true. The books were right. If you think positive thoughts, your destiny, thereafter, follows.

The next day, and the day after, my father is in high spirits. But by the third day, his euphoria turns to fear because the accounts payable department still has not called. On the fourth day, a panic sets in because the phone still has not rung. He anxiously tells my mother that in his eagerness, he may have written down the wrong phone number.

I'm walking home from school along Main Street when a man exits Stanley's Grocery. He pauses, studies my face, then asks if my father is the owner of Bill's Grocery. I nod.

"Talked to your dad the other day about ordering some food, but the phone number he gave me don't work. Kept getting the busy signal. My accounts people called all day and the next, but they couldn't get through. I tried too, even found it in the Yellow Pages to make sure the number was right. Anyways, the cook needed food right away, so we had to call the other store in town, and they were willing to set up an account right there and deliver us food," he says. "Tell your dad Joe tried calling, but for whatever reason, the phone line was always busy and we couldn't get through. Should get your dad to look into that."

I don't say anything that evening, even though my father is now convinced that he wrote down the wrong phone number and is considering driving around the dirt roads near town to intuitively find this remote lumber camp and personally take the order from Joe. It's only when some labourers enter our store—my father eagerly asks them if they belong to Joe's crew and where their camp is located and which unmarked dirt roads need to be taken to get there and then gives each of them his business card that has been express-shipped from a print shop in Fort Athabasca—that I speak to him after they leave.

"Joe stopped me on the street and told me he kept calling you for several days to make an order, but the phone line was busy, so he set up an account at Stanley's."

"Why phone busy?" he asks. Then he picks up the phone and hears the screaming shrills from Charles's modem. He looks at me, bewildered.

"That's a modem," I say tersely, trying not to show my terror. From there, I have to explain what has happened in a backward sequence of events: what a modem is, where Charles got the modem, where he got the computer, why the phone wouldn't work during the day if Charles was supposed to be at school. I answer my father's questions with as few words as possible, watching his anger grow. Only then, when he fully comprehends that he's lost the biggest account he's ever encountered because of Charles, and that Charles has been missing school to be on his computer, does he walk down the aisle and slam the door so fiercely that the front store windows rattle.

I quietly follow my father into Charles's room. My father speaks in a controlled voice, which hides the magnitude of his anger.

"There's a computer revolution going on!" Charles exclaims as he looks up from his computer monitor. He begins to talk about the World Wide Web and explains the new opportunities that will result. Charles lets out a nervous giggle before revealing that he's sold limited-edition comics sent to our store from $1.75 to $175! I stare at Charles in disbelief that he can't sense my father's rage.

"No more computer. Focus on school," my father says in a calm manner, but I know he is going to great lengths to restrain his wrath.

"Dad, aren't you proud of me? I made one thousand dollars and I didn't lift a finger."

"Who give you one thousand dollars?" my father asks suspiciously.

"Gregory Anderson from Thunder Bay, that's who. He's mailing me a cheque for six comic books."

"No more. Focus on the school."

"Clint's mom doesn't have a problem with her sons being interested in computers."

"Clint is loser. His dad is my best customer at liquor store."

"You're the one selling it to him."

My father stares hard at Charles. After a long pause, my father guffaws. "So, will this *com-pu-tah*," he says, spitting out each syllable derisively, "get you into medical school?"

"No, Dad, but . . ." Charles stutters, recalibrates as he finally sees my father's glowering eyes. "I don't want to go to med school," he confesses quietly.

"I don't work hard so you can play bee-dee-oh game all day."

"It's not video games, Dad. It's coding. This is something entirely different. Right now I'm part of something that's going to change the world!"

My father laughs. "My son gonna change the world?"

"Yes, this technology is going to change all industries, and now is the time to take advantage of all this opportunity and make money!"

"Son will be rich!"

"Yes, Dad! And once I make money, I'm going to help you. Your honourable son is going to pay off the rest of the money you owe to Mr. Kang!"

Something about this logic makes my father finally snap. Perhaps my father has detected a hidden jab that he is not competent enough to financially take care of the family. Or perhaps it's the sheer arrogance of Charles thinking that this computer, just a glorified video game, is somehow for the good of the family. It's then that my father roars in anguish about his son who has squandered money, time, and talents on this useless hobby that will destroy him.

"Pay back Mr. Kang? Ha! Is that why you work so hard to play the bee-dee-oh game? No, you help by getting A, you go to Essex Academy, you go to good university, you become doctor. Is that too much to ask?" my father shouts.

"Yes," Charles hisses.

Then both father and son begin yelling at each other, and I'm unsure if my father is asking Charles to leave, or if Charles is telling my father that he's leaving. As my father screams, "GET OUT! YOU NO SON OF MINE! HERE NO LONGER YOUR HOME!" Charles shouts back, "I'M LEAVING! I CAN'T LIVE HERE ANYMORE!"

Charles grabs his backpack and begins filling it with his clothes. "It's my life! I can do whatever I want with it!"

"No, your life don't just belong to you. It belong to our family. If you don't understand that, get out. I don't come all the way here so you can ruin your life and become loser."

"Going to med school would be a waste of my life. It's your dream, not mine. My dream is computers. If I don't do computers, I will die inside."

My father laughs. "Good! Die inside. That will be better for everyone!"

"Just because you run a grocery store and never amounted to anything doesn't mean I have to devote my entire life to compensate for you being a failure!"

My father looks at him as if he's just been struck. The colour in Charles's face drains, and his lower lip begins to tremble. After a succession of hard blinks, my father exits Charles's room, goes into the hallway closet, and digs through his toolbox. He returns with a hammer, and it's only after he swings it into the computer monitor does Charles unleash a terrifying scream.

FOURTEEN

2014

It's late. I'm watching a movie, which I rarely have time to do in New York. One of the actors reminds me of Richard: his height, his breadth of chest, his eyes. I think about Richard and am seized with a desire to curl next to him. I miss rubbing my cheek against his stubble, and have a sudden urge to talk to him, to make amends. I grab my phone and call him, but after many rings it goes to voice mail. I try again, then again. Finally, he picks up. I hear the background of music blasting, people chattering. This sudden burst of merriment drains my feeling of urgency. My apology can wait.

"Everything okay?" he shouts.

"Nothing important. Just wanted to chat. Where are you?"

"Out with a client."

"Sounds nice. Who?" I ask and notice a pause.

"I did a favour for a client, and they wanted to thank me. Listen, it's super loud in here. Can I call you back later?" he asks.

"Sure."

After I hang up, I'm unsettled. Was his pause a hesitancy? Why didn't he say who he was with? I wait for him to call, but he doesn't.

I fall asleep, and when I wake up the next morning, the first thing I do is reach for my phone to see if Richard called. He didn't. I wait by my phone, and the longer I wait, the more this becomes a test: When will he ring me back? I text Cathy, asking her, "How's it going?" She begins typing, then is on typing mode for a long time before she stops. I send her a question mark, but she doesn't respond. For the entire day, I'm consumed thinking about the reason for her reticence. When I don't hear from Richard the following day, I finally dial his number in the evening.

"How was dinner?" I ask after we greet one another.

He pauses. "I didn't get back to you, did I? I'm sorry. I've been distracted. Are you mad?"

I'm too proud to say yes, yet have too much integrity to say no, so I say nothing.

The pause becomes uncomfortable, so Richard starts talking. "It's been chaotic. The dishwasher broke and flooded the kitchen. The wood warped all the way into the living room. Everything has to be pulled out now." He talks about outrageous quotes from contractors, advice from litigator friends on who he should sue. I wait for a pause in speech to reinforce my displeasure that he didn't call, but it doesn't come.

"And to top it all off, the dishes are piling up. Unlike you, I actually use my dishwasher," he says with mock accusation.

"What do you mean?"

"I've looked inside your dishwasher."

I smile at how well he knows me.

"Even after all-nighters in the office, you never ran that damn thing. I know you store your shoes in there. But I find it endearing," he says tenderly. "Endearing but strange."

“Cathy wouldn’t do that,” I say, trying to steer the conversation back to why I called, which is to figure out why he did not call. The past two days, I have been fearing that Richard had dinner with Cathy and that something transpired. She mentioned how she wanted to buy us dinner if she got the referred business, which she did, and I wonder if she offered to take Richard out without me. Yet the more I thought of this scenario, the more I realized how she is more of Richard’s type: her pedigree, her ability to make him feel wanted. I cannot give the way Richard wants me to. I listen carefully for his response, but there’s only a weighty silence. “Is there something going on between you two?” I ask. There, I’ve said it. I’ve placed my last card on the table.

“Did she say something?”

“No, I just guessed.”

There’s a long pause. “I wanted to tell you this in person. She wanted to buy me dinner to thank me for bringing her that project. We had a lot of drinks that night. I had no intentions other than hanging out, but she got really drunk and all of a sudden she came on to me and I didn’t know how to stop her. I’m a guy. I know that’s no excuse, but I’m not in love with her. I screwed up. I’m sorry.”

Surprisingly, I’m not angry. I wonder where my next words will take us. “I think she’s a better fit for you.”

“She means nothing to me. This is about us. You keep pushing me away, and it’s hard to keep standing around. I know what I did was wrong, but I want to work things out, if you’re willing.”

I’m silent for a long time.

“Please say something.”

“I have nothing to say right now. Let’s talk another day,” I say with calm. He protests, says we need to talk this out, but I hang up. I sit still for a long time. I pick up my phone. Cathy will likely never call or text me again, but just to be sure, I block her number, more angry with myself for, yet again, lacking discernment in selecting friends.

When Richard calls back that evening, I turn off my phone. Early the next morning, he makes multiple calls, which I mute and allow to go to voice mail. Later in the afternoon, I find my old cassette player and a box of mixtapes. I listen to them and lie on my bed with my father's letters and the Korean-English dictionary beside me. There's a soft knock on my door, and my mother appears.

"I don't feel like talking," I say, annoyed. This morning, I asked both her and my brother to leave me alone. Luckily, my brother left for the gym and hasn't returned.

"It's Richard."

"Tell him to call back another time."

"He here. He sitting in the living room waiting for you."

Richard is out of place in my mother's living room: His tall frame hunches forward on the sofa, where he is seated on a wooden bead cover, which supposedly helps with circulation.

"What are you doing here?" I say in shock.

"You asked me not to come because you didn't want me to burden your mom. I respect that. I booked myself a hotel room so your mom doesn't have to worry about me. We need to talk."

I hear my mother clattering pots and pans in the background. She reenters the living room and addresses Richard. "You like the Korean food? I'm not good cook, but I make something simple you can eat. You stay for dinner," she says with uncharacteristic cheer.

Richard's eyes gauge mine to see if he can accept this offer.

"Mom, we're going out. Richard is staying at a hotel, so you don't have to worry about him."

"You sleep here," my mother insists, looking at Richard, her eyes brimming with offence. "Charles can sleep on sofa." I imagine Richard sleeping on my brother's twin bed preserved from the nineties, complete with Superman sheets.

"He's okay," I say.

"You sure?" my mother asks, her voice hurt. Again, my mother insists that Richard eat or sleep at our house, and I refuse on his behalf. She finally leaves.

Richard surveys my mother's living room, which I also scan through his eyes: the lace doilies that cover most surfaces, my framed diplomas and awards that hang on the wall, photos of me as a girl growing into a young woman. I'm struck that the only signs of Charles are photos of him as a child. Richard stares at a cluster of my high school portraits. "You were cute as a teenager. Just needed to smile more," he says, examining my photos, where I stare with intensity.

"This might surprise you, but I was also unhappy throughout my youth," I say in a deadpan voice, though I'm attempting to be funny.

"I find it endearing," he says, and moves towards me to give me a kiss. I refrain from leaning into him like I normally would. "We need to talk," he whispers.

"Let's go outside."

We leave the house and walk towards the ravine. Normally, I would go into the woods to be along the water, but with Richard I stay on the walking path: His wool blazer is too thin for the branches, which could tear at the fine fabric; his tan leather shoes would get ruined from the mud.

"Why this grand gesture, Richard? You didn't need to come all the way here."

"I came to tell you in person that I'm sorry. It was a stupid mistake. I'm willing to do whatever it takes to make it up to you. I just need to know that you want me."

I know that now is the moment I need to fight for this relationship, if I truly want it. I also need to apologize for the little and big aggressions, to say that I love him and that I need him. But something inside of me fails.

"Being back made me realize there's still stuff I need to deal with," I say.

"You've been sounding like a different person over the phone. I'm worried about you. I can tell that being back is changing you."

"I'm getting sucked into a world I have spent my life trying to escape."

"I wish you could let me in so I could be there for you."

"I don't think I can let anyone in."

"Why?" Richard asks, looking hurt.

"I feel a lot of guilt for what happened to my family, especially to my brother. I need to figure out how I can absolve myself."

"Babe, tell me what that is. Talk to me."

"I can't. I've never spoken to anyone about it. It's something I need to figure out on my own. I don't have the space to deal with this relationship right now. I think you're better off with Cathy. She can be there for you. I can't. Besides, I'm going to leave the city."

Richard stops walking. "Like take a leave of absence or move?"

"I'm done with New York. It's a life that doesn't belong to me. I need to start creating a life on my own terms."

"What about us?"

I look into Richard's bewildered face. "I don't want us. I think I've felt this for a while, even before the whole Cathy thing happened."

"You're being rash. Your father just passed. You need to think about this more."

"No, I realized that I've been lost for a really long time, and I need to start finding my way out."

Clouds move away from the sun, casting a harsh light that makes Richard's skin paler, his eyes more aqua, his hair silver. I will miss the elegance of this face. Yet I feel only relief. For the first time, I am making a decision that feels like my own, that finally feels right.

"All I know is that I'm unhappy," I murmur, not having the energy to clarify it's not only this relationship but also my job, my life.

"I don't know what happened in the past, but whatever you went through, you don't have to be on survival mode any longer. You have to start letting people in," Richard says.

"You're the person I've shared the most with."

"I need more. You're completely enclosed, and those walls are going to destroy that beauty inside of you."

"It's been happening since I was a kid. And I need to untwist myself. That will take some time."

"Do you want to take a break from this relationship?"

I shake my head. "That would be unfair for you to wait around when I can't promise you I'll want to get back together."

He sighs and looks off at the distance so I can't see his frustration. "You sure you can find someone who loves you as much as me?"

I shrug. "I'm not afraid of being alone."

"I wish you needed people. But I can't fight for the both of us anymore, especially if you're telling me that you don't want to be with me."

"Right now, I have too much going on and I don't have space for you."

We're quiet as we consider the words that have now created a slender fracture that will inevitably widen into a chasm. "What are you planning to do then?" he asks.

"I've been thinking a lot about North Korea, about how no one cares and carries on while this brutal regime continues. I might join some humanitarian organization that helps defectors. Or go to film school so I can make a documentary and bring awareness about North Korea, though I don't know a thing about operating a camera. We'll see." Richard's eyebrows rise. "You seem surprised."

"You once told me that you didn't have any hobbies or passions. I never understood that. I mean, how can anyone go through life without any interests? But I sense fire behind what you've just said, and I haven't heard that from you. Ever," he says. "Will your mom be okay with that?"

"I haven't told her yet. But she doesn't have a choice."

"Who's going to support her and Charles?"

"I'm realizing they can figure it out. I can't provide the answers for everyone anymore."

We stand in silence, staring at one another. Then he leans forward and presses his forehead against mine and lifts a finger to tilt my chin upwards.

"You're going to be okay?" he asks.

I nod.

"Remember our first date when we went out for dinner and the waiter thought we were married?" he says.

I break into a smile. "Yes."

"Afterwards, I remember calling my mom and telling her about you. For the first time in my life, I felt that I found the one. You brought that out in me. Can you just think about it a little more before making all these drastic decisions?"

"No, Richard, I've been waiting my whole life to be freed. I need to do this."

Little splashes of water start dropping on us, and we look up at the sky, now covered in dark grey. We walk briskly back to my mother's house, where his rental car is parked in the driveway. Thunder cracks, and the rain begins to fall harder and heavier. I wish him well, he wishes me well. On instinct, I stretch my arm to shake his hand. If someone was witnessing this, they would think that I had just sold Richard life insurance or real estate: Our final goodbye is that bland and that nice.

When I go inside, my mother is standing by the living room window, watching Richard drive away.

"Where he going? I make dinner. It's ready."

"He's going back to New York."

"He just come!"

"We broke up, Mom."

My mother's eyes widen. "Why you break him?"

I wish I could articulate the reasons but know my mother would not understand. "I just have too much going on right now," I say simply as I head towards my room.

"Richard good man. Success, tall, lawyer, everything! Why you break him? Call him back, tell him dinner ready!" she says angrily as she opens the front door, only to find the driveway empty. She comes to my room, widening the door.

"He cheated on me with Cathy," I say. Though this isn't the only reason, it is a reason she would understand, enough so that she will leave me alone.

My mother winces. "Your friend Cathy?"

"Yeah."

"So he coming to apologize?"

"Yes."

She leans against the door, quiet in thought. "He telling the truth, he spending the money to come here. If he say sorry, you forgive."

"I told him I'm leaving New York."

"What about your job?"

"I'm quitting. I need to take some time off and figure things out. All I know is that I don't want this life anymore. It's never been mine. It's built on a lie."

"You got everything. You went to best school, have good job, find successful man. Why you throw away like that?"

"I'm stuck at my job. Even though I'm as smart as Richard, I'm never going to make partner."

My mother looks confused. "You have everything and still complaining."

"Also, I hate what I do."

"You think I like working the grocery?"

"I want to do something more creative."

"I wanted to paint too, but then, how do I feed the family?" She gives out a frustrated sigh. "You gonna try to be an artist?"

I feel a pang of regret. I wish I had the courage to say yes, but I'm too old and too used to my comfortable lifestyle to go to art school; maybe if I were young, I could romanticize an artist's poverty, but not now. Living impoverished at my age would make me miserable. And I already know what it's like to be poor. "It's too late for that. I just want a job that has a bigger goal than making my clients rich. I want more meaningful work. When I was young, all I wanted was to make you and dad happy, and it bent me out of shape. Now, I need to straighten myself out."

My mother looks hurt. "So many people want your life."

I know no words can convince her to think otherwise.

She shakes her head and begins to snicker. I'm jarred by this response. "I don't understand your generation. You have so much, maybe too much."

"You could be right about that," I say and walk out my room before my resentment releases.

1994

Charles doesn't return that night, nor the following night. My mother weeps continually. Tears fall at inopportune moments, like when she's at the front counter packing groceries.

"Are you okay?" a customer asks, concerned.

"She fine," my father answers on her behalf, then waits until the customer leaves before berating my mother for exhibiting such emotions in public.

Neither of my parents speak about Charles, so I don't either. I avoid them both: I'm angry at my mother for being loyal to a son who doesn't care about her loyalty, and I fear my father, whose anger is getting more unpredictable and unhinged. My parents don't speak to one another unless absolutely necessary, so a silence descends in our household.

The following week, my mother waits until the store closes and my father is on the sofa watching the evening news before approaching him. Since Charles's departure, my father drinks more, and he has finished several shots of whiskey. "Why don't we just let our son explore this hobby until he gets bored of it?" she asks in Korean. Because we have been operating in silence, my ears perk up when I hear them speaking to one another.

"No."

"All his friends play these games. It must not be that bad. We could give him time limits," she pleads.

"It's your fault that Charles rebelled! You made him rotten and spoiled!" he roars. Unable to bear a wife who would defend their wayward son, my father flips the coffee table. I hear the glass ashtray land, then spin violently onto the kitchen floor.

Alarmed, I tiptoe into the living room and watch as my father grabs a chair and is about to smash it against the wall when my mother cries, "Stop. Stop. I'll stop. I'm sorry. I won't speak about this again."

"Are you going to find him and give him money?" my father yells.

She looks down and shakes her head in quiet defeat. But I don't believe her, and seeing how hard my father glowers at her, I doubt he does either.

"Even if he comes begging, you must never give him anything. If he thinks he's a man, he has to accept the responsibilities of one. Let him starve, I don't care. He is no longer allowed here. This is not his home, he is no longer our son."

She nods, her bottom lip trembling.

"Don't ever speak about him again," he says with finality.

My mother nods meekly as her posture caves.

My father throws the smashed computer with all its wired accessories into the garbage bin outside. My mother goes into Charles's room and sweeps up the glass shards from the broken monitor. She organizes his desk, makes his bed, folds his laundry and arranges it in his wardrobe drawers. And true to her word, my mother says nothing. Her grief cannot be expressed, so my mother's thoughts push inward, warping her insides. My father begins to ignore her—not looking at her, nor speaking to her—so that only I can see her look of derangement. I try not to meet her eyes, lest her craziness enters into me.

That night, when I know my parents are asleep, I go to the garbage bin. I delicately lift the smashed monitor until I find the case, the keyboard, the mouse, the modem. I bring these back to my room and hide them in my closet until I can figure out where I can resell them. I'm furious at how Charles has devastated my mother, enraged my father, shattered our family. I have been thinking nonstop of how to be recompensed, not only for the money that Charles took from me but also the destruction that he has left for me to deal with.

Every day, my mother asks me the same question when I return home. "You see Charles?"

"No."

"You pass by his classroom? His locker?"

"Yes, Mom. He wasn't at school."

One day, she asks a daring question. "What's Clint's last name?"

"I don't know."

"Tell me," my mother says, sounding desperate.

I try not to show my annoyance. "I have no idea."

My mother frowns at me, then picks up the phone and calls the pizza parlour. "Hello? What is last name of waitress who has son name Clint?"

I look at her in disbelief. Any townsperson would recognize the caller as my mother with her demanding and crude speech.

"My son at Clint home and I have to call him," she says, a shrill taking over her voice. "It's emergency. Have to talk to my son but dunno how to reach." A pause follows and then I hear the owner speak. "Thank you, thank you, can you spell?" She scribbles down the last name. Then she flips open the White Pages, finds Clint's mother's entry, writes down the address, and goes for a walk that evening carrying a box of canned ravioli. I'm scared for her, lest my father finds out.

Another day, she comes into my room and hands me an envelope thick with money. "Go to Clint's house and give to Charles. Don't tell Daddy."

"No," I say as I push back her hand.

Her eyes brim with hurt. "You want Mommy to go to Clint's house and make Daddy mad?"

"He doesn't need money. He needs to apologize to Dad and come back home. Money will just prevent him from returning sooner."

"Give to him," she says as she throws the envelope onto my bed and closes the door.

I sit at my desk trying to quash the impulse to obey my mother. Because I'm conflicted, I can't study, so in frustration I decide to rid myself of this money. I jam the bills in my back pocket and walk through the falling snow to Clint's trailer house. Once there, I knock several times before I hear footsteps approaching the door. I hear the door viewer open, then these footsteps retreat and another set approaches. Charles cracks open the door. He blinks rapidly as the cold air rushes to his face.

"Hey." I dig my hands into my pocket. I smell the metallic scent of electricity from inside. My brother has lost weight, and his bangs are tucked behind his ears. He looks older.

"Hey."

"Haven't seen you around."

"I've been busy."

"Doing what?"

Charles shrugs. "Stuff."

"You're going to flunk out of high school," I say, exasperated.

"People are still contacting me for the comics that I've listed on my website. I'm talking with a comic book distributor about lowering their minimum orders so I can sell more titles. I just need to figure out how I'm going to pay for my first order."

"You're chasing a stupid idea. People won't buy things they haven't first touched. Go to school," I say, feeling the heavy wad of money in my back pocket. I decide then that I will not give this money to him. Any money he receives will be used to buy comic books and continue his foolish dream. As a result, he will not graduate and my parents will be devastated.

"You sound just like Dad."

"Yeah, well, maybe you should think about your family over yourself for once."

"Dad's brainwashed you. Putting the family over myself is destroying me."

"You're the adeul, not me. It's your job to take care of Mom and Dad, not mine." As I say these words, Charles's face hardens. "Come home, Charles."

"Nah, I'm going to listen to Dad on this one. He's right, I shouldn't consider that place my home anymore," he says, closing the door, then locking the latch. As I walk out of Clint's yard, out of frustration, I kick the garbage can, which falls onto the ground, scattering a heap of empty ravioli cans.

When I enter the store, my mother nervously glances at my father, then at me with hopeful eyes. I ignore her, and as soon as my back is towards her, I roll my eyes and go to my room. I store the envelope of money in my closet, unsure of what I will do with it. True to her promise to my father, my mother never asks me about my visit to Charles.

At the store, at home, my mother sits lifelessly, staring blankly at the wall. I overhear my father scolding her after the store closes that customers stand in front of her, unloading their baskets and carts, but my mother does not smile or say hello, she only stares at them with her haunted eyes. She barely eats, and her pale complexion against her unkempt, static hair make her look like a *gwisin*, a ghost.

It's only when the Songs visit that I realize the extent of my mother's madness: Mrs. Song is shocked at my mother's sallow cheeks, thinning hair, the dark shadows beneath her eyes. Mrs. Song inspects the kitchen and shakes her head disapprovingly at the bare cupboards save the packages of ramen. Luckily, she's brought a bag of Korean groceries from a recent trip to Edmonton. She boils a vat of water and drops meaty bones into the bubbling pot to make a bone broth. She gathers some vegetables and teaches me how to make banchan: to mince garlic, slice scallions, blanch vegetables, and season them with just enough salt and sesame oil. Before she leaves, she pulls me aside.

"Your father tell me you doing good job at school. You good daughter, Anne. Keep studying hard, because your parents going through hard time."

I nod politely, say, yes, yes, even though each word she utters pushes me deeper into my self-imposed inferno.

After she leaves, I mince garlic. I steam spinach and pickle cucumbers and make mounds of marinated vegetables, which I set on the table. I ladle the soup into serving bowls. I go to the store to get my mother to eat. Her face is blank as she sits down at the table. She pushes the food away and returns to work.

The next morning, my father wakes me. It's Sunday, and I'm surprised he's not at the store. He holds a cigarette in his mouth and fumbles to put on his winter coat.

"We need to find Mommy," he says. My heart tightens and I know not to ask questions. The only sign of worry he shows is chain-smoking cigarettes as he gets ready.

It's one of the coldest days of the year. When I step outside, inhaling the air creates tiny icicles inside my nostrils. Exhaling makes my breath visible. When I touch the metal car door handle with my bare hand, it sticks.

My mother's footsteps are nonexistent. The backyard, the alley, the roads are covered in an unbroken layer of snow. We drive down Main Street, the smaller streets, then the outskirts of town. There are no other cars or people. Despite the overcast sky, the brightness of the snow dazzles me, mocks me with its indifference. We start driving through rural roads, and as we pass a field, I see her: a black figure in her wool coat. When she sees our car, she turns her back towards us and tries to run the opposite direction, but the snowbanks are so high that she has to raise each leg and plunk it back into the deep whiteness. My father stops by the road and watches her scramble. He scowls at her, then looks away. "Tell Mommy to come home," he says with irritation.

I open the car door and stand in the snow. The cold air enters me, instantly draining away any accumulated warmth. "Mom," I say gently. I can hear her whimper. "It's cold. Let's go home."

She turns around, as delicate snowflakes catch in her hair, eyebrows, eyelashes, dust her black coat. Her hair hangs loose. She speaks to me in a Korean that I don't follow.

"I don't understand what you're saying, Mom," I say tersely, my growing frustration steeling me against her. Would she ever grieve like this for me, her daughter? I wish I had the courage to test her, to rebel and carry out an act of defiance. My unhappiness is on the brink of the insanity that I see in my mother's eyes.

My father rolls down the window and yells impatiently, "Yeobo, get inside now."

Her lower lip trembles, and the tears that stream down her cheeks solidify midway. She looks like a child I need to protect. She reluctantly takes a step toward us, then another. She makes her way slowly into the car, then slides into the passenger's seat, refusing to look at my father.

"Let him lead his life. Let us lead ours," my father says dispassionately, and then we drive home in silence.

"Mom," I say with exaggerated cheer as I return from school.

She remains still, sitting behind the front counter, gazing straight ahead with hollow eyes as if I'm not there.

"Mom, guess what?" I say louder, with more animation as I stand in front of her. I open my backpack and pull out an exam. "I scored perfect!"

Her torpor momentarily breaks, and some vigour returns to her as she briefly comes back to life. "Perfect?"

"Yes, look!" I point to the 100% that my teacher, Mr. Stevenson, has marked prominently in red felt.

"I know you working hard. I appreciate."

I bask in her brief happiness.

"Dad!" I call, energized by my mother's reaction. He's restocking the vegetables. "I got 100 percent on my test!"

He takes my test and smiles. “Good job!” he exclaims. He turns and sees a customer selecting apples. “My daughter get perfect on math test.”

“Wow! Congratulations, you have such a smart daughter,” the customer says, and my father beams, as if he is the one being complimented. He glances at my mother, pleased to see her smiling.

“You need to keep bringing home the marks to make Mommy happy,” my father says.

“Yes, of course,” I say, nodding eagerly.

“Who needs son? Daughter best. Because of you we get the strength to wake up every morning and work hard.”

Spurred on by his words, I bend my mind to reshape itself to the logic and reasoning of my textbooks. In the name of sacrifice, I no longer draw so I can use all my energy to study. Studying becomes a moral act: I, alone, need to repay an unpayable debt. This energy—anxiety, fear, insecurity—is being transformed into pure virtue. My quizzes, tests, and essays are offerings that I make, that somehow extend salvation to our entire family. The misery at home distills into a perfectionism that purifies. But these triumphs are always short-lived, because there is always another quiz or test that I need to perfect. There is no end to the sacrifice I can make or the level of virtue I can attain.

The school calls frequently to ask about Charles’s lack of attendance until one day, my father tells the secretary that Charles no longer lives at this address, that this is no longer his home, and he is no longer my father’s son. An awkward exchange follows and ends with the secretary advising my father to call the police to report his missing son. When the conversation ends, my father slams down the phone, muttering, “Why call police for son no longer yours?”

One day, Mrs. Reeves comes to the store. Her face brightens when she sees me behind the counter.

"Do you remember last spring when you showed me those portraits of your parents?"

"Sure," I say. I vaguely recall giving her my drawings.

"I took photos of your portraits and sent them to Glenda, my friend with the gallery in Edmonton. Well, yesterday she called and said she wanted to include your works in an upcoming show. She got funding from the government for an exhibit to celebrate multiculturalism, and she's having a hard time finding artists from different cultures. She loves your drawings. She couldn't believe you were only in high school. She said your portraits were haunting, strong enough to stand along with her professional artists. She wants the ones of your mother and father. The show opens on the last Saturday of February, and there'll be an opening reception party. Because you'd be from out-of-town and it would be hard to go back and forth on this, I gave her the dimensions of your drawings, so she's going to get the frames ready beforehand. You just need to show up a few hours before the reception and she can slide them into the frames. She's never extended this privilege to a minor," Mrs. Reeves says, and hands me a piece of paper with the name and address of the gallery.

I force a smile even though inside, my heart sinks. It doesn't occur to her that I won't be going. Aside from the intense pressure I have now to study, there are also practical hurdles: Saturday is our busiest day. An art show would not warrant the inconvenience involved in making the trip. Also, exhibiting portraits of my parents would be seen, by them, as an act of betrayal; they would be horrified, not proud, at the privileged patrons viewing them in their vulnerability and exhaustion. Finally, it doesn't occur to Mrs. Reeves that my parents would see my art hobby as a lavish waste of time because there is no practical value to it. I need to study to become a lawyer, and drawing is irrelevant to this destiny. I want to tell her this, but instead, I meekly say, "Thank you."

She slides a paperback across the counter. On the cover is a black-robed figure floating above a bridge, holding a glowing orb. "This is one of my favourite novels. I think you might like it," she says before she leaves the store.

When the invitation arrives in the mail, I toss it into the garbage before my parents can see it. Despite the cold, my mother continues to disappear on walks, and I dread when my father comes into my room to tell me that I need to watch the store while he drives around looking for her. I try to read the novel that Mrs. Reeves gave me. It's *Cat's Eye*, by Margaret Atwood, a name that I have seen in enough magazines to know that she's an important writer. Elaine, the story's protagonist, wants to become a painter. However, she doesn't struggle very much with her parents or with herself about this desire. I'm puzzled by this lack of conflict on what I assume should be a bigger problem. I lose interest and am unable to finish the book.

The day of the art show's opening, I wake and study throughout the morning, listening to the store and helping to pack groceries when there are rushes. After lunch, I stock candies; my mother observes that I have arranged them in a rainbow sequence of Swedish red berries, peach rings, banana marshmallows, gummy green frogs, and blue whales. Later in the afternoon, I am at the front counter studying my flashcards, when Mrs. Reeves comes in, looking upset.

"What are you doing here? Glenda just called. She's expecting you. She has the empty frames ready and hanging in the exhibition space. What happened?"

"I'm sorry, Mrs. Reeves. I couldn't attend."

"Why not?"

"My parents had to work, and they didn't have the time to drive me to Edmonton."

She presses her lips together, spreading them thinly. "You should have told me. I could have driven you. This was such an honour, a big opportunity."

I look into her warm, generous eyes, but then I pull back, as if touching fire. "Plus, I have a lot to study this weekend."

"Glenda represents some of the most famous artists in Alberta and knows top collectors across Canada. I've never heard her extend this offer to an unknown artist, never mind a minor."

"I'm sorry, Mrs. Reeves. Please give Glenda my apologies."

"Anne, is everything alright?"

"Yes."

"Then why are you crying?"

Only then do I realize tears are rolling down my cheeks. "I have to focus on my studies right now," I say, my voice squeaky.

Her eyes soften. "Anne, I see this gift so plainly in you. It would be a shame to waste it."

"Drawing won't help me become a lawyer."

"Maybe becoming a lawyer wouldn't be the best fit for someone with your talent."

"You don't need to give me career advice. I'm not your daughter," I say. I instantly regret those words, wanting to follow up with the sentence, *I wish I were.* Her pupils shrink, and I feel a door inside of her slam shut.

A coolness enters her eyes, then her voice. "You're right, Anne, I'm sorry," she mutters, then leaves the store. I want to follow her and apologize, but instead, I sit on my stool sensing the loss of not only her support for my art but also her kindness. But perhaps it's for the better, as I feel a hardness growing inside of me, and I will need it to get me through this time.

Mrs. Sweeney visits the store and mentions how she misses having me over, hinting at something darker that's happening to her daughter. "You are always welcome to come over. I miss your influence over Meredith. Since dating *him*, she's changed so much," she says, then pauses as if she wants to say more, but does not. I notice her increased purchases of wine.

One day, I stay late after class to work on the newspaper. I'm initiating our first edition—largely because I want to add "editor in chief" to my application to Essex Academy. I've stayed late, making the final layout, cutting and gluing printed columns onto ledger paper so it can be photocopied. As I walk outside, I see Meredith standing by herself in the cold, shivering in her knit stockings and short skirt, smoking a cigarette. As I pass by her, I'm about to give a friendly "hi," when I notice her eyes are streaked with black mascara circles—they look like a pair of exploding dark stars.

"Everything okay?"

"I'm fine," she says in her adult voice.

"Are you sure? Do you want to talk?" I ask, concerned.

She knots her eyebrows as tears roll down her cheeks. "I said I'm fine."

I nod my head and am about to walk away.

"What's wrong with your mom?" she asks in a taunting voice.

"What do you mean?"

"I've seen her walking along the country roads, and she looks spooked."

I glare at Meredith, who is intent on hurting me. I want to return this hurt. "She's got some health issues," I say. "How're your parents doing? Your mom comes by our store, and judging by all the booze she's been buying, she seems stressed."

"I hate them," Meredith says, exaggerating her gloomy face. "They're ruining my life. They're doing everything in their powers to keep me and Trevor apart."

"They care about you," I say, trying to mask my envy.

"I'm lucky when I can get them to care about me. They're too absorbed in their own drama. My father hasn't been home for months because he's in love with another woman. He moved in with her and her son in Fort Athabasca." She snorts. "My mom plans to move to Edmonton and live with her sister, so I have to either move in with her or my dad. Either way, I'm moving this summer, and I won't be able to see Trevor anymore. To top it all off, neither of my parents are willing to take care of Mystique, so we have to sell her. So you see, my life isn't so perfect after all." She looks at me, then asks in a raised voice, "Do you still want to have my life?"

I'm shaken by the news of Mr. Sweeney's infidelity and the breakup of her family. But because of the cruelty I sense in her inflection, I want to hurt her back. "Yeah, I'm jealous these are your problems," I say with equal malice.

Her face crumples, as if she's swallowed something unpleasant. "She's Oriental, the woman who's ruining our family," she says, almost accusingly. "My mom was right about your type." And with that, she storms off, our relationship destroyed by the finality of these words.

FIFTEEN

My mother descends deeper into her darkness. My father prohibits her from being at the front counter, as she is no longer presentable to our customers. My father begins drinking more, and oftentimes, I see empty shot glasses and bottles scattered on the back office desk and the kitchen table. My good marks are no longer enough to cheer them—at most my father may tell me I'm doing a good job, but my mother refuses to be comforted. So when Mr. Stevenson announces the science competition and tells us that the winner will compete at the provincial science fair in Edmonton, and that winner will be flown to Ottawa to represent Alberta at the National Science Fair Championships, I realize that I need to win this competition. Yes, this will bring back my parents. And I will use Charles's computer.

No matter I would be using Charles's work as my own. Besides, I own half the computer. Moreover, Charles has left me with the tremendous burden of being the sole source of relief to my parents, so his programming code is fair compensation. I absolve myself from any guilt because my motive is not only moral but noble. I go into his room to get his coding books and magazine articles. Even though his notes on using CGI scripts to create dynamic websites don't make sense to me, I reason it probably won't make sense to my audience either. In Charles's room, I also find a journal where he has scribbled down his thoughts.

My plan is to memorize, then recite all these terms. To give examples of how coding can make a website interactive, then give a speech taken from his feverish notes about the future, where the computer will bring interconnectedness, which will beget globalization, which will beget economic prosperity and then, finally, usher in world peace. Though these ideas are not mine, they become mine. I need to win: My mother's recovery depends on it.

I call Future Shop at Fort Athabasca and order a computer monitor to be delivered. I purchase it using the money my mother intended for me to give to Charles. I convert this to a bank note, then mail it, then check the post office every day for the monitor to arrive. When it does, I hoist it onto our grocery trolley and pull it to school.

On the day of the presentation, I connect the monitor and modem to the case, and the modem to the classroom phone jack. The principal is the judge and sits at the back: He will select the winner to go on to the science fair in Edmonton. When I present, I begin by explaining what a BBS is, then move to the World Wide Web and its potential to change the way people interact and consume. I describe the internet as the great democratizer, which will remove geographic boundaries. Socio-economic barriers will fall, and industries that do not adapt will fail. But the world will finally unite because of this technology.

I see Crystal scribbling on a piece of paper, then passing the note to Meredith, who, upon reading it, snickers. However, the principal watches me intently and nods throughout my impassioned speech. When it ends, he excitedly walks up to me and asks if he can explore the website that Charles created. He clicks on the mouse, his eyes widening with curiosity.

Later that week, it's announced that I have been selected to represent our school at the provincial science fair in Edmonton. I am thrilled.

I run to the store with this news. Although both my parents respond enthusiastically, my mother's happiness is short-lived, and she soon sinks back into her misery.

For the fair, I ask Mr. Stevenson to arrange to have a monitor lent to me at the arena, and to have my booth close to a phone jack, so I will only have to bring the computer case, modem, and keyboard, which all fit into my brother's duffle bag. I haven't foreseen a dilemma: How will either parent drive me to Edmonton without them knowing that my presentation is about the computer? The solution comes easily: A week before the fair, our soda cooler breaks down. My father apologetically tells me that when we go to Edmonton, he will need to drop me off so he can search for mechanical parts around the city in addition to purchasing sundry goods at the local cash and carry. I tell him that he does not need to attend the science fair, that most parents won't be in attendance—even though I doubt this to be true—and we both hide our relief. I try my best not to sound too pleased when my father commends me for being so independent, and we agree on a time he should pick me up.

On the day of the science fair, I wake up full of excitement. I have washed and ironed my navy dress with a red sash—one of the choicest hand-me-downs from Yura—which used to fit loosely but now fits tightly. I put on my matching velvet blue headband, which I've bought from the drugstore. I pack my laminated charts and diagrams. I recite my memorized speech in the bathroom mirror, and even practise how I will appear modest. I place the duffle bag into the car's trunk before we leave for the two-hour ride to Edmonton. While we drive, an awkward silence descends. I stare out of the window at the uninterrupted stretches of snow which covers the farm fields. At some point, my father asks what my project is about. I use technical jargon: I talk about connecting human beings through CGI scripts and use abstruse terms until he loses interest.

When we reach the venue, I rush out to the trunk and lift out the duffle bag and folded poster boards. I say goodbye to my father. Inside, the arena teems with other contestants setting up their booths, and all of them are with at least one parent. After registering and setting up, I walk along the aisles noting all the ethnic students—so far I see two Chinese boys and an Indian boy in a turban. I also note that a few of these participants, despite their pale skin and fair-coloured hair, are also immigrants, betrayed by their Eastern European accents. But they are preferable to kids like me, with our obvious differences.

I'm in awe at how some contestants have such polished presentations: Whereas I was proud of how I purchased self-adhesive laminating sheets for my charts and photos, others have charts and diagrams seamlessly fused onto glossy three-fold poster boards as if made for a corporate meeting—I marvel at this technical feat and overhear one of the parents complaining to the other how her work's print department almost screwed up her order last minute.

The boy in the booth next to mine stands with his parents. They are a good-looking white family, the type that could advertise butter or cereal. I observe his neatly combed hair, the starched collar with a red bow tie in the middle, the ironed pleats on his pants. He talks with the same ease I've seen Meredith speak with her parents. Throughout the day, I watch his interaction with the judges: The judges speak in a more relaxed, informal manner with him and leave his booth chuckling. No matter how many A's I earn, or how many quizzes and tests I perfect, this is a skill that I will never master, and that not even Yura would be able to pull off: to speak with white adults in a way that would make them want to champion you. But I know I have a compelling topic, and this conviction gives me a small but growing confidence. I am the grocer's daughter. I have nothing to lose.

When the first pair of judges comes to my booth, I deliver my rehearsed speech, giving equal eye contact to each judge. One judge nods in approval, while the other enthusiastically scribbles onto his clipboard and leaves. I become more poised and polished with each visiting judge. One of the judges leans over as if to give me the ultimate compliment: "On top of having such a great presentation, you speak English very well," she says warmly. I nod meekly, and smile complicitly: I don't correct her, I just want to win.

I only have two more judges left to show my presentation when I see my father walking towards me. His face is tight and he walks with urgency. I quickly push the cardboard presentation in front of the computer.

"I phoned your mom. Charles has come home, so she is making dinner. I'm going to the wholesalers, but get ready to leave in two hours. I will pick you up then," he says in Korean. I nod. Without taking an interest in my booth, he walks out.

My heart sinks: All the excitement and anticipation that has built up dissipates with these words. Charles not only disobeyed our parents but left behind a dysfunction that I have tried my best to fix, and yet all my hard work will fade as they honour Charles tonight. Rather than punish Charles, they will almost certainly celebrate him for simply walking through the door.

When the final two judges visit my table, my mind is dysregulated as I stutter and apologize for my disorderly booth. I straighten the poster board. I forget my rehearsed speech, so I take out my index cards and read my notes in a flattened monotone. When I finish, I try my best to focus and answer their questions. They calmly scratch their pens onto their clipboards.

"I have one last question," says a judge who, despite my disarray, has been giving me encouraging looks. "I'm a computer hobbyist myself and

I tinker on the side. For your hit counter, what CGI script did you use? I write my own custom Perl script but use someone else's odometer graphics."

I stand there opening my mouth, but no sounds come out. The judge patiently waits, and entire minutes pass before he gently says, "Well, I think we have all the information that we need."

"It's too bad, because it's a very interesting topic," I hear the other judge say as they walk off.

"Her website was very sophisticated," the computer hobbyist judge says. "But, just like her computer, her speech felt programmed, and when the code veered off script, it just crashed. That's the problem with people like her—they can copy, but they can't innovate."

I come in third place. The neighbouring boy with the red bow tie comes in first place. I'm not surprised as I watch both him and his parents talk jovially with the judges. I am the only winner without a parent. I leave the podium as soon as I receive my ribbon.

I place the computer case and accessories into the duffle bag, toss the laminated sheets and cardboard display boards into the garbage, and hoist the monitor onto a trolley to be returned to the AV room. My father arrives when I have finished packing everything, and I tell him that I came in third place. He says, "Good job," but his distracted silence reveals that he's preoccupied thinking about Charles's return. I fall asleep on the drive home, waking intermittently to my own sobs, which my father doesn't notice.

When we reach home, I open the door and smell deep-fried foods, savoury soup, and sesame oil. Charles sits at the table, spread with his favourite dishes: fish stew, battered shrimp, grilled octopus, and glass noodles. My first thought is how my mother has procured so much seafood, last minute, in the middle of the prairies. Also, when did she find the time to cook?

"You closed the store early to cook him dinner?" I ask, incredulous.

"Good to see you too," he says. He's changed in appearance. He's taller, and his hair is tied into a ponytail. His face has hardened and stretched, as if it's been pulled taut.

I look at Charles. "I don't know if you care, but after you left, Mom got pretty depressed, Dad's been drinking more, and oh yeah, we haven't been doing well."

"Anne, no negative talking. We happy family now," my mother says, wiping her glistening cheeks.

"I'm glad you missed me," he says as he widens his arms and walks towards me. When he hugs me, I smell the faint scent of tobacco. I shut my eyes against a rush of angry tears.

"Why did you come back?" I whisper as I lead him to my bedroom so we can speak privately.

"Somebody broke into Clint's house and took my stuff," he confides quietly.

"What did they take?"

"Everything. That's why I'm back. I was working for Paul's friend, helping him with some projects, and I scraped enough money to buy another computer. Well, yesterday, someone broke into Paul's house and stole that computer along with all my accessories and disks. They wiped Paul clean of all his electronics too. I'm pretty sure it was Jeff."

"He's so dumb. The last thing on earth he'd be capable of understanding is how to use a computer."

"Jeff and his friends are druggies now, and they're desperate for cash. His old man kicked Jeff out for stealing from him. He's drilling holes in car tanks to sell the gasoline. But because his uncle is the RCMP officer, he's pretty much untouchable. We didn't even bother reporting the robbery."

"How would he even know you had a computer?"

"Jeff and his buddies were hanging around the parking lot at the mall when we picked up my second computer. They saw us carrying the boxes into Paul's car. Jeff kept looking at us, sizing us up, knowing there was some expensive stuff to be had. Then I saw Jeff's car loitering around Clint's house just before the robbery. He knew that every Friday we went to the pizza parlour for their two-for-one pizza special. The break-in happened while we were there, so whoever stole from us knew our schedule and knew what they were after," he says, sounding tired.

My mother tells us that dinner is ready.

"This is new chapter. Carry your sister's bag at the door, and then we eat," my father says in English.

I look at Charles's unrepentant face. For months, he's brought on dysfunction to our family and I've tried my best to carry on his duties. But now that he's back, he's been so easily forgiven, my self-sacrifice so easily forgotten. "Just leave it, Charles. I don't need it anymore," I say as I grab the duffle bag, open the door, and toss his computer into the garbage.

Charles transforms into the perfect son. His lack of defiance and his abundance of deference is unreal. My father and Charles meet with the principal, and Charles convinces the principal not to keep him behind. He breezes through his textbooks in one read and effortlessly perfects each make-up test and assignment.

The secretary, a devout Catholic, stops me in the hall with a triumphant smile. "Your brother is truly the prodigal son. There must have been so much rejoicing in your house."

In anger, I say nothing and walk away as I reflect on this famous parable in the Bible.

The story begins with a father and his two sons: The youngest asks for his inheritance, so the father divides it among them. The youngest travels to a distant country and squanders his money, living a life of debauchery. He eventually becomes broke and finds a job feeding pigs; his situation is so destitute, he longs to eat the pigs' food. It's then that he decides to return home, not to be a son—because he knows he's no longer worthy of that title—but to work as a hired hand. The father sees his youngest return from a distance, so he runs and embraces his son, then orders his servants to prepare a great feast to celebrate his homecoming. When the oldest reacts angrily to this extravagant reception, the father rebukes him, saying he should be happy for his brother's return. I have always found this story problematic because of its end: The wayward son is celebrated, the loyal son is dismissed. I rage with the older brother, whose dedication hasn't been rewarded.

The principal writes a glowing letter to Essex Academy endorsing Charles, stating he's one of the brightest students they have ever taught, and asks the admissions officer to overlook his late application and absence due to personal circumstances. This is mailed along with a letter, which has Charles's perfect SSAT scores. It's almost as if the drama of the past months never happened.

But, inevitably, Charles becomes bored again. Although he's in his room, I don't sense he's actually studying, more than sitting at his desk, in position in case my father opens the door. One day, while I walk home with him after school, Clint runs up to Charles, hands him a wad of cash, then leaves.

"What's that for?" I ask.

"Just something that came in the mail for me."

"You're still selling comic books?"

"I'm just raising a little side cash."

"I thought you let go of that, Charles," I say, exasperated.

"Don't say anything to Mom or Dad, but I'm only here until I can buy a one-way ticket to San Francisco."

"Why are you going there?"

"One of my friends is starting a company that's going to sell things online. He likes my ideas. He says if I come to San Francisco, I can stay in a spare room at his house and work for his company."

"How did you meet him?"

"On a BBS."

"Charles, he's a complete stranger! Does he know you're still in high school?"

"You don't understand this community. They're like my family even though I've never physically met any of them. If I can get to San Francisco, I know I'm going to be a part of something that will revolutionize the world. So much is happening there right now. They're living in the future." He looks at me with his pleading eyes. "Do you believe in me? Do you think I can make it?"

"I believe you can do anything. But at least graduate high school."

"I can finish high school through correspondence while I work down there. I don't want to go to Essex Academy. If I go, I'll decide why not go to university, then go to med school, then become a doctor. I'll become an adult living a life that's not mine, that I never wanted. I want this. I know if I pursue computers, I'll never regret it. Even if I fail, at least I failed chasing my dreams. Do you understand?"

"You know what the difference is between you and me? I think about Mom and Dad, whereas you just think about yourself. You get all the benefits of being the adeul, yet you do nothing for us. You only cause problems because you're so selfish. Grow up. Start acting like a man and take up your responsibilities to our family."

These words have their desired effects, as Charles's face darkens and he storms off. Once home, I sit at my desk, fuming. I think about the destruction Charles is about to create and how I will be left with another mess to clean up. Last time, at least my mother knew Charles was at Clint's. How much worse off would my mother be, knowing that Charles is in a different country, staying with strangers? It would destroy her. I need to convince him to stay, even if I have to blackmail him. If I can figure out who this friend is, I could threaten to show up in San Francisco with the police and have them arrest his friend for hosting a minor. There are laws. I go into Charles's bedroom and search for this friend's contact information. His notepads and scribbling reveal nothing. Maybe he would tell me his friend's information if I pretended to support him.

I run to Clint's house, and knock on the door, but no one answers. I gather some wooden crates from their yard, stack them in front of the living room window, and take a peek inside. No one is home. I hurry to Main Street, where I see Charles, Clint, and Paul about to enter the arcade.

I rush to catch up to them, and I'm about to tap Charles on the shoulder when Jeff and two of his friends walk out. A teenage girl with curly red hair and her friends follow behind. Then I hear a faint whistle, but I don't know from whom.

Jeff stops. He glares at Charles, then walks up to him and stands in front of him with folded arms. The redhead teen tries to push Jeff, but he stands firm, staring at Charles and snarls, "He just disrespected you."

"Jeff, he didn't whistle. It was someone else, I swear," the redhead teen says.

Jeff doesn't move. "This fucking chink disrespected you. I can't do nothing."

Charles glowers at Jeff, then spits. The bystanders gasp as slime slides down Jeff's bewildered face. Then all bodies go into motion. Jeff pounds his fist into Charles's stomach. Charles's body crumples but he then rushes at Jeff, pushing him with both hands, and then, Charles kicks Jeff in the balls. Jeff howls in pain.

One of Jeff's friends slams Clint against the window, and he falls limply to the ground. Another of Jeff's friends pummels Paul's head—Paul covers his face with his hands and shrinks into a crouching position. The girls are screaming, trying to restrain Jeff and his two friends. The redhead teen grabs Jeff from behind, trying to hold him down, but he throws her off. In this moment of distraction, Charles takes a swing at Jeff's jaw. A loud cracking sound rings out. Jeff wipes his mouth with the back of his hand, and is stunned to see blood. Jeff wraps one arm around Charles's neck, and with the other fisted hand, begins beating on Charles's head. I stand there, helpless, as these bodies tumble and break before me, needing to help, but unsure how.

Suddenly, sirens shriek. An RCMP car drives towards us and everyone flees except for Charles, Jeff and me. Jeff momentarily stops to look up at the flashing lights, and it's then that I reach towards Charles. Upon seeing this, Jeff pushes Charles to the ground, then sees a cement block that is used to prop open the door. He runs to it, lifts the cement block, turns around, and charges towards Charles, aiming to smash it into his head. Charles crawls backwards, his eyes wide and white with fear. His fingers desperately frisk the sidewalk, searching for anything to protect him. Abruptly, Charles lifts his arm and stabs Jeff with a knife.

SIXTEEN

2014

Charles takes a walk by the ravine after dinner as part of his daily routine. It's one of the healthy habits his recovery mentor has recommended, to help regulate his moods and keep sober. After dinner, he asks me to join him.

"Sure," I say, trying to sound pleased. Though I want to support him, I'm slightly irked: I was hoping to spend this evening packing for my flight back to New York. I'm leaving in two days, but tomorrow will be a full day driving my mother to the gravesite, then afterwards taking her to Costco. Also, I have been avoiding Charles, not wanting to engage with him too deeply, lest he probe into why I broke up with Richard.

Although the days are hot, the evenings get chilly, so I put on my mother's light parka, which I'm surprised she wears regularly—on the left chest is the logo of the Alaskan cruise I sent them on over a decade ago to celebrate my father's sixtieth birthday.

We walk in silence along the narrow path as joggers and elderly walkers pass us with a smile or a nod.

"Mom told me Richard came yesterday and that you guys broke up," Charles says gently.

"Yeah, he slept with my friend."

Charles nods, his unruffled reaction revealing he already knows this. Charles enters the forested area that leads to the ravine. We're alone, walking around bushes and trees, the rustling of the leaves muffling any sound beyond.

"I actually wanted to share some news with you. And I need to ask you for a favour," he says casually, without turning around.

Fear rushes through me as I realize he's invited me on this walk to ask for something. "What do you want?" I ask nervously, bracing myself for him to express his financial needs.

"Do you remember a girl named Patty Kwon?" he asks.

My mind draws a blank. "No, should I?"

"She played competitive lacrosse and is your age but she grew up in Calgary," he says, glancing at me, to which I shake my head. "Well, Mina is her younger sister. We hung out right before I went to the centre again. I called Mina the other day to tell her about Dad's passing. That's when she told me that she's pregnant."

I stop walking. My jaw drops. "As in, you could be the father?"

His voice softens. "I am the father."

"So, what's going to happen?"

"We're figuring that out."

"Does Mom know?"

"Not yet."

He gives a sheepish grin, and I realize that he's happy. "That's big news Charles. Are you ready to be a father?"

"I have no choice, do I?" he says with a laugh, but I don't join in.

"Well, congratulations," I say, trying to sound happy for him while my mind races. He can barely take care of himself. How can he be responsible for another person, a baby?

"You know I've always dated white girls. Mina was just a friend. I never thought anything like this would happen: That I'd get her pregnant, or that she would want to keep it. Anyway, my kid's going to be a purebred Korean. Isn't that what Mom and Dad wanted from me?"

I smile weakly and nod. "Do you know the gender?"

"No, she wants it to be a surprise, but I hope we get a daughter. It would be a lot easier."

"What do you mean?" I ask.

"It's better being an Asian woman—at least the white man wants you."

"Let's not play this game. You've dated plenty of white women who've wanted you."

"Tell me that being a desired minority woman hasn't helped you in life."

"Are you talking about my career? I hope I was hired for my intelligence and not for my ethnicity. Besides, I always feel objectified. It's so different now than when we were growing up and all the boys thought I was ugly. I'm pretty sure Richard has an Asian fetish. That's another reason I broke up with him."

"Yeah, but you got to do the breaking up. I'd rather be objectified than ignored. I read online that Asian women are at the top of the food chain for desirability, while Asian men are at the bottom."

"Charles, I don't think it's because of race that you're unemployed and struggling. I think it's because you're an alcoholic," I say lightly, trying to rein in my irritation.

"And why do you think I became an alcoholic?"

"Because you made some bad choices," I say, feeling unease. I don't want to be discussing this right now, or ever, really.

"I think a lot about that last night in Crow Plains, about who whistled and started everything. I'm pretty sure it was Paul, though he never admitted to it. He did stupid stuff like that when it came to girls. Back then, Paul would always drop by whenever he was in Edmonton. I felt like he visited me out of guilt."

"So, what's this favour you need?" I ask, wanting to change the topic. I'm unsure why he's bringing up that night, especially since we've never spoken about what happened.

He stops walking and looks at me in earnest. "Now that I'm going to be a father, I need to make peace with my past."

My back tenses, and my chin lifts. I turn to stare at the ravine. Without direct sunlight, the water is sinister and black. The meandering curves resemble a serpent waiting to attack.

"After I stabbed Jeff, I don't remember much. I was driven straight to Edmonton, and I just shut down and did whatever my lawyer told me to do. I never saw you or Dad again for years. What do you remember from that night?"

"I have no recollection. It happened so long ago," I say too quickly, without any pause to consider this request.

"I've been wondering about how it all went down."

I have a sensation of plunging into darkness as I grasp for a response. "I'm not a criminal lawyer," I say, trying to ground myself through these words.

"Haven't you ever been curious about my case? Didn't you study this in law school? I want to know if my lawyer was any good and if you think justice was served."

"Not now, Charles. Tomorrow, I promised Mom I'd take her out all day, so I need to pack tonight."

"When can we talk about it?"

"How about the next time I come?" I haven't told him yet that I plan to quit my job and move back home. This realization is still too new and I need some time to get used to it before I tell him.

"When's that going to be? Your last visit was five years ago."

I look away.

"You always sent tickets to Mom and Dad to go to New York but you rarely came out here."

"I didn't have money when I was in school. And then, when I started working . . . You don't know how crazy my hours are."

"Or were you avoiding me so you wouldn't feel any guilt?"

"For what?"

"You never visited me."

"Dad wouldn't let me."

"Even when I got out, you never visited me."

"I had to survive too; it wasn't just you. Do you know how much pressure I was under to succeed because you were in jail?" I try to remember that period, but it's all a blur. All I remember about those years following Charles's incarceration was how much I studied. I became a machine, studying even more than I did at Crow Plains. Succeeding felt like the only way to tame the darkness overtaking our family. Getting into Essex Academy provided no relief. Once there, I became editor in chief of our school paper, captain of the debate team, an attacker for the lacrosse team, where we went on to compete in the world finals in Ottawa: all these efforts to impress a faceless college admissions officer. My teachers and coaches commented on my relentless drive, my ferocious appetite to win at all costs. When I received my acceptance letter to Yale, my parents called our relatives in Korea, waking them up in the wee hours of the morning to share the news. In their excitement, my parents forgot the time difference. But I recall so little of that time.

"Mom was the only one who visited me."

"I never visited you, Charles. But I took on your duties."

"You studied hard for me?" He snorts aloud. "Even your selfish acts have become selfless."

"Mom and Dad were in so much despair. I remember how happy Dad was when I wired him my first paycheque after I started at the firm. He called to clarify if my paycheque was for one month, and he was ecstatic when I told him that it was for two weeks' pay. I felt like my entire life was made for that moment. But all that bent me out of shape, and now I'm trying to figure out how to straighten myself back out."

Charles's voice softens. "I know you also had it hard. Mom told me you struggled with depression."

"What did she say?"

"She said even though you went to these fancy schools and worked at a prestigious law firm, you were always on medication for depression." We fall silent and stare at the ravine.

"You threw me that knife, didn't you?"

I look at him blankly.

Charles continues. "What I remember about that night was that Jeff was coming at me. Then, suddenly, I felt a knife handle in my hand. I know you wore it as a necklace."

"Did I?" I try to remember that moment. My thoughts race but nothing comes to mind. I feel as if a cord has been cut and I am free-falling into an endless void.

Charles waits for an answer, but I'm unable to say anything.

"I mean, that's the only explanation. There's no other way I would have gotten that knife."

"I don't remember that night, Charles. That was more than two decades ago," I say too quickly, too firmly. I can't afford to have doubts, not now. I refuse to look him in the eyes as my world becomes blurry.

"You can admit it now. Besides, I never told anyone. And too much time has passed for it to have any consequences."

I blink quickly, but I recall nothing. "I have no memory of what happened."

"I'm not asking for a confession or even an apology. It's just when that knife appeared, the fight changed from just a fight to a killing."

"It happened decades ago, so you're a little late cross-examining me now," I say, steeling myself, refusing to allow this unease that I've dodged for so long to enter.

"I went to the courthouse and found the records under my file. Could you at least take a look and tell me what you think?" Charles reaches into his coat pocket and hands over a stack of folded papers.

I feel a surge of panic, and I close my eyes to stop the chaos. Charles holds the folded papers, waiting for me to accept them. A long moment passes before I reluctantly take them. "Sure," I say as my voice trembles. I turn around to begin the ascent home, first walking, then breaking into a run, hoping that Charles is not behind me.

Charles doesn't return home that evening. I don't attempt to find him. I tell my mother he needs some space to be alone because we just had a heated exchange. Despite her curiosity, I don't say more. I lie in bed. The folded court records are on the dresser. I haven't read them because they fill me with dread. I have blocked out any memories of that night as a matter of survival. Even in law school, I avoided criminal law as much as possible, as it always brought me great distress.

I don't sleep that night. When I look at the alarm clock, it's early morning. I go to the kitchen, make coffee, and drink it, watching the crepuscular sky transform. Light glows at the horizon, which slowly takes over, brightening the world into morning. I have a sudden urge to visit the ravine. I go to my dresser to pick up the court records and leave before my mother wakes. I walk along the wooded path, to a small clearing overlooking the ravine, where there is a bench. I take out the court records and begin to read the sentences that forever altered my family.

I'm hunched over, my hands on my knees, trying not to collapse, when my mother calls. Before answering her call, I force my breathing to regulate. She asks where I am, complains that both her children are missing this morning, says she's ready to visit my father's grave, then go to Costco, and she begins to list the items that she needs to buy. She doesn't realize how hard I am struggling to temper my voice. It's only after we hang up that I begin to sob.

When I return home, my mother is at the kitchen table reading her Bible.

"What's wrong, you sick?" she asks.

"Is Charles back?"

"No. His phone off. What happen yesterday with him?"

I sit down at the table. "Charles asked me to read his court records. So this morning, I took a walk and read them."

My mother's eyes widen with anger. "Why you looking at that?"

"His case got botched," I say quietly. My mother looks confused. "His case got screwed up," I say for her clarification.

"Charles stab Jeff. Jeff die. Charles go to court. Judge tell him to go to jail. That's what happen."

"Last night, I tried to recollect what happened. What I remembered is that Jeff picked up a cement block and was charging at Charles, about to smash his head in. That's why Charles stabbed Jeff, to protect himself. But Charles voluntarily pled guilty to manslaughter."

"What this mean?"

"This case should have gone to trial. His lawyer should have argued that Charles acted out of self-defence. If he argued that, Charles likely wouldn't have gone to jail, or at least for that long."

"Why it screw up?"

"I don't know." Panic enters, and my voice shakes. "The police reports and witness statements don't exist anymore. If Charles didn't mention the cement block to anyone, his lawyer probably told him to plead guilty to manslaughter, to lessen a murder charge. But I searched for his lawyer online and found his obituary. He passed away a decade later from Huntington's Disease. What if Charles mentioned it to his lawyer and he didn't act on it because his lawyer was mentally deteriorating?"

"Didn't anyone else see what happen?"

"Right after the stabbing, Jeff's uncle arrived in his car but I don't know what he saw. But what if he did see the cement block, and omitted it out while making the report? He was the only officer on the scene, and Charles just killed his nephew." I draw a blank, knowing that no matter how desperately I grasp, I will never gain certainty on this. Isolated and alone, Charles didn't understand what was going on and probably forgot to mention or emphasize enough that right before the stabbing, Jeff was about to smash his head in.

"Why you don't say anything?"

I shake my head as tears freely flow down. "I don't remember what I said that night. I was so scared." I stop there and it's then that I realize I threw the knife towards Charles. Charles must have kept quiet about it all these years in order to not incriminate me. And I must have blocked this from my memory out of fear that I would be implicated and also end up in jail. *This must have been the reason I refused to talk about that night afterwards to anyone.* And it has haunted all that I have done since. "Did Charles ever say anything about the cement block?"

"How do I remember? Was so long ago."

"Charles served the wrong sentence."

My mother is gripping the side of the table as she processes my words. "You gonna tell him?"

"What good would it do? He's already served his time. I can't reopen this case because, two decades later, I suddenly remember some new detail." I cover my face with my fingers and start to cry. "Remember when Charles was taken to Edmonton, Dad wouldn't allow us to visit him? He was just a kid. He had no idea how the courts worked."

My mother violently shakes her head as she processes what I have said. "What can we do?"

"Nothing. It's too late."

"Only me go see Charles after Jeff die. I don't understand all the talking. All I do is show up for my son. I tell him don't cause any more trouble, just listen to lawyer and do everything lawyer says. I never thinking maybe he has another way out."

"Charles could have done anything. Remember after he went to jail, the acceptance letter from Essex Academy came with a full scholarship? But he wouldn't have gone because he had a job waiting for him in San Francisco. He was planning to run away again, Mom. And if he did, he would have been the success. We didn't understand how big the internet was going to be back then."

We weep bitterly at the table. It's the first time we've spoken about that night and what we recollect. My mother starts recounting the past, how they had to hastily sell their store at a loss, then move to

Edmonton so she could visit him at the city's Young Offender's Centre and then to the prison in Bowden, where he was eventually transferred. My father never visited him.

She tells me that once, she ran into Mrs. Song at a rehabilitation centre. It was a brief encounter. Neither dared ask the other why they were there, but Charles later found out that her oldest son was there for outpatient help.

My mother speaks of how the hardest part was my parents' self-imposed isolation. They stopped attending church, and they shopped at the city's sole Korean food store right after the store opened or before it closed so there would be less chance of running into acquaintances. Once, they ran into the Yoons at a mall where Mrs. Yoon's sincere greeting was met with a reticence which probably came off as rude. My mother promised to call Mrs. Yoon with her new phone number but never did. After that, they stopped going to malls in the city altogether. I remember our annual drives to Fort Athabasca Mall for my clothes and school supplies. Those retail trips were the highlight of my year.

"It's funny, when I was a child I wanted so badly to be invisible, but when I finally got it, all I wanted was to be seen. The only time I felt real was when I brought home my report card," I say more as a confession to myself. I search my mother's face to see if she comprehends what I have just said. She sits helplessly beside me, unable to unknot the tangles inside of me. We're surrounded by crumpled balls of Kleenex wet with our tears and mucus.

She sighs. "No use thinking about another path. This is the only life we have. Charles struggling, but things will get better for him. He can still make it."

Eventually, we dry up our tears and calm down, though I'm hiccupping from crying so hard. My mother glances at her watch and reminds me that I still need to visit my father's grave before I leave, so we get ready and drive to the cemetery. When we arrive, I'm relieved to see Charles's car parked next to the lawn where my father is buried.

As we walk towards him, I'm taken aback by how much older he looks, slouched in front of the gravestone. Is this what my lost uncle would have looked like?

My mother embraces him. "Where you go last night?" she asks.

"Slept here in my car," he answers without turning his head. I can tell from his lethargic voice that he's tired.

"You come home," my mother says gently. "You served the time. Everything is over."

"Charles, I'm sorry," I say.

He turns around to look at me. "For what?"

"Even though I've forgotten most of that night, I must have thrown that knife to you. It had to have come from me, and once it did, that changed everything."

My mother looks at me but says nothing. Charles stares at me and is silent, so I keep talking. Words that have been desperate to escape for so long burst forth. "My success is built on a lie," I blurt out. I tell my brother that I stole the computer that my father tried to destroy. I confess about the science fair: how I submitted his work pretending it was mine and that allowed me to win third place at the provincial tournament, which led to my acceptance to Essex Academy, then to Yale, and now here, where I'm a lawyer working for one of the top law firms in America.

"What happened to that computer?" Charles asks when I'm done talking, his voice hard.

"What do you mean?"

"You won third place at the science fair. I remember I came home that day. Where did that computer go?"

"I threw it away," I say meekly, wishing I could answer differently. I know he is thinking what I have also thought: Had I given Charles back his computer after the science fair rather than throwing it away, he wouldn't have had the anger to start a fight with Jeff. He would have been the success, not me.

"Your sister apologize. Now, you forgive," my mother says.

"There's nothing I can do to change the past," he says. "The past is the past. But I appreciate your apology. It helps put things to rest."

We stare at the gravestone in silence. I glance over at Charles because I want to see the expression on his face, but he turns his head away. After some time passes, I ask him the question that is burning inside of me.

"Did you tell anyone about the cement block?" I ask cautiously, trying not to show how desperately I want this information.

Charles looks at me, confused. "What are you talking about?"

"Right before you stabbed Jeff, he was coming at you with a cement block. It was a door stopper at the arcade."

He frowns. "Is that what happened?"

"I mean, that's what I remembered."

He shrugs, then shakes his head. The fatigue is slowing him down, and he doesn't catch the edge in my voice. I stop myself from saying more. To say more would possibly inject a poison in him so great that it would kill the little resolve he has left. He's already served his time. He doesn't need to know how wrong it all went.

"You do the bow yet?" my mother asks Charles, her obvious attempt to change the topic. I wonder if my brother senses my discomfort.

My brother shakes his head.

"You and Anne need to do the bow. Follow Eomma," she says as she stands in front of the grave, kneels to the ground, then bows. She rises again and does this two more times. When she's done, she stands to the side and waits for us to do the same. We awkwardly follow her movements: standing in front of the gravestone and bowing thrice.

"Yeobo, Charles has happy news," she shouts, competing with the wind which makes soft whistling noises. She looks at Charles. "You tell him," she says, nodding her chin towards the gravestone.

"Mom, he can't hear us."

"That's what you think. You tell Appa the big news."

Charles takes a deep sigh. He stuffs his knuckles into his front jean pockets and stares down at the gravestone. "Dad, I'm going to be a father. The mother's Korean, so the baby will be a hundred percent purebred," he says, then forces a smile.

"I'm gonna write baby name in *jokbo.* Make sure we have next generation recorded in family book. Finally, we have grandbaby coming," my mother says happily. My mother turns to me. "How about you sharing your news with father?"

I feel ridiculous standing in front of the heavy granite slab, engraved with my father's name in both Korean and English. "Dad, I broke up with Richard and I'm going to quit my job," I say in a formal tone, as if I'm reporting to a boss. Charles looks at me, surprised.

"Anne needs a break to think about her life," my mother says gently, as if talking to someone who is protesting my update. We stand there staring at the ground. A gust of wind blows against a nearby tree releasing dead leaves, which spiral down and scamper over the gravestone. My mother bends down and brushes them away.

"Charles gonna be father. Anne is finding her way. We all happy. No need to worry about us. Things getting better for everyone," my mother says, speaking cheerfully to my father's gravestone.

SEVENTEEN

2015

It is spring, though nature is being indecisive as the snow falls, then melts, then falls again. As a result of these shifting temperatures, the sidewalks can get very icy. I bought my mother ice grippers and a walking pole, but she refuses to use these and stubbornly wears her neon-pink nylon sneakers—she bought half a dozen of the same pair during Target's liquidation sale.

My mother is preparing for her garden: Egg cartons line our living room floor, their small pockets stuffed with dirt, the fluorescent lamps placed strategically throughout the room. Even I have begun checking on them daily. Viewing the tiny green shoots that rise from the black earth fill me with hope. Sometimes I catch her speaking to her seedlings with a tenderness that she never used with her own children or husband.

It has been six months since I arrived at my mother's house, my furniture sold, my belongings packed in boxes and stored in the garage. These days, I'm searching for nonprofit advocacy jobs on the internet while also taking an online documentary filmmaking course—I like that making a documentary is creative but doesn't require a mastery of technique like drawing or painting. It's easier to learn software than to retrain my brain or hands to learn a craft. I take pleasure in making short videos for my class assignments and appreciate the instant results. I'm considering making a documentary about separated families from North Korea, perhaps even about my father's past life and my lost uncle, though I lack material on this and don't know where I would get it from. I'm trying to keep busy, as my days are slow.

My mother is excited for her new grandchild. She approves of Mina, who comes from a similar background: Mina was raised in Calgary to Korean immigrant parents who ran a sushi restaurant. Her father is an elder at one of the largest Korean churches in Calgary and is reputed to be righteous despite being estranged from his two daughters. Even though Mina lives in Calgary, she does not speak to her family and has not told them that she is expecting. Charles visits her every weekend. Although he recently enrolled in a program to become an oil and gas production operator, the price of oil has dropped dramatically and companies are doing mass layoffs, making his studies useless. He is now studying for the computer network certification he previously started but stopped. He hopes to get accredited before the baby's birth and has taped the baby's sonogram above his desk to motivate his sobriety and his studies. He has been sober since finding out about Mina's pregnancy. My mother is hopeful that the baby will inspire him to finally become a responsible adult.

Widowhood has brought a new vitality to my mother. When my parents returned to Edmonton, after much pleading from my mother, my father finally permitted my mother to attend church, but only the service. He forbade her from joining the various Bible studies and volunteering groups because he did not want to engage so deeply as to exchange life stories and be forced to talk about their son. Now, without my father, she has joined the diaconate and is busy cooking at church events and attending various meetings. For Mother's Day, she is requesting a forty-quart stock pot to keep pace with her culinary outputs. My mother's *sikhye* is renowned among the congregants, and it is rumoured that attendance surges on the Sundays that she is scheduled to prepare post-service refreshments.

After my father's death, my mother contacted her high school friends to share the news of her husband's passing and they decided it was time to visit my mother and see the famous Canadian Rockies. They came early spring and stayed with us for a week. When they arrived, the many decades of being absent from each others' lives vanished and they reverted to being the schoolgirls they once were, that I never fathomed my mother to be. I would eavesdrop as they spoke about what became of their childhood peers, exchanged tips on improving their skin and digestion, recommended which Korean drama series to watch. My mother was bright-eyed and giggling in a way that I had never seen her in Canada.

One friend had a passion for "freestyle" dancing, which seemed to be a form of aerobics set against the backdrop of K-pop music. She was taking classes in Seoul, where a young man—whose handsome face this friend kept gushing about—started a class specifically for elderly women wanting to learn how to dance. Somehow, in the midst of postwar and rapid modernization, a generation of Korean women grew up never dancing in their youth and now need to make up for lost time. The next day, I woke up to a pounding bass vibrating the walls and found these elderly women in the living room dancing to "Gangnam Style." After they left, my mother started blasting music in the living room and doing her own interpretation of freestyle dance. "We never think about dancing. We study, study, study, then work, work, work, that's all we do. We don't think, maybe we dance. So now, why not?" she explains one morning at seven A.M. when I ask her to turn down the volume.

After they left, she found a ballroom dance group through a community flyer and began attending drop-in sessions. It's there that she met Mr. Ju. Last weekend, Charles came running home, out of breath.

"Anne, you're never going to believe this, but I think Mom is seeing somebody."

"What?"

"I was taking a walk, and I saw Mom in front of me with someone. When I called her name, she pretended she didn't hear me, and then finally turned around. She was acting all weird. She was with this old Korean man who she introduced as Mr. Ju. He was holding a bunch of dandelions in his hands. He was startled to see me, but then he asked me questions about my job search, and even questions about you."

My mother is not in love, but in friendship, with Mr. Ju. At this age, she is too old to fall in love, and she just needs companionship. He helps pass the time, she explains impatiently even though I have seen her jump when her phone vibrates, fumble with her glasses as she reads her text messages, pause in the mirror to inspect her wrinkles and sunspots. Charles and I are too eager to label something as love. It is hard work and requires a lifetime of sacrifice. "Besides, I need to fulfill mourning period," she tells me grudgingly, though I'm unsure if it is to remind herself or me. When I press more questions—How did they meet? How often do they see one another?—she answers hesitantly.

Mr. Ju is a widower. He sings in the choir of a rival church, though they did not have any mutual acquaintances as he immigrated more than a decade after my parents and belonged to a separate social group—from the wave of Korean immigrants who came during the nineties.

I try not to ask who picked the crocuses that are in a jar on our kitchen windowsill. I don't stare when my mother comes home from Marshalls with bags full of brightly patterned polyester clothes bought on sale or when she returns from the hairdresser's with her tight curls and burgundy highlights. I have never seen my mother giggle so much, and her newfound vigour unnerves me. But perhaps, after a lifetime of struggles, this is deserved, a youth in reverse.

With all my free time, I recently connected with Meredith and Crystal on Facebook, though we haven't exchanged any messages—they only approved my friend requests. According to what I've gleaned from their photos, Meredith married an oil executive and lives near Calgary. In her profile photo, she wears a tank top that says, "I ♥ ALBERTA OIL & GAS." Her eldest son, who is a teenager, has a striking resemblance to Trevor. Her two other children, both daughters, are much younger, and she prominently features them: in their matching swimsuits on beaches along the Mexican Riviera, in their private school plaids, riding horses on their acreage. Crystal is a musician and travels with a band to remote bars and taverns in Northern Alberta flush with money from oil workers. She posts numerous selfies where her hair and eye colour keep changing. I scrutinize their photos with the understanding that if I met either of them now, we would never entertain being friends with one another.

I also searched for Euphemia, who is now a journalist at the *Globe and Mail.* According to her bio, she lives in Toronto, is married to a man of Indian descent, and has two kids. I read through her articles, enjoying the ones which explored the dynamics of a bi-cultural household. I was impressed with her acerbic wit, even found myself chuckling aloud while reading through her opinion essays. Afterwards, I was left with a feeling of longing. I wished we could meet now and exchange our life experiences. I would tell her I have also thought her thoughts, yet pinpoint areas where I didn't fully agree with her arguments. Afterwards, I found her on Facebook, where her profile was set to private. I sent her a friend request and am waiting for her to accept.

My mother scours the clearance section for baby clothes and toys for her future grandchild. She buys things that are marked down even though she has no idea what they are used for: infant mitts, leak pads, peepee teepees.

"Mom, we're not going to find out what gender the baby is until Mina gives birth, so these pink clothes might all be a waste of money."

"They having daughter."

"How do you know?"

"I have dream of red bird holding charcoal in her foot. You know, charcoal means daughter. In olden day Korea, when baby born, the family announce gender by tying a rope outside home: If rope hold coal means daughter, and pepper means boy because it looks like penis."

"Why coal for daughters?"

"Maybe disappointment? Back then, everyone think son is better. You have daughter, once she marry, she leaves you and become stranger. Son different, he stay with you. Anyway, my dream means Mina will have daughter. Koreans believe dream before birth of baby is prophecy. But maybe I'm not good dreamer, because I thought you would be son."

"Why?"

"Before you born, I dream me and your father sinking on a boat. Then, dragon come and put us to safety. I remember I wake up and tell your father we having another son. Dragon means son, you know."

I want to tell her that the dream came true because she had a daughter who took on the roles of a son, but I decide to stay silent. I fold the tiny clothes. I think of the few times I've met Mina in her trendy cropped sweatshirts exposing a naval ring. "Even if she has a daughter, Mina might be picky about what sort of clothes her daughter wears."

"This is good quality cotton. She should be thankful. When you baby, we have no money to buy new clothes for you. Everyone thinking you boy because you always wearing Charles's clothes." She hands me a box from her pile. "What this for?" she asks. The box is labeled "Organic Cotton Peepee Teepees." I read the packaging in amusement.

"You're supposed to put this over the boy's penis while changing his diaper so he doesn't urinate on you. This is only useful if they have a son."

"Regular price fifteen dollar. I pay only five."

"Yeah, but if Mina has a daughter, then you've wasted five dollars."

"She should appreciate any gift from me," she says, clipping the price tags off her bargain bin finds. "You looking for job yet?" she asks.

Surprisingly, this is the first time she's asked me about my job plan since I've been back. I wonder if, in part, she's too busy with her flourishing social life. I have been looking at local lawyer jobs, and have considered getting certified so I can practice in Alberta. Although I don't want to raise her hope that I'll return to law, I'm open to discussing my ambivalence with her. "I'm all over the place. I don't know if I want to go back to school and start something new entirely, or work at some humanitarian organization, or go back to corporate law and do meaningful volunteer work on the side. I recently found a therapist that I'm seeing."

"Therapist?" Her eyes twinkle as if I'm telling her a joke.

"Yes, Mom," I say, indignation leaking through my voice.

"How much you pay?" she asks.

"Two hundred dollars."

"For how many session?"

"For one session."

"How long each session?"

"An hour."

She guffaws, then shakes her head. "To pay someone two hundred dollars to listen to you complain for one hour is luxury." After some time passes, she asks, "You still thinking about doing the law?"

"I just need a backup in case my other plans don't amount to anything," I say. I've saved enough money so I can afford this break from working, but with all this time, I've also been panicking. Most jobs that interest me don't pay well and require entry-level experience. I'm giving myself a year to find a creative job that can turn into a financially viable career. Though I want to follow a passion, at my age, I question if pursuing it would be worth an enormous salary drop, especially since there are no guarantees I would succeed or even create anything meaningful.

"What is other option?"

"I was thinking of studying filmmaking. I want to make a documentary on separated families from North Korea. I'm taking an online course right now, and I'm really enjoying it."

"Do people care?"

"I'm sure a lot of people want to hear about it. We need to remember what happened in the past. I actually donate to a group that is lobbying the Japanese government to pay reparations to comfort women."

"What mean reparation?"

"Payment. They're asking the Japanese government to pay the women who were raped by the Japanese soldiers before and during World War II. But most of them have died and only a few are left."

My mother smacks the table and huffs in frustration. "Why you hold on to pain that don't belong to you? Your generation have no pain, is that why you need to go to past? We give you the gift to forget and you turn it down. Japan never record what happen so feel no guilt. Good strategy: just forget, no guilt!"

My mother looks away, her eyebrows knotted, her arms crossed. I take a deep breath. "So, I have this class project and I need to make a short film. I was wondering if I could interview you. Maybe you could share some past family stories, both yours and Dad's. Afterwards, I promise I'll put a lid on it and forget. I just have to exorcise this ghost."

"A decade ago, people care. Canadian journalist contact pastor and ask if he can speak to any church member with family from North Korea, but your father don't wanna talk. Why talk about pain? Now, no one care. South Korea don't want reunification. It will hurt economy. New generation don't care. Our generation care but we dead or dying."

"I care. Is that enough? Your daughter caring and wanting to know about her past?"

After a long pause, she sighs, exasperated, "Okay. I will tell stories but only so you can finish class project and get an A. Hopefully, that will help you get good job." She rises from her chair and digs through the kitchen drawers and pulls out a white envelope. "Perhaps this make your documentally interesting," she says, handing me a letter written in Korean.

"You know I can't read this."

"Remember my friends come last month? One friend has son who works for Ministry of Unification. He think he find Maknae, your uncle."

"When did you get this?"

"Last week."

"Why didn't you say anything to me or Charles?"

She puts on her reading glasses, then opens the envelope. There's a photo of a man who looks like an elderly version of Charles. "My friend's son spend lots of time researching to find him. Your father always say Charles is Maknae. He has so much dream for Charles. All break."

I study the photo. "Can we meet him?"

"We see. Right now, no one know if Kim Jong-un allow more reunification. But if there is opportunity, we take Gomo and visit. But I dunno which family member is allowed for meeting, so need to ask my friend's son first. We have to go to China to get to Pyongyang. If we go there, no asking funny questions. Probably don't mention you making documentally."

"This is great. If we can go, should we visit Seoul too?"

"No. Last time I go to Seoul with Father, too crowded. We don't recognize anything and we can't wait to leave. I guess your mother is Canadian now. This is my home." She sighs.

I study the photo. The resemblance to Charles is uncanny, the soft, rounded eyes, the square jawline, even the intensity of his gaze.

"How much money you make?" she asks.

"For what?"

"Documentally."

"Mom, there's no money in documentaries. Everything I'm remotely interested in doesn't make money."

She stands there looking at me in disbelief. She begins laughing as if I'm telling her a joke and walks off shaking her head.

The call arrives at night and wakes me. Mina has given birth to a daughter. They rushed to the hospital the night before when her water broke. She had complications, which led to an emergency C-section. Charles assures us that Mina is fine. They've just settled into their hospital room and she's on pain medication.

We wake early in the morning and drive to the hospital in Calgary. We find Mina asleep. The baby is in a clear bassinette beside her bed. An IV is inserted into Mina's right arm, which lies bare, revealing an intricate dragon tattoo. My mother sees the tattoo and winces. Charles quickly places a blanket over Mina's arm. I have never held a newborn before, and I refrain from touching her, lest I drop her. My mother gently brings the baby to her chest. We hear the infant gurgle.

"Do you have a name for her yet?" I ask.

"We both like the name Sasha."

"Isn't that a Russian name?"

"Yeah, it means 'Defender of Mankind.' I like that meaning."

"You not Russian, it mean nothing," my mother protests. "What about Korean name?"

"Nah. Neither of us speak Korean. It wouldn't be true to who we are."

"What you mean? You and Mina one hundred percent Korean blood, so your daughter is also pure Korean."

"Whatever that means, Mom," Charles snaps, and I can tell that he is tired and hasn't slept.

"Sasha Kim. Sounds like a promising future accountant," I say with a smirk.

"She can be anything she wants," Charles says, stooping to gaze at his daughter. "You are free from the past. It's only the future for you."

"He will wipe away every tear. No mourning, no crying, no pain. Old things, they all pass away," my mother whispers as she rocks the newborn gently in the oversized vinyl chair.

"You'll be a good dad. Nothing can beat what we went through," I say.

There's a long pause before my mother asks, "What you mean?"

"Dad was abusive," I say.

"You accuse Father of abuse? That's how you thank him?"

"He ruined Charles's life by killing his dreams," I say, turning to my brother. "He could have been Jeff Bezos."

"You grow up in Canada, have happy childhood, so much privilege, so lucky. Don't ever say abuse. Father did his best. You need to thank him for all the sacrifice he make for you and Charles," my mother says defensively.

"Mom, do you remember Paul?" I ask.

"Anne, just drop it," my brother mumbles, annoyed.

My mother looks confused and shakes her head.

"Paul was the brother of Clint, Charles's best friend from Crow Plains. Well, Paul took the job Charles had lined up in San Francisco. This is him now," I say as I Google Paul's name into my phone and show her the results.

My mother adjusts her bifocals and studies the images of a slender white male talking on a stage, hugging a beautiful woman, standing in a group of important-looking men. "He from Crow Plains?"

"Yes, Mom," I say, nodding vigorously.

"You thinking you could have been Jeff Bezos and Father stop you?" she asks Charles.

"I wouldn't have become a billionaire, but I could have done something more with my life. I know Dad was only doing his best, but I missed out on a lot of opportunities," he says.

My mother shakes her head. "I couldn't stop him. Even if I try, I couldn't stop your father." Bitter tears roll down her cheek.

"Mom, I don't want to dwell on what could have happened. The past is the past, right? Sasha's here now, and I'm going to put my hope in her. Whatever she wants to do with her life, she'll have our support," he says. My mother stares at the newborn. When their eyes meet, my mother beams joyfully. She begins humming a Korean melody. Charles sits on a hard chair and stares ahead. I'm unsure if it's fatigue or contemplation that makes his eyes distant.

After a while, Charles says, "You used to sing that to me when I was at the centre. Can you teach me it? I don't know any lullabies for Sasha."

"Arirang is sad. No more sadness for next generation. You learn your own happy songs for her," my mother says resolutely.

"I don't even know what the words mean. I just liked the melody."

My phone rings. It's the HR director from an accounting firm I interviewed at a few weeks ago in Calgary. They were looking for a consultant familiar with American tax law, and I applied on a whim. She congratulates me and offers me a sum that I know is generous and would allow me to live comfortably. I feign enthusiasm and ask for a few days to deliberate.

"You're going back to tax law?" Charles asks when I hang up.

"I don't know what I want," I say, confused now that I have this option. I miss having a stable income and the security that affords. Recently, my mother was asked to join a group of church ladies for a Caribbean cruise, and she declined—likely because I no longer have money to give her an allowance and finances are now tight.

"How much did they offer?" Charles asks. I tell him the amount, and he raises his eyebrows. "You lawyers get paid way too much for a job that theoretically shouldn't exist."

The amount would allow me to continue taking care of my mother. She could go on that Caribbean cruise. I could work on my documentary on the side and even volunteer for social justice causes. Also, because I would be a consultant, I could still decide if I wanted to go back to law or not. What if I hated my job because of my firm? Or am I fooling myself and further getting stuck in a career that I hate?

"I thought you say no lawyer job, too depressing?" my mother asks softly.

"For now, it would just be a consulting job. I would need to get certified if I wanted to practice law here," I say.

"You should take it. We're in Calgary and Sasha needs an aunt," Charles says.

"I'll visit Sasha regardless of if I take this job or not."

We hear Mina murmur. We turn around, and she's stirring from her sleep. Her eyes open.

"Mina, congratulations," I say.

"Thanks," Mina says, and upon seeing my mother, immediately reaches for the blanket that fell from her shoulders and covers up her tattoo. We spend another hour there. My mother insists that Mina calls her parents so they can meet their granddaughter. Mina surprisingly acquiesces, and from the stilted conversation over the phone, I can tell she hasn't spoken with her parents for a while. When she hangs up, she announces that her parents are on their way to the hospital and admits that it's been a few years since she's last seen them. We don't inquire as to why. She asks Charles to get her long-sleeve cardigan from her suitcase. My mother and I get ready to leave. As I give Charles an embrace, I slip an envelope with a cheque into his hand.

"What's this?"

"I didn't get anything for Sasha."

"You're not working, Anne. I wasn't expecting anything from you."

I press the envelope into his hand and let go.

He opens the flap and looks at the amount. "This is your inheritance. I already got my half for the Crow Plains land."

"Save it for Sasha's college fund. This is the least I can do," I say. Tears begin to form so that when I blink, Charles appears as a coloured blob against the backdrop of the hospital's white. "I'm sorry for everything, Charles. I should have done more."

Charles stares at me, then leans forward and gives me a hug. Sasha begins to cry and interrupts the solemn mood.

A long moment passes before he says, "It's okay."

I take my mother's arm and guide her to the door. "Well, we're off," I say brightly.

Charles whispers into Mina's ear.

"Oh my gosh, thank you, Anne, you totally didn't have to. Goodbye, Mrs. Kim." Mina bows her head from her hospital bed. She brings her swaddled daughter to her chest.

While we're waiting for the elevator, we're both quiet in thought. "So, you think Charles has tattoo?" my mother playfully asks. We burst out laughing.

"You haven't checked, Mom?"

"No!"

"Well, then maybe you should go into his room while he's sleeping sometime and check his body parts for any tattoos," I say, and we giggle uncontrollably as people look our way.

"I am hopeful about Mina. She seems like nice girl," my mother murmurs and nods her head in approval to no one in particular.

We drive by the yellow fields, the pastures dotted with lazy cattle chewing on hay. As we near Red Deer, dark grey clouds overtake the cornflower-blue skies and then everything turns black. Thunder booms. Slivers of lightning pierce through the clouds, which release an intense shower. The traffic stalls on Highway 2 as many cars pull into the ditch. I slowly exit the highway and park next to a fast-food restaurant. We get drenched running inside. We order coffees and gaze through the foggy glass windows displaying variations of the colour grey. My mother is pensive and says little. Then, just as suddenly, the showers stop and the blue sky returns. We spot a rainbow along the highway, and I feel like I'm chasing it as I drive. My mother watches in silent delight.

When we arrive home, my mother announces that she's ready. I set up the tripod and a lighting kit I bought online while my mother powders her face, pencils in her eyebrows, lacquers her lips.

"Are you sure you wanna hear? Lots of sadness and pain. Happening so long ago."

"I'll just record you talking and see what comes out of it. I want to know your stories from Korea, then Dad's stories, and then the stories after you immigrated to Canada. Like, remember when we took over that store in Crow Plains and the town stopped shopping there? We almost went bankrupt. That was so racist."

"Not racist. Town people don't know us yet. Eventually, your father and I win them over and we make the money. Why you always remember things the worst way? Good things happen too. Maybe if we stay in Korea, you don't have opportunity. Canada is good to our daughters, that's what church ladies agree on. Try to remember positive and let go of negative thinking. You always hold on to the bad. No wonder you depressing all the time."

"Sometimes you need to process the bad in order to get to the good."

"After making documentally, promise you stop being sad?" She sits on the armchair in front of the video camera.

I nod impatiently. "Sure, Mom. I'm taping now."

Her eyes twinkle as she straightens her posture and breaks into a smile that is too wide and full of mischief.

"Are you ready?"

"Yes."

"Okay, tell me everything. Tell me all your stories."

ACKNOWLEDGMENTS

This novel took a long time to write. Through the many dry spells, I want to thank Shyam Selvadurai. For the longest time, your encouragement and edits were the only thing that kept me going and what got me to the finish line. Thank you for believing in me and this book.

Thanks to Nino Ricci, Greg Hollingshead, and Dr. Bill Reeves who used to teach German Literature at Queen's University. Thanks to my agent, Chris Casuccio at Westwood Creative Artists, with gratitude for finding two homes for my book.

I completed this novel before starting an MFA, and want to acknowledge and thank the organizations that support emerging writers, even though emerging, for me, spanned almost two decades: the Banff Centre, MacDowell, Humber School for Writers, Diaspora Dialogues, and Canada Council for the Arts—which helped me get through a difficult time during COVID. These organizations provided time, space, and validation knowing someone in the adjudication process saw promise in my work.

To Jessica Case at Pegasus Books and Shivaun Hearne at House of Anansi Press, a heartfelt thanks for championing my humble grocer family and taking on an unknown writer with a little over 100 Instagram followers. Also, for seeing importance in stories like mine.

Thanks to Julia Romero at Pegasus Books and Carla Bruce at Lavender Public Relations for all the energy you bring in promoting my novel in the US. Finally, a shout out to the amazing team at House of Anansi Press: Melissa Shirley, Jessey Glibbery, Emma Davis, Leah Swalwell, Christina Valenzuela, Quinn Baker, and Emma Rhodes. Also, thanks to Karen Brochu and Shirarose Wilensky. I feel very lucky to be working with you all.

Thanks to people who lent their expertise for this book including Mona T. Duckett, K.C. at DDSG Criminal Law for your invaluable legal expertise, Scott Campbell at the University of Waterloo Computer Museum for your knowledge about 90s internet, Becky Toyne, Tyson Brown at the University of Saskatchewan, OWW, and Bora Kim.

I want to acknowledge the land on which I reside: on the traditional territories of the peoples of Treaty 7, which include the Blackfoot Confederacy (Siksika, Piikani, and the Kainai First Nations), the Tsuut'ina First Nation, the Stoney Nakoda (including Chiniki, Bearspaw, and Goodstoney First Nations). This also includes the homeland of the Métis (Calgary Nose Hill Métis District and Calgary Elbow Métis District) in the Battle River Territory.

I also want to acknowledge that the date of the privatization of Alberta liquor stores was moved up in my novel.

Suzi Chun-Turley, thank you for holding the flashlight.

Finally, thank you to my family, especially my parents, for immigrating to Canada, and to my mother, for riding shotgun.